ANNA OF BETHSAIDA

ANNA OF BETHSAIDA

THE ARIMATHEA CHRONICLES

BOOK TWO

SUSANNE BLUMER

SUTTON AVENUE
PRESS

Published by Sutton Avenue Press

Black Mountain, North Carolina

ISBN: 978-1-945065-23-1

Cover design by Hannah Linder Designs

This is a work of historical fiction. While it draws on known events and historical figures of the first century, all characters' thoughts, motivations, conversations, and specific actions are imaginative interpretations. Any resemblance to persons living or dead, apart from documented historical individuals, is coincidental.

Scripture quotations, whether spoken or paraphrased in dialogue, are taken from the Holy Bible, New International Version®, NIV®. Copyright © 1973, 1978, 1984, 2011 by Biblica, Inc.™ Used by permission, or are taken from the King James Version of the Bible. Public domain. All rights reserved worldwide.

Printed in the United States of America 10 9 8 7 6 5 4 3 2 1

For the ones who break but are not broken,
And the ones brave enough to hope again.

And for my Thursday morning Bible Study ladies, thank you
for the support and encouragement! Especially Rosemary, who
has been my biggest cheerleader every step of the way.

"He heals the brokenhearted and binds up their wounds."
Psalm 147:3

PROLOGUE

Joseph of Arimathea reached Jerusalem by midday, the Temple officers riding in formation around him like an honor guard that felt more like a threat.

They had come for him the night before, arriving at his gate during Anna's wedding celebration with torches and official scrolls and voices that turned joy to sorrow. He had negotiated with them, buying himself those few precious hours to finish celebrating his daughter's marriage, to hold onto normalcy for just a little longer.

But dawn had come anyway, as it always did.

He had left Anna standing in the courtyard, Andrew's arm around her waist, her face pale in the early light. She had not slept. None of them had. The wedding night had turned into a vigil, the household keeping watch through the dark hours, waiting for when Joseph would have to go.

He had not said goodbye. What words could possibly be adequate? Instead, he had embraced her, kissed her forehead, and walked through the gate before she could see him break.

The road from Arimathea to Jerusalem was familiar. He had traveled it countless times. But today, the officers flanked him, silent and watchful, ensuring he kept his word. Their presence turned the journey into something else entirely. He was not a councilman traveling to the city for business but a man being escorted to answer charges he did not fully understand.

The morning sun should have warmed him. It did not.

Now he waited in the Court of the Gentiles, travel dust still on his robes, exhaustion sitting heavy in his bones. The officers had brought him here directly—no time to wash, no time to compose himself, no time to prepare a defense for accusations he did not yet know.

A different guard approached, one who had clearly been waiting. "Joseph of Arimathea." His expression was neutral, but his tone carried a warning. "The high priest is waiting."

Waiting. As if Caiaphas had been counting the hours until Joseph arrived.

This was not routine council business.

Joseph followed the guard through the Temple complex, past the Court of Women, where pilgrims gathered for the midday prayers, and past the Court of Israel, where the smell of burned offerings hung thick in the air. His sandals whispered against stone worn smooth by generations of feet, each step taking him deeper into the heart of power that now viewed him with suspicion.

They should have been heading toward the council chamber if this were routine business. Instead, the guard led him to a smaller room tucked behind the treasury, the space where the chief priests held private conversations that never made it into official records.

The door was open. Joseph stepped inside.

Caiaphas sat behind a low table, scrolls spread before him like evidence at a trial. Two other chief priests flanked him—Annas the Elder on his right, Eleazar on his left. All three men had held the high priesthood within Joseph's lifetime. All three watched him with the focused attention of predators.

Matthias lingered by the window, arms crossed, satisfaction evident in his posture. He was the Pharisee who had confronted Joseph in Capernaum, who had questioned his loyalties while Jesus listened. He had reported back, as Joseph had known he would. And now here was the fruit of that encounter.

Nicodemus positioned himself near the opposite wall, his expression carefully blank. But Joseph caught the slight tension around his features. *Be careful*, that look said. *This is not what it seems.*

"Joseph." Caiaphas gestured to the cushion across from him. "Sit. We have matters to discuss."

Joseph lowered himself onto the cushion, maintaining his composure. His pulse roared in his ears, but he kept his breathing regular. "I am at your service, as always."

"Are you?" Annas leaned forward, jeweled rings catching lamplight. "We have wondered."

"My commitment to this council has never wavered."

Caiaphas selected a scroll from the table. The parchment was long, unrolling in stages as he spread it across the low table between them. Joseph watched the columns appear—dates in one, amounts in another, names in a third, all in his own steward's handwriting. Ezra's careful recordkeeping, meant to keep the household accounts in order, now turned into evidence.

Fifteen denarii had gone to a teacher in Capernaum. Twenty to an itinerant rabbi in Bethsaida. Thirty-five for provisions sent north. The amounts climbed down the page. Joseph's mind raced, calculating how much they knew, how much they could prove. Had Ezra been questioned? Arrested? The scroll kept unrolling.

"The Law commands generosity," Joseph said. His voice came out steady despite the roaring in his ears.

Eleazar lifted a second scroll from the table and set it beside the first without opening it. Then a third. The scrolls lay between them like weapons waiting to be drawn.

Caiaphas's finger moved down the first column before stopping at an entry. "Galilean teachers." His nail tapped the parchment. "Itinerant preachers." Another tap. "Men who gather crowds."

"I support many causes." Joseph kept his voice level. "Education. Care for widows. Travelers in need. If some of these funds reached—"

"We are not speaking of vague charity." Caiaphas set down the scroll and fixed Joseph with a penetrating stare. The high priest's gaze was sharp enough to draw blood. "We are speaking of a Nazarene carpenter who calls God his Father and claims authority to forgive sins. A man who breaks the Sabbath and gathers crowds. A man who undermines the authority of this council."

The room fell silent except for the distant chanting of prayers from the outer courts.

Joseph felt the trap closing. They already knew too much —Matthias had seen him with Jesus in Capernaum. Denying the meeting would be foolish. But admitting the depth of his conviction would be fatal.

"I have heard of this teacher," he said carefully. "As has all of Jerusalem."

"Have you met him?"

Joseph glanced at Matthias, who watched with the same satisfied expression. No point in lying about what Matthias had witnessed. "Once. In Capernaum. My daughter believed he might help her dying servant. I accompanied her out of duty, though I was skeptical of the claims being made."

"And did he help this servant?"

"The woman recovered." Joseph kept his tone neutral. "Whether through this teacher's intervention or through natural means, I cannot say with certainty."

"But you spoke with him."

"Briefly. He addressed me as family. We share distant kinship through my late sister." Joseph held Caiaphas's stare. "It would have been discourteous to refuse acknowledgment of that connection, regardless of my opinion of his teachings."

Matthias stepped forward from his place by the window. "Joseph speaks modestly of the encounter. I observed them in lengthy conversation. The Nazarene called him 'uncle.' They spoke with the ease of family, not strangers observing courtesy."

Joseph's jaw clenched. "We are family. That does not mean I endorse his claims."

"Yet you sought him out for healing," Caiaphas said. "Your daughter's servant was ill, and you brought her to this Nazarene. That suggests a measure of faith in his abilities."

"My daughter insisted. She believed he could help when nothing else had worked." Joseph maintained his even tone.

"I went to indulge her request, not because I shared her conviction. A father does not always refuse his daughter, even when he thinks her faith misplaced."

"And what did you find?"

"A man who speaks with authority. Whether that authority comes from God or his own presumption, I cannot judge." Joseph chose his words with extreme care. "That is for this council to determine, not me."

"Very diplomatic." Annas's expression was arctic. "But you have not answered the question. Have you sent this man money?"

"I give to many charitable causes. It is possible some of these funds reached this teacher. I cannot account for where every coin travels once it leaves my possession." The lie tasted like ash. "Surely you do not hold councilmen responsible for every shekel we donate."

Caiaphas and Annas exchanged a look. Some silent communication passed between them.

"Your steward," Eleazar said. "This would be Ezra ben Solomon?"

Dread settled into Joseph's gut. They had been asking questions. Tracking payments. Building their case with the thoroughness of men who meant to see it through.

"Yes."

Annas reached for another scroll, smaller than the others. Newer. The wax seal was still fresh.

Joseph's hands curled into fists against his thighs. *Not that one. Please, not that.*

Annas broke the seal. "Your daughter married yesterday."

Joseph saw Anna as he had left her that morning—pale in the courtyard after celebrating through the night, Andrew's arm around her waist, trying to be brave as her father rode away to answer this summons. He had blessed the marriage knowing full well what it would cost them both.

He had made his choice. Now Caiaphas would make him pay for it.

"Andrew bar Jonah." Caiaphas's voice cut through Joseph's thoughts. "One of the twelve."

The room spun. Joseph gripped the edge of the cushion to steady himself. They knew Andrew's name. They had been waiting to see if Joseph would be foolish enough to approve the marriage.

"She loved him. A father does not refuse—"

"A father who values his seat on this council does." Annas set the scroll down with the others. The small one with Anna's name on it was laid out like all the rest. Evidence. Damning. Permanent.

"I approved my daughter's marriage to a good man. His religious associations are his own concern." Joseph ground his teeth to stop from saying more.

"Are they?" Annas settled back, fingers steepled. "Or are they yours as well?"

The accusation hung in the air, unspoken but clear. Joseph sensed Nicodemus's tension from across the room, though his friend remained motionless and silent.

"I do not understand what you are suggesting." The words came without emotion, though his fists wanted to clench.

"We are suggesting nothing." Caiaphas rolled up the scroll with precise, controlled actions. "We are simply... curious. About the pattern we are seeing. Charitable donations that seem to find their way to Galilean troublemakers. A daughter married into their inner circle. Your defense of certain controversial positions in council sessions."

"I defend the Law. As we all do."

"Do you?" Eleazar's voice was soft, dangerous. "Because it seems to us that you defend this Nazarene more than you defend the Law."

Joseph's mind raced. What had he said in council? When had he spoken too freely? He had been careful, or thought he had been, to frame every objection in terms of legal procedure, not personal conviction. But apparently, he had not been careful enough.

"If I have given that impression, it is unintentional. I seek only to ensure we follow the proper legal process in all matters."

"Legal process." Caiaphas set the scroll aside and pinned Joseph with a look that could have cracked stone. "Let me be direct, Joseph of Arimathea. This Nazarene is a problem. He gathers crowds. He speaks against the Temple. He claims authority he does not have. If we allow him to continue, Rome will take notice. And when Rome takes notice, we all suffer."

"If he is breaking the Law—"

"He is. We have witnesses. What we need is unity among the council when we bring charges." Caiaphas paused. "We need to know that every member of this body understands what is at stake. That one's personal connections will not interfere with their judgment."

There it was. The threat wrapped in courtesy. *Choose your loyalties. Now.*

Joseph looked at Nicodemus, who stood quietly by the wall. His friend's expression revealed nothing, but Joseph knew him well enough to read the warning in his stillness. *Do not give them ammunition.*

"I understand perfectly," Joseph said. "When evidence is

brought before the council, I will evaluate it according to the Law. As I always have."

"Will you?" Annas's lips curved upward. "Even if the accused is part of your own family?"

"The Law does not change based on personal relationships."

"Good." Caiaphas collected his scrolls then looked up at Joseph with icy finality. "We will be watching, Joseph of Arimathea. Your votes in council. Your associations. Your household's expenditures. Everything. If your loyalty to this body wavers even slightly, we will know." He paused. "Do we understand each other?"

"Perfectly." Joseph forced the word past the constriction in his throat.

"Then you may go."

Joseph rose, maintaining his unhurried pace though everything in him wanted to flee. He bowed slightly, the courtesy required of a junior councilman to the high priest, and turned toward the door.

"Joseph."

He stopped.

Caiaphas's voice came from behind him, deceptively mild. "Give your daughter our regards. It would be unfortunate if your family's reputation suffered because of... poor associations."

The threat was clear. *Your daughter is married to one of the Twelve. That connection makes you vulnerable. We can use her against you.*

Joseph did not turn around. "I will convey your greetings."

He walked out, Nicodemus falling into step beside him. Neither man spoke. They passed through the first courtyard, where midday prayers filled the air, then the second, where merchants counted coins. Joseph's legs moved without thought, carrying him away from that room, those scrolls, Caiaphas's cold certainty.

Only when they reached the columned walkway did Joseph stop. His back hit the column, and he slid partway down it before catching himself. His hands were shaking. He pressed them flat against the stone behind him.

Nicodemus checked both directions down the walkway. Empty. But his eyes kept moving, scanning the shadows between columns.

"They have been tracking everything." Joseph's voice came out hoarse. "The donations. Anna's marriage. Every word I have spoken in council." His mind replayed the scrolls spreading across the table. How many had there been? Four? Five? How deep did their evidence go?

"Your defense of legal procedure has been noted." Nicodemus's voice was barely above a whisper. He stepped closer, blocking Joseph from the view of anyone who might pass. "They are watching for sympathy."

Joseph pushed off the column. His robe was twisted at the shoulder where he had pulled at the fabric during the interrogation. He forced his hands to smooth it, to stop their trembling.

"I defend the Law."

"Then defend it more quietly." Nicodemus glanced back again toward the treasury rooms. "For a time. I have heard things about this Nazarene. Troubling things. Impressive things. I confess I do not know what to make of him."

Joseph studied his fellow councilman. "Have you met him?"

"No." The answer came quickly. Too quickly. "But I am curious. As are others, whether or not they admit it."

"Curiosity can be dangerous these days."

"So can family connections." Nicodemus met his gaze. "Be careful, Joseph. Whatever you believe about this teacher, keep it to yourself. They are looking for proof. Do not give it to them."

Joseph pushed off the column, straightening his robes. The shaking in his limbs was easing. "And you? What will you do if they bring charges?"

"I will insist on proper legal procedure. As I always do." Nicodemus's voice was carefully neutral. "Beyond that... I do not know yet."

It was not an alliance. Not quite. But it was something. Two men uncertain, watching each other, wondering if they occupied the same side of a divide neither fully understood yet.

"Go home," Nicodemus said finally. "See your daughter. And Joseph, whatever you are doing with your charitable donations, perhaps it is time to be more discreet."

Joseph's stomach lurched. Nicodemus suspected Joseph was funding Jesus directly, not just making general charitable donations. Yet here he was, offering caution instead of condemnation. Not reporting his suspicions to Caiaphas nor adding his voice to the accusations.

The silence between them held weight.

Joseph nodded, but he did not leave immediately. He looked out over the Temple complex, the golden afternoon light turning everything to honey. He had spent his adult life here, building influence, earning respect, gaining power. And all of it, every connection, every carefully cultivated relationship, was about to crumble.

But when he thought of Jesus in Capernaum, speaking with such authority, calling him "uncle" with genuine affection, Joseph felt something shift inside him. Not certainty, not yet, but the beginning of something that might become conviction if he let it.

Caiaphas was right about one thing. The time for pretending was almost over.

Joseph left the Temple as afternoon shadows lengthened across the stones. In a few days, perhaps a week, he would travel to Bethsaida to check on Anna. He would give her and Andrew time to settle, and he would see Naomi again. Andrew's mother had somehow, in the span of one wedding celebration, made him think about second chances.

He did not know how long he had before the council's patience ran out, before they gathered enough evidence to question his loyalty. Before he would have to choose, publicly and irrevocably, between the power he had spent his life accumulating and the truth that had arrested his soul.

But he knew it would not be long.

The storm was coming. He could feel it in the way Caiaphas had surveyed him and in the weight of those scrolls documenting his donations. In the veiled threat against his daughter.

All he could do now was prepare. And pray that when the moment came, he would have the courage to stand.

Even if it cost him everything.

CHAPTER 1

The voice that pulled me from sleep was not one I expected to hear in Bethsaida.

"My lord," Andrew said from somewhere near our window, his voice lifting with surprise.

The formality in Andrew's greeting pulled me upright, my palms pressing into the woven rushes of our sleeping mat. The mat was still warm where his body had been moments before, and my shift clung to my skin where I had slept nestled against him. Through the window, cool morning air touched my face, carrying salt and the yeasty smell of Naomi's baking. The harbor lay pearl-colored in the early light, fishing boats rocking at their moorings, masts making dark lines against the brightening sky. Men's voices drifted up from the docks, accompanied by the creak of wood and rope that had become the rhythm of my mornings these past months.

Three months married. Three months of waking to these sounds, of learning the rhythms of this place. The scrape of nets against stone in the pre-dawn dark. Andrew's careful footsteps as he tried not to wake me. The way Naomi hummed wordlessly while she worked dough for the day's bread.

I pulled the blue tunic over my head, the wool sliding cool and soft against my bare arms, the faint scratch of good fabric against my skin. It still smelled of lavender. My mother's belt came next, the leather supple and warm in my hands, worn smooth by years of her touch and then mine. I cinched it at my waist, feeling it settle into its familiar place. The silver bracelets were last—two from my mother, one from Naomi. I slid them over my hand, and they came to rest at my wrist with soft metallic whispers, warm circles that marked me as belonging.

In the courtyard, my father sat at our small table with Andrew and Naomi. Road dust darkened his traveling cloak and lined the creases of his face. His eyes were shadowed with weariness from the hard road, but they lit up when he saw me.

"Anna." He pulled me close, and I laid my face against his chest, breathing in the smell of him—road dust and donkey, leather and sweat, and underneath it all the faint spice of Temple incense that never quite left his clothes. His arms were solid around me, his heart beating steady under my ear. When he released me, his hands lingered on my shoulders, warm through the wool of my tunic. "I hope you do not mind the early hour."

"You are always welcome, Abba." I sat beside him on the

bench, the wood smooth and sun-warmed beneath my palms. Naomi had already set out bread, still warm, its crust crackling softly as she tore it, honey the color of amber in a small clay pot, and wine. "But what brings you from Jerusalem?"

"First, tell me how you are." He broke the bread, honey pooling golden in the torn center. The bread was still warm when I tore a piece, steam rising from the soft interior. The first bite was sweet enough to make my teeth ache, the honey cutting through the grain's earthiness. Abba turned to Andrew. "How has the fishing been?"

"Good this month," Andrew said. His hands shaped the water, the depths. "The fish run deep now, following the cold currents."

"And the harvest in Judea?" I asked.

"Fair. The early rains came when they should." He met Naomi's eyes. "Your figs?"

"Sweet this year." She smiled, and for a moment, so did he.

But his eyes stayed shadowed, and his hands were not quite steady on his cup.

"I came because I heard you might soon be called to join the traveling ministry," he said finally, setting down his cup with a soft *thud* against the table. "I wanted to see you both before you left."

Andrew and I exchanged glances across the table, and his foot brushed against mine. "How could you know that?" Andrew asked carefully. "Jesus has not sent word."

Abba was quiet for a moment, his fingers turning his cup slowly, watching the wine catch the strengthening light. "I spoke with him two days ago. In Jerusalem."

"Jesus was in Jerusalem?" Surprise sharpened my voice.

"He came quietly to pray at the Temple." Abba's voice grew heavy. "But he could not stay hidden. A man brought his paralyzed son to the Temple courts, and when Jesus saw him..." He shook his head. "The boy walked away carrying his own mat. In full view of the priests and teachers of the law."

Andrew leaned forward, his elbows on the table. "What happened?"

"What always happens when Jesus performs miracles in Jerusalem. The council erupted. Some called it God's work. Most accused him of blasphemy." Abba met my eyes. The weariness in them had nothing to do with the road. "The hatred grows daily. Before he left, Jesus sought me out. Said your time in Bethsaida was ending. That you would both be called soon."

Andrew's hand found mine beneath the table, his fingers squeezing tight.

Naomi set down her cup with trembling hands, tears bright in her dark eyes, eyes so like Andrew's. "How soon?"

"Soon."

We sat with that knowledge, silent. The bread lay forgotten on the table, and somewhere in the village, a rooster crowed his late-morning challenge. Then Abba looked at me.

"Anna, might we walk?"

"Yes, of course, Abba."

We made our way through the village as the morning light strengthened from pearl to gold. The narrow streets were coming alive. Women shook out sleeping mats in door-ways, sending up small clouds of dust that caught the slanting sun. Men checked their nets while children chased chickens through narrow courtyards that still held the coolness of night in their shadowed corners.

The harbor spread before us, the water catching light like beaten copper. I climbed onto the low stone wall, the rock cool and rough under my palms. Even through my tunic, I felt the chill of stone that had not yet caught the sun's warmth. My feet dangled above the ground. The air tasted of salt and fish and the wild herbs that grew in the cracks between the stones. Small waves slapped against the quay, as rhythmic as breathing.

My father sat beside me, close enough that our shoulders nearly touched. His weight made the stone shift slightly beneath us.

"You look happy," my father said, his voice soft. "More than happy. Content."

"I am." I studied his profile and found lines around his eyes, lines I had not seen at my wedding. Shadows under his eyes. His shoulders sagged beneath something I could not see. "But there is more troubling you than just our leaving. What is it?"

He was quiet for a long moment, his hands clasped loosely in his lap. A fishing boat was leaving the harbor, its sail catching the morning breeze with a snap of canvas. The boat heeled slightly, cutting through water that broke white at its bow. When he spoke, he paused between thoughts, choosing his words carefully.

"The council grows more suspicious of Jesus with each passing day. They watch his movements like hawks circling prey, count his followers, measure the size of the crowds." He looked at me then, his dark eyes serious. "They ask questions about who funds his ministry."

My hands tightened on the edge of the stone wall, the

rough surface biting into my palms. The breath went out of me. "They already suspect you. The Temple officers came to my wedding…"

"And since then, they watch me even more closely. They note every word I speak in council, every vote I cast, every shekel that leaves my treasury." His mouth grew grim. "That questioning was just the beginning."

The morning suddenly felt colder despite the sun's warmth on my back. "Why tell me this? Are you trying to warn me away?"

"I am not warning you away. I am telling you to be careful. To understand what you are choosing."

"What am I choosing?"

"To be known as his followers. To travel openly with him, to be seen using your gifts in his service." He reached for my hand, his fingers warm and ink-stained against mine. "Once you take that step, there will be no hiding. No pretending neutrality."

I had thought only of the joy, traveling beside Andrew, using my healing skills where they were needed desperately, being part of something that mattered beyond my small circle of patients and domestic routines. The danger had always been there. I had simply not looked at it directly.

"My following him will put you in a more precarious position." I said it aloud, the truth I had been avoiding. "The council will use that against you."

"They already use it against me. It could get worse." He paused, and I heard him draw breath as if preparing to lift something heavy. "But fear is not a reason to turn away from what God calls us to do."

"Then you think I should go?"

He turned to face me fully, his hands finding my shoulders with a grip that was firm but gentle. "I think you were called to this. Your husband is one of the Twelve. To follow the Messiah, to be part of what God is doing in our time, is an honor beyond anything we could have imagined." His grip tightened slightly. "To turn away from such a calling would be unthinkable."

Relief came, as warm as wine. "Then you give us your blessing?"

"I give you my blessing and more than that." He withdrew a leather bag from his traveling pouch. It clinked softly with the unmistakable sound of coins. "For your journey. For whatever needs you have on the road."

"Abba, this is too much..."

"It is not nearly enough. I cannot travel with you, cannot protect you, cannot ease the hardships you will face. But I can provide this."

I took the bag, feeling its heaviness in my hands. Not just silver and copper but what it represented. My father's investment in our mission. His belief in what we were doing, even as it put him in danger.

"There is something else." From inside his cloak, he produced a small wrapped bundle, the cloth soft and worn with age. "From Deborah. She made me promise to give it to you."

My fingers trembled as I unwrapped the cloth. It fell away in my lap, and there in my palm lay a small silver pendant on a fine chain.

I lifted it carefully. The chain slipped through my fingers like water, impossibly delicate. The pendant was shaped like an olive branch, each tiny leaf catching the morning light and throwing it back at me in sparks. I turned it in my hand, feeling the warmth of it—my father's body heat from his journey still trapped in the metal. The leaves had been etched with such care that I could feel the raised lines under my fingertip.

"It was your mother's," he said softly, and his voice was thick with memory. "Sarah wore it every day until she died. Deborah has been keeping it safe, waiting for the right moment."

I remembered this necklace. Playing with it when I was small, when she would hold me on her lap while she worked her embroidery. How I would make the leaves dance across the walls, catching sunlight. How she would laugh. The pendant was more beautiful than I remembered, each leaf detailed with tiny lines that some long-dead craftsman had etched with painstaking care.

My eyes burned and filled. The pendant blurred in my hand, silver swimming in my vision.

"She would want you to have it now." His hands were gentle as he lifted the chain, drawing it over my head.

The silver was cool for just a moment against my throat then warmed. The pendant settled just above my heart. I pressed my palm over it, feeling its shape through my tunic, feeling my heartbeat beneath.

"A reminder that you carry her gifts. Her compassion. Her courage."

We sat in silence, watching the water change color as the sun climbed higher, from copper to bronze to a blue that hurt to look at directly. I fingered the pendant, tracing its delicate leaves, thinking of my mother, who had died too young, of Deborah, who had raised me with such fierce love, of all the women who had shaped me into who I was becoming.

A few houses down, Tabitha's door stood open to catch the morning breeze. For three months, the village midwife had been teaching me the mysteries of bringing new life into the world, how to read a baby's position and how to ease a birth when complications arose. Yesterday, she had said I had the steadiest hands she had ever taught.

When the time came to leave, saying goodbye to her would be one of the hardest things I would have to do.

"Anna."

The voice came from behind us, and we turned to see Simon approaching with the long-legged stride of a man used to covering miles.

"Andrew said I would find you here." He nodded respectfully to my father then met my eyes. "Jesus sent me. He wants you both to join the group now. He said your time in Bethsaida has ended."

"Today?"

"Andrew is already gathering your things," Simon said. There was sympathy in his voice but no yielding. "I will walk back with you."

I looked at my father.

"Go." His hand found my shoulder. "This is what you were made for."

I stood, my legs uncertain, the stone wall that had been solid under me suddenly feeling insubstantial. This morning, I had woken in my bed with Andrew's warmth beside me, thinking I had time. Now everything was changing.

"I am ready," I said.

We walked back through the village together, Simon

striding ahead, while my father and I followed more slowly, our steps measured by the impending goodbye. I tried to memorize everything. The narrow streets where I had learned to belong after a lifetime of not belonging anywhere, the green doors and climbing roses, the way the shadows fell across the worn stone thresholds. The scents of bread baking and fish drying and herbs growing in careful rows behind the houses, all of it weaving together into the smell of home.

The morning sun painted everything golden. Perhaps this was how journeys began: beauty and sorrow woven together, the road ahead bright with dust and promise.

At our house, Andrew was loading our few possessions into traveling packs. He looked up when we entered, and his face was equal parts excitement and concern, eyes bright but mouth tight, like a man standing at the edge of something he both wants and fears.

"I see Simon found you."

"He did." My hands moved without thought, reaching for the leather satchel. The leather was soft and oil-darkened from years of use, the straps worn smooth where my hands had gripped them a thousand times. I opened each compartment, checking. The dried herbs sat in their small cloth bags —yarrow, shepherd's purse, pennyroyal, chamomile. I lifted each one, testing its weight, breathing in its scent. The yarrow was still pungent and sharp. The chamomile was sweet and dusty. The clean linen strips came next, as soft as silk from being boiled and dried in the sun. I rolled them tight and tucked them into their pockets, my fingers remembering the motion. My hands found each item without thought, even as my mind reeled.

In the corner, I spotted the honey cakes Naomi had made yesterday, their tops still golden and perfect, smelling of cinnamon and sweetness. The cloth came away smelling of cinnamon when I wrapped them. I had meant to take them to young Amos this morning, to check how his broken arm was healing. The bones had been setting beautifully when I saw him yesterday, the swelling nearly gone, the new growth strong under my fingertips when I felt gently along the break.

I wrapped two cakes quickly and handed them to Naomi. "For Amos. His arm needs another week in the splint, no matter how much he protests."

Naomi pulled me close, and I went into her arms. Her body was soft and warm, flour dusting my tunic where we met. Tears wet my neck where her face pressed against me. She smelled of yeast and salt and the woodsmoke that lived in her clothes from tending the oven. Her arms squeezed tight enough that my ribs ached.

"You come back to us." Her breath was hot against my ear, her voice breaking on the words. "Promise me. You will come back."

The dampness of her tears soaked through to my skin.

"I will," I promised, though we both knew I could not be certain. Though we both knew the roads were dangerous and Jesus's ministry was drawing hostile attention.

My father embraced me one final time, wrapping me in his arms the way he had when I was small and the world had seemed too large and frightening. "Be careful. Be wise. And remember that you carry not just your own gifts but the prayers and love of everyone who believes in what you are doing."

"Including yours?"

"Especially mine."

Andrew helped me lift the pack onto my shoulders. The leather straps bit into my flesh immediately, the weight of everything I owned pressing down on my back. Spare clothes, my mother's journal wrapped in oiled cloth, Naomi's blanket, my healing supplies. I shifted, trying to find a position where the straps did not cut so deeply, but there was none.

Within the hour, we were walking away from Bethsaida. The road stretched before us, pale and dusty in the strengthening sun. We walked.

The pack grew heavier with each step. My shoulders began to ache then burn. Sweat gathered at my hairline and trickled down my temples. The sun beat on the back of my neck, and I felt my skin beginning to tighten with it. Dust rose with each footfall, coating my sandals, my ankles, working its way up the hem of my tunic. It caught in the back of my throat, gritty and mineral.

Beside me, Andrew's breathing was steady. His pack was larger than mine, heavier, but he carried it as if it weighed nothing. Our shadows stretched long on the road ahead of us, walking figures that led the way.

Behind us, Bethsaida's sounds faded. Children's voices calling to each other. The rhythmic *clang* of a hammer on metal from the smith's workshop. A dog barking. All of it grew softer, more distant, pulled away by each step we took.

I did not look back. Some instinct warned me that to turn would break something inside me, would make the leaving impossible. So I kept my eyes forward on the road and walked.

But I felt it all anyway. The place on my cheek where Naomi had pressed her face against mine was still damp with her tears, the salt of them drying on my skin. My father's last words echoed in my ears, his voice steady even as his hands had trembled. And the pendant swung with each step, solid against my breastbone. I felt its weight with every breath, a small pressure that said, *You are not alone. You were loved. You are loved still.*

Andrew's hand found mine. His palm was rough with calluses and slick with sweat, but his grip was firm.

The road stretched ahead, white in the sun.

CHAPTER 2

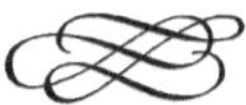

"Try to keep up, little brother," Simon called back over his shoulder, his voice booming despite the heat. "I know married life has made you soft, but we still have ground to cover before the sun sets. These roads do not walk themselves!"

Andrew's laugh carried forward. "Soft? I pulled nets this morning. What did you do? Talk?"

"Talk?" Simon's voice rose in mock outrage. "I will have you know I walked more miles last month than you have walked in your entire life! Every step serving the Kingdom while you sat comfortable in Bethsaida!"

"You are right," Andrew said mildly. "Walking is much harder than hauling fish."

Three hours had passed since we left Bethsaida, and my feet had gone numb inside my sandals, which was almost a mercy. The blisters I knew were forming would make themselves known tonight. For now, I concentrated on putting one foot in front of the other, on breathing through the ache in my shoulders, on not thinking about how much farther we had to go.

When we rounded the last bend, the camp spread across the valley below—tents of rough goat hair scattered near a stream that caught the afternoon light like hammered silver, cooking fires sending thin columns of smoke into still air that carried the smell of roasting fish and bread baking on hot stones. My mouth flooded with saliva.

Women moved between the fires with the rhythm of those who had done this many times before, and men gathered in clusters near the tents, their voices a low rumble beneath the crackle and hiss of flame. Perhaps twenty people, maybe more.

My steps slowed.

This was nothing like Arimathea with its stone walls and ordered household, nothing like Bethsaida with its neat houses and familiar rhythms. These people lived on the road, their homes packed and unpacked with each sunrise. A woman I did not know stirred a pot over the fire while another kneaded dough on a flat stone, her hands pressing and folding the pale mass in the rhythm of someone who had done this a thousand times. They belonged here. They knew where the water was kept, which pot held the salt, and whose bedroll went where.

I did not.

Andrew's hand found the small of my back. "I am right here with you."

We descended into the valley. The air changed as we dropped lower—cooler near the water, carrying the green smell of the stream and wet earth. Woodsmoke drifted across my face, and underneath the smoke came the savory smell of cooking lentils.

As we drew closer, faces became familiar. Mary Magdalene worked near one of the cooking fires, her dark hair tied back and sleeves rolled to her elbows, tending flames that sent curls into the still air. Miriam sat in the shade sorting dried beans, Joanna moved between the tents with a water jar balanced on her shoulder, Susanna, close behind, carried kindling, and near the stream, Tirzah crouched among scattered waterskins, filling them one by one.

Mary saw us first and came toward us, wiping her hands on her tunic as she straightened from her work. When she reached me, her face broke into a smile. "Shalom, Anna." She pulled the pack from my shoulders in one smooth motion, and the weight fell away, my spine lengthening, my shoulders lifting, breath coming easier as the ache between my shoulder blades finally eased.

She set the pack on the ground at my feet then pulled me into a brief embrace. Her body was solid and warm, woodsmoke clinging to her hair, the sharp scent of crushed herbs on her hands and tunic. "I am so glad you are here. We need another pair of hands."

I breathed easier. "Thank you."

Joanna approached more slowly. She moved like water, the jar still balanced perfectly on her shoulder. When she reached me, she set the jar down carefully then took my hands in hers. Her skin was soft, her grip gentle. She kissed both my cheeks, her lips cool against my dusty sun-heated skin.

"Welcome, Anna," she said, her voice carrying the careful courtesy I remembered from when we had first met in Arimathea. "We are glad you have joined us."

"Anna."

The voice was quiet, but I knew it instantly. Miriam

stood a few paces away, her hands at her sides, just looking at me. Her mouth trembled, caught between a smile and tears that already brimmed in her eyes. For a moment, neither of us moved. Then she crossed the space between us and wrapped her arms around me.

I held her just as hard.

"Three months is too long," she whispered against my shoulder.

"I am here now."

She pulled back just far enough to look at me, her hands still gripping my arms. "Tonight. After the meal. We have so much to talk about."

"We do."

A splash from the stream sounded then running footsteps. Tirzah abandoned her waterskins and ran toward me, her tunic hiking up above her knees, her feet kicking up dust. She collided with me hard enough that I stumbled back a step, her arms going around my neck, her face against my shoulder.

"You are here!" Her voice was muffled against my tunic, breathless and joyful. "Finally!"

I wrapped my arms around her, steadying us both. She was all angles and energy, her heart beating fast against my chest. "I am here."

She stepped back, still holding my arms, grinning through her tears.

I looked across the camp. Near one of the fires, a woman I did not recognize sat with a bowl in her lap, sorting through dried beans. She was older, with gray streaking her dark hair. "Who is that?" I asked.

Tirzah followed my gaze. "Salome. James and John's mother. You will like her."

Andrew caught sight of Matthew across the camp and moved toward him, their embrace the grip of brothers reunited. Simon's voice already rose in animated discussion with Thomas and Nathanael, gesturing with both hands as he recounted some story that made Thomas shake his head and laugh.

I turned to Mary. "Where is Jesus?"

"He left before dawn to pray," Mary said. "He often goes off alone in the early morning. He will return before sundown." She slipped her arm through mine. "Come. Let me show you where you will sleep."

The small tent sat slightly apart from the others, its patched goat hair worn but whole, the seams mended with careful stitching. Mary ducked inside, and I followed, bending low into a space dim and close, barely enough room for two people to lie down, smelling of musty wool and the salt of male sweat and leather and oil. Two bedrolls lay on the ground with a small oil lamp in the corner between them.

"We borrowed it from Thomas," Mary said. "He is sleeping with some of the other men. He said marriage deserves some measure of privacy, even on the road."

This was home now. This space that still held the scent of other men's labor, where I would sleep beside Andrew on ground that would leave me aching each morning.

"Thank you," I said. "This is perfect."

"It will seem less strange in time." She smiled. "Now come. Let us get you some food before the men return."

Mary led me to a spot by the fire's warmth and handed me bread and dried fish. The bread was still slightly warm and the fish salty and satisfying. I ate gratefully, my body demanding fuel after the long walk.

The conversation flowed around me—talk of the grain

supply running lower than expected, the stream that fed the camp shallower than last time they camped here, wondering aloud if Jesus would lead them north to Capernaum soon. Simple concerns of daily life, the ordinary woven through the extraordinary. I listened more than I spoke, learning the rhythms of this new world, watching how these women moved together with the ease of sisters who had learned each other's ways through shared labor and shared road.

Then came movement at the camp's edge.

A man approached from the south, moving fast. His cloak was dark with sweat and plastered to his back. Even from a distance, I could see the dust rising in clouds with each step, his pace urgent despite the way his shoulders sagged. His face was set and grim.

He stopped at the edge of the gathering. His eyes swept across the camp, searching. "I seek Anna of Arimathea." His voice carried, roughened by road grit and hard breathing. "Joseph of Arimathea's daughter."

The surrounding conversations died. Every gaze landed on me, heat crawling up my neck and flooding my face. My first day here, and already I was being called out, marked as different, as the daughter of someone important.

I stood. My legs trembled slightly, whether from the long walk or sudden nerves, I could not tell. "I am Anna."

Andrew was already moving toward us from across the camp, concern on his face. When he reached me, he placed himself slightly between me and the stranger. "I am Andrew, her husband. What business do you have with my wife?"

"My lord," the messenger said, slightly breathless. "My lady, your father bids me bring urgent news to the camp." He glanced at the women then back to me and Andrew. "John the Baptizer has been arrested. Herod has thrown him in prison at Machaerus. Word reached your father this afternoon shortly after you left—a messenger from his contacts in Jerusalem. He sent me at once to warn the Teacher."

John. My cousin. In Herod's dungeon.

I remembered his hands on my shoulders in the Jordan, rough and strong, pushing me down into the water. The shock of cold. His voice when I came up gasping, as fierce as always: "Die to what was. Rise to what shall be."

The man who had baptized me, who feared neither Pharisee nor Herod nor any man, was now caged like an animal.

My hands shook.

"Does my father say anything else?" I managed to ask the messenger, though my eyes stayed on Andrew. He stood frozen beside me, his face gone blank as if the words had not yet reached him.

"Only that it happened quickly. That Herod struck without warning." He hesitated. "And that others may be in danger. Your father reminds you to be safe."

Mary stood so quickly her stool tipped backward into the dirt. She looked toward the path where Jesus had disappeared that morning then back at the messenger. "When did this happen?"

"I do not know exactly, my lady."

Beside me, Joanna swayed. I saw the color drain from her face, leaving it the hue of old parchment. Her hand shot out before grabbing a fistful of her tunic at her chest, twisting the fabric.

"Machaerus," she said, and her voice was barely a whisper. "He has him at Machaerus."

I knew that fortress. Everyone knew Machaerus, Herod's stronghold, where enemies disappeared into cells carved from rock, where screams echoed up from dungeons that never saw daylight.

Tirzah made a sound, half gasp, half sob. Her hand flew to her mouth. "But John—he has done nothing wrong. He only spoke truth."

"That is precisely what makes him dangerous to Herod." Joanna's eyes were distant, seeing something the rest of us could not. "I have seen men taken to Machaerus. They do not return."

Miriam rose from her place by the fire. "Does the Teacher know?"

"Jesus left before dawn to pray," Mary said. Her hands hung at her sides, fingers twitching. "He should return before sundown."

"Should we send someone to find him?" Salome asked, her voice tight with worry.

"No." Mary shook her head. "He will know. He always knows."

Running footsteps sounded behind us. The other disciples arrived together—Simon first, Matthew and the Zebedee brothers close on his heels, drawn by the commotion. Simon's eyes swept the scene, taking in the messenger, the women's stricken faces, and Andrew standing rigid beside me.

"What has happened?"

"John the Baptist." Mary's voice was steady, though her hands were not. "Herod has arrested him. He is in the prison at Machaerus."

Simon stopped mid-stride. James went still, his face blank, one hand gripping his belt. John turned his head away, staring at nothing, his shoulders drawn tight, his breath coming shallow and quick.

Andrew said nothing. Just stood there, staring at the messenger as if the man had spoken in a language he did not understand. Then he turned and walked away, moving toward the edge of camp. His steps were measured as if he were carrying something fragile that might break.

Mary's eyes met mine, and she nodded once. I followed Andrew into the scrub.

We moved past the last tent and the boundary stones that marked the edge of camp. Andrew kept walking into the scrub brush, where wild growth caught at my tunic and small stones rolled beneath my sandals.

When we were far enough that the camp sounds became a distant murmur, he stopped with his back to me. His breath came quick and ragged, catching in his chest, the sound of a man trying to hold something too large inside.

"Andrew—"

"John." His voice cracked on the name. He pressed the heels of his hands against his eyes. "John."

I moved closer. Close enough to touch, but I did not touch yet. Just stood there, waiting.

"He was my teacher." The words came out ragged. "Before Jesus. Before any of this. John looked at me by the river and said I was ready. Said the Lamb of God was coming and I needed to follow him." He dropped his hands, staring out at nothing. "Everything I am—everything—started with John pointing me toward Jesus."

His voice broke completely. "They have him in chains, Anna. In the dark. John lived in the open places. He never bowed to anyone." He turned to face me then, and tears were running down his face, unchecked. "They will kill him."

I closed the distance between us. My hand found his arm. The muscles beneath were rigid. He trembled under my palm, not just his arm but his whole body shaking with the effort of not falling apart completely.

"I know," I said, though the words felt useless.

His knees gave, and I caught him with both hands, fingers digging into his arms.

Behind us, the camp sounds changed—voices rising sharp with fear and questions, footsteps running, then silence fell, not gradual but sudden and complete as if someone had pressed a hand over the camp's mouth.

I turned.

Jesus was there, walking through the camp. People stepped aside without being asked, their bodies making a path. His mouth was set in a thin line, and he walked slowly, his sandals stirring dust with each step, his shoulders bent forward under some invisible weight.

He already knew.

He stopped to speak with Mary, his hand on her shoulder. She nodded, gesturing toward where we stood. His eyes found us across the camp, wetness tracking down his cheeks even from the distance.

Andrew's whole body went stiff beside me.

Jesus came directly to us. Simon, John, and James followed close behind, their faces grim. They said nothing, just came and stood nearby. Brothers in grief.

When Jesus reached Andrew, he put both hands on Andrew's shoulders and looked into his face. For a long moment, neither of them spoke. I watched my cousin's face, and what I saw there made my chest ache. His eyes were red, his cheeks still wet with tears. Jesus, who had healed me and commanded storms and driven out demons, stood before us weeping for John.

"I know," Jesus said. "I know, brother."

A sound tore out of Andrew, raw and broken, and Jesus pulled him into an embrace. Andrew's shoulders shook, his breath coming in harsh gasps as he pressed his face against my cousin's shoulder, all the control he had been fighting for finally giving way.

Jesus held him and let him cry.

When Andrew's breathing slowed, Jesus drew back, holding him at arm's length, his hands still on Andrew's shoulders. "John fulfilled everything asked of him. His testimony stands. He knew the cost when he chose to speak."

"They will kill him." Andrew's voice was hoarse.

Jesus did not deny it. His fingers tightened on Andrew's shoulders. "John did what he was born to do. What he started, we will finish."

Andrew's cheeks were tracked with tears. Jesus cupped his face with both hands, the way a father might. "Do you understand me? His work is not in vain."

Andrew nodded, but no sound came out.

Jesus released him and turned toward the camp. "Come. Let us join the others."

We walked back together. The camp had gathered, a loose circle of faces, waiting. Jesus moved to the center, where everyone could see him. "Tonight we mourn. Tomorrow we continue what John began." His eyes moved across every face. "This is what it means to follow. John knew. He chose it anyway. Just as you have all chosen."

No one spoke. The silence stretched.

Then Jesus's gaze found me, and something in his expression softened. He came to where I stood and placed both hands on my shoulders. "Anna, my cousin. I am sorry I am just now greeting you. You join us at last."

"Yes. Though the welcome is heavier than I expected."

"It is. And it will be heavier still before the end." His hands squeezed gently. "But welcome anyway. The road will not be easy, but it is good. You chose well in coming."

He pulled me into a brief embrace. His beard scratched against my forehead when he kissed it. Then he looked into my eyes, his voice dropping lower, meant only for me. "Your husband needs you tonight. Be with him in his grief. That is sacred work too."

"I will," I whispered.

"Tomorrow brings its own work." He said it loud enough for others to hear then turned and walked toward the woods beyond camp. His figure grew smaller until the trees swallowed him.

Around us, people stood uncertain. No one knew what to do, whether to disperse or wait. Mary began moving between the fires, banking coals, checking supplies. Others followed her lead. The camp settled into uneasy quiet.

Shadows stretched long across the valley. The air grew cooler. Then Jesus emerged from the trees, walking slowly back toward camp. He said nothing, just took his place by the fire.

The women served the evening meal. Bread from the baking stones, still warm enough to steam when torn. Lentil stew with onions and garlic. Dried fish. I took what was offered and sat by the fire.

The bread was fresh, the inside soft and yielding, but when I swallowed, it caught halfway down my throat. I tore another piece and dipped it into the stew, thick and savory, the lentils soft, forcing myself to chew, to swallow. The taste was good, but each bite felt like a betrayal while John sat below ground, chained in Herod's dungeon.

Around the fire, others ate in silence broken only by the

scrape of wooden spoons against bowls, someone coughing, the crackle and hiss of the flames. No voices rose. No one lifted their eyes from their food.

Andrew sat beside me, close enough that our shoulders touched. He held a bowl of stew in his lap, lifting the spoon halfway to his mouth then lowering it again, lifting and lowering without ever tasting. The stew had formed a skin on top now, gone cold and thick. He stared into the flames, his face drawn and pale, the grief still etched in every line.

I wanted to comfort him but did not know how. This grief was too large for words. So I sat next to him and let my shoulder press against his, let him feel that he was not alone.

Someone added wood to the fire, and sparks spiraled up into the darkening sky, orange and gold against deepening blue, the flames leaping high before dropping back to low, even light.

Then Simon spoke. His voice was rough, like something dragged over stones. "John would not want this."

Heads turned toward him.

"This." He gestured at the subdued gathering, the untouched food, the downcast faces. "John was not a man who sat in silence and waited for death. He proclaimed. He celebrated. He lived." His voice grew stronger. "Herod can cage him. But he cannot cage us. Not unless we let him."

Jesus looked at Simon across the fire and nodded once.

Andrew set down his bowl. He cleared his throat. "My brother is right. John baptized me in the Jordan and told me life was waiting. He would not want us to stop living because he cannot."

Salome's face was wet with tears, the firelight catching them on her cheeks. She wiped them away with the back of her hand, leaving a smear of ash from the fire. "Then we honor him by continuing."

Around the circle, heads nodded. Miriam reached for her bowl again. Matthew poured wine into cups and passed them. The fire danced, and someone laughed—a small sound, tentative but real. The sorrow was still there, pressing on all of us, but we could breathe beneath it now.

After we had eaten, James rose. He walked slowly around the fire toward where Jesus sat, wiping his palms on his tunic. His eyes found Tirzah once, held for a heartbeat, then looked away.

"Rabbi, may I speak with you privately?"

The camp quieted. Jesus looked up at him. The sorrow gave way to something gentler. "Of course."

They walked toward the edge of camp together, disappearing into the shadows beyond the firelight.

Simon and John exchanged glances. John's face split into a grin. He leaned toward Simon and whispered something I could not hear. Simon's eyebrows rose.

Andrew took my hand. "I think James is asking for permission to marry Tirzah."

"Tonight? After everything?"

"He has been planning this." Andrew watched his friend disappear into the darkness. "But yes. Life continues, even when we mourn."

Across the fire, Tirzah sat utterly still. Her face was pale in the firelight, her breathing shallow and quick. She stared beyond the firelight where James had gone, unblinking.

Mary sat beside her. She reached over and squeezed Tirzah's hand, but Tirzah barely seemed to notice. Her eyes never left that spot beyond the fire's reach.

The conversations around the fire continued in low

voices, words about ordinary things that no one seemed to hear, sentences trailing off mid-thought with long silences falling between. The fire popped, sending up a shower of sparks. Everyone waited.

Jesus and James emerged from the darkness, stepping back into the firelight.

James's face was transformed. His eyes were bright, too bright, shining with unshed tears of joy. He could not seem to stop smiling. His mouth kept pulling wider, like he was trying to contain something too large to hold. He moved quickly, his feet unsteady, nearly tripping over a stone. Jesus kept a hand on his shoulder to keep him steady.

When they reached the fire, Jesus was smiling, too, the first smile I had seen from him since he arrived.

Jesus spoke loudly enough for all to hear.

"James, son of Zebedee, has asked permission to marry Tirzah."

Tirzah stood, her hands flying to her chest, clasped together. For a moment, she went perfectly still.

"As Tirzah has no father or mother to give blessing to this union, I will stand in their place." Jesus looked toward Salome. She was crying openly now, not bothering to wipe the tears away. "His mother has given her blessing as well. They wish to marry soon, to bypass the long betrothal."

His gaze swept across all of us. "Today we learned that John the Baptist is in chains. Tomorrow is promised to no one. In times like these, to choose love, to bind yourselves in covenant is not foolishness but faith." His voice strengthened. "Let us celebrate with them. A new household is being formed in the Kingdom."

The camp erupted. Voices rose in congratulations and laughter that pushed back against the darkness itself. The fire blazed higher as someone added fuel, flames leaping, heat washing over me in a wave.

Salome went to her son first. She pulled him into an embrace. When she released him, she turned to Tirzah.

She took both of Tirzah's hands, drawing them away from her chest. Her grip was so firm I saw Tirzah wince. "I prayed for you," she said, loud enough for those nearby to hear. "Before I knew who you were, before James knew his own heart, I prayed God would send him a woman strong enough for this life."

She released one hand to cup Tirzah's face, her palm against Tirzah's cheek. "And here you are. Welcome, daughter. Welcome to our family."

Tirzah smiled, then the tears came. Salome pulled her close, cradling the back of her head. Tirzah shook against her chest, hands clutching at Salome's tunic.

The women surged forward, embracing and celebrating, and I moved into their midst. Their bodies crowded close, warm and smelling of woodsmoke, their voices rising in joy that pushed back against the grief we had been holding.

I took Tirzah's hand when I reached her. She squeezed back, her fingers trembling but strong.

Night had fully settled over the valley by the time someone began singing—a psalm I knew from childhood, the words carried into the night on voices that wove together, some strong, some wavering, all speaking the same prayer toward heaven.

I leaned against Andrew's shoulder. His arm came around me, pulling me close. The fire had burned down to coals now, glowing red and orange, pulsing brighter when the wind touched them.

I tilted my head back. Stars covered the sky, more than I

had ever seen in Arimathea, more than in Bethsaida. Here in the valley with no lamps to dim them, they blazed. Thousands of them. Tens of thousands. A vast river of light across the darkness.

"This is good," Andrew said. His breath was warm against my ear. "We needed this. Joy even in the darkness."

"Yes," I said. "We did."

One by one, people rose and moved toward their tents. Quiet good nights were called across the camp. Salome banked the cooking fires, covering them with ash, while others stretched and yawned, their movements heavy with exhaustion.

Andrew pulled me to my feet. My legs protested, stiff from the long walk and from sitting too long by the fire.

We walked toward our tent. The night air was cold and bit at my arms where my sleeves ended, raising bumps on my skin. I wrapped my arms around myself.

Inside, the darkness was complete. I stood still, waiting for my eyes to adjust, but they did not. The tent blocked even the starlight.

The air was close and thick, holding canvas and damp earth and male sweat that had settled deep into the fabric and bedrolls —old and musty, not the fresh salt of labor but something that had soaked into wool and leather over many nights. The scents mingled with lamp oil and the worn-leather smell of straps and sandals, remnants of other men's bodies, their work, their sleep. This space where strangers had lain now belonged to us.

I heard Andrew moving in the darkness—the soft *thud* of something being set down, the rustle of fabric, his breathing close in the blackness but his body still beyond reach.

"The bedrolls are right here," he said. His voice came from my left.

I took one step forward. My outstretched hand touched canvas, and I crouched, feeling along the ground until my fingers found the bedroll.

The ground was hard beneath my knees. I unlaced my sandals and set them aside then lay down.

The bedroll was thin, just wool batting wrapped in rough fabric, barely thicker than my hand. Beneath it, the ground pressed up. Every pebble, every root, every irregularity made itself known through the padding. I shifted onto my side. My hip bone ground against something hard. I reached beneath the bedroll and found a stone, pulled it out, tossed it aside, and tried again.

Better. Not good but better.

The night air moved through the tent's weave, finding my skin through my tunic, wrapping cold against my arms and legs. I pulled the blanket up—Naomi's blanket that smelled faintly of home—and wrapped it tight. But the cold came from below, too, from the earth itself, seeping up through the bedroll into my bones.

Outside, voices murmured too low for me to make out words, just the rhythm of people speaking, the cadence familiar even when the meaning was lost. A woman laughed softly. Someone coughed, the sound sharp then fading. The last embers of the fire crackled and sparked. Night insects sang, a pulsing drone that seemed to come from everywhere and nowhere.

Andrew lay down beside me. The bedroll rustled and shifted with his weight. He was near enough that warmth from his body reached across the small space between us, near enough that I smelled the salt of his sweat and the dust of the road still clinging to him.

"I keep thinking about him in that cell." His voice came out of the blackness beside me, barely more than a whisper. "John. He lived in the wilderness. He was freer than any man I ever knew." A pause, a shaky breath. "And now he is caged like an animal. For speaking the truth."

I had no words. Nothing I could say would make this smaller, more bearable. So I moved closer, turning onto my side, fitting my body against his. My head found the hollow of his shoulder, my cheek against his chest. His heart beat through his tunic—too fast, too hard, a frantic rhythm that matched the quick rise and fall of his ribs beneath my ear.

"He does not deserve it." Andrew's voice broke on the last word.

My arm went across his chest. His arm came around me, his hand gripping my shoulder, pulling me tighter.

A tremor ran through his body. His chest hitched once, hard. Then again. His breathing went ragged, torn, catching on each inhale. A muffled sound released against my hair, and his whole body shook with it.

He wept against me, fighting to stay silent, to hold it in, but his body betrayed him. His chest jerked beneath my cheek, his hand gripping my shoulder until it hurt, the bedroll shifting and rustling with the force of his grief.

I moved against him, as close as I could get. My lips found his neck, tasting salt, sweat and tears mixed. "I am here," I whispered against his skin. "I am right here."

His other arm came around me, both of them now, holding me until I could barely breathe. Like I might disappear if he loosened his grip. Like I was all that kept him tethered.

I held him. There was nothing else to do. Time passed. I did not know how much. Slowly, the shaking eased. His breathing evened out, and his grip on me loosened slightly, though he did not let go.

Sleep was pulling him under. His body grew heavier against the bedroll, his arms slack around me even as his hands still held on. His breath deepened and slowed, becoming even, measured, the frantic pace finally easing.

He was asleep. But still, he held me.

I lay there in the darkness, listening to him breathe. Outside, the camp had gone quiet. No more voices. Just the night insects singing their endless song, and the sound of wind moving through the valley.

Adonai. I formed the word in my mind, not daring to speak it aloud. *I do not know what is coming. But let me be enough. For him. For this.*

My hand found the pendant at my throat. My mother's olive branch, warm from my skin. I traced the tiny etched leaves in the darkness, over and over, until finally, sleep came.

CHAPTER 3

Morning light shone through the olive branches overhead, painting shifting patterns across my hands as I sorted dried herbs. Thyme sharp enough to water my eyes, the scent almost medicinal. Yarrow with its tiny white flowers gone brittle and brown. Chamomile that crumbled when I touched it, releasing the smell of apples left too long in the sun. The work stained my fingers green, the oils from the plants seeping into my skin, and when I wiped my forehead, I smelled it there, too, earthy and bitter.

"Anna, look!"

Tirzah held the tunic she had been embroidering, turning it so light caught the stitches. The linen rough-woven, undyed, the color of old cream, and around the neck-line, she had worked blue flowers in thread the color of deep water. Her small, careful stitches rose slightly beneath my touch, each tiny knot smooth and even. The fabric smelled faintly of cedar from the box where she kept it.

"It is beautiful. James will treasure it."

Tirzah's thumb traced the stitching, checking for loose threads, her nail catching on the weave. "I finished the last flower just before dawn." She brought the fabric to her face, breathing in the scent. "I wanted it ready for tomorrow."

Mary approached carrying a basket of dried figs, the sweet, sticky smell reaching us before she did, honeyed and thick. She set the basket down, and figs tumbled against each other, wrinkled skins catching the light.

"Tirzah, that is exquisite work. Your aunt taught you well."

"Thank you." Tirzah folded the tunic with care, smoothing each crease between her palms. The linen made soft rustling sounds as she pressed it flat. She placed it in her wooden box. I glimpsed inside of it a bone comb, a spare head covering gone gray with washing, and a pair of sandals with worn soles. "I wish we had wine for the blessing cup. A wedding without wine feels..."

"Incomplete." Mary sat beside us, the movement releasing a scent of woodsmoke from her clothes.

Jesus emerged from the trees beyond camp, prayer shawl still draped over his shoulders, tassels swaying with each step. He caught the end of their words. "What troubles you, Tirzah?"

"Nothing that matters, Rabbi." Her hands went still on the box lid.

"All concerns matter to those who bear them." He sat on the ground beside us, settling cross-legged, his tunic pooling around him, dusty at the hem. "Tell me."

Tirzah worried the edge of her tunic between her fingers, the linen making small creaking sounds as she twisted it. "We have no wine for the blessing cup. And James has only his traveling tunic." She gestured across camp.

I followed her gaze. James sat with John beneath another olive tree, mending a tear in his cloak. His outer tunic was faded almost colorless, the hem frayed to individual threads. Dark stains marked the front, either wine or oil, set deep into the weave. A patch on the shoulder was coming loose, the stitches visible even from here.

"He would never complain," Tirzah continued, her voice soft. "But I wish..."

Jesus was quiet. The only sound was the morning breeze moving through the olive branches overhead, leaves rustling like rain. "The town of Nain is less than a half a day's journey. They have both a cloth merchant and a wine seller."

"I could go." Andrew's voice came from behind me. His hand rested on my back, warm through the fabric of my tunic.

James crossed to us, dust puffing around his feet. "If I am to have a new tunic, I should select it myself." He smiled at Tirzah, showing the gap between his front teeth. "And choose wine worthy of our covenant."

John rose and stretched, joints cracking. "It is too far to go alone. The three of us could make the journey and return by evening."

Tirzah's face went still, then something passed across it—disappointment, perhaps, or fear she would not name. Her shoulders drew up toward her ears then dropped. "You would leave now? The day before our wedding?"

James took her hands. His were large and rough, rope-scarred across the palms. Hers looked small and smooth in his grip, her fingers pale against his sun-darkened skin. "We will return well before sunset. You deserve a proper wedding cup." He glanced down at his worn garment. A flush crept up his neck. "And I should look my best when I make you my wife."

Jesus nodded. "Go, then. Return before darkness falls. We will continue preparations here."

James leaned forward and kissed Tirzah's cheek. His beard scratched against her skin, and she blinked. Then he was moving away, calling to Andrew and John, checking his sandal straps, and shaking out his traveling cloak until dust fell in a small cloud.

Tirzah watched him go. Her smile stayed fixed and bright, but her shoulders sagged. She twisted her fingers together, then apart, then together again.

I moved next to her and our arms brushed. "They will return before you have finished the wedding bread."

"I know." She tucked a strand of hair behind her ear then tucked it again though it had not come loose. Her voice was too light. "I just thought we would spend today together. Foolish of me."

"Not foolish. Just hopeful."

The men gathered their things—waterskins that sloshed when lifted, a small leather purse that clinked with coins, walking sticks that tapped against the ground as the men tested them. The morning had grown warmer. Sweat gathered at my hairline and trickled down my temples.

James turned back to wave once from the edge of camp and again when the path bent before the trees swallowed them. Andrew's figure grew smaller with each step, until I could not tell which of the three was which. Just moving shapes against the dust. Then nothing.

My chest tightened.

"It is never easy to watch them leave."

Mary stood beside me. Her hands kept working a piece of

linen, fingers moving without pause even as she looked toward where the men had disappeared, threads catching on her calluses with soft scraping sounds.

"Does it become easier?"

"No. But you become stronger."

The camp settled into work. Susanna and Joanna mixed flour with honey and dried figs, their hands sticky with the paste. It clung to their fingers in golden strings, and the smell was so sweet it made my mouth water. Mary directed the clearing of space beneath two ancient olive trees. Women swept the ground with bundles of dried grass, raising dust that hung golden in the slanting light, making me cough when I breathed it in.

Miriam sat apart from the others. I perched beside her, the ground hard beneath me. She was weaving late-autumn wildflowers into a crown, her fingers moving with precision, tucking stems between stems, testing placement. Small white blooms shaped like stars. Hardy purple blossoms that had survived the turning season. They smelled faintly sweet, like honey diluted with water.

The sight pulled at me with a memory of another flower crown, years ago, when I lay broken after my mother's death. Miriam had brought me one then. I could still remember how the petals had felt against my forehead, cool and soft.

"Is that for Tirzah?"

She nodded, not looking up. A purple bloom broke in her fingers, the stem oozing clear sap. She set it aside and chose another. "A bride should wear flowers in her hair. It is tradition." A smile touched her mouth. "Do you remember the one I made for you? After..."

"I do." I touched her hand briefly. My fingers came away

dusted with yellow pollen and sticky. "Some traditions carry healing in them."

Her eyes sparked with sudden mischief. "Would you like to try making this one? Though as I recall, yours always came apart."

I laughed. The sound was loud in the quiet, startling me. "Some things never change. My skills with needle and cloth have improved, but flowers still refuse to obey my fingers."

"Just as well." Miriam tucked a purple bloom between two white ones, testing, adjusting. "You have other gifts. We cannot all be masters of flower crowns."

Salome joined us. Her arms were full of fresh-gathered blooms. The stems dripped dew onto her tunic, leaving dark spots that spread slowly through the fabric. "The small purple ones smell sweetest." She added them to Miriam's pile, wet stems soaking into the dry earth. "They grow in protected places even as winter approaches. My mother sought these same flowers for my wedding crown, and her mother before her."

Tirzah drifted over from the cooking fire. She sat down beside me with a basket, and we began sorting through the flowers, discarding any with brown spots on the petals. Any with wilting edges. Her hands moved without seeing. She crushed a white bloom between her fingers absently, and the smell rose sharp and green.

"Tell me about your first meeting with James."

Color rose in her cheeks. "It was at the Sea of Galilee. My father's fishing boat had damaged oarlocks and a broken rowing bench. We could not afford repairs." She turned a broken stem between her fingers. "James and John were mending their nets nearby. James offered to help. By evening, his hands were bleeding from splinters, but the work was finished. My father invited him to share our meal."

"And that was the beginning?"

"For me, perhaps." She kept her eyes on the flowers in her lap. "I found him kind and thoughtful. He differed from the other fishermen. But I kept these feelings to myself." She twirled a small white flower between her fingers, the petals spinning, casting tiny shadows. "Weeks later, he arrived in our village with news about a rabbi named Jesus. Said he was leaving his fishing boats behind to follow him. He invited several families to hear this teacher speak. I wanted to go, but my father was ill and needed care. James left, promising to return."

"When did you finally hear Jesus teach?"

The smile faded. "After my father died that winter, my aunt insisted I join her household in Capernaum. While there, I heard people speaking of Jesus's teachings by the lakeshore. My aunt permitted me to attend." She paused. "I never expected to see James there, standing among the disciples."

"Did you think he had an interest in you?"

"No." Tirzah laughed quietly. "I thought he was simply kind to everyone. It was not until after I had been following the Rabbi for nearly a month that James confessed he had hoped I would join the group. Even at your wedding, I was not entirely certain of his feelings. It took his proposal to finally convince me his heart was truly mine."

"He seems devoted to you."

"I believe he is." She crushed a flower between her fingers, and the scent grew stronger. "My life has taken such an unexpected path. My father worked the fishing boats. I expected a simple life—safety, stability, a fisherman husband with a home by the sea." Her gesture took in the tents, the cooking fires, the dusty ground beaten hard by many feet. "Not this. Sometimes I still wonder if I am truly prepared for what lies ahead."

"Do you regret your choice?"

Her gaze shifted to the horizon, where the men had vanished. "No. I believe in the Rabbi's teachings with all my heart. Following him gave my life meaning after my father died. And finding James here was an unexpected gift." She paused. "But sometimes I wonder what awaits us. Children raised on dusty roads? Always moving, never setting roots?" A small laugh escaped her. "Listen to me worry about the future when we have not even spoken our vows."

"It is natural to wonder. I have had the same thoughts."

"You have? But you seem so certain."

"I love Andrew. I want to be where he is. That is my certainty." I touched her arm. "But the questions come in the quiet moments."

The sun climbed higher, and the heat built, pressing down from above and rising from the baked earth until sweat gathered between my shoulder blades and soaked into my tunic. The bread had been shaped into rounds and set on flat stones to rise. I covered them with damp cloths, linen cool and wet against my hands, already drying at the edges. We swept the ceremony space clean again and decorated it with branches still holding a few green leaves and late blooms wilting in the heat.

The immediate tasks were done.

Salome paced at the camp's edge, eyes returning again and again to the road, searching the dust and shimmer. "They should have reached Nain by now."

"The market will be busy." Mary crushed lentils in a

stone bowl. The rhythmic grinding punctuated her words—crush, grind, crush, grind. The smell of the lentils was earthy and dry. "Finding the right merchant takes time."

The sun eventually began its slow descent. Shadows stretched from stumps at midday to long dark shapes reaching halfway across camp. The risen bread was covered with fresh damp cloths. The stew bubbled over the fire, onions and herbs, garlic and cumin rising in the steam. My stomach growled despite the knot of tension there.

Still no sign of the men.

Tirzah stirred a pot by the cooking fire, the wooden spoon scraping harshly against the bottom. The dried figs for the wedding bread sat beside her, soaked and prepared, untouched, dark and swollen with water. She had checked the rising loaves three times in the past hour—lifting the cloth, peering beneath, letting it fall again.

"They are later than expected." Worry threaded her voice.

"The town might be crowded. Or perhaps the first merchant did not have what they needed," I said, though I was worrying too.

She nodded. Her knuckles were white around the spoon handle, the tendons standing out like cords beneath her skin.

Jesus had been teaching a small group of followers from a nearby village. Now he approached, his sandals making soft sounds on the packed earth. "Your bread smells wonderful."

Tirzah managed a smile. "Thank you, Rabbi. I hope it tastes as good."

"It will nourish body and spirit." He sat on a stone near the fire. The heat made the air shimmer between us, distorting his features. Sweat beaded on his forehead. "You are concerned about James."

The spoon went still. "They should have returned by now."

"Yes. They should have."

"Do you think something has happened?" The words tumbled out fast, tripping over each other.

"I think James is resourceful, as are Andrew and John. The roads are not always predictable."

"That is not very reassuring." Her hand flew to her mouth. "I am sorry, I should not—"

Jesus laughed, the sound warm and genuine. "No, it is not, is it? But tell me, Tirzah, will your worry bring them back faster?"

She shook her head.

"Then finish your bread. Prepare your garlands. When they return, let them find the wedding ready." He stood, brushing dust from his tunic. A small cloud rose and dispersed. "Your work matters, especially when fear whispers otherwise."

The sun dropped lower. The hills turned gold, then amber, then deep orange bleeding into red. The heat of the day faded, but a different kind of tension wound through the camp—tight, coiled, ready to snap.

"Should we send someone to look for them?" Simon stood with Nathanael and Philip near the camp's edge. Their voices were low but urgent, carrying on the still air.

"If we send more men, we risk spreading ourselves too thin," Philip replied.

"And if something has happened to them?" Salome's calm had finally cracked. "My sons, both my sons, are out there."

I moved toward Tirzah. She stood apart from the others, facing the path. The evening light painted her in shades of light and shadow. She did not acknowledge me, but when I reached her side, her hand found mine. Her fingers were cold despite the day's warmth, trembling slightly.

"If they are not back by sunset," Simon decided, his voice hard, "three of us will go."

Jesus had been watching the horizon. Now he turned to face the anxious group. "Wait a little longer. Trust a little deeper."

"Rabbi," Salome began, "it grows dark soon. The roads—"

"Look!" Miriam pointed toward the distant path. "Someone is coming!"

Three figures appeared. Even at this distance, I knew Andrew's walk—the slight favor of his left leg, the cant of his head when tired. Relief struck first, then concern. They were moving too slowly, too carefully, supporting each other.

"James!" Tirzah broke away. Her sandals slapped the ground as she ran, kicking up dust that hung in the evening air.

As they drew closer, details emerged. James walked with Andrew's support, one arm over Andrew's shoulders, his face bruised and swollen, one eye nearly shut, his lip split and crusted with dried blood. A makeshift bandage wrapped his forearm, the linen dark with dried blood—rust-colored, the edges fraying. John carried all their bundles slung across his back, a fresh scratch marking his cheekbone.

I was already moving, already thinking about what I would need.

"What happened?" Salome reached her sons first, tilting John's face to examine the scratch.

"Trouble in town." John's voice was clipped. "Some men recognized James from Jesus's teaching by the lake."

Andrew eased James down onto a flat stone. James sat with a sharp intake of breath, color draining from his face. "They followed us from the marketplace. Called us heretics. Said Jesus was leading people astray from the true faith."

"Words followed by fists when James defended our Rabbi's honor," John added.

"How many were there?" Simon's hand moved to the knife at his belt, leather scraping.

"Five." Andrew's voice was grim. "Locals, not Temple guards or Roman soldiers. But they spoke with authority, as if someone had instructed them to watch for us. One claimed to be a cousin of a priest in Jerusalem."

Thomas shook his head, his thin face pinched. "First the merchants refused us in Bethsaida, then the questions in Magdala, now this. The pattern grows clearer each week."

Philip nodded. His fingers found the wooden beads at his belt—*click, click, click* as he moved them, an old habit. "They are becoming more organized in their opposition."

Several other disciples exchanged knowing glances. This was not the first such encounter, but it was the most violent yet.

Tirzah kneeled beside James. Her fingers hovered over his bruised face, not quite touching, as if afraid contact would hurt him. "You fought?"

"Not willingly." James winced as she gently touched his split lip. Fresh blood welled at the corner. "They did not give us much choice."

I kneeled on his other side. The ground was warm, still holding the day's heat. I examined the bandage on his arm. The linen was crusted to the wound beneath, stiff with dried blood. It would need to be soaked before removal or the scab would tear. "This needs proper cleaning."

"I will get your healing supplies." Mary was already moving toward my tent.

"Did you get the wine and tunic?" Thomas asked, ever practical.

Andrew nodded. "We did. Though we paid for it with more than coin."

Jesus approached. His face was solemn as he looked at James's injuries. He touched James's uninjured shoulder, his hand gentle. "Was anyone else harmed?"

"The merchant who sold us the wine," John said. His hands curled at his sides. "They knocked over his stall when they came after us. Called him a collaborator. His wares were everywhere—jars broken, wine soaking into the dust."

James looked up at Tirzah. Pain lived in his eyes. "I am sorry. This is not how I wanted to begin our marriage. All bruised and bloodied."

"Hush." She pressed her fingers gently to his uninjured cheek. Her touch was featherlight. "You are here. That is what matters."

Mary returned with my healing supplies. The leather satchel was familiar in my hands, worn smooth from use. I began my work. Tirzah held James's other hand while I soaked the bandage with clean water from a clay jug, the water cool and smelling faintly of the stream. I poured it slowly, watching it darken the linen, loosen the crusted blood. James's breath came sharp through his teeth.

"Almost done."

The bandage finally came free. The gash across his forearm was angry and red, the edges swollen—not deep enough for stitches but almost. I cleaned it with wine, the sharp smell filling the air. James jerked at the sting. I worked quickly, my fingers steady even as my heart pounded.

"Will this delay the wedding?" someone asked from the gathering crowd.

Before James could answer, Tirzah spoke. "No. We will marry tomorrow as planned. I will not let fear or hatred dictate our joy."

I applied a poultice of crushed herbs to his arm, a mixture of calendula and yarrow ground into a green paste, smelling sharp and medicinal.

James winced. "That hurts."

"Good." I wrapped a clean bandage around the wound, winding it carefully, tucking the end. "It means it is working."

"Will I have full use of my arm for the ceremony tomorrow?" He flexed his fingers. They moved stiffly.

I secured the bandage with a small knot, testing the tension. "You will be sore, but you will present Tirzah with the marriage token tomorrow."

"And hold a cup of wine." Andrew unrolled a bundle of deep-blue fabric, the cloth catching the last golden rays of sunlight. "Which we procured despite our welcome."

The tunic was finely woven, the traditional wedding blue, simple but beautiful, the fabric soft and supple. John placed a small clay flask of wine on the ground with a soft *clink*, the flask unbroken despite the scuffle.

Tirzah touched the fabric, her fingers reverent on the weave, tracing the threads. "You did all this for me?"

"For us." James covered her hand with his, his fingers rough and bruised against her smooth skin. "A proper beginning, even in improper times."

The camp quieted as night fell. As I put my supplies back into the satchel, Jesus gathered the disciples near.

"Opposition grows stronger... must be wise... gentle as doves..."

Andrew found me later as I washed blood from my hands. The basin water turned pink, then red, then slowly clear as I scrubbed, the blood sticky beneath my nails. He sat beside me on a fallen log, the wood rough beneath us, his knee brushing mine warm through the fabric.

"I am sorry we worried you."

"I was not worried." The lie came easily. Then I caught his eye. "Well, perhaps a little."

"Only a little?" His shoulder pushed against mine. "Your face tells a different story. I could see your worry from halfway up the path."

"You were the one in danger, not me."

His mouth twitched. "I would rather face a dozen angry townsmen than return to Salome's wrath when we were late. The way she paced..." He shook his head, a wry smile playing at his lips. "Like a hawk circling prey."

I laughed despite myself. "She wore a path in the ground."

Andrew took my damp hands in his, his palms rough and calloused and warm despite the cooling evening. "This is the reality of the life we have chosen, Anna. There will be danger. Separation. Uncertainty."

"I know."

His gaze grew serious, searching my face. "Today was a small taste. The hostility will only grow. Jesus has warned us of this."

I thought of James's bruised face, the merchant's destroyed stall, the hatred strong enough to drive men to violence over differences in belief, and the blood I had just washed from my hands. "I understand better now than I did this morning."

"And still you stay?"

"Of course I stay." I turned my hands to clasp his, lacing our fingers together. "I will not be separated from you. We both knew the cost when I came. Today does not change that."

He exhaled, his shoulders relaxing, the tension flowing out. "Good. Because I need you here. Especially now, with what is coming."

"What is coming?"

Andrew looked toward where Jesus sat with Simon, their heads bent close in conversation. "I do not know exactly. But Jesus speaks more frequently of Jerusalem and of confrontation." He shook his head. "Whatever lies ahead, it will not be easier than today."

The breeze carried the scent of night-blooming flowers, sweet and heavy, almost cloying, and woodsmoke from the cooking fires. The air was cooling rapidly now, raising gooseflesh on my arms. Stars appeared one by one in the darkening sky, familiar patterns emerging from the blue. In the center of camp, Tirzah sat beside James, her head resting on his shoulder. Mary sang a quiet evening hymn, her voice rising and falling like water over stones.

"Not everyone finds joy in the approach of a wedding."

I turned. Judas stood a few paces away, his refined features shadowed in the deepening twilight, his robes finer than those of the other disciples, less dusty, better maintained. He often kept himself apart, observing more than participating.

"Tomorrow brings happiness to many," he continued, his

words careful, each syllable precise. "But such celebrations remind others of what they have sacrificed."

"We have all sacrificed," Andrew said. "It is the cost of following."

Judas smiled, teeth catching the last of the light, white against shadow. "Some sacrifices are heavier than others. Some of us had positions of respect, family connections, futures secured by wealth and influence."

"And you regret your choice?"

His gaze shifted to me, assessing. "I regret nothing that serves a greater purpose. But I wonder if our Rabbi understands how quickly doors are closing." He gestured toward James, the motion languid. "Today's incident is not isolated. The authorities in Jerusalem send inquiries about us to every town. They watch, they record, they prepare."

"For what?" Andrew's voice sharpened.

"For whatever they deem necessary to protect their power. The Romans grow nervous about gatherings like ours. They fear another uprising." He paused. "I still hear things from my time in Jerusalem. The Temple treasury keeps careful accounts of more than just coins. Our numbers grow. That makes some nervous." He glanced toward where Jesus sat. "Our Rabbi means well, but..." He let the thought linger, unfinished, then nodded curtly and moved away.

"I do not trust him." I said it softly, barely above a whisper.

Andrew sighed. "He manages our funds with skill. Jesus values his perspective."

"That does not mean you trust him."

"No." He squeezed my hand. "It does not."

I shivered, and Andrew wrapped an arm around my shoulders, his body heat welcome. "Let us join the others."

Around the main fire, the community had gathered. Thomas played a simple melody on a wooden flute, the notes swirling in the night air, sweet and plaintive, merging with the crackling fire and distant nightbirds calling to each other in the darkness. Philip tapped a gentle rhythm on a small handheld drum, the sound like a heartbeat. Mary led the women in traditional wedding songs, her clear voice rising above the others, the Hebrew words ancient, worn smooth by generations of voices.

Tirzah sat beside James, the blue tunic folded carefully in her lap. Her fingers occasionally touched it as if to confirm its reality, moving over the fabric with care. Firelight painted her face in shifting shades of gold and ochre, making her eyes shine.

"Tomorrow," Andrew whispered in my ear, his breath warm against my skin, "they begin their journey together, whatever paths lie ahead."

"As we did."

"Yes." He kissed my temple, his lips soft and warm. "Though our path seems to grow stonier by the day."

I watched the flames dance, their amber light warming the circle of faces. The fire blazed, sending up sparks that died before reaching the stars.

When Jesus joined our circle, his presence brought a deeper quiet. The talking stopped, and the songs trailed off. He sat between James and John, his hands resting on both their shoulders.

"Today you have tasted the world's rejection." His voice carried to all gathered. "It will not be the last time." His gaze moved around the circle, meeting each person's eyes, holding them with quiet intensity before moving on. "Those who cannot bear what lies ahead will fall away.

Those who remain will find burdens they did not expect to carry."

He looked at James and Tirzah, his face warming, the harsh lines softening. "Yet even in shadow, light persists. Even in struggle, love endures. Tomorrow we celebrate that endurance, that persistence." He smiled, the warmth reaching his eyes. "Tonight, we rest knowing that what we build together matters. The world does not fight against what holds no power to change it."

The fire eventually burned lower. Coals glowed red and orange, pulsing like a heartbeat. People drifted toward their tents, calling soft good nights, their silhouettes dark against the dying light. I watched Tirzah and James, their hands intertwined, fingers laced tight. Their faces turned toward each other in conversation too quiet for others to hear, their foreheads nearly touching. Tomorrow they would pledge themselves to each other and to this uncertain path.

Like Andrew and I had done. Like many others would do.

Mary's voice rose in a final blessing song. The ancient Hebrew words carried into the night, rising toward the stars. A prayer for protection. For faithfulness. For courage in the face of whatever might come.

The words faded, and the fire died to embers. Andrew's hand found mine in the darkness.

CHAPTER 4

Jerusalem, February, 31 AD

Water trickled down the back of my neck, cold against my skin beneath the collar of my wool cloak. The garment hung heavy against my shoulders, its fibers soaked through after five days of persistent winter rain. Three months of hard travel had transformed it into a poor imitation of its former self.

Around me, the others hunched forward against the downpour, heads bowed as we made our slow progress toward Jerusalem. The road had dissolved into a quagmire of rust-colored mud that sucked at our sandals with each step, releasing them with reluctant squelching sounds. The earthy scent of wet soil mingled with the sour tang of unwashed bodies and damp wool. Days of unrelenting rain had even dampened Simon's cheerful commentary.

"There," Andrew said, pointing toward the crest of the hill before us. "Jerusalem."

I raised my eyes, blinking against the rain. Jerusalem gradually emerged through the mist, pale limestone buildings rising on the hillside, the massive form of the Temple Mount dominating the skyline. After weeks of small villages and crude shelters, the rain-darkened silhouette made my breath catch.

"The Holy City," Tirzah murmured beside me, her voice carrying the same reverent tone it held whenever she spoke of Jerusalem.

"The city of roofs that do not leak," Joanna added with a practical longing that drew weary laughter from the women around us.

As we entered the main square, Jesus turned to address the group, rain streaming down his face. "We shall stay three days. I will teach in the Temple courts each day."

Simon stepped forward. "A friend has offered his home near the Temple. It will be crowded, but we should all stay together as a community during our time in Jerusalem."

The others nodded in agreement. The prospect of shelter, even crowded shelter, was clearly appealing after days of travel in the rain.

As the others began discussing arrangements, a hand touched my arm. Andrew stood beside me. "You look exhausted," he said, his voice low.

"Just the journey," I assured him, though the constant rain had chilled me through.

"Perhaps we should—" Andrew began, but his words faltered, and his face brightened. "Joseph!"

There, making his way toward us through the crowd of pilgrims, came my father. Even from a distance, the rich blue of his councilman's cloak set him apart. He moved with the confident stride of a man accustomed to respect, yet the moment his eyes found mine, his face broke into a smile.

"Anna," he said, embracing me without regard for my sodden state.

"Abba." I returned his embrace. I had missed him. "How did you know we had arrived?"

"I have friends who watch the roads," he said then turned to clasp Andrew's arm in greeting. "Son. You look…"

"Like a shepherd caught in the flood?" Andrew supplied with a rueful smile.

"I was going to say 'well-traveled,'" my father replied, "but your description may be more accurate." He looked us both over, then to the bedraggled group beyond. "My house has room for several of you, at least. You are all welcome to whatever comfort I can provide."

Jesus approached, inclining his head with familial warmth to my father. "Your generosity honors us, Uncle. We have arranged lodging near the Temple, where we can remain together during our teaching days." His eyes moved between my father and me. "But surely Anna and Andrew should accept your hospitality. Family bonds are sacred."

"It is decided, then," my father said. He turned back to us. "You will both come to the house. I have had chambers prepared since I heard you were coming to Jerusalem."

"The house," I echoed. I had not seen my father's Jerusalem residence since I was five years old, when my mother still lived. A courtyard with a small fig tree. Cool stone floors beneath my feet. Servants who slipped me treats when Ima was not looking.

"It stands ready for you," my father said, his face softening at whatever he saw in mine. "For both of you."

Andrew frowned slightly, glancing between my father and the group of disciples still clustered around Jesus.

We stared at each other, the rain streaming between us, while my father maintained a diplomatic silence. Finally, Andrew exhaled slowly. "I should return to the others now." He hesitated then added, "And I should stay with them tonight. We have matters to discuss for tomorrow's teaching."

"You would stay with them and refuse my father's hospitality?"

"I am not refusing," Andrew corrected. "Just... I have responsibilities to the group."

"I see." I turned toward my father.

Andrew caught my arm. "Anna—"

I pulled free. "Do as you feel you must. My father's house will remain where it is."

"Anna—"

"The eastern market," my father interjected smoothly. "When you are ready to join us, ask for the councilman's residence. Any local can direct you."

Andrew nodded. "Thank you. I will... I will see you both tomorrow."

He turned and walked back to the group, his shoulders hunched against more than just the rain.

"He may yet change his mind," my father said quietly.

"He will not come," I said, pulling my sodden cloak tighter. "He has made his choice."

My father led me through streets that grew more familiar with each turn, memories surfacing with each corner turned. Here was the spice merchant's corner where my mother had once purchased cinnamon that made our bread taste like festival treats. There stood the well where women still gathered to draw water, just as they had when I was small. The city had changed yet remained essentially the same, much like my relationship with it.

The house, when we reached it, proved both familiar and strange. The courtyard was smaller than I remembered, and the fig tree taller. The main room, with its richly colored wall hangings and carefully placed oil lamps, struck me with its opulence only because I had grown accustomed to the simplicity of tents and village homes.

A serving woman took my cloak, promising a bath and fresh garments. The guest chamber held a copper bathtub, steam rising from the surface. I had not seen one since leaving Arimathea.

The hot water embraced me. I sank deeper until it lapped at my collarbone, the heat penetrating bone-deep chill. I remembered three months of washing in cold streams where my fingers turned blue. Three months of rationing precious cupfuls of heated water, choosing between my face or my feet but never both. Three months of mud worked into the creases of my skin until I forgot what it felt like to be clean.

I closed my eyes. The warmth pulled at me, loosening tension I had not known I carried.

By the time I emerged, dressed in clean robes that felt impossibly soft against my skin, the rain had stopped, and evening approached. I found my father in the small garden that occupied one corner of the courtyard, tending to a collection of herbs I recognized as healing plants.

"Your color is better," he observed as I joined him. "Are you hungry?"

"I am very hungry," I admitted.

My father hesitated. "Do you think Andrew might still come tonight?"

I shook my head. "He made his choice clear. He is staying with the others."

"I see." My father studied me for a moment. "Then let us eat. Tomorrow is another day."

We sat in the dining area, reclining on cushions that felt absurdly luxurious after months of sitting on ground cloths. Servants brought fresh wheat bread still warm from the oven, roasted lamb fragrant with spices, stewed vegetables gleaming with olive oil, soft cheese, dates and almonds, and wine—actual wine, not the watered version we rationed on the road.

"How fares life on the road?" Abba asked after we had eaten in silence for several minutes. "The few messages I have received from travelers have been selective in their details."

"It is harder than I expected," I said finally. "The physical demands alone are considerable. The distances we walk each day, the weather, the uncertain shelter."

"And Andrew? Is he attentive to your needs?"

I broke off another piece of bread. "He tries. But he has responsibilities to Jesus that often take precedence."

"Over his responsibilities to you?" My father's tone remained neutral, but he looked at me more intently than he had been.

"Like tonight," I admitted, staring into my cup. "This is not the first time, just the most obvious example." I sighed. "When we married, I knew he followed Jesus. I knew what I was choosing." My voice softened. "At least, I thought I did."

"And now?"

"Now I understand there is a difference between visiting the ministry and living it," I admitted. "Between admiring a man's devotion and competing with it."

My father nodded slowly. "I wondered if you would discover that distinction. Your mother did, in her way."

"What do you mean?"

"Your mother married a man devoted to the Law, to the Temple, to the Council of elders. She learned, as you are learning, that such devotions create divided loyalties."

I stared at him. "I never thought of it that way."

"Few do until they experience it directly." He refilled my cup with wine. "Tell me about your journey since we last met. I understand there was a wedding?"

The change of subject lightened my mood immediately. "Yes! Tirzah and James were married just after Sukkot, when the fall harvest ended. Jesus himself conducted the ceremony. It was simple but beautiful."

As I described the wedding and the events since, I chose my words carefully, emphasizing the positive aspects while minimizing the hardships. The women's companionship, not the lack of privacy. The local families who offered food, not the days without proper meals. The occasional village home with space for everyone, not the more frequent nights crowded under makeshift shelters.

My father listened attentively, his keen eyes suggesting he detected the omissions in my narrative. When I finished, he merely nodded. "And the healing work? Have you had the opportunity to use your skills?"

"Some," I said, the question touching on a sensitive point. "There is always a need. Fevers, injuries, skin ailments."

"Jesus is fortunate to count you among his followers."

A servant appeared to clear away our meal. The evening grew late, and though I tried to hide my repeated glances toward the door, my father noticed.

"It appears he will not arrive this evening. And despite your earlier certainty that he would not come, I know you still hoped he would. The choice he made was difficult for him. Give him time."

I nodded, fighting back tears. "I should rest. The day has been long."

That night, alone in the guest chamber prepared for both Andrew and me, I lay awake staring at the ceiling. The bed felt too large, too empty.

I turned onto my side, watching moonlight filter through the window shutters. Tomorrow. Tomorrow I would see him at the Temple and perhaps understand better why he had chosen as he had.

THE NEXT MORNING, I stood with Tirzah and the other women at the edge of a growing assembly, the smooth paving stones beneath our feet still damp from yesterday's rain. Beneath the open sky, the vast expanse of the Temple courtyard accommodated hundreds yet still felt crowded with humanity. The mingled scents of incense, animal sacrifice, and too many bodies pressed together created a distinctive perfume I associated with Jerusalem itself.

Jesus sat on a low wall near Solomon's Portico, disciples arranged in a loose semicircle around him. Andrew sat among them, looking tired but attentive, the shadows beneath his eyes speaking of a night spent on a hard floor with too many bodies in too small a space. A small, uncharitable part of me felt satisfied. Our eyes met briefly across the distance before he turned back to Jesus's teaching.

"You look different today," Tirzah observed, studying my face with frank curiosity.

"Different how?"

"More... distant," she said. "I noticed Andrew stayed with us last night while you went with your father."

"Yes. We had a disagreement," I admitted with a sigh. "About where his priorities should lie."

Tirzah nodded, understanding immediately. "James said Andrew was torn about it. Andrew moped around all evening." She lowered her voice. "James told me he might have made the same choice if my father had a home in Jerusalem."

"And what would you have wanted?" I asked.

"A night away from twenty people sleeping in one room?" Tirzah raised an eyebrow. "What do you think?"

I smiled despite myself. "I had an actual bath, and it was peaceful."

"I imagine it was," she said wistfully. "Sometimes I think the men forget there is more to marriage than just duty." She glanced toward where James sat among the disciples. "They do not always see what we sacrifice to be here."

"They have their own sacrifices," I said, feeling compelled to be fair despite my lingering hurt.

"True," Tirzah conceded. "But theirs are celebrated while ours are merely expected."

Before I could respond, the crowd shifted and murmured. A group of men in the formal garb of the Pharisees approached, their faces ranging from curious to openly hostile.

"Gamaliel is with them," my father murmured from beside me, having appeared so quietly I had not noticed his approach. "And Eleazar. This is no casual encounter."

"Who are they?" I asked, watching as the group positioned themselves prominently within hearing distance of Jesus.

"Influential teachers from the Sanhedrin. Members I have sat in council with many times," he explained. "But their presence here is a troubling sign."

His tone made me glance up sharply. "What has changed?"

"The opposition is organizing," he said, his voice barely audible. "They are actively seeking ways to trap him, to document his teachings for evidence against him."

"And your position on the council?"

"No longer secure," he admitted grimly. "As you know, after they interrupted your wedding with their summons, they have grown more suspicious. I have begun preparing for whatever comes next."

Before I could press further, Jesus began to speak. His voice, though not loud, echoed clearly across the courtyard. He was teaching about the Sabbath, a frequent point of contention between him and the religious authorities.

"The Sabbath was made for man, not man for the Sabbath," Jesus said. "So the Son of Man is Lord even of the Sabbath."

A murmur ran through the crowd. This teaching was indeed controversial—suggesting the Sabbath laws should serve human well-being rather than rigid adherence to tradition challenged fundamental interpretations.

"You speak against the Law," one of the Pharisees called out. "Moses gave us these commands directly from God."

Jesus regarded the man with a steady gaze that held neither defensiveness nor challenge. "Have you not read what David did when he and his companions were hungry? How he entered the house of God and ate the consecrated bread, which was not lawful for him to eat but only for the priests?"

The Pharisee's face flushed with anger. "You compare yourself to David?"

"I tell you that one greater than the Temple is here," Jesus replied calmly. "If you had understood what these words mean, 'I desire mercy, not sacrifice', you would not have condemned the innocent."

The Pharisees conferred among themselves, their discomfort evident at Jesus's skillful use of their own scriptures to counter their accusation. Most turned away, muttering complaints about twisted interpretations and dangerous teachings. But one of the younger Pharisees remained, standing apart from his colleagues. His face held none of their anger—only a deep, troubled thoughtfulness. He watched Jesus with an intensity that made his knuckles white on the edges of his prayer shawl. When the others called to him to leave, he hesitated then slowly followed but not before glancing back once more at Jesus.

"He walks a dangerous line," my father whispered. "Using their own traditions to refute them while making claims they consider blasphemous."

"Which increases the danger to you as well," I said, unable to keep worry from my voice. "Have you considered withdrawing from the council before they force you out?"

He shook his head firmly. "I can do more good from within, for now. Nicodemus and I provide information Jesus needs about their plans." His eyes took on a distant look. "When the time comes for open declaration, I will be ready. But that moment has not arrived yet."

"You have spoken with Nicodemus about this?"

"We meet privately, away from Jerusalem. He faces the same choices I do." My father's face softened. "Do not worry for me, Anna. I have had decades to prepare for this moment.

My wealth is secured, my position planned for. The only true cost will be status, and that seems a small price compared to what others will sacrifice."

Before our conversation could continue, a commotion erupted on the far side of the courtyard. A man pushed through the crowd, his movements desperate and uncoordinated. He fell at Jesus's feet, his body contorting in violent spasms.

"Master!" someone cried out. "My son! He has been like this since childhood. He cannot speak. The spirits throw him into fire or water to destroy him. If you can do anything, have compassion and help us!"

The man's affliction was familiar to me—the violent trembling, the speechlessness, the loss of control that most attributed to unclean spirits. I had encountered such suffering in my healing work, though my treatments brought only modest relief. The most I could offer was soothing herbs after an episode and prayers to ward off the spirits' return.

Jesus kneeled beside the suffering man, his face compassionate rather than alarmed. "All things are possible to him who believes," he said to the desperate father.

"Lord, I believe," the man cried, tears streaming down his face. "Help my unbelief!"

Jesus placed his hand on the convulsing man's forehead. "You mute and deaf spirit, I command you, come out of him and enter him no more."

The man's body went rigid then relaxed completely. For a terrible moment, I thought he had died. Then his eyes opened, clear and aware in a way they had not been before. He sat up slowly, looking around in confusion that gradually gave way to wonder.

"Stand," Jesus said gently, helping him to his feet. "You are healed."

The crowd erupted with exclamations of amazement. I watched in awe, my heart filled with joy for the man now standing whole before us.

"It is remarkable," Tirzah said beside me.

"Truly a blessing to witness," I agreed, my voice hushed with wonder. "His power reminds me why we are here. To witness God's work in the world."

"And your own healing gifts?" Tirzah asked.

I smiled. "Are given by the same God, though in smaller measure. When I treat someone successfully, I see now it is His work through my hands." I touched the small pouch of healing herbs at my belt. "My skills and His miracles serve the same purpose of relieving suffering and showing God's mercy."

The crowd dispersed as Jesus concluded his teaching for the morning. I saw Andrew hesitate before making his way toward us, his face uncertain. When he reached my side, there was a moment of awkward silence between us.

"Did you sleep well?" he finally asked, his voice carrying a hint of discomfort.

"Yes," I answered, not elaborating further. "And you?"

"The floor was hard," he admitted with a small, conciliatory smile. "Simon snores louder than the Temple trumpets."

Despite myself, I felt the corner of my mouth twitch upward. "Perhaps you might reconsider your choices tonight."

Before he could respond, my father intervened smoothly. "Is something wrong, Andrew? You seem troubled."

Andrew's face shifted back to seriousness. "Jesus wishes to speak with you," he said to my father. "Privately."

My father nodded as if he had been expecting this. "I shall join him momentarily." He glanced between Andrew and me, clearly sensing the tension. "Andrew, would you accompany Anna to the market? There are supplies I wish to provide for your journey onward. Perhaps you two might... talk."

"Of course," Andrew agreed, though I noted the concern still evident in his eyes.

As my father moved away to join Jesus, Andrew took my hand. "Let us find Judas as well. He manages the group's funds and will know what we need most."

We found Judas in the outer courtyard, engaged in what appeared to be an intense discussion with a man I did not recognize. As we approached, I caught fragments of their conversation.

"—gathering significant support among the common people—"

"—cannot act prematurely—"

They fell silent at our approach, the stranger departing with a curt nod that acknowledged our presence without welcoming it.

"Andrew." Judas greeted him with his characteristic charm, though I noted he did not extend the same warmth to me. "And Anna. What brings you here?"

"Joseph wishes to provide supplies for our journey," Andrew explained. "We thought you might know what the group needs most."

Judas's face brightened with genuine interest. "How generous of your father! We could use new waterskins, certainly. And perhaps oil for lamps. The nights remain long this time of year."

"Who was that man you were speaking with?" I asked during a lull in their conversation.

Judas's smile remained unchanged, but his posture shifted subtly. "A supporter of our work. He has connections among those who wait for Israel's redemption."

"What kind of connections?" Andrew asked.

"The kind that matter when change comes," Judas replied. "When Jesus claims his true authority, many will discover how powerless they actually are."

There was nothing overtly alarming in his words, yet his expectations felt misaligned with Jesus's teachings as I understood them.

"Jesus speaks of a kingdom not of this world," I said carefully.

Judas laughed, the sound not unkind but somehow dismissive. "Naturally, he must be circumspect in public. The Romans crucify those who challenge their authority openly."

Andrew frowned slightly. "I have not heard Jesus speak of such things, even in private."

"Perhaps you have not been listening with the right ears," Judas suggested before returning to the matter of supplies.

As we made our way through the crowded marketplace while selecting supplies, I thought of my father. By now he would have met with Jesus.

"They will not speak where they might be overheard," Andrew had said. "Too dangerous for them both."

THAT EVENING, back at my father's house, Andrew appeared at the door. "Am I welcome?"

"Always." I stepped aside to let him enter. We sat with my

father in his garden among the herb beds, the evening air carrying the mingled scents of rosemary and mint.

"The council is watching him more closely than ever," my father said, his voice low despite the privacy of his garden. "There are those among the Pharisees who seek any pretext to discredit him, and those among the Sadducees who fear he will provoke Roman intervention."

"How great is the danger?" Andrew asked, his face grave.

"Significant and growing. Jesus speaks openly against hypocrisy, challenges traditional interpretations of the Law, and attracts crowds that make both religious and Roman authorities nervous." My father sighed. "And now there are rumors he may claim messianic authority."

"He has never said this directly," Andrew objected.

"What he has not said matters less than what people believe he represents," my father replied. "There are many who see in him the fulfillment of prophecy—the promised king who will restore Israel."

I thought of Judas and his barely concealed expectations of political revolution. "Does Jesus know of these perceptions?"

"He is fully aware," my father confirmed. "And undeterred."

When my father finally excused himself for the night, leaving us alone in the garden, silence fell between us.

"I am sorry," Andrew said at last, his voice quiet in the darkness. "For not coming here last night."

"And I am sorry for not understanding your reluctance," I replied.

He looked up. "You understand now?"

"Not entirely," I admitted. "But I have been thinking about it all day."

Andrew moved to sit beside me rather than across from me in the garden. "When I thought about this house, when I realized the difference between your world and mine..."

"This house has nothing to do with us," I began, but he raised a hand gently, the calluses on his palm catching the amber light from nearby oil lamps.

"But it does," he said. "It reminds me of what you left behind. For me." His hands worked unconsciously, fingers flexing as if seeking the familiar resistance of nets. "These past months on the road. The cold that seeps into your bones until you forget what warmth feels like. The mud that never truly washes away. The hunger that becomes a companion. Watching you struggle with it all..."

He fell silent, his face as pained as if the words themselves were stones too heavy to carry. I waited, sensing he needed to find his own way through this tangle of emotions, like navigating a boat through rocky shallows.

"When we married, I told myself you understood what you were choosing," he finally continued. "The hardships seemed like nothing to me. I had grown accustomed to them. But watching you endure them..." His eyes met mine. "Seeing you sleep in rain-soaked tents, go hungry when villages turned us away, walk until your feet bled. It is different when it is someone you love suffering these things. Someone who gave up comfort and safety because of you."

I began to understand. "So you stayed away last night. Because being here reminded you of what I gave up."

"I told myself it was about duty to the group," he admitted. "That was... easier than facing the guilt I feel when I see you struggle."

A small, painful laugh escaped me. "And I believed the

worst. That you chose them because I was not—" I stopped abruptly.

"Not enough?"

All this time, we had been carrying the same fear.

"All my life," I said softly, "I have tried to be enough. For my father after Ima died. For Deborah. For everyone." I touched my scarred face reflexively. "Always proving my worth."

"And I have spent my life knowing I would never have much to offer," he said. "When your father welcomed me, despite having nothing..."

"He saw what I see," I said, reaching for his hands.

He looked up. "How could you think you are not enough?"

"How could you think I would regret marrying you because of material comforts?"

We stared at each other, the absurdity of our mutual misunderstanding suddenly apparent. A laugh escaped me, small at first then growing. Andrew's mouth twitched, then he smiled.

"We are both afraid of the same thing," I said when I could speak again. "That we are not enough for each other."

"I am a simple fisherman," he said, his smile fading. "Nothing will change that."

"And I am a woman whose face bears scars that make children stare," I countered. "Nothing will change that either. Yet you chose me knowing this."

"Your scars are beautiful to me," he said, the words so simple and true.

"And your hands," I said, reaching for them, "are beautiful to me. Strong enough to haul nets, gentle enough to ease pain, faithful enough to follow Jesus even when the path is difficult." I held his rough palms against my cheeks. "These hands sheltered me when I needed shelter. These hands will build our home someday. These hands I chose, knowing exactly what they are."

His shoulders dropped, the tension flowing out. "I fear I will never give you the life you deserve."

"The life I deserve is the one I chose," I said. "With you. Following Jesus, wherever that leads us."

He leaned forward until his forehead rested against mine, our shared breath creating an intimate space between us. "Forgive me for staying away last night."

"Forgive me for not understanding your concerns," I replied. "For making it about my worth rather than your fears."

"We have much to learn about each other still," he said, drawing back slightly to meet my eyes.

"We have time," I assured him, though I wondered if we would ever fully bridge the gap between our worlds.

His response came not in words but in the gentle pressure of his lips against mine, tentative at first as if seeking permission, then with growing certainty as I answered in kind.

That night, in the unfamiliar comfort of my father's guest chamber, we came together with the tenderness of those who have wounded and been wounded, who have spoken truth and been heard. His hands traced careful paths across my skin, learning me anew. When his fingers found my scars, he did not pass over them but lingered there, and I understood what he had tried to tell me in words—that these marks were not flaws to overlook but part of what he loved. My scars became sacred ground beneath his touch.

In the flickering lamplight, we found each other again.

The day's hurt fell away, replaced by this—skin against skin, breath mingling, the quiet sounds of reunion.

Afterward, as moonlight spilled through the narrow window and painted silver patterns across the woven blanket, I placed my hand over my abdomen. Beneath my palm, I felt the gift of this night taking root.

Andrew slept beside me, his face relaxed in a way it rarely was during waking hours, the sharp lines of worry smoothed away.

The rain had returned by the time we left Jerusalem. It streamed down around us as we continued northward, away from comforts and toward whatever awaited us on the road ahead. My new cloak kept the worst of the downpour at bay, the tightly woven wool shedding water like a duck's feathers.

Andrew reached for my hand as we navigated a treacherous section where the road had become a shallow stream, stones slick with green slime beneath our feet. "Are you all right?"

"Yes." I laid my free hand against my abdomen, warmth blooming there despite the rain soaking through my cloak.

Andrew squeezed my hand, and we continued north, water streaming down our faces.

CHAPTER 5

Ministry Camp, April, 31 AD

The bile rose in my throat before I was fully awake, bitter and flooding my mouth without warning, the taste of copper and last night's bread mixing with the sour churn of my empty stomach. I scrambled from my sleeping mat, one hand clamped over my lips while the other braced on the tent pole. The cool predawn air slid over my face as I stumbled away from camp, seeking privacy among the olive trees that bordered our site, their old trunks dark in the gray light filtering through leaves overhead.

I barely made it far enough before my stomach heaved, emptying its meager contents onto the rocky ground beneath a gnarled tree. The spasm left me trembling, sweat beading cold on my forehead despite the morning chill, my knees digging into damp earth that smelled of wet stone and crushed grass. I braced myself on the trunk, its bark scoring my palm as another wave of nausea washed over me, and I closed my eyes while the world spun liquid and uncertain.

"You too?"

I turned at Tirzah's voice, finding her several paces away, her silhouette visible in the gray light of approaching dawn, the sky behind her beginning to lighten from black to pearl. She wiped her mouth with the back of her hand, her face as pale as the waning moon that hung like a remnant above us, and in that moment, we were two women sharing the oldest secret in the world without speaking a word of it.

"Three mornings now," I said, straightening slowly, my belly muscles aching from the strain, the metallic taste still coating my tongue.

"Five for me." She pushed her dark braid back over her shoulder, the plait fraying at the edges where she had slept on it, tiny wisps escaping around her temples. She moved closer, her sandals crunching on the rocky soil, and the faint scent of sickness clung to her breath mixed with night's sleep. "Though yesterday was not as bad."

We looked at each other, and in that look passed everything we both knew but had not yet said aloud. The knowing sank into my bones, as certain as the sunrise that was even now gilding the high branches with gold. Her mouth curved at one edge, and I smiled in return despite the lingering sour taste and the shaking in my legs.

"Here." She offered me a small skin of water, its leather worn soft from use. "Rinse your mouth. It helps."

The water was cool and sweet, washing away the bitterness, and I held it in my mouth for a moment before spitting carefully onto the ground. I handed the skin back to her, our fingers brushing in the exchange.

"Thank you."

The sky lightened around us as we stood together, the first rays catching the leaves overhead and turning them to flame, casting long shadows across the ground. Birds began their morning songs, tentative at first and then building to a chorus, and somewhere in the distance, a rooster crowed, its call echoing across the hills. The camp would stir soon, and we would need to return before anyone noticed our absence.

"We should get back," Tirzah said, though she made no move to leave.

"Yes." I remained where I was, uncertain what to say next, the words knotting in my throat. I did not want to tell Tirzah what I had not yet told Andrew, did not want to speak the certainty aloud before he knew it first.

Instead of speaking, she reached for my hand and squeezed it once, her palm against mine, then released it. We walked back to camp together in silence, our footsteps crunching softly on the path while the world woke around us and the sky turned from gray to rose to gold.

After helping prepare breakfast, I slipped away from the bustling camp, drawn to the sound of water nearby, the gentle rush and gurgle that promised coolness and clarity. The scent of bread and honey had turned my stomach again, though I forced myself to eat a little. The small stream ran cold and clear over smooth stones worn round by years of water and time, its surface catching the morning light in silver flashes. I dipped my hands into the icy water, the shock of cold making me gasp as I splashed my face and neck, letting droplets cling to my eyelashes and run down my throat, washing away the night's sweat and the lingering taste of sickness.

I sat down on a flat rock beside the stream, the stone still holding the night's chill, and for a moment, I just breathed, letting the sound of the water and the smell of wet stone calm the churning in my belly. I closed my eyes and counted backward through the phases of the moon, feeling the rhythm of my body's timing the way a healer learns to track such things, measuring the days and nights since my last bleeding. Two cycles missed now, and before that, the subtle changes I had tried to ignore. The tenderness in my breasts. The way certain smells upset my stomach. The bone-deep weariness that claimed me by midday. There was no doubt.

The certainty took root in my chest, as real as the stone beneath me. Tears came, running down my cheeks to mix with the water still clinging to my skin. I laid both hands flat on my belly, feeling my flesh, the slight softness there that would grow and swell in the months to come. A tiny, perfect baby, already real and already mine. Already Andrew's. The joy that rushed up through my chest was so sharp it stole my breath, leaving me gasping like I had been running, my heart pounding hard.

I had to tell Andrew. Now. I could not hold this secret another moment or sit alone by this stream knowing what I knew while he worked unknowing it back at camp.

I found him helping Simon mend a torn pack, their heads bent together over the leather. The morning sun caught in Andrew's hair, turning the dark strands to copper and bronze, and I stopped to watch him for a moment before he sensed my presence and glanced up. His entire face changed when he saw me, the dimples appearing in his cheeks, his eyes crinkling at the corners in the way that sent heat flooding through my chest.

"Anna." He set aside his work, rising to greet me, his hands dusty from the leather and rope. "I missed you at breakfast."

"Walk with me?" I took his hand, my fingers curling around his, and led him away from Simon and the other men working nearby.

We followed a narrow path that wound through the olive grove, morning light dappling the ground beneath our feet in patterns of gold and shadow, the leaves overhead rustling in the slight breeze that brought the scent of wild thyme and warming earth. When we were far enough from camp that no one would overhear, I stopped beneath the spread of a tree, its branches offering a canopy of silver-green leaves that whispered secrets to the wind.

"What is it?" Andrew asked, studying my face with those brown eyes that never missed anything. Except this.

I took both his hands in mine, feeling my fingers tremble in his palms. We had spoken of children before, of course, but only briefly in the quiet moments before sleep claimed us, fleeting references to some distant future when we might expand our small family beyond the two of us. But they had just been dreams and whispered hopes, words spoken into darkness with no weight behind them.

Until now.

"Andrew." My heart hammered so hard the pulse of it filled my mouth. "Have you ever thought about what our children might be like?"

His expression softened, grew distant, his gaze turning inward. A pulse beat at the hinge of his jaw, quick and visible, and I wanted to touch my fingers there, to feel the rhythm of his blood beneath the skin, to know what he was thinking in this moment before everything changed.

"Many times." His voice dropped and went as soft as wind through wheat. "I have imagined teaching our son to fish, the way my father taught me. The secrets of the deep water, where the fish run in spring, how to read the sky and the wind, when to cast the nets and when to wait." His eyes lightened, the brown turning to amber in the sunlight that filtered through the leaves. "Or a daughter who could learn your herbs, who could watch your hands and understand the healing in them. How to recognize sickness before it takes hold, how to bring comfort to those in pain." His mouth curved, crooked and dimpled, in the smile that was mine alone. "A child with your eyes and my stubbornness. Or your wisdom and my height."

"I am glad you did not say my stubbornness." I squeezed his hands tighter to stop mine from shaking, my palms slick.

He reached up to touch my cheek, his fingertips rough on my skin, and the scent of cedar and sweat and sun rose from him, the smell that had become as familiar as my own. "But those were always thoughts for someday. For when we are settled, when the time is right, when we have a home of our own instead of sleeping in tents and traveling from place to place." He tilted his head, curiosity stirring in his gaze, in the slight furrow between his brows. "Why do you ask now?"

My excitement faltered. *Someday. When we were settled. When the time was right.* And here I was, about to tell him the time had already come, whether we were ready or not. Fear flickered through me.

Instead of trying to explain, I took his hand—that hand I knew so well now, the hardened ridge below his fingers from years of rope work, the crescent scar where a fish hook had caught him as a boy, the deep lines etched by salt water and sun and labor—and I guided it lower then laid it flat on my belly where our child grew.

"Because it is no longer just a thought," I whispered.

His hand tensed beneath mine. The heat of it burned

through my tunic, the heaviness of his palm where everything had changed. His face went still, absolutely motionless, every muscle freezing as his mind worked to understand what I was telling him without words. Then understanding broke across his features like dawn breaking over the sea. His eyes widened, pupils swallowing the brown until only a thin rim remained. A flush climbed from his neck, as dark as wine spreading through linen, creeping up into his face until his cheeks burned with it.

The moment stretched as tight as a bowstring. I could not read him. Fear cut through me, sharp beneath my ribs like a blade finding the spaces between bones. Too soon? Too uncertain? Our lives too unsettled, our future too unclear for this news to bring anything but worry and doubt?

Then joy flooded his face, changing him from my husband into a father, from the man I had married into something new and fierce and protective I had never seen before.

"A baby?" His voice emerged hoarse. "We are having a baby?"

I nodded and let my eyes speak what my voice could not, let him see the happiness and fear and wonder all tangled together in my chest.

He lifted me off the ground in a single fluid motion, his strong arms circling my waist as he spun me in a circle beneath the trees, his laughter ringing out clear and bright, echoing among the olive branches. Birds scattered from the canopy above us, startled into flight by the sound.

"A baby!" He set me down carefully, gently, then dropped to his knees before me on the hard ground. His hands cupped my hips, his thumbs resting lightly on the curve of my belly, and a faint quiver ran through his fingers.

"Hello in there," he said to my belly, his voice full of tenderness. "I am your father."

The simple words broke something open in me. Tears spilled hot down my cheeks as I rested my hands on his head, feeling the texture of his sun-warmed hair between my fingers.

"When?" he asked, rising to his feet but keeping his hands at my waist, his fingers gentle there.

"November. Mid-November, I think, if I have counted correctly."

"A child of autumn." He traced the line of my jaw with his fingertip, the gesture so sweet it brought fresh tears to my eyes. "With your eyes, I hope. And your compassion, your gentleness with those who suffer."

"With your heart," I said, my voice catching. "Your courage and your faith, your certainty that Adonai is good even when nothing makes sense."

"You have always been the courageous one, Anna. I knew that from the moment I met you, standing in your father's courtyard with your staff and your scarred face and your eyes that looked straight through me."

He pulled me close, burying his face in my hair, and the rapid beat of his heart matched the tempo of my own, both of us racing together. One of his hands remained at the small of my back, while the other moved to rest lightly on my hip, his thumb tracing small circles there.

"I never knew I could feel this," he murmured into my hair, his breath against my scalp. "I thought I understood joy when you became my wife, when you said yes to me that day in your father's garden. I was wrong. This is... There are no words for this."

I understood perfectly because I felt it, too, this thing

that was beyond language, beyond anything I had known or imagined. I had thought myself complete when my hip was healed, when I married Andrew, when I found my place in this community of travelers. Yet here was a new wholeness I had not known to seek, a fullness I had not known I lacked.

"We have to tell Jesus," Andrew said suddenly, pulling back to look at me, his hands framing my face. "He should be the first to know after us. He should bless our child."

WE FOUND Jesus alone beneath an old sycamore, its trunk thick and twisted with age, his eyes closed in prayer. A stillness hung in the air around him that made me slow my steps, that made the ordinary sounds of morning fade into background noise. His eyes opened as we approached, and he was already smiling, a knowing smile that told me he understood why we sought him, that perhaps he had been waiting for us to arrive at exactly this moment.

"Master," Andrew began, his voice quivering. "We have news."

"Anna carries a child," Jesus said simply.

Andrew's hand tightened around mine, his fingers digging into my palm.

"Come, sit with me." Jesus patted the ground beside him, and we sat cross-legged in the grass that was still damp with dew, the earth cool beneath us. The normal sounds of camp faded further until we might have been alone in the world, just the three of us beneath this tree. Jesus studied me with eyes that bore both gentleness and unfathomable depth, eyes that had seen things I could not imagine.

"New life is our greatest reminder of hope," he said and

reached out to rest his hand on my belly, his touch gentle but sure. "It reminds us that Adonai is always creating, always bringing forth new things, always beginning again."

The nausea that had shadowed me all morning lifted like fog burning away in sunlight. Andrew's fingers found mine and wrapped around them, and we sat in silence while something beyond words passed between heaven and earth, something that made the air shimmer though nothing visibly changed.

"Children are our greatest teachers about faith," Jesus continued, his voice taking on the cadence we had come to know, the rhythm that made his words burrow deep and stay. "They show us how to trust without questioning, how to wonder without cynicism, and how to forgive without keeping accounts of wrongs. They teach us what the Kingdom is like—pure and honest and fully present in each moment."

"Will you bless our child?" I asked, my voice a whisper.

"Before I formed you in the womb, I knew you, Anna." His hand moved from my belly to rest on my head, and his voice took on the weight of Scripture made new. "And I know this child. He is fearfully and wonderfully made, knit together in secret in the hidden places. Every day of this child's life has been written in God's book before even one of them came to be. Your child is already loved dearly by the Father, already known and chosen and precious."

The heat beneath his hands deepened, soaking through me like sunlight warming stone that has been cold all night, like fire penetrating cold bones. My breath caught. Something fluttered inside me, too early to be actual movement yet unmistakable in its presence, the baby stirring in recognition.

I gasped, the sound escaping unbidden. Andrew's hand tightened around mine.

"The child is known to God even now," Jesus said, his voice resonating through my bones, through the earth beneath us, through the very air we breathed. "May wisdom grow alongside the body. May this little one's life shine bright, as a lamp on a stand gives light to all in the house, not hidden but proclaimed for all to see. May your light so shine before others that they may see your good works and glorify your Father in heaven." His voice deepened further, taking on a quality that made the hair on my arms stand up. "This child is precious. Guard him well."

A chill touched my spine despite the heat soaking through me, as unexpected as winter wind cutting through summer, sharp and cold and carrying a warning I could not quite hear. But it passed quickly, swallowed up in the lingering glow of his blessing.

"Share your joy with the community," Jesus said, lifting his hand from my head. "This blessing is not meant to be held in secret. Let others celebrate with you. Let them share in the wonder of new life."

I FOUND Tirzah near the cooking fires, where she had returned after our morning encounter, grinding grain, the rhythmic scrape of stone on stone a sound as old as bread itself. Her cheeks had regained some of their color, though a shadow of fatigue still lingered beneath her eyes, and a slight tremor ran through her hands that told me the morning's sickness had taken more from her than she wanted to admit.

"May I join you?" I asked, sitting beside her, reaching for a handful of grain to add to her pile.

"Of course." She continued her work, the grain crushing between the stones into powder as fine as dust. "You look better than you did at dawn."

"So do you." I took more grain and began helping her grind, letting the familiar rhythm soothe something in me that still felt uncertain and new. "I think we both know why we were sick this morning."

Her hands stilled, the stones going silent. She looked up at me, and a smile crept across her face like sunrise, starting at her eyes and moving down to curve her mouth. "I thought maybe, but... you too?"

I nodded, unable to keep my smile contained, feeling it break across my face wide and joyful. "Andrew knows. And Jesus blessed the baby."

"James told Jesus last night." She set the grinding stones aside and turned to face me fully, abandoning the pretense of work. "I have only known for certain these past few days, though I suspected longer. James said Jesus smiled when he heard and said he had been expecting the news, that he had known before we did."

"When do you think?" I asked, already knowing but needing to hear it confirmed.

"Mid-November, by my counting." Her hand moved to her belly in that protective gesture I recognized because I had been doing the same thing myself. "You?"

"The same. We will walk this road together."

A look passed between us that was deeper than friendship, deeper than sisterhood, even, this shared journey beginning at the same moment, our bodies changing in tandem, our children side by side in the hidden darkness. A bond was forming that would tie us together for the rest of our lives.

"Our children will grow together," Tirzah said, her voice hushed with wonder, with the weight of what we were only beginning to understand. "Like family."

"They will be family," I replied, reaching for her hand. "In all the ways that matter most."

She gripped my hand fiercely, her fingers strong despite their earlier trembling. "I never thought I would have this. A husband who loves me not for what I can give him but for who I am. A child within me that I already love more than my life. A place where I belong, where I am wanted and valued." Her eyes filled with tears that she did not hide. "It feels too much."

I understood because I had felt the same way, had spent years believing marriage and children were gifts meant for other women, women whose faces were whole and whose bodies moved without pain. We had both lost our mothers too young, had both carried that absence like a hole in the center of our lives. And now we would become what we had missed, would fill that space for our own children. There was both terror and triumph in that circle being completed, in becoming the mothers we missed.

BY THE EVENING MEAL, our small camp was abuzz with quiet excitement, the news spreading through whispered conversations and knowing glances. Susanna embraced me with motherly affection, her ample bosom soft and comforting, the scent of bread and smoke and cooking oil clinging to her clothes.

"My daughter gave birth to three sons," she told me, her eyes bright with remembered joy. "Each one different, each one a blessing in his own way. The first always changes you the most, though. Nothing is ever the same after the first." She tucked a small bundle of dried leaves into my palm, the stems scratchy. "Morning sickness? Chew a leaf of this with your bread before you rise. An old remedy from my savta, passed down through the women in my family. It will not take away the sickness entirely, but it helps take the edge off."

Across the fire, Salome wept joyful tears as she drew Tirzah close, already speaking of her grandchild with wonder in her voice, her hands framing Tirzah's face. The men were more reserved in their congratulations, as was proper, though Simon clapped Andrew on the shoulder with enough force to make him stagger slightly, grinning wide. John caught his brother James in a crushing embrace, the firelight catching the glint of their matching eyes, their similar features that marked them as sons of the same father. Two new lives were beginning in our close-knit band of followers, two children who would hear Jesus teach from their earliest days, who would know no other life than this strange wandering existence we had chosen.

Throughout the evening, I found my gaze drawn to Miriam across the firelight. While the others gathered close with excited chatter and advice and stories of their own children, she kept to the edge of the circle. She raised her cup in toasts and joined in the laughter when it came, but when she thought no one looked, her face went still, settling into lines of sorrow she quickly smoothed away when anyone glanced in her direction. Miriam had told me once that she and Philip hoped for a child, that they had been hoping for years now with nothing to show for it but disappointment and monthly bleeding that came as regular as the moon. Philip tracked her from across the gathering, a helpless furrow between his brows. Their eyes met briefly across the flames and lingered for a moment filled with unspoken things, then Miriam looked away. She raised her cup to me, and I raised mine in return, and we acknowledged each other for a breath before she turned away.

Jesus sat slightly apart from the main gathering, observing the celebration, a small smile playing at his lips. When he caught me looking his way, he nodded once, and I felt the certainty that what was happening inside me was holy and precious and known.

The night air brought the scent of roasting meat and fresh bread, the sound of laughter and conversation, and the crackling of the fire. I leaned into Andrew, his arm secure around my shoulders, and thought of how far I had traveled from the isolated gardens of Arimathea, where I had spent so many years alone with only Deborah and my herbs for company.

"What are you thinking?" Andrew murmured, his lips close to my ear.

"How happy I am. It seems a story, something that happens to other people in tales told around fires. But then I stop and remember that it is true. I am the woman in the story now." I turned to look at him, the firelight casting his features in bronze and shadow, making him look older somehow, already becoming the father he would be. "I can hardly believe how blessed I am. How blessed we are."

His hand found mine in the dark. "We are going to be a family. A real family, not just you and me but three of us and then maybe more someday if Adonai wills it."

"We already are," I replied, looking around at the circle of faces illuminated by firelight, at Simon and John and James, at the women gathered close, at Jesus sitting apart but still present, still over us all. "Our strange, beautiful family of followers, bound by something stronger than blood, something that will keep us together no matter what comes."

Later, lying beside Andrew in our small tent, I listened to the camp winding down for the night. Someone laughed softly, the sound drifting through the thin walls. An owl called from the trees, its voice lonely and wild. Wind stirred the tent flaps, bringing the scent of smoke and earth and the lingering smell of roasted meat from dinner.

Andrew's hand rested over my belly, his palm spread wide across the place where our child grew. Nothing to feel yet beneath his touch, no movement or swelling to mark the presence of new life, but he kept it there anyway. "Do you think it is a boy or a girl?"

"Does it matter?"

"No." His cheek moved, and the smile was there in the movement. "A healthy one is all I ask. Whole and strong."

"Yes." I turned my face into the curve of his throat, where his pulse beat sure and even, that rhythm I had learned to recognize even in sleep. "A healthy one."

He pulled me closer, his body sheltering mine in the dark. We spoke of names then, testing different sounds on our tongues, imagining calling a child by this name or that.

"The road ahead will not be easy," Andrew said after a silence had stretched between us. "Bringing a child into this life of travel and uncertainty, never knowing where we will sleep or what we will eat, always moving from place to place with no home to call our own..."

I touched my fingers to his mouth, feeling his lips, stopping the words before they could take root and become real fear. "We have each other. We have this community that has become our family. And we have faith that Adonai brought us to this place, that he has a plan for us and for this child. We will make it work because we must, because there is no other choice we can make."

He nodded, the movement slight in the dark, his chin bumping my head. "Yes. We will find a way. We always do."

Sleep claimed him first, his breathing evening out into the slow, deep rhythm that meant he was truly gone, his arm heavy across my waist, his fingers curved into my ribs. I lay awake a while longer, my hand covering his where it still rested on my belly, feeling the rise and fall of his chest.

Outside, the stars traversed the heavens in their appointed patterns, keeping silent watch over this new miracle. These same stars that had seen Abraham count his descendants would shine on our child's first night in this world.

"Adonai, keep my baby safe," I whispered into the darkness. "Watch over us in all we do, in all the days ahead of us. Guide us on this road we have chosen, and help us be worthy of the gift you have given us. And thank you. Thank you for all of this—for Andrew, for this community, for the life inside me, for bringing me from loneliness to belonging, from isolation to family. Thank you."

I closed my eyes and let sleep come, Andrew's breathing pulling me down into dreams.

CHAPTER 6

Galilean Camp, April, 31 AD

The Galilean afternoon heat pressed down as heavy as a smith's hammer, unusual for early April, and the crowd moved around Jesus like water seeking its level, bodies pressing close enough that I could smell the salt of their sweat and feel the weight of their desperation in the thickness of the air. My tunic clung damp to my back, my head ached from the glare of sun on pale stone, and the constant queasiness in my belly made me grateful for the slight breeze that stirred occasionally from the lake. I kept to the edges where the desperate and uncertain gathered, those not yet brave enough to approach but too burdened to turn away, finding space where I could breathe more freely.

The woman moved along the periphery with the hunched caution of someone who expected to be driven off, and something in her movement caught my attention—the way she kept her distance even from those of us at the edges, the furtive glances, the body held as though expecting a blow. Her shawl had gone gray with age and covered half her face. Her spine curved forward, her eyes skirted from face to face, and her hands twisted in the fraying threads of her cloak. The smell of old blood clung to her, faint beneath the sharper scents of sweat and dust but unmistakable to anyone who knew the scent of sickness.

I moved closer, stepping carefully through the crowded space. Blue veins showed through the translucent skin of her hands where they twisted in her cloak, the threads fraying, her pallor speaking of years spent indoors.

"Are you seeking healing?"

She startled, her deep brown eyes met mine, looking almost black in the shadows of her veil, the rims reddened in the way that comes from years of weeping.

"I cannot speak with him directly." Her voice came hoarse from disuse. "I am unclean."

"What makes you unclean?"

Her eyes darted around us, checking who might overhear. "My bleeding. It never ceases."

Twelve years, she told me when I asked, her voice dropping to barely a whisper. Twelve years of physicians who took her money and sent her away no better than she came. Twelve years of blood flowing from her body, sapping her vitality, staining everything she touched. The Law was explicit about such things: She must live apart, and anyone who brushed against her carried her impurity until evening.

My hand moved to my belly, still flat beneath my tunic, feeling the faint flutter of nausea that never quite left me these days. My few weeks of sickness seemed trivial beside twelve years of this.

"What do you mean to do?"

She looked toward Jesus where he stood among the crowd. "If I could just touch the edge of his robe, the tzitzit, I believe that would be enough. I need not trouble him directly."

"I could speak to him for you. Jesus welcomes—"

"No." She had already begun moving. "I must touch his garment myself."

She made her way toward Jesus, keeping low, moving quickly between bodies. When the crowd shifted, she dropped to her knees and crawled between feet and robes, dust rising around her. Jesus had slowed to speak with a synagogue leader. She stretched forward on the ground, reaching from below the notice of those standing nearby. Her hand trembled as it brushed the fringe of his cloak, the blue threads twisting around her fingers before falling free.

Jesus stopped mid-step, his shoulders going taut. He turned, one hand pressed to his side. "Who touched me?"

His disciples stared. "Master," Simon said, spreading his hands wide, "the people are all around you and pressing against you from every side."

"Someone touched me. I felt power go out from me."

The woman went still where she kneeled in the dust. She raised her face to him, her features bone-white. "I am the one, Lord. For twelve years, I have bled without ceasing. I have been to every physician, spent all I had. When I heard about you, I thought, 'If I just touch his clothes, I will be healed.' The moment I touched your cloak, the bleeding stopped."

The crowd drew back from her, leaving her kneeling alone in a widening circle of dirt.

Jesus looked down at her, his face gentle. "Daughter,

your faith has healed you. Go in peace and be freed from your suffering."

She lifted her face, tears cutting clean paths through the dust on her cheeks. "Master—"

Jesus extended his hand and helped her to her feet. The crowd gasped, drawing back farther. A rabbi touching a bleeding woman.

"What is your name?"

"Damaris."

"Damaris. Today you are made whole." He smiled at her and turned back to the waiting synagogue leader.

The throng's attention returned to Jesus, people shifting away from where we lingered. Damaris stood apart, her hands moving repeatedly to her midsection as though testing for wounds that had vanished. Sweat trickled down my back despite the shade we stood in, my throat dry from the heat and dust.

I offered her water from my skin, the leather warm from the sun. "You must be thirsty."

Her hands shook so badly I had to help her lift the skin to her lips, steadying it while she drank, the water running down her chin. I took a drink myself when she finished, the water tepid but welcome, washing away some of the dust that coated my throat. "Twelve years," she whispered after she drank, her voice stronger now, "and in one moment, it is gone."

"Where will you go now?"

Her expression shifted. "I do not know. My husband died years ago. I have used all my money on physicians. My family grew tired of my uncleanness."

Joanna joined us. "You have nowhere to go?"

Damaris shook her head.

"Then you will come with us."

"But I cannot. I have nothing to offer."

Joanna smiled. "You have yourself. The Lord has made you whole. We who follow the Rabbi understand the value of one redeemed life."

Damaris's face changed, the lines of despair easing into something softer, uncertain, like the first tentative hope after a long winter. Twelve years of being defined by her illness, twelve years of being told to keep her distance, and now she was being invited into community.

As the crowd dispersed and we began our journey back to camp, I walked beside this woman whose steps grew steadier with each passing hour, though my own grew heavier. The afternoon sun beat down on my head and shoulders, and by the time we reached the outskirts of camp, the nausea that had been merely present all day rose in waves that made me grateful when camp finally came into view.

By late afternoon, the shadows lengthened across the dusty ground, and my body cried out for rest. The evening air carried the scent of bread baking in clay ovens, mixed with cumin and coriander from the cooking pots, the bleating of flocks being brought in from the hillside, and the distant call of shepherds above the valley. After the day's travel, my sandals were covered in dust, fine and red-gold in the fading light, coating my feet and ankles, working its way into every fold of my garments.

Mary and Susanna prepared the evening meal while several disciples sat with Jesus near the central fire, their voices rising in bursts of laughter that carried across the camp. I lowered myself carefully onto a low stool near the women's area, my back protesting, and reached for my bundle of herbs, grateful to be still, to let my feet stop moving.

Andrew kept looking at me then looking away when I caught him, concern written plain on his face. His expression was the one he wore when he worried but did not want to hover.

"You need more rest." Miriam sat beside me with a basket of mending, her eyes taking in the way I held myself, the pallor I could feel in my cheeks. "Your color is better today, but the shadows beneath your eyes remain."

"There never seems to be time." I bound a bundle of rosemary with thin cord. The sharp green scent cleared my head slightly, my fingers moving through the familiar motions. "The crowds grow larger each day."

Her needle flashed in the dappled light. "Jesus spoke of finding a quiet place soon. Perhaps then you might rest properly."

A rider appeared at the edge of camp, his horse breathing hard from swift travel, foam flecking its mouth and chest, the sound of hooves on packed earth cutting through the evening sounds. Conversations stopped mid-sentence, hands stilling in their work, heads turning. The rider dismounted, and the silence spread, reaching from the edge of camp to the central fire where Jesus sat, until even the cooking fires seemed to burn more quietly.

Joanna rose from her place by the cooking fire and crossed to him, her movements urgent. The man bowed his head.

"Elias," Miriam murmured beside me, her needle pausing mid-stitch. "He serves Joanna's husband in Herod's court."

The messenger handed Joanna a small rolled parchment sealed with dark wax. She broke the seal, and as she read, her hands began to shake, the parchment rattling loud enough in the silence that I could hear it from where I sat. She spoke to him briefly, pressed something into his palm, and he mounted and rode away, fading into the gathering dusk.

When she turned toward camp, all the color had drained from her face, leaving her skin as gray as old linen, and my stomach dropped in response, knowing before she spoke that whatever news she carried would change everything.

She walked to Jesus and interrupted the disciples' conversation. Her hands trembled as she extended the parchment. Jesus took it and unrolled it slowly. As he read, the warmth left his face. He placed a hand on her shoulder and asked a question too quiet to hear. Whatever she answered made him bow his head and close his eyes.

Andrew stood and moved closer. Jesus handed him the parchment. Andrew read it, and his legs folded beneath him. He sank to the ground, the parchment falling from his hand.

I gathered my herbs and started to rise.

Miriam caught my wrist. "Wait a moment."

Jesus placed a hand on Andrew's shoulder, leaned down to murmur in his ear, then turned and walked toward the empty hillside beyond camp.

The disciples sat without moving, looking at one another, at Andrew on the ground, at Jesus's retreating figure. Simon spoke first. "We should go to him."

"No." Andrew's voice came raw. "He needs to be alone with his Father."

Joanna made her way toward the women's area.

Mary rose to meet her, her hand reaching out to steady Joanna's arm. "What is it?"

"John has been executed." Joanna said, each word distinct and terrible in the heavy silence. "Beheaded at Herod's palace. Chuza sent details."

The women drew sharp breaths almost as one, and I felt my breath catch and hold. My skin went cold despite the day's lingering heat, a coldness that started in my chest and spread outward until my fingers felt numb, tingling as though I had plunged them into winter water.

Beheaded. The word itself, like the stroke of a blade, sharp and final and absolute. John's fierce eyes, his voice crying in the wilderness, calling us to repent, his absolute conviction that had drawn Andrew to the Jordan years ago—all silenced by Herod's executioner in one swift motion.

"Herodias arranged it," Joanna said. "Her daughter danced for Herod during his birthday feast. When he offered her any reward, prompted by her mother, she asked for John's head. On a platter."

The last words came out broken.

"Chuza writes that Herod gave the order reluctantly. The Tetrarch feared John, knowing him righteous, but he feared losing face before his guests more."

I rose, my herbs forgotten, and moved through the stunned women toward where Andrew sat with the other disciples, the ground seeming to tilt slightly with each step. The smell of dust and sweat clung to him when I reached him. His face had taken on the color of aged stone.

Simon sat beside him, one arm around his brother's shoulders, his own face wet with tears.

I kneeled before Andrew on the hard-packed earth, feeling small stones press into my flesh. "Andrew."

He lifted his gaze to mine, slowly as though it required great effort. "They killed him." The desolation in his eyes was complete, emptied out, like a house left abandoned after a fire. "John knew the price. He always knew what speaking truth would cost."

He turned to Simon. "The day I left him to follow Jesus, he told me, 'I must decrease, that he might increase.' I thought he meant his influence, his following. I never imagined—" He stopped. "When Herod imprisoned him, we thought... We hoped..." His head shook slowly. "Jesus once said John was the greatest man ever born of a woman."

"He was a prophet." Simon's voice came rough with grief. "The first true prophet Israel had seen in generations. And now his voice is silenced."

Around us, the other disciples spoke in hushed tones, their words threading through the evening air.

"If they have killed John, will we be next?"

"He never compromised, not even for a king."

"I did not think Herod would dare."

"He died because he spoke the truth."

The women had drawn closer, gathering around the disciples. Tirzah found James and kneeled beside him. Susanna wept openly. Even Judas, who usually held himself apart, sat with his head bowed.

John's death had cut deep. Andrew shook as he tried to steady himself. Simon sat beside him, his jaw tight. Thomas shook his head again and again, denying what could not be denied. Nathanael whispered scripture under his breath, fragments of psalms. Each face around the fire reflected a different shade of loss—some numb, some openly weeping, some hardened into anger.

My baptism rose in my memory. John's fierce eyes, the shock of cold water, his hands pressing me backward as he baptized me. He had come to Simon's courtyard specifically for me. "I have come for the daughter of Joseph," he had declared, knowing me by name though we had never met. Now I would never have the chance to know him.

And he had been Jesus's cousin. He had been my cousin. Family.

On the hillside, Jesus stood as a silhouette against the darkening sky.

Hours passed. The cooking fires burned low, their light insufficient against the darkness gathering around us. When stars appeared overhead, they looked more distant than normal, as though heaven itself had drawn back.

Andrew remained with the disciples long after others had retired. When he finally returned to our tent, the goat-hair walls still held the day's heat, close and stifling, the air thick with the smell of dust and old smoke. He lay beside me on the rough wool blanket without speaking. I placed my hand on his chest and felt the steady thump of his heart beneath my palm, his tunic damp with sweat, the weave coarse under my fingers. His body shook with grief he would not show the others, his breath catching in his throat, wetness on his cheeks that I felt when I touched his face in the darkness. I held him, my fingers moving through his hair where the dust of the day still clung, my voice low with words that meant little but offered what comfort they could. Outside, the camp had gone quiet except for the occasional crack of a dying fire and the distant call of a night bird across the valley. His breathing steadied at last, and he drifted into fitful sleep while I lay awake listening to the familiar sounds of his rest and the unfamiliar weight of grief that filled the space between us.

~

MORNING ARRIVED WITHOUT RENEWAL, the light gray and heavy, pressing down through clouds that had gathered overnight. The camp stirred slowly, moving beneath the weight of what had happened at Machaerus. I had spent much of the night awake, torn between my nausea and Andrew's restless grief, and now my eyes felt gritty, my head thick with exhaustion. The air tasted metallic, like coming rain, and hung close and damp against my skin, carrying the smell of cold ash from last night's fires and the sourness of unwashed bodies too long on the road.

With the first light, Jesus gathered all his followers in the open space at the center of camp. We came slowly, some still wrapping cloaks around shoulders, others moving with the stiffness of those who had slept poorly or not at all. Faces bore the marks of grief, eyes reddened from tears or sleeplessness, some looking at one another as though seeking permission to feel what they felt. I stood near the back with the other women, Andrew somewhere ahead of me among the disciples, near enough that I could see the set of his shoulders, the way he held his head.

Jesus stood in their midst, his face lined with weariness but alive with something undiminished, his voice carrying clearly in the morning stillness. "You have heard what happened to John. Herod has cut his life short. This is the fate of prophets in a world that fears truth more than it loves righteousness."

A murmur passed through the group. Some nodded, their faces hard. Others looked away.

"The powers of this world believe they can stop God's message with the sword. They are wrong. Where one voice is silenced, many must now speak. The time has come to spread our message beyond what I alone can reach."

The disciples leaned forward, attention sharpening.

"The harvest is plentiful, but the workers are few. What I have taught you in private, proclaim from the housetops. What you have heard whispered in your ear, shout from the rooftops for all to hear."

His gaze moved across the assembly.

"I send you out as sheep among wolves. Be shrewd as serpents, innocent as doves. Take nothing for the journey— no staff, no bag, no bread, no money, no extra tunic. Whatever house welcomes you, stay there until you leave that town."

He extended his hands over the disciples. "I give you authority over all the power of the enemy. The same power that works through me will work through you. Heal the sick. Cast out demons. Proclaim that the kingdom of God has come near. Some will welcome you. Stay in their homes, eat what they offer, minister to their needs. But others will reject you. When a town refuses to hear, shake the dust from your feet and move on."

"And if we are threatened?" Thomas asked. "If Herod's men question us?"

"Then you speak the truth and trust your Father in heaven. Do not be anxious about what to say. The Spirit will give you the words when you need them. But be wise. You are sheep among wolves. Do not seek out danger, but do not flee from it either when it finds you."

The disciples exchanged glances, the reality of what he asked settling over them.

"It is time for you to carry this message without me beside you. You have watched, and you have learned. Now you must go."

Judas spoke up. "But Rabbi, is it wise to scatter now? With Herod's hostility so clear?"

"It is precisely because of Herod's actions that we must spread our efforts. Herod ended John's voice, thinking to stop the message of repentance and preparation. But now, where there was one voice crying in the wilderness, there will be many spread across the villages and towns of Galilee, too many to silence with a single sword stroke. What my cousin began, you will continue."

Andrew lifted his head, meeting Jesus's eyes. "We are ready. John prepared us for this moment, even before we met you. He always said he was making ready your path."

Jesus's eyes softened. "Yes, and he did so until the very end."

He assigned them in pairs: Simon with his brother Andrew, James with John, Philip with Nathanael, and so on until all twelve had been matched. He spoke to each pair individually, giving specific instructions about which villages to visit, which roads to take, and when to return.

Andrew's face changed as he received his assignment. Despite his grief, or perhaps because of it, something had hardened in him, a resolve that had not been there yesterday.

When Jesus finished, the disciples embraced one another, checked their sandals, and emptied their pouches of coins and provisions in obedience to Jesus's command. The women gathered around them, offering final blessings and prayers. Damaris watched, her eyes wide, as though witnessing something she had never imagined she would see.

Andrew found me packing dried figs into a small cloth pouch.

"I cannot take that. We are to take nothing, as you heard. We leave within the hour."

"How long?"

"Two weeks, perhaps three. We are to visit seven villages between here and Capernaum then circle back." He stopped, his eyes searching my face. "Anna, I worry about leaving you. You rise before dawn to be sick where you think no one will notice. You rest your hand on your belly when you think no one is looking. The pallor beneath your skin tells what your lips will not. This journey, this child, is harder than either of us imagined."

"I will be fine." The constant churning in my belly suggested otherwise, but I kept my voice steady. "The women will look after me."

"The child takes much from you. I see your strength but also your struggle."

Jesus approached before I could protest.

"Andrew, a moment with you and Anna."

We stepped aside.

"Anna, you carry new life at a difficult time. The weeks ahead will be arduous even for those at full strength."

"I can manage." Another wave of nausea rose within me even as I spoke.

Jesus studied my face. "Do the lilies of the field toil to bloom? Does the sparrow strive to be worthy of its nest? There is no failure in honoring the vessel that carries new life. The kingdom is served in seasons of action and seasons of waiting."

"What are you suggesting, Rabbi?"

"Bethsaida is less than a day's journey from here. Your mother would welcome Anna, would she not?"

Andrew's expression lightened. "Of course. She would love to have Anna for a visit and hear about her first grandchild."

"Then it is decided. Anna will rest in Bethsaida while you complete your mission. When you return, we will collect her on our way north." He looked toward Damaris. "And I think our new sister would benefit from time away as well. Two women healing together often find greater strength than one alone."

The thought of a proper bed, of Naomi's motherly care, pulled at me with undeniable appeal, my body crying out for rest I had not allowed it in weeks. Yet I had found my place among the followers. To leave now felt like retreat, like admitting I could not keep pace and proving true all the doubts I carried about my strength.

Jesus's gaze met mine, steady and knowing. "The olive branch bent by the wind does not break. While it rests low, it gathers strength to rise again."

I felt the truth of it in my bones, in the exhaustion that made my hands tremble slightly as I set down the cloth pouch. "When will we leave for Bethsaida?"

"Today. I will take you there myself, along with any of the women who wish to accompany us. The rest will remain here with Mary to keep the camp until our return."

I looked over at Damaris. She caught my eye and offered a small smile.

CHAPTER 7

Bᴇᴛʜsᴀɪᴅᴀ, April, 31 AD

Bʏ ᴍɪᴅᴍᴏʀɴɪɴɢ, the disciples had departed, their forms growing smaller in the distance, Andrew and Simon side by side on the southern road, their staffs moving in rhythm with their steps. I stood long after the others had turned away, the sun hot on my head despite the early hour, the dust they raised hanging in the still air. My hand moved to my belly without thinking as I watched until they disappeared entirely around a bend in the road, taking with them the familiar comfort of Andrew's presence and leaving me with an emptiness that burrowed deep in my chest.

Jesus led our smaller group to Bethsaida, a quieter company without the rest of our group. Joanna joined us, needing to return to her husband's household. Miriam had relatives near the lakeshore. And Damaris stayed close to those who had welcomed her, uncertain of her place but no longer alone.

We set out as the day's heat built, traveling the well-worn path that followed the lake's western shore, our shadows shortening as the sun climbed higher. The morning breeze carried the scent of water and wild sage, fish and salt from the waterline where fishermen mended nets, their hands moving with the ease of lifelong labor, wild herbs crushed beneath our feet releasing their sharp green fragrance with each step. Children ran along the shore, collecting shells and smooth pebbles, their voices rising bright above the lap of waves, their laughter a different sound from the somber tones of camp. Scattered clouds drifted across the sky, casting fleeting shadows on the hills that rolled down to the water's edge.

Women sang as they washed linens along the shore, their melody carrying on the breeze, and I hummed along, my hand resting absently on my middle where new life grew hidden and mysterious. The sound reminded me of Deborah in the garden at Arimathea, the same ancient rhythms that mothers had sung over their washing stones since Sarah first drew water from Abraham's well.

Beside me, Damaris walked with careful steps, her gait stronger than yesterday but testing, as though her body needed convincing it could move freely after years of confinement. Her face turned toward every new sensation—the cool splash of lake water against her ankles when our path dropped close to shore, the scent of baking bread from a village we passed, the brush of wildflowers against her palm as she reached out to touch their petals. Each small pleasure seemed to catch her by surprise, like a gift she had not expected to receive.

"It is strange and wonderful to be healed, is it not?" I asked her. "I have had my own healing."

"Yes, it is." She dipped her fingers in the lake water where the path met the shore, watching the ripples spread. "It is like I have a new life." She hesitated then gestured toward my face, her fingers tracing in the air an invisible line that mirrored the path of my scar. "I have wondered... about your face. I did not wish to ask, but—"

"It is all right." I touched the jagged line that ran from my temple down my cheek to the edge of my jaw. "This is where my story begins. As a child in Jerusalem, I was injured in the marketplace. The Romans left their mark that day."

I told her how for years afterward, I had walked with a staff, my hip and spine damaged beyond what physicians could repair. "People would stare. In Arimathea, I rarely left my father's estate."

Damaris nodded, her eyes on my face. "For twelve years, people crossed to the other side of the street when they saw me coming. They feared becoming unclean through mere proximity."

"I am sorry you lived like that for so long." I leaned over to pick a flower, raising the petals to my face and inhaling the sweet scent.

"Jesus healed me at my wedding feast," I continued, remembering that moment when pain had vanished like morning mist burned away by sun. "My hip and spine were made whole in an instant. I had lived so long with that staff, with that limp, they had become part of who I was." I traced the scar. "This mark remains, and these as well," I added, raising my hands so the light illuminated the web of lines on their backs.

"He knew the right moment."

"Yes. He said my healing was not a condition for love but a celebration of it."

As we rounded a bend in the path, my foot caught on an exposed root. My hand instinctively reached to my side, grasping at empty air where my staff had once been. Damaris caught my arm, steadying me.

I laughed. "Even now, my body forgets it is whole."

"I understand. This morning, I woke and immediately reached for my rags before remembering I no longer need them. Twelve years of habit does not vanish in a day."

"Our bodies remember what our minds wish to forget. But each day, the memory grows dimmer."

We walked in companionable silence then, two women joined by the common thread of having been remade by the same hands. Jesus and the others moved ahead of us on the path, giving us this moment of quiet connection.

By late afternoon, we arrived at Bethsaida, the town spreading along the lakeshore, whitewashed houses catching the slanting light, fishing nets hung to dry between the dwellings. The smell of the town reached us first—fish and woodsmoke, baking bread and the ever-present salt water, the mineral tang of Galilean mud mixing with the sweeter scent of ripening grain from fields beyond the town. Naomi stood in her doorway, wiping flour-dusted hands on her apron, her face breaking into a wide smile when she saw us. She opened her arms, the smell of fresh bread and dried herbs reaching us before she did.

"Anna!" She pulled me into an embrace, her body sturdy against mine, her hands strong on my back. She took in our small group. "I did not expect visitors today, least of all my son's wife." She turned to Jesus, wiping her hands on her apron. "Rabbi, you honor my home again. But where is my son?"

"The disciples have been sent out to spread the word. Andrew accompanies his brother on their first independent mission."

Naomi's face grew solemn. She looked from Jesus to me and back again. "So it has begun in earnest, then."

"It has."

Jesus promised to return in two or three weeks, his hand resting briefly on my shoulder in farewell, then departed with Joanna and Miriam, their figures growing distant along the lakeshore path. Damaris and I stood in Naomi's doorway, the afternoon sun on our faces, watching until they disappeared around the bend where the path turned inland toward the hills.

"Come inside, both of you. The sea air grows cool as evening approaches."

Naomi busied herself preparing the evening meal, the movements of her hands speaking of decades spent in this kitchen—the way she reached for the knife without looking, knew by touch which clay pot held the olive oil, moved from hearth to table with an economy of motion that came only from years of repetition. Damaris excused herself, retreating to the small guest chamber to rest, leaving me alone with Andrew's mother in the gathering twilight. My pulse quickened, a flutter in my throat like a trapped bird. This news belonged to Andrew to share with his mother, yet here I was, carrying both his child and the burden of telling her without him. The words sat heavy on my tongue, sweet and terrifying at once.

"You are hovering in doorways like a spirit." Her knife

stopped moving, the rhythmic chopping of leeks pausing. "Come. Sit. Something weighs on you."

I sat on the low stool near the cooking hearth, the familiar scent of dill and garlic rising from the pot she stirred. The words lodged in my throat, neither advancing nor retreating.

"Is it Andrew?" Her fingers tightened around the knife handle as she turned to face me fully. "Has something happened to my son?"

"No, Andrew is well. It is..." I put my palm against my abdomen, the gesture unconscious but revealing.

Naomi went still. The knife clattered against the wooden board as she set it down. Her eyes, the same warm brown as Andrew's, lowered to where my hand rested then rose to meet my gaze.

"Anna?" A single word, barely above a whisper.

"We wanted to tell you together. I am with child. Your grandchild. By the time of the olive harvest."

For a heartbeat, Naomi stood perfectly still as though any movement might shatter this moment like a clay pot dropped on stone. Then her face transformed, lines smoothing, eyes brightening, her whole being seeming to lighten. She crossed the space between us in two quick steps, flour billowing from her apron. Her hands, rough from decades of labor yet impossibly gentle, cupped my face.

"Oh, Anna! A child." Tears gathered in the creases at the corners of her eyes, catching the lamplight. "My son's child."

Her hands moved down to clasp mine then, with reverent hesitation, came to rest on my belly. Though it was still flat, we both knew the miracle growing beneath her touch.

"May the God of our mothers Sarah and Rebecca bless this child."

She pulled me into an embrace, her body solid and warm against mine, the familiar scent of bread and spices wrapping around me. When she released me, she wiped her eyes with the corner of her apron then took my hands in hers, squeezing them with surprising strength.

"I have prayed for this day. To see my son blessed with a child of his own." She smiled, the lines around her eyes deepening. "And with you as the mother, a woman of healing and strength, this child will be doubly blessed. You have made me very happy, Anna."

She squeezed my hands once more before returning to her cooking, but the movements now had a lightness, almost a dance to them. As she worked, she began humming a lullaby, one I had heard Deborah sing during my childhood when she thought I slept. From time to time, Naomi would glance at me and smile as if confirming I was still there, that this moment was real.

Naomi led me down the familiar hallway to the chamber Andrew and I had used during our previous visit, where the walls smelled faintly of lime wash and the floor tiles felt cool beneath my feet. The stone walls were hung with woven tapestries in shades of blue and green that reminded me of the sea. Opening the door, I felt a strange tightness in my throat. The room remained exactly as we had left it months ago—my comb on the small table, Andrew's spare fishing knife tucked in the wall niche, a water jug still standing in the corner. Even the shell he had found on the shore, as pale as bone and spiraled like a ram's horn, lay undisturbed on the windowsill. These small signs of belonging brought unexpected comfort, like finding something precious you thought you had lost.

"For you, this is already home." Naomi's hand rested briefly on my shoulder, her palm pressing there with a gentle presence. "Your things waited for your return, as I did." She brushed my cheek lightly before turning to leave. "I will finish the meal."

I sat on the edge of the sleeping mat, running my hands over the familiar woolen blanket, the weave rough beneath my fingers. After months of voices carrying through thin tent walls, animals stirring in the night, and wind rattling through canvas, the stillness of the house enveloped me like a cloak. Only the distant murmur of the lake against the shore and the occasional call of a bird punctuated the quiet, their rhythm a balm rather than a disturbance.

As evening approached, Naomi called us to gather for the meal. The small table was laid with simple fare—fish stew simmering in a clay pot, the steam rising fragrant with herbs, fresh bread still warm from the oven, its crust crackling when I touched it, and a plate of early spring greens dressed with oil and salt. The familiar scene stirred something in me, a longing I had not allowed myself to acknowledge during our months of travel.

While Damaris helped set out wooden bowls, I helped Naomi pour watered wine into clay cups, the liquid catching the lamplight as it fell.

She ladled the fish stew with extra care, making sure my portion was generous, chunks of white fish floating in the broth alongside lentils and chopped vegetables. "You need strength now. The child is forming bones and flesh within you."

We shared the meal in comfortable quiet, broken only by

the occasional question Damaris asked about the town or Naomi's gentle observations about the fishing season. The simple domesticity wrapped around me like a warm cloak after months of uncertain roads and makeshift camps. Here, in Andrew's childhood home, I could almost pretend he would walk through the door at any moment, smelling of lake water and sun on his skin.

That night, the steady rhythm of the sea beyond the town murmured through the window, rising and falling like breath, and the solid walls around me shut out the night wind that had whistled through the goat-hair tents. The linen sheets carried the scent of sun and lavender, smooth against my skin, a luxury after weeks of sleeping on thin pallets in the open air where dust settled over everything and the sounds of the camp never quite ceased. Here, the only sounds were the sea and the occasional *creak* of the house settling. My body sank into the sleeping mat, releasing all the tension of the previous months, and sleep came easily, deep and without dreams—more soundly than I had slept in weeks.

In the morning, Naomi greeted me with ginger tea steeped with honey and mint, the steam rising fragrant and soothing, the heat seeping through the clay cup into my hands. I sipped slowly, feeling the warmth spread through my chest, the sharpness of ginger cutting through the constant queasiness that had become my companion, the honey coating my throat with sweetness. "An old remedy. It served me well through two difficult pregnancies."

Damaris moved about the household with growing confidence, lifting a water jug carefully, sweeping the court-yard with strong strokes, her movements deliberate and measured, testing what her body could do. I sat near the herb garden, noticing the way she paused sometimes to touch things—the rough texture of the courtyard wall, the smooth handle of the broom, the cool water when she dipped her hand in the washing basin—reminding herself that she could.

"Did you have family in your village?" We sat in the afternoon shade of Naomi's courtyard wall, the stones holding the morning's coolness, a welcome relief from the heat that pressed down on the open spaces beyond. Between us sat a wide basket of lentils, the small round seeds clicking softly as we worked through them, sorting out pebbles and broken pieces, the repetitive motion soothing after the chaos of recent days. The air smelled of dust and the sharp scents of the herb garden nearby, mixed with the ever-present salt from the lake.

She paused before resuming her work, her fingers stilling in the lentils. "I did. My parents died while I was living apart. My brothers inherited the family land." Her eyes remained on the lentils, watching her hands move through them. "I would like to find them again someday. To see if they will take me back now that I am healed."

"Do you think they will?"

"I do not know. Twelve years is a lifetime. They have their own families now. Their wives never knew me as I was before." She looked up, hope and fear mingling in her expression, her hands going still again. "But I am clean now. Perhaps that will be enough."

"You have wisdom in you, Damaris. The years watching the world from its edges have taught you to see what others miss."

"When you cannot take part, you observe." She passed me a handful of sorted lentils, the seeds sliding through my fingers into the basket with a soft pattering sound. "I have watched how quickly people judge, how easily they exclude. But I have also seen unexpected kindness." Her voice grew softer. "The Rabbi sees people, does he not? Truly sees them. I wish to learn that sight."

"Yes, he does. He sees far more than I could ever hope to see."

"Maybe someday I will have the courage to seek my family out." She stopped sorting lentils and looked up at me with tears in her eyes . "Do you believe I will?"

"I do, Damaris. You are one of the bravest women I have ever met." I reached over and grasped her hand, feeling the calluses on her palm, the strength in her fingers. "When the time is right, you will find them."

THREE DAYS PASSED in the gentle rhythm of home life—kneading bread until the dough grew smooth and elastic beneath my hands, hanging linens in the sun-drenched courtyard where they snapped and billowed in the breeze, watching fishermen from the shore as they hauled their nets aboard, the scales of their catch flashing silver in the afternoon light. My body regained strength as Naomi's care and nourishing meals restored what had been depleted by travel and morning sickness. The nausea eased, coming only in the early hours now rather than lasting all day, and my appetite returned with surprising force.

On the fourth day, the afternoon sun had just begun its descent toward the mountains when the sound of a donkey braying and hooves on the path preceded a familiar voice calling a greeting.

"Naomi? Are you at home?"

I stepped from behind Naomi into the doorway, scarcely believing my eyes. "Abba?"

Joseph of Arimathea stood in the shade of the path, dressed in traveling clothes, his normally immaculate appearance disheveled from the road, dust coating his sandals and the hem of his robe. His eyes widened at the sight of me, his mouth opening in surprise.

"Anna?" Surprise and concern filled his voice. "What are you doing here? Is Andrew—"

"Andrew is well." I stepped forward to embrace him, crossing the space between us quickly. The familiar scent of cedar and sandalwood wrapped around me as his arms closed tentatively, then with greater certainty, his hands firm on my back. "He travels with the disciples."

The worry lines around my father's eyes softened, though the furrow in his brow remained. He drew a breath as if to speak then simply shook his head, his eyes moving past me to where Naomi stood.

He smiled then, a genuine smile rarely seen in the formal halls of our home in Arimathea, the stern lines of his face easing. "I was passing through the region on business," he explained, though the explanation seemed thin. Bethsaida was hardly on any direct trade route he normally took. "I thought perhaps..." He trailed off, glancing again at Naomi.

"You thought to call on me." Naomi stepped forward, her eyes bright with barely suppressed amusement. "How fortunate that you should find your daughter here as well."

My father's face colored slightly, warmth spreading across his cheeks. He recovered quickly, gesturing toward his donkey, where bundles were tied to the saddle. "I have brought some provisions from the south. Including some spices I recall you mentioned were difficult to obtain here."

"Abba, this is Damaris." I drew her forward with a light touch on her arm. "The Lord healed her several days ago. She travels with us now. Damaris, this is my father, Joseph of Arimathea."

My father inclined his head respectfully. "Peace be with you, Damaris. It is good to meet any friend of my daughter."

Damaris bowed slightly, her eyes downcast in the presence of such an important man. "Thank you, my lord. I am honored." She glanced at the bundles. "May I help with your provisions?"

"Of course. My thanks."

Damaris stepped forward to unload the bundles, leaving me momentarily alone with my father.

"You look different." He studied my face with the intensity I remembered from childhood, when he would assess whether I was telling the whole truth, his eyes moving over my features as though examining any changes. "There is something changed in you, despite..." He paused. "I heard about John the Baptist. I assumed you all might be grieving." He moved toward the donkey to help Damaris with the parcels.

"We are. But there is something else. And I am glad you are here now so I can tell you the news myself." I took a steadying breath. "Abba, I am with child."

Abba went completely still, his hand frozen in the act of untying a bundle from his saddle. When he turned to me, his face had gone blank.

"A child." He tested the word as if for hidden flaws.

"Yes. Your grandchild. Due by the time of the olive harvest."

He reached out, his hand hovering uncertainly before me.

"May I?"

I nodded, taking his hand and placing it against my still-flat abdomen. The gesture felt foreign. My father had rarely shown physical affection, even when I was small. His palm rested there, warm and steady against me. His hand trembled slightly beneath my touch.

"Anna," he whispered.

After a moment, he gently withdrew his hand from my abdomen and clasped my arm instead. He straightened, his fingers still maintaining their gentle grip, as if reluctant to break the connection between us. "I am to be a grandfather." His voice carried the formal tone he typically reserved for council meetings, though it cracked slightly on the word *grandfather*.

The soft scrape of a sandal against stone drew my attention. Naomi stood in the courtyard entrance, a pitcher of water in her hands, her eyes bright with unshed tears. How long she had been standing there, I could not tell, but her face told me she had witnessed enough to understand. "Yes, you are." She stepped closer, offering him the water, her smile luminous. "And I will be a grandmother. It seems we share something unexpected."

My father accepted the water, his fingers brushing hers as he took the cup, the contact lasting a heartbeat longer than necessary.

That evening, we sat together around Naomi's table—an unlikely family assembled by circumstance and choice. Abba had shed his outer traveling robes and sat comfortably beside Naomi, occasionally leaning toward her to share a comment that made her laugh, the sound unguarded and easy. Damaris, initially intimidated by my father's formal bearing, gradually relaxed as he showed genuine interest in her story, asking questions and listening with the attention he gave to important council matters.

"Twelve years." He shook his head after she shared her history, his jaw tightening. "The physicians of Jerusalem would have bankrupted you even faster. I have seen their prices." His attempt at levity carried genuine anger beneath it. "And now?" He glanced at me. "You both stay here while Andrew travels?"

"Jesus sent us here to rest. After the news of John's death, he dispatched the disciples in pairs to spread the message. He thought Naomi's home would offer sanctuary while they traveled, especially with Damaris newly healed and joining our company."

"A wise decision." He was quiet for a moment, his fingers tracing the rim of his cup. "Though I worry about you traveling with the ministry while you carry a child, especially with the authorities growing more hostile."

"Andrew will protect me. As will Jesus. This is but a brief pause in our journey together."

Abba studied my face for a long moment. "The Sanhedrin's scrutiny intensifies weekly. This path you have chosen..." He faltered, then started again. "I support Jesus's work. You know I do. But as your father, I fear for your safety. Both of you." His eyes dropped briefly to my middle.

"I understand your fears. But this is the path I am meant to walk. Even when it grows difficult. I will not be swayed."

Naomi reached across the table and touched my hand. "Sometimes wisdom means knowing when to rest and when to journey. This time in Bethsaida may be the Lord's provision for both."

Abba's face grew tender as he looked between us. "I remember when you were born. Your mother was ill for months before your arrival. I feared—" He broke off then continued more evenly. "She said you were worth every moment of discomfort. That bringing new life into the world was worth any price."

The mention of my mother sent a ripple of emotion through me. My father rarely spoke of her.

"I wish she could be here. To know she would be a grandmother."

"She knows." Abba spoke with surprising certainty. "Wherever her spirit dwells in Abraham's bosom, she knows." He cleared his throat. "And she would be proud of your strength, if not your stubbornness, which, I might add, you inherited from her, not me."

This unexpected admission drew a laugh from me, breaking the solemn moment. My own memories of my mother were few—I had been so young when she died—but I remembered her once in the marketplace, her hand tight around mine, refusing to move from a merchant's stall until he admitted his scales were weighted wrong. She had stood there in the sun, her voice calm but immovable, while other customers passed by and the merchant's face grew red with anger and then pale with shame. I must have been four, maybe five, but I remembered the fierce protectiveness in her grip, the way she would not budge, and how the merchant finally emptied his measure and began again with honest weights. Deborah always said I had inherited that same stubborn tilt of the chin, that same refusal to be moved when I knew I was right.

Naomi chuckled, giving Abba a sidelong glance. "I find that difficult to believe. Having witnessed your own considerable determination."

He turned to her with mock affront. "I am merely persistent in matters of importance."

"As you showed by happening to pass through Bethsaida?" Naomi raised her eyebrows.

To my astonishment, my father actually grinned, a boyish expression I had not seen from him. "The importance of the visit justified the deviation from my route."

"A deviation of, what, thirty miles?"

"At least forty. But well worth every step."

Their easy banter continued as we cleared the meal, Damaris and I exchanging glances as we carried bowls to the washing basin. I could not wait to tell Andrew.

Later, as the lamps burned low and we prepared for sleep, I drew my father aside in the small courtyard. Above us, stars scattered across the black sky, and the lake lapped against the shore below, a steady rhythm beneath our voices.

"How does the council view Jesus these days? Has there been any change?"

My father's face grew grave. "The situation worsens, I am afraid. Caiaphas has become more determined in his scrutiny. The number of spies attending your teacher's gatherings has increased threefold."

"But you still attend the council. They suspect but have not moved against you."

A faint smile crossed his lips. "They have not. I remain cautious. Those who speak too forcefully against the tide find themselves removed from influence entirely. I can temper their worst impulses only by maintaining my position. Though I must be increasingly careful. Questions have been raised about my reluctance to support harsher measures, about resources from my caravans disappearing and somehow finding their way to the poor where Jesus teaches. There are whispers of more serious charges being contemplated against him, not merely blasphemy but suggestions that your Rabbi threatens the established order Rome demands we maintain."

I gripped the edge of my shawl, twisting the fabric between my fingers. "I put myself at risk the moment I recognized my nephew taught truth," he said. "Blood and faith bind me to this path. As they do you."

I looked down at my belly. "And now there is another life to consider."

My father followed my gaze, his face softening. "Yes. A life that may change everything." He placed a hand on my shoulder. "Anna, I came to Bethsaida seeking Naomi, not knowing I would find you. But perhaps the Lord arranged this meeting. Perhaps this separation from the group provides an opportunity—"

"I will not abandon my husband or my calling." I cut him off, already sensing where his thoughts led.

He sighed, the sound heavy with resignation. "I expected no less. You are indeed your mother's daughter." His fingers tightened around my shoulder. "But promise me you will be careful. The child you carry is precious beyond measure, not just to you and Andrew but to me as well."

Something in his voice made me look up sharply. "You are not disappointed? That I will bear a child while following Jesus and away from the security of Arimathea?"

Abba was quiet for a long moment, his face turned toward the stars. "I would have chosen a different path for you. A safer one. But I cannot deny the change in you since you began following him. There is a light in you I have not seen before. A purpose that transcends the ordinary concerns that occupy most lives. Including my own."

"Then you understand why I must continue."

"I understand. Though I may never fully approve." His lips quirked up. "Parents rarely do. It is our nature to worry, to imagine dangers, to see storm clouds where our children see only adventure."

"Will you stay?"

He nodded. "For a few days. I have arranged lodging with a merchant friend in town." A hint of vulnerability crossed his features. "But I hope to call on Naomi while I am here. I find her company... invigorating."

I smiled, recognizing the admission for the rare confidence it was. "She seems equally pleased with yours."

A comfortable silence fell between us. The coming child had changed something fundamental, creating a bridge where barriers had stood. Here in this courtyard under Galilean stars, we had become something new to each other —father and daughter still but also participants in a shared future.

"I am glad you came."

"As am I." Then, with uncharacteristic tenderness, he pressed a kiss to my forehead. "Rest well, daughter. Guard yourself and the life within you."

That night, moonlight spilled through the narrow window, casting silver patterns on the floor. I lay awake, my hand drifting to my belly, feeling for movement too faint yet to detect. The skin there felt different, tighter, warmer, as if the hidden life beneath had already begun to change me from within.

The world beyond these walls grew more dangerous by the day. The Sanhedrin watched. Herod's sword had already fallen. But for now, in this house by the sea, we had found sanctuary.

CHAPTER 8

BETHSAIDA , May, 31 AD

THE BREAD TASTED SWEETER this morning, as if honey had been kneaded into the dough, though Naomi swore she had used none.

I broke another piece from the loaf Naomi had baked at dawn, steam rising when the crust gave way, the bread carrying a richness I had not noticed before, the mint in yesterday's tea singing against my teeth in ways it never had, even the olive oil at last night's meal tasting fuller, like I could taste the entire hillside in its gold, the sun and soil and ancient roots. Everything had sharpened.

The sickness that had bent me double in those first weeks had passed, leaving this strange vitality. At night, lying on my side brought a new awareness—the weight of my breasts against my ribs, tender, making me shift position through the dark hours, my arm curved beneath them through the darkness before sleep, my palm finding the place below my navel where the curve had begun, as firm as risen dough beneath the skin. Life, there. Growing. A secret written on my flesh.

Each day, Damaris ventured farther from the safety of Naomi's walls. First to the neighbor's gate to borrow a cup of oil, then to the well at the edge of the square, where other women gathered in the morning cool, and yesterday, all the way to the potter's shop to fetch a replacement bowl. They were small steps toward rejoining a world that had been denied her for so long, though too many people still made her hands shake and her breathing quicken.

"Will you come to the market with me today?" I asked as we sat in the courtyard, the morning sun casting leaf-shadows through the olive branches overhead.

Her shuttle stopped mid-pass, the thread hanging slack between her fingers. "The market?" Her voice climbed at the end, testing the edges of possibility. "There will be many people."

"Yes. But none who knew you before. And I will be with you."

She said nothing for a long moment, only wound the loose thread back onto the shuttle with movements so slow the wood barely moved in her fingers, her face turning east toward where heat already wavered above the hills. "What do we need?"

"Naomi mentioned needing more oil, and I would like to find some fresh dill." I did not mention my true purpose was to continue drawing her back into the rhythms of regular life, one morning at a time.

"Very well." She set aside her work and smoothed her shawl. "But not for too long."

The market pressed close around us, thick with sound

and scent and movement. Fishermen displayed their catches on beds of reeds, the fish still wet with lake water, tilapia and sardines with scales like beaten silver. Merchants called their prices in the distinctive lift and fall of Galilean traders, hands moving as they praised their wares to the sky. Women tested figs for ripeness and hefted grain sacks, their baskets already heavy with provisions for the day's meals. The morning air carried fish and salt, fresh bread from stone ovens, the sharp bite of pickled vegetables in their clay jars, all layered as thick as wool. At a nearby stall, a woman ground spices, releasing the scent of cumin and coriander into the air. Damaris tensed as the crowd thickened, her fingers finding and refinding the edge of her shawl.

I touched her arm as a group of boys ran past, their shouts echoing off the stone walls. "You are doing well. Remember the Rabbi told you that your faith has made you well. These people see only a woman going to market."

Damaris drew a breath that lifted her entire frame, her fingers stilling on the fabric. "Years of hiding," she said, barely audible beneath the market noise. "I still expect someone to point and cry out 'Unclean.'"

"But they will not. That life is behind you now. Each day brings new strength."

I guided her toward a merchant selling oils, positioning myself between her and a cluster of men debating wool prices, their voices rising with each point scored.

"Two measures of olive oil," I told the merchant, an older man whose face bore decades of Galilean sun in its deep lines and permanent squint.

He peered at me as he reached for his measuring vessel. "You are the healer who married Andrew, yes? You have not heard the news? The Rabbi's disciples returned this morning.

Fishermen spotted them crossing the lake at dawn." He leaned closer, voice dropping. "They landed north of town, in that deserted stretch where the hills meet the water. The crowds are gathering there now."

My pulse kicked. I quickly put coins into his palm as he handed me the filled jar. "Thank you for telling me. The Lord bless your kindness."

Damaris met my eyes, questions written there.

"Let us return to Naomi's," I said. "Andrew will come for us when he can."

We made our way back through the streets with quickened steps, the oil jar heavy against my hip, anticipation threading through my limbs like wine.

I had just entered Naomi's yard when his voice called a greeting to a neighbor beyond the wall. I set the oil jar on the ground and was across the yard before he finished speaking, reaching him as he appeared in the gateway.

His arms came around me, and I buried my face against his shoulder, breathing in dust and sweat and lake water and woodsmoke—Andrew. His tunic was sun-faded and travel-worn, frayed at the hem, with a tear hastily mended near the shoulder. But his arms were solid, his hands steady against my back, and beneath the rough weave, his heart beat as strong and constant as the rhythm of oars.

"My heart has longed for you," he said near my ear.

"As mine has for you. Each day stretched like seven."

He drew back enough to see my face, his brown eyes moving over me with the careful attention of someone taking inventory after a long absence, his gaze falling briefly to where the child had changed my shape, then lifting again to meet my eyes. He pressed his forehead to mine, our breaths mingling.

Naomi emerged from the house, and we broke apart. She embraced her son, her eyes shining with tears. "You look tired."

"Is that not what mothers always say?" Andrew laughed as Naomi inspected him thoroughly.

"Perhaps, but in this case, it is true. And you look thin."

"The work has been good but demanding. The Rabbi sent us to every village within a two days' journey. People were hungry for hope after news of John spread." He turned to Damaris, who hung back near the house. "Are you well, sister?"

She nodded. "Your mother has been kind."

"Will you eat something?" Naomi asked, hands already moving toward the bread basket.

"I wish we could stay longer, Ima. Your food is what I have dreamed of for weeks. But Jesus has asked for both Anna and Damaris to join us. He says he has need of them today." He glanced back toward the gate. "We will come back tonight if we can."

Naomi patted his face, the gesture so tender it made my chest ache. "Go. Do what the Rabbi asks. I will have food ready whenever you return."

While Andrew stepped outside to wash the dust from his hands and face, Naomi pulled me inside to a corner of the room where the morning light fell softly through the high window. "You carry more than just a child," she said. "You carry the future of our family."

"I know. To carry your future, to be given such a place in your family, is a blessing I scarcely dared hope for. I do not take it lightly."

Naomi studied my face then reached up to tuck a strand of hair behind my ear, the touch so motherly my throat tightened. "The glow of new life suits you. When I carried Andrew, I blossomed like you. When I carried Simon, well —" She laughed softly. "His father said he made his presence known early. Even then, Simon was not one to go unnoticed."

"The child gives me strength now rather than taking it. Is that common?"

"For some, yes. The Lord blesses each mother differently." She laid her palm gently against my cheek. "Your body knows what it is doing, Anna. Trust its wisdom."

My hand strayed to where the curve now formed beneath my tunic, still modest enough to conceal with loose garments but unmistakable to my touch, this possibility growing inside me.

"What is meant to be, will be," she said. "But remember that a mother's prayers have power. Mine go with you, daughter of my heart."

As we prepared to depart, she brought out packets of dried fish and bread and handed them to Andrew before catching my hand and holding it a moment longer. "For the journey to wherever you are going. And extra for you. You carry the blessing of our house."

I kissed her cheek then turned to Damaris. "Are you ready for this?"

She squared her shoulders with a determination that had not been there three weeks ago. "I am no longer the woman who hides. I will go."

WE FOLLOWED Andrew through Bethsaida and north along the lakeshore path. The afternoon sun was warm on my shoulders, and the dust rose with each step to coat my sandals, my ankles, the hem of my robe. The lake stretched to our left, its surface beaten silver in the small waves lapping at the reed beds with a sound like whispered secrets. Damaris walked nearby, her face turned toward the water, her breathing easier here away from the confines of town walls and watching eyes.

As we walked, Andrew told us fragments of his journey, his voice following the beat of our steps. Villages where they had been welcomed with open doors and shared meals, bread broken and passed from hand to hand, sleeping mats unrolled in courtyards under stars. Others where doors had been shut in their faces before they could finish speaking, where stones had been gathered and threats muttered and they had shaken the dust from their feet and moved on. And the power that had worked through their hands: evil spirits driven out at a word, fevers breaking beneath their touch, the lame rising to walk.

"It was as Jesus promised. Demons fled at our command. Sickness vanished beneath our hands." He paused, trying to shape wonder into words that could hold it. "Simon and I went out as fishermen playing at being messengers. We returned changed."

Before I could ask what he meant, the path rose beneath our feet, climbing a gentle slope where wild grasses grew thick and green, still lush from spring rains, the air here carrying the scent of crushed thyme and stone heated by sun and the ever-present tang of the lake. My body had found its walking rhythm, the child within adding weight but lending strength, my hips swaying to accommodate what grew there.

The path crested the rise, and I stopped.

The sound reached me first, a low murmur like distant

thunder, the collective voice of thousands blending until the air itself vibrated with it. Then I saw them—a vast multitude spread across the grassy slope that descended to the lakeshore, people as numerous as the grains of sand Abraham had been promised, sitting in clusters beneath sparse terebinth trees or exposed to the afternoon sun. Even from here, the smell reached me, unwashed wool and the sourness of bodies that had been sitting for hours. At the center of this human sea was Jesus, his figure small but unmistakable, surrounded by the disciples.

"There are thousands," Damaris whispered.

We made our way down the hillside, Andrew guiding us through the seated crowds toward where Jesus taught. The ground was cool and slightly damp beneath us as we lowered ourselves onto the grass at the edge of the inner circle. Simon glanced up as we approached, acknowledging his brother with a brief nod before returning his attention to Jesus. James and John sat nearby, their faces weathered from weeks on the road. Philip caught my eye and offered a quick smile of welcome. Matthew sat with his writing materials, Thomas beside him, and beyond them, Nathanael and Judas, all dust-covered and weary from their journeys. Simon the Zealot stood slightly apart, arms crossed, his eyes scanning the crowd like a man who had not forgotten how to watch for trouble. From here, Jesus was clear, his arms occasionally lifting to emphasize points as his voice carried across the multitude.

"The kingdom of heaven is like a mustard seed," he was saying, "which a man took and planted in his field. Though it is the smallest of all seeds, when it grows, it becomes the largest of garden plants, with branches so large that the birds of the air can make nests in its shade."

The crowd leaned forward as he continued, moving from

one parable to another. "The kingdom of heaven is also like yeast that a woman took and mixed into a large amount of flour until it worked throughout the dough." His eyes swept over the gathering. "Do you have ears to hear? Then listen!"

A child near us whispered a question to his mother, who quietly explained the meaning.

"Blessed are the poor in spirit," he taught, "for theirs is the kingdom of heaven. Blessed are those who hunger and thirst for righteousness, for they will be filled."

As the afternoon lengthened, the disciples conferred with each other, glancing toward the descending sun and then at the vast crowd. Several approached Jesus.

"This is a remote place," Thomas said, his voice carrying to where I sat, "and it is already very late. The sun will set soon. Send the crowds away so they can go to the surrounding villages and buy themselves something to eat before darkness falls. These people have nowhere to stay for the night."

Jesus studied the disciples gathered around him, his expression calm despite the obvious urgency. The golden light of approaching evening cast long shadows across the hillside, emphasizing just how remote this place was, how far from any village with food to sell. Thousands of people, including many children and elderly, would be stranded as night approached.

"They do not need to go away," he said. "You give them something to eat."

Philip stepped forward, his hands spread wide. "That would take more than eight months' wages! Are we to go and spend that much on bread for them to eat?"

"How many loaves do you have? Go and see."

The disciples dispersed among the crowd. Andrew

moved through the groups nearest us, kneeling beside families, murmuring. He paused beside a young boy several rows away, his hands gesturing in a way I recognized, making a request that mattered.

Damaris leaned close. "The boy is eager to help. See how he listens?"

The boy considered then nodded and reached for a small basket at his side. Andrew smiled, and he gently guided the boy forward, returning with him to where Jesus waited.

"Here is a boy with five small barley loaves and two fish," Andrew told Jesus. "But how far will they go among so many?"

The boy stood before Jesus holding his small offering, his eyes bright, his hands gripping the basket. Jesus accepted it and looked inside before lifting his gaze to the vast crowd spread across the hillside. He spoke to the disciples, who began moving through the multitude.

"Have everyone sit down in groups. Fifty here, a hundred there."

The chaotic gathering transformed into an organized assembly, people arranging themselves on the green grass in orderly sections. From above, they must have resembled the encampments of our ancestors in the wilderness, twelve tribes arranged by their standards. The sun had begun its descent toward the horizon.

"Come," Andrew said, returning to us. "Jesus has asked for your help. We are to feed these people."

"Feed them? With what?" I asked.

"Five barley loaves and two small fish."

"That cannot possibly—"

"With Jesus," Andrew interrupted, his eyes alight, "we have learned to set aside what is impossible."

We joined the other disciples, forming a circle around Jesus. He stood in our midst, holding the boy's small offering. His face turned upward to the sky as he blessed the food with words both ancient and new.

"Blessed are You, Lord our God, King of the Universe, who brings forth bread from the earth. We give You thanks, Father, for these gifts which we are about to receive from Your bounty."

Then he broke the bread, placing pieces into the baskets we held. I picked a piece out and held it.

The bread in my hands was warm.

Not sun-warmed. Not the fading heat of something baked hours ago and carried in a basket. Oven-warm. Fresh-from-the-coals warm, the interior soft enough that my thumb left an impression when I gripped it. I tore a piece, and the scent rose, the way it smells when the baker pulls the first loaves before dawn and the stones are still learning their heat.

I moved among the seated groups. Each time I reached into the basket, my fingers closed on more bread and more fish. The weight never changed. The supply never diminished. I gave pieces to a woman with three children clinging to her robe, their eyes enormous in thin faces. The smallest one bit into his portion and crumbs tumbled down his tunic, and he laughed and reached for more. There was more. There was always more. I reached into the basket, and bread that should not exist burned against my palm like a promise made flesh.

An old man took bread from my basket and held it in trembling hands. Tears ran down into his beard. A girl pointed at my basket and tugged at her father's sleeve, chattering too quickly for me to follow. He shushed her gently, but he had gone pale.

When Andrew reached us with his basket, wonder filled his eyes despite him having taken part directly in the miracle. He held out the basket, still filled with bread and fish.

"Eat," he said.

The bread steamed in my hands, still hot from whatever fire had formed it out of nothing. The fish flaked at my touch, perfectly cooked. I bit into the bread, teeth sinking through to the soft interior, the taste of grain and salt filling my mouth, mingled with the salt-rich flesh of lake fish. My empty stomach clenched with gratitude. I ate slowly, watching as the same scene repeated itself thousands of times across the hillside. They simply ate with the grateful hunger of people who had spent a long day listening to teachings that fed their souls.

Only after everyone had eaten did the magnitude settle over me. Jesus instructed the disciples to gather the leftovers, and I joined Andrew in collecting pieces of bread and fish that remained scattered across our section of the hillside. We filled a large basket, and around us, eleven other baskets were similarly filled.

"Twelve baskets," I said. "One for each tribe of Israel."

Andrew nodded. "He said to gather the pieces, that nothing be lost."

As the sun reached the edge of the hills, voices rippled through the crowd. People gathered in clusters, animated despite exhaustion. Fragments reached me: prophecy fulfilled, Moses and manna, the promised king who would feed his people.

"Some of them want to make him king," Andrew said,

having returned from delivering the basket of leftovers. "By force, if necessary."

A coldness moved through me despite the evening warmth. "What will he do?"

Before Andrew could answer, Jesus withdrew from the crowd, climbing higher up the mountain alone. The disciples stood watching him go.

"He goes to pray," Andrew explained. "The others are taking the boats across to Capernaum. He told them to go ahead, that he would join them later."

"And us?"

"He told me to walk you and Damaris home. Simon and the others can manage the crossing. There is not enough room in the boat for all of us, so I will see us safely to my mother's house. Simon will bring the boat back to get us in the morning."

We joined the dispersing crowd, making our way toward Bethsaida on foot with those who lived in or near the town, our shadows stretching long and thin before us as the sun sank into the western hills. The mood was jubilant, feverish, voices rising and falling despite the day's fatigue. My legs protested after hours of sitting on the damp ground, but I walked on, one hand on Andrew's arm, the other pressed to where the child rested.

The road was thick with people, dust rising in clouds that caught the amber light and hung in the air like smoke, coating our throats and turning our robes from blue and brown to uniform gray.

"Surely he is the Prophet who is to come into the world," one man declared loudly, his voice carrying over the general noise.

"Greater than Moses," another responded, walking just

ahead of us. "Moses brought manna from heaven, but Jesus created food from nearly nothing."

"If he can feed thousands with five loaves, imagine what he could do with the resources of the Temple," a third added, his hands gesturing wildly as he walked. "The Romans would be driven out within weeks!"

The talk swirled around us, dangerous and intoxicating in its fervor. Andrew kept his head down as we walked, his jaw tight, saying nothing as the speculative voices rose and fell. I slipped my hand into his, our fingers intertwining. Damaris walked on my other side, her face thoughtful, taking in the talk but offering no words of her own.

The evening air shifted as we walked, the day's heat giving way to a coolness that carried a metallic taste, like copper on the tongue. The stillness broke. A breeze off the lake pulled at my veil and sent dust devils spinning across the road. The clouds gathering over the water darkened against the fading light, their bellies heavy and bruised purple. Lightning flickered in the distance, silent at first then followed by the low rumble of thunder rolling across the hills. The wind picked up, no longer a breeze but a true wind that made the terebinth trees thrash and sent people clutching at their cloaks.

Andrew glanced toward the water, his brow creasing. "The others are out there somewhere. Rowing across to Capernaum."

I followed his gaze. The usually calm surface of the Galilee had begun to chop, whitecaps visible even from this distance, growing larger with each gust, the water changing from silver to iron gray to nearly black. Lightning split the sky over the far shore, a jagged white tear that illuminated the churning waves for a heartbeat before darkness swallowed them again. Thunder cracked, closer now. "Will they be safe?"

"They are fishermen. Simon and James and John have weathered worse." But Andrew's hand tightened on mine.

He pulled me closer as the wind gusted harder, and I leaned into his solidity, grateful for the protection of him beside me. The first drops of rain hit my face, cold and heavy, and within moments, the sky opened, drenching us, turning the road to mud beneath our feet.

When we finally reached Naomi's house, water streamed from our robes, pooling on the courtyard stones. My hair hung in wet ropes against my neck, cold rivulets running down my spine. Andrew's tunic clung to his shoulders, darkened to near-black with rain.

Naomi appeared in the doorway, took one look, and began issuing orders. "Out of those wet things. Andrew, the chest—you know where. Anna, Damaris, with me."

She pulled us inside and handed lengths of rough linen to us. I peeled the sodden robe from my shoulders, the wool so heavy with water it took both hands to lift it away. The air hit my damp skin and I shivered, wrapping my arms across my chest. Naomi's hands were already in my hair, squeezing water from the thick strands, working the linen through until it came away merely damp rather than dripping.

"Dry robe there," she said, pointing. "Quickly now, before you catch a chill."

The dry fabric was rough against skin that had gone cold and prickled with gooseflesh, but it was blessedly warm. Around me, the smell of wet wool hung thick in the air, mingling with the steam rising from the lentil stew Naomi had prepared, the scent of cumin and coriander, fresh bread from the stones, olives glistening with oil, dried fruits.

"Sit. Eat. You must be hungry after such a long day," she said once we were settled around her table, the wood worn smooth by years of family meals. Naomi listened in silence as Andrew described the thousands gathered, the boy's small offering, the bread and fish that never stopped multiplying in our hands. When he finished, she set down her cup and shook her head slowly.

"With twelve baskets of fragments remaining," Andrew said. "One for each tribe."

Naomi looked at me. "You saw this with your own eyes?"

"I helped distribute the food. It never diminished, no matter how many times I reached into the basket."

She nodded slowly as if confirming something she had already suspected. "The signs are becoming impossible to ignore."

As night deepened, weariness overtook us one by one. Damaris retired first, her steps slow as she climbed to the upper room. Naomi followed soon after, kissing Andrew's forehead before she went, leaving Andrew and me alone in the main room lit only by the dying fire, the flames casting shifting shadows on the walls, the smell of woodsmoke thick in the air, mingling with the sharper scent of the lamp oil burning low.

"Come," Andrew said, extending his hand. "You need rest."

The room was cool after the house's lingering heat, the stone walls holding the chill of night. Rain drummed against the shutters, wind whistling through cracks in the wood. The clay lamp on the small table beside the sleeping mat burned low, its flame guttering with each gust, casting unsteady shadows across the worn wool blankets. The air smelled of the lavender Naomi had scattered among the linens and the mustiness of a room that had been closed during the heat of day.

I sat on the mat, and the wool blanket beneath me was rough against my palms, the weave coarse but clean. Andrew sat beside me, and I could sense the heat of his body after the long day, the dust of the road still clinging to him along with the salt of dried sweat, his skin holding the sun's touch from hours of exposure. In the dim light, tiredness marked every line of his face, the hollows beneath his cheekbones more pronounced from weeks of sparse meals on the road, the new creases at the corners of his eyes. His hands rested on his knees.

"What does it mean, Andrew? What happens now?"

"I do not know. The crowds grow larger each day. The demands increase. And now, with what happened today..." He shook his head slowly. "They want to make him king."

"Would that be so wrong? If he is the Messiah—"

"He is." Andrew spoke with quiet certainty, the words carrying the importance of all he had witnessed. "But he is not the king they seek. Not the king any of us expected." He studied his hands that had somehow distributed bread to thousands. Lightning flashed through the cracks in the shutters, briefly illuminating the lamplight that revealed the small scar on his thumb from a fishing hook years ago, the permanent staining of his fingers from net dye, the thickening at the base of his palm from gripping wood, before darkness closed in again.

"When we were sent out, he told us the kingdom of heaven was near. I thought I understood what that meant. Now I am less certain."

I rested my head on his shoulder, the weave of his tunic rough against my cheek, breathing in his presence after the weeks of separation. The solid warmth of him anchored me, his heartbeat steady beneath my ear. His arm came around me, his hand spreading wide against my back.

"When I saw the bread multiply in my hands today," Andrew said finally, the words rumbling through his chest, "when I felt it as warm as if it had just come from the fire, though no fire had touched it—" His fingers stilled on my arm. "Creation happened in my hands, Anna. I felt it form from nothing. Like the beginning of all things." A long pause came, filled only by rain and the lamp's wavering flame. "I do not know what manner of man can speak and bread appears. I only know I held it, and it burned."

"We bring what little we have," I whispered against his shoulder. "He makes it enough."

"Yes, he does."

Outside, the wind rose to a howl, and lightning split the darkness, each white flash revealing the shutters straining against their latches, rain lashing the courtyard stones, before thunder shook the walls and darkness fell again.

CHAPTER 9

I woke to silence. The wind had died sometime in the dark hours before dawn, leaving behind an unnatural stillness more ominous than the howling had been. The shutters no longer rattled against their frames, and the house had stopped its creaking protest against the storm's assault, settling into itself with the relief of something that has survived. Even the usual morning sounds of the village were muted—no donkeys brayed from the streets below, no roosters called out their territorial claims, no women's voices echoed in the comfortable rhythm of drawing water from the well.

Andrew was not next to me.

I rose, my bare feet finding the cool stone floor, smooth from generations of others rising, the chill seeping into my soles and traveling up through my legs. I wrapped my shawl around my shoulders against the morning cold that lingered despite the season, the wool scratchy against my skin but welcome. Looking through the narrow window, I could see the lake spread out below the town in the growing light, its surface unbroken and smooth and gray under the colorless dawn sky, empty of boats, silent of fishermen's voices.

I found Andrew in the courtyard, standing beneath the olive tree with his arms crossed over his chest, his body carved from stone. His tunic was rumpled from sleep, his hair uncombed, and he stared eastward across the water without blinking.

"That storm," he said. "I kept thinking about them out there."

I moved to stand beside him, slipping my hand into his, his fingers cold against mine. "They are fishermen. They know the lake."

"I know the lake too." His jaw flexed, the muscle jumping beneath his beard. "I have seen what it can do when the wind funnels down between the hills. The waves rise higher than a man. The boat fills faster than you can bail."

"Andrew."

He stopped himself, drew a breath that expanded his chest, and then released. "Simon is the best sailor among us. If anyone can bring them through, it is him."

The line of his throat moved when he swallowed, tension held across his shoulders as he stared at the calm water that had raged through the night.

Naomi appeared in the doorway with bread and olives, her face drawn tight with worry, the lines around her mouth deeper than they had been the day before. "Come. You must eat."

Andrew shook his head. "I am not hungry."

"Neither am I." She set the tray on the bench anyway, the clay dishes rattling slightly. "But we will sit together, and we will eat, and we will wait for word."

Damaris joined us, moving quietly, her presence gentle and unobtrusive. We sat in that courtyard as the sun climbed higher, turning the stones warm beneath our feet, the heat seeping up through the packed earth, and we spoke little because there was nothing to say that would ease the waiting.

It was midmorning when we heard the footsteps, quick and heavy on the stone street. Andrew was on his feet before the gate banged open. Simon appeared in the courtyard, breathing hard and disheveled.

His tunic was stained with salt, his hair uncombed and standing in every direction. But his face was alight with an energy I had rarely seen, his eyes feverish, his hands shaking when he gripped the gate.

"Brother." The word came out gasping. "You will never believe—I need to tell you—" He stopped, gulped air, then started again with words tumbling over each other in his haste. "The others are breaking camp. Jesus sent me to fetch you both. But I would have come, anyway. I had to tell you what happened."

Andrew gripped his brother's shoulder, his fingers digging in hard enough to leave marks. "Simon, what is it? Are you hurt? Is anyone—"

"No. No, we are all safe. But Andrew—" Simon's laugh caught in his throat. "Brother, I walked on the water."

The courtyard went very still.

Naomi's hand had gone to her mouth, her other hand pressing against her chest. Damaris sat frozen on the bench, her eyes wide.

Andrew's grip on Simon's shoulder loosened, his hand falling away slowly. "You what?"

"I walked on the water." Simon said it again, slower this

time, each word deliberate. "On the surface of the lake. Jesus called me out of the boat, and I walked to him."

"Come inside." Naomi's voice was unsteady. "Come in and tell us properly."

We moved into the main room, dim and cool after the brightness of the courtyard. Simon sank onto a bench, and Naomi took him a damp cloth to wipe his face. Andrew sat across from him, leaning forward with his forearms on his knees, his whole body tilted toward his brother, and I stood behind him with my hand on his shoulder, the rigid line of muscle beneath my palm thrumming like a bowstring pulled taut.

"Tell us. Tell us everything."

Simon dragged his hands through his hair, sending bits of dried salt flaking onto his shoulders, making the uncombed strands stand even wilder. "The storm came up fast after you left. We were perhaps halfway across when the wind shifted and came straight at us from the west. The kind that churns the water white." His hands moved, describing what his words could not fully capture. "The waves kept coming, crashing over the bow, filling the boat faster than we could bail. Thomas was vomiting over the side." He looked at his mother. "Pardon me, Ima. Matthew was praying. James and John and I rowed, trying to keep us pointed into the wind, but it kept pushing us back toward the eastern shore."

He paused, his gaze fixed on something beyond the wall. "We rowed for hours. The wood tore my hands raw. The blisters broke. I kept rowing because what else could we do? We were going to die out there. I was certain of it. The lake was going to take us all down, and our bodies would wash up on some shore days from now, bloated and picked at by birds."

Naomi made a soft sound of distress. Andrew said nothing, his jaw clenched so tightly I could see the muscle jumping beneath his beard.

"It was the fourth watch, just before dawn, when we saw him. At first, we thought it was a spirit. A ghost walking on the waves." Simon's voice dropped lower. "You have to understand, we were exhausted. Half mad with fear and effort. And then Jesus comes walking toward us over the water, walking as calm as if he strolled through a marketplace and the waves that were tossing our boat to pieces just held him up."

My breath caught. Naomi pressed her hand to her chest.

"Jesus was walking," Andrew repeated slowly. "On the water."

"On the surface of the lake." Simon's laugh came out sharp and disbelieving. "We screamed. Grown men, fishermen who have faced many storms before, and we screamed like children. But then he spoke. He said, 'Take courage. It is I. Do not be afraid.' And I knew that voice. I knew him."

He leaned forward, his hands gripping his knees. "So I called out. I said, 'Lord, if it is you, command me to come to you on the water.' And he said, 'Come.'"

Simon's eyes were on Andrew, holding his brother's gaze. "I climbed over the side of the boat. John tried to grab me, but I did not stop. I heard Jesus saying 'Come,' and so I put my foot down on the water." His voice broke. "It held me. The water held me up as though it were solid stone. I took another step and another. And I was walking. Brother, I was walking on the surface of the lake. It does not seem real."

Andrew had gone very pale, the color draining from his face until even his lips looked bloodless, his hands tightening on his knees.

"I kept my eyes on him. On Jesus. And as long as I looked at him, I could do it. I could walk where no man should be able to walk. But then—" Simon shook his head. "Then, I looked down. I saw the waves, saw how high they were, felt the wind tearing at my clothes, and I remembered where I was. What I was doing. How impossible it all was. And then I sank."

"You sank."

"Like a stone." Simon's hands were shaking now, trembling so badly he had to clench them into fists. "The water closed over my head, and there was no air, no light, just water everywhere. I have never known terror like that. I was going to drown. I knew it. So I cried out. Just one word, 'Lord!'"

"He caught me. Grabbed my hand and pulled me up out of the water. I gasped air into my lungs. And he looked at me and said—"

"What did he say, Simon?" Andrew asked.

"He said, 'You of little faith. Why did you doubt?'"

Andrew stiffened beneath my touch.

"Then he put me back in the boat and climbed in after me. And the moment he stepped aboard, the wind died. Just stopped. The waves calmed. And we were at the shore. At Gennesaret, miles from where we should have been, but there we were, safe on the beach."

No one moved. I tightened my grip on Andrew's shoulder, but he shook me off and stood. He crossed the space between the benches and pulled his brother into an embrace, his arms tight around Simon's shoulders.

"If I understand the story correctly, you walked on water. The storm stopped the moment he entered the boat. Miles crossed in a heartbeat. And you witnessed all of it."

His hands trembled on Simon's shoulders.

"I wish you had been there. I wish you could have seen it."

Andrew's smile held. "I am glad you are safe. That is enough."

But the tone of his voice said differently. And from the way Simon's eyes searched his brother's face, I suspected he knew it too.

Naomi broke the moment by bustling out of the room and coming back with fresh clothes and more food. "You look half-starved and covered in salt, my son. Change, eat, and then you can take these two to Jesus if that is the plan."

"It is. Thank you, Ima."

While Simon changed in the other room, I drew Andrew aside, my hand on his arm.

"You do not have to pretend with me."

He looked down at where my fingers curled around his sleeve. "What do you want me to say?"

"That you wish you had been there."

His eyes met mine. "You think I am jealous of my own brother?"

"I think you love him and still wish you could have seen it."

The words stopped him. He closed his eyes, his shoulders sagging. "I do wish I had been there. I wish I could have seen it."

"I know."

He pulled me against his chest, his arms coming around me, and he breathed in the scent of my hair, his face laid against the top of my head. Simon had returned to the main room, his voice carrying while he talked to Naomi about the storm and the miracle and Jesus's words. The story spilled out of him again.

"He will tell this story until we are old and gray."

Despite everything, my lips curved. "And we will listen every time."

"I might not." A small laugh escaped him. "But probably."

When we emerged, Damaris was waiting with our traveling packs already prepared, the leather straps buckled tight. She had been busy while we spoke, gathering our few possessions, rolling our blankets, filling waterskins from the courtyard cistern.

I looked around. "You are ready to go? Where are your things?"

She looked up from where she kneeled beside the packs, her hands stilling. "I am not going."

"What? What will you do?"

"I am staying here." Her voice was strong in a way I had not heard before. "With Naomi. For a time, at least."

I crouched beside her and searched her face. "Damaris, you do not have to—"

"I want to." She reached out and took my hand, her grip warm and firm. "You gave me back my life when you took me to Jesus. You helped me learn to walk in the world again when I did not know if I could. But now I need to finish what you started. I need to find my family. To see if there is a place for me with them after all these years."

"Are you certain?"

"Naomi has offered to help me. She knows people in my village. She will send word, will help me prepare them. And while I wait, I can help her here. She should not be alone."

Naomi came to stand behind Damaris. "It is settled. She will stay as long as she needs. And when the time is right, we will see about her family."

Naomi's hand rested on Damaris's shoulder, and Damaris leaned into that touch, no longer the frightened woman who had hidden from crowds but someone beginning to remember her own shape. She needed roots before she could walk the roads again. I would miss her, but being with her family again would be good for her.

"Then I am glad. Glad you will have each other and glad you will find your people again."

When it came time to leave, Damaris embraced me tightly, her arms strong around me. "Thank you. For seeing me when I was invisible. For taking me to him."

"You did the reaching. I only walked beside you."

She pulled back, her eyes full of unshed tears. "If you ever need me, send word. I will come."

"And if you need us, we are never far. We are also family now. Do not forget that."

We left her standing in the courtyard with Naomi, the two of them waving when we turned the corner. They disappeared from sight, swallowed by the narrow streets.

Simon led us down to the harbor where a fishing boat waited, pulled up on the stones, its wood dark with water from the storm and smelling of fish and lake weed and wet timber that never quite dries in the damp air near the water. He talked the entire way through the narrow streets, the words tumbling out of him, his hands moving in the air. When we pushed off from shore, the boat rocking gently beneath us, he took up the oars and told the story again.

Andrew sat across from him, listening and responding when needed, asking the right questions, nodding at the right moments. But his eyes stayed focused on the far shore, his jaw tightening when Simon described Jesus reaching out his hand. He went motionless when Simon said again, "You of little faith. Why did you doubt?"

The rhythmic splash of the oars marked our passage, the blades dipping and pulling, water dripping from them with each stroke, the boat cutting through the lake's glassy surface and leaving a wake that spread behind us in perfect chevrons. The sun was warm on my face and arms, pleasant after the morning's chill, and the water smelled clean and mineral, and beneath it the ever-present smell of fish and weed. I watched the coastline slip past—rocky outcroppings where herons stood as motionless as statues, stretches of sandy beach marked with countless footsteps, villages clustering around natural harbors with their fishing boats drawn up on shore.

WE REACHED GENNESARET BY MIDDAY, the sun directly overhead and beating down with the intensity it has at this season, making the water shimmer and dance with light.

The crowd was already there.

Hundreds of them gathered along the waterfront and spilled back into the narrow streets that led up from the shore, filling the air with their voices, a constant roar of expectation that crashed over us like a wave when we approached, making it impossible to think or breathe.

We found Jesus near the synagogue, surrounded by the disciples and a throng of people pushing in from all sides. Someone shouted from the back, "Rabbi, when did you get here?" Others took up the cry, their voices overlapping.

"Teacher, give us more bread!" A man near the front raised his hands. "Show us another sign!"

Jesus stood in their midst, his jaw set, his eyes moving over the crowd without warmth, and when he spoke, his voice cut through the noise like a blade through fabric.

"Truly I tell you, you are looking for me not because you saw signs but because you ate the loaves and had your fill. Do not work for food that spoils but for food that endures to eternal life, which the Son of Man will give you."

The crowd surged forward, bodies packed so tightly I could smell their sweat and breath, the sour tang of desperation. "What must we do to perform the works of God?"

"The work of God is to believe in the one He has sent."

"What sign, then, will you give us? Our fathers ate manna in the wilderness. What will you do?"

Jesus's eyes swept over them, grief etched into the lines around his mouth. "Truly I tell you, it is not Moses who has given you the bread from heaven, but it is my Father who gives you the true bread from heaven. For the bread of God is the one who comes down from heaven and gives life to the world."

"Sir," they called out, their voices rising in pitch, urgent and demanding, "always give us this bread!"

And then Jesus said the words that changed everything.

"I am the bread of life. Whoever comes to me will never go hungry, and whoever believes in me will never be thirsty."

The murmuring started then, low and uncertain, a rustling through the crowd like wind through dry grass, spreading from the front to the back, voices rising in confusion and doubt. Faces shifted from anticipation to confusion, from hope to doubt.

Jesus continued, his voice growing harder, more uncompromising, pushing into territory that made people shuffle their feet and glance at each other. "I am the living bread that came down from heaven. Whoever eats this bread will live forever. This bread is my flesh, which I will give for the life of the world."

People started talking all at once. "How can this man give us his flesh to eat?" someone demanded. Another voice rose above the rest. "This is a hard teaching! Who can accept it?" From somewhere in the crowd, a man shouted, "He speaks blasphemy!"

But Jesus did not soften his words, did not backtrack or explain or make it easier for them to swallow. If anything, he pushed further. "Very truly I tell you, unless you eat the flesh of the Son of Man and drink his blood, you have no life in you. Whoever eats my flesh and drinks my blood has eternal life, and I will raise them up at the last day. For my flesh is real food and my blood is real drink."

Andrew tensed beside me, his whole body going rigid. Around us, people were backing away, shaking their heads, their faces twisted with disgust or anger. A man near me muttered, "This is too much. I cannot follow a man who speaks such things." Someone else agreed loudly. "He has gone too far. Eating flesh? Drinking blood? This is madness."

And they began to leave.

Not just one or two but whole families, clusters of people who had followed Jesus for weeks or months, who had listened to his teaching and witnessed his miracles. They turned their backs and walked away, their voices carrying while they went, discussing among themselves whether Jesus had always been mad or if this was something new, some breaking point that had finally been crossed. Footsteps and muttered conversations gathered momentum with each person who turned away, an exodus building with each moment.

A woman I recognized from the feeding, the one who had held her child up to see Jesus with her face glowing with hope, gathered her little ones and hurried back toward town, her children running to keep up. A man who had sat at Jesus's feet just yesterday spat in the dust and strode away without looking back, his shoulders set with righteous indignation. Others followed in groups, some arguing quietly among themselves and others silent with disappointment. Their departure created a wake through the crowd until what had been hundreds dwindled to dozens and then to tens, the space opening up around us while the number of bodies thinned.

The air grew chilly despite the midday sun, or perhaps that was only me.

When the last of them had disappeared into the town, Jesus turned to face the disciples, his voice level but his eyes giving nothing away.

"Do you also wish to go away?"

The disciples looked at each other, then at the empty road where so many had just traveled, then at Jesus standing alone before them with the question waiting to be answered.

Andrew shifted beside me, his shoulders squaring. But then Simon moved, his voice already rising.

"Lord, to whom shall we go? You have the words of eternal life. We have come to believe and to know that you are the Holy One of God."

Andrew went motionless. He stepped back slightly, making space for his brother, his face carefully neutral. But his hands curled into fists at his sides, just for a moment, before releasing.

Jesus looked at Simon for a long moment. "Have I not chosen you, the Twelve? Yet one of you is a devil."

The words sent a chill through me, raising the hair on my arms despite the day's warmth. Jesus did not elaborate, but his eyes moved over the Twelve, each man shifting when that gaze passed over him.

Then Thomas gestured toward the empty road. "We just watched hundreds walk away. We are all that is left."

Andrew's voice was quiet. "We chose to stay."

"But did we choose rightly?" Thomas's voice was raw. "They all left, Andrew. Families who followed him for months. Men who witnessed his miracles. They heard what we heard and walked away. And now he tells us one of us is a devil." He looked around at the other disciples. "Which one? How do we know we are not standing beside him right now?"

Andrew's jaw tightened. "We cannot know. Not yet."

"Then how do we trust each other?"

"We trust him." Andrew looked at Jesus. "Lord, we stayed when the others left. But if one of us betrays you—" He stopped. "What are we to do?"

Jesus looked at Andrew. "You will know when the time comes. Until then, you follow me. Even when you do not understand." He turned toward the synagogue. "Come. There is work to do."

The disciples followed him toward the synagogue, leaving Andrew and me standing in the emptied street. Around us lay the debris of the crowd—trampled grass, a wooden animal lying forgotten in the dust where some child had dropped it. The water lapped quietly against the shore with the eternal rhythm that continues regardless of human concerns. A gull cried overhead, its call sharp and lonely in the sudden quiet.

"It is only going to get harder, is it not?" I asked.

Andrew did not answer right away. He was looking at Jesus's retreating figure.

"Yes," he said finally. "Yes, I think it is."

CHAPTER 10

Galilee , June, 31 AD

I could hear Andrew breathing beside me.

Not labored—just the even rhythm of a man used to walking, in and out, as constant as his stride. A month ago I would not have noticed. A month ago there had been too many voices, too many bodies packed around us, too much noise to hear anything so small as one man's breath. But the crowds had thinned through June, and now we were twenty, maybe fewer. Few enough that I knew the sound of each person who walked with us: Salome humming something from my childhood, James and John arguing about nothing that mattered, Simon's occasional laugh that carried over everyone else's.

Quiet enough that when Andrew leaned close, I caught wild thyme from the hillside on his clothes and the salt-warm smell of his skin beneath it.

My hand rested on the low curve where our child grew. My body had grown heavier this past week, the weight riding lower, and I found myself walking with one palm always curved over that place, as if I could hold the baby through my touch alone. She had been still all morning—or he, Andrew would correct, grinning—but now I felt it: the faintest flutter, soft as moth wings.

Andrew's hand found the small of my back as the road climbed through a rocky stretch.

"Better?" he asked when we reached level ground. His hand stayed.

"I was fine before."

"I know." His thumb traced a small circle against my spine. "But now I am closer."

I looked up at him. His beard had grown longer in these months of travel, wilder than he used to keep it. The sun had darkened his skin. Fine lines creased the corners of his eyes when he smiled, as he did now, his dimples deepening, reading something in my face that made him grin.

"What?" I asked.

"You are staring at me."

"I am allowed to stare at my husband."

"You are." He caught my hand and pressed his lips to my knuckles. "Stare all you wish. I will not complain."

Behind us, John made a sound of disgust. "Must we watch this all day?"

"Yes," Andrew said without turning. "Marriage is a holy sacrament. You should take notes."

Simon laughed. James called out something rude in Aramaic that made Salome swat at him with her walking stick.

We stopped for the night beside a stream where willows

grew thick enough to give shade, their branches trailing in water so clear I could see smooth stones on the bottom, brown and gray and speckled white. The women spread out to gather wood while the men hauled water. I helped Joanna lay out our few cooking pots then sat on a flat stone to rest, the rock still warm. The baby had been still all afternoon, but now came that quickening again, as gentle as breath, there and gone.

Mary kneeled beside the stream, filling a waterskin, her hair falling forward over her shoulder. She looked up and caught me watching, water dripping from her hands.

"How do you feel?" she asked. "The sickness has passed?"

"Mostly. Though the smell of fish in the morning still turns my stomach." I pressed my hand to where the child grew beneath my tunic. "Sometimes I feel something. Like a butterfly trapped inside."

"A butterfly?" Mary smiled and came to sit beside me, sitting so our hips touched. "That is a good sign. It means the baby grows strong."

"I hope so. It is still so early. Just these small flutters. Nothing more."

"Give it time," Mary said. "In another month or two, he will kick hard enough to wake you at night."

"She," I corrected.

Mary laughed. "You sound certain."

"I am not. But if I must carry this child through the summer heat and have swollen feet and an aching back, I want a daughter at the end of it. Someone who will remember me when I am old."

"Daughters remember their mothers," Mary agreed. "Sons forget."

Joanna came to sit beside us, wiping sweat from her forehead. "My son did not forget me. He wrote letters every week when he went to study in Jerusalem."

"How old was he?"

"Eight when he went to Jerusalem."

Mary's eyebrows rose. "Eight? So young."

"Chuza wanted him to have a proper education. The best teachers." Joanna's face softened. "I cried for a month. But he comes home when he can, taller each time, full of stories about the Temple and his studies."

"You must miss him," I said.

"Every day. I miss them both—my son and Chuza." She looked down at her hands. "But they understand. Chuza knows why I follow Jesus, why I use our resources to support this. He does not always like it, but he understands."

We sat without speaking. The stream murmured over stones, and I felt that movement again, a secret beneath my hand.

The sun sank lower. Shadows stretched long across our clearing, and the light turned everything golden: the white of Simon's tunic, the silver in the stream, even the dust on our feet. Across the clearing, Jesus sat with Simon and John, their heads bent close in conversation. Andrew and James were arguing about something near the fire, their voices carrying the cadence of men who disagreed about nothing important, more music than debate.

Matthew sat apart, writing in his small book. I watched his stylus move across the page, recording what only he seemed to think worth preserving. Nearby, Thomas and Nathanael spoke in low voices, heads together over some question I could not hear. Philip kneeled by the fire, coaxing the flames higher with bits of dry grass.

Simon the Zealot and Thaddaeus returned from gathering wood, their arms laden with fallen branches. They dropped their loads beside the fire with satisfied grunts, brushing bark from their tunics. Judas Iscariot moved among the packs, taking inventory of our dwindling supplies with the careful eye of someone who had learned to make much from little. James, son of Alphaeus, sat near the water's edge, his hands working a torn sandal strap through a leather awl, pull and twist, pull and twist.

This was all of us now. A remnant.

I thought of all who had walked away. The ones who wanted only the miracles, who ate the bread yet turned from the teaching.

These few had stayed.

We ate simply that night. Flatbread, olives and dried fish, and some cheese that Salome produced from the depths of her pack. Jesus blessed the food with words so plain they sounded like poetry. "Father, thank you for this bread. For these friends. For this night together. Amen."

We sat in a loose circle around the fire. The flames threw shadows across faces I knew and loved. Simon gestured with bread in one hand, too loud as always, arguing about fishing with John, who rolled his eyes but smiled. Judas passed the end pieces to Matthew without being asked, remembering. Tirzah laughed at something James said, her face tender in the firelight. Conversations wove around the circle, punctuated by laughter or quiet agreement. Salome moved among us refilling cups, her hand gentle on shoulders as she passed.

And Andrew beside me, our knees touching, his hand resting on my leg with comfortable possession.

"Tell us something, Teacher," Thomas said. "Something we can hold on to. These days—" He stopped and shook his head. "These days are hard."

Jesus looked at him across the fire. "What do you want to hold on to, Thomas? A sign? A promise that this path will grow easier?"

"Yes," Thomas said. "I would welcome it."

"I cannot give you that." Jesus slowly broke bread between his hands. "But I can tell you about a farmer I knew once in Nazareth."

We all stopped and leaned in.

"This man," Jesus said, "planted a field of wheat. He prepared the ground, scattered the seed, and prayed for rain. And the rain came. The wheat grew. But then flocks of birds came, stripping the young plants. Then the sun beat down, scorching what the birds had left. Then weeds sprang up, choking the wheat that struggled toward harvest."

"Did he get any grain?" Andrew asked.

"Yes. Some of the wheat survived. It grew strong and produced a harvest thirty, sixty, even a hundred times what he planted." Jesus looked around at us, his eyes catching the firelight. "But here is what I remember most about this man. Every morning, while the wheat was still growing, he walked his field. Examined each stalk. Spoke to them."

James snorted. "He spoke to wheat?"

"He did. I asked him once why he bothered. The wheat could not hear him, could it?" Jesus smiled. "He said, 'They do not need to hear. I need to speak. I need to see each one, know each one, love each one. Otherwise, they are just crops. Just a harvest. Just numbers.'"

No one spoke.

"You are not just a crowd to me," Jesus said. "You are not numbers. You are Philip who asks good questions and Nathanael who speaks truth even when it cuts. You are Simon who runs hot as fire and John who burns slow and deep. You are Matthew who writes the rhythm of our days. You are Mary who knows what it costs to be forgiven and Joanna who left comfort for truth. You are Thomas who doubts out loud and Andrew who believes quietly."

He looked at each of us and spoke a truth over us. Then his eyes found mine across the fire. "You are Anna who carries life while learning to walk in mine."

Andrew's hand tightened on my leg.

"No, you are not numbers," Jesus said. "I see each of you. I know each of you. And I love each of you. Not because you are many but because you are mine."

The fire burned low. Conversations drifted into silence. People rose one by one to prepare their sleeping places— spreading cloaks on the ground, banking coals, checking water supplies for morning.

Andrew stood and held out his hand. "Come with me."

I let him pull me to my feet. We walked away from camp, following the stream into deeper shadow where branches hung low enough to brush our shoulders, their leaves cool and smooth against my arms. The water ran clear over stones, catching starlight. The air smelled of green growing things, wet earth, and smoke from the fire we had left behind.

Andrew sat on a fallen log and drew me down beside him. I leaned into his chest, and his arms came around me, both palms resting over the curve where our child slept.

"Our child heard him tonight," Andrew said against my hair. "Jesus said you carry life while learning to walk in his. Our son will remember that, even if he does not know it."

"Or daughter."

"Or daughter." His lips pressed softly against my temple. "Either way, they will be born into this. Into what we are building."

"What are we building?"

He was quiet for a long moment. The stream murmured. An owl called somewhere in the darkness.

"I do not know yet," he said finally. "But I know it matters. It is worth everything we have given and everything we will give. I know that when I am old and my hands shake too much to fish, I will look back on these days, walking rough roads with my pregnant wife, sleeping under stars with a handful of stubborn fools who would not leave when the rest did, and I will say, 'That was when I lived. That was when I was most alive.'"

I turned in his arms to look at him. His face was half in shadow, but I could see his eyes, dark and serious.

"You are a poet," I said.

"I am a fisherman."

"You can be both."

He kissed me then, slow and sure, his hand cradling my head. When he pulled back, he was smiling. "Tomorrow, before the others wake, I will teach you to fish properly."

"You think I need teaching?"

"I think you have never held a net in your life."

"True."

"Then come with me at first light. I will show you how to read the water, how to feel the weight of the line, how to wait." He tucked a strand of hair behind my ear. "And maybe if there is time, I will teach you to skip stones. Though I suspect you will be terrible at it."

"Probably," I admitted.

"But I will love watching you try."

Dawn came cold and gray, the air soft with mist rising from the stream. I woke to Andrew's hand on my shoulder, his finger to his lips. Around us, the camp still slept, dark shapes wrapped in cloaks around a fire burned down to ash and glowing coals. We rose quietly, stepping around huddled forms, and made our way to the stream.

The water looked dark in this light, the current stronger than it had seemed by starlight. Mist hung low over the surface, turning everything soft and strange. Andrew carried a small net slung over his shoulder, old and mended in a dozen places, the mesh worn soft with use.

"This was my father's," he said, running the mesh through his hands with a tenderness I recognized. "My brother has his good nets now. This one is mine."

He waded into the stream, his tunic tied up around his thighs, and I saw the water darken the linen, saw gooseflesh rise on his legs from the cold. "Stream fishing is not like the sea. The water is shallower and the fish more cautious. But the principle is the same. You watch, you wait, you learn what the water will give you."

He showed me where fish would gather in the calm pockets behind rocks, how to cast without tangling the net.

"You cannot muscle the water," he said, his voice low in the morning quiet. "You have to work with it. Let it help you."

I stood on the bank, my arms wrapped around myself against the chill, watching him move through the stream. His movements came without thought, the net blooming in the air like a flower opening and floating down to the water with barely a sound. He waited, reading the surface with eyes that knew every ripple and current, then pulled slowly. The net came up empty, water streaming from the mesh, catching the gray light.

"Sometimes they do not come," he said. "Sometimes you

throw a hundred casts and catch nothing. But you keep throwing."

"Why?"

He looked at me over his shoulder, water dripping from his hands. "Because the hundred-and-first cast might fill the net. Because the act of casting matters as much as the catching. Because—" He stopped and smiled, and in that moment, he looked so young, the way he must have looked when his father first taught him to fish. "Because you are a fisherman, and fishermen fish. Even when the water is empty."

He cast again and again. On the fourth try, the net came up thrashing with silver fish. He laughed, as delighted as a child, and waded back to show me, water sluicing from his legs and the net, the fish flashing and flipping in the mesh.

"See? The water provides."

I helped him lay the fish on the grass. They gasped and flipped, catching the early light, their scales iridescent. He moved quickly through them, choosing which to keep and which to throw back, his hands sure and gentle even in the killing. A quick twist and they were still.

He stood and gathered the net again, shaking water from the mesh. "Now. Your turn to learn." He waded back into the stream, and I followed, the cold water shocking against my legs, soaking the hem of my tunic. He stood behind me in the shallows, close enough that I could feel the warmth of him.

"Put your hands on the net," he said.

I did. I felt the rough weave of the net and smelled the fish and river still clinging to the fibers. He placed his hands over mine and showed me how to feel the weight and balance of it, how the mesh should hang, where to grip for the throw.

"Now cast."

"I will tangle it."

"Probably. Cast anyway."

I gathered the net awkwardly and tried to mimic the fluid motion I had watched him make a dozen times. The net left my hands in a clump and landed in a sad heap at the water's edge.

Andrew grinned. "That was even worse than I expected."

"I hate you."

"No, you do not." He waded over and began untangling the mesh. "Try again."

We tried again. My second cast was marginally better. At least the net opened before it hit the water. The third almost looked like I knew what I was doing. Andrew stood behind me, his hands guiding my arms through the motion, his breath warm against my neck.

"Like this. Feel the rhythm. Cast and gather, cast and gather."

The fourth cast opened properly, spreading across the water like it should, and this time, I felt the difference.

Andrew made an approving sound low in his throat. "There. You felt that?"

"Yes."

"That is what you are looking for. The net wants to open. You just have to let it." He kissed my shoulder. "You will never love it the way I do. But you understand it now. That is enough."

"I understand I am an expert net caster now."

He laughed and grabbed my hand. "And we would both know that is a lie. Now," he said, wading to the bank and towing me along with him, "let me teach you something you will be even worse at."

He found a smooth stone on the bank, flat and round, and tested its weight in his palm. "Stone skipping. Watch."

He sent it flying low across the water—one, two, three, four, five bounces before it sank. The splashes caught the morning light, perfect circles spreading and overlapping.

"Show me," I said.

He placed a stone in my hand then stood behind me again, his arms coming around to guide my throw. "Same principle as the net. Low angle, flick of the wrist. Let the stone do the work."

I threw. The stone plunked straight down.

"That was terrible," I said.

"Worse than terrible," he agreed cheerfully. "Try again."

We tried again. And again. My stones dove like drunken birds, kerplunking into the water with no grace whatsoever. Andrew's laughter tickled the back of my neck.

"You have no talent for this," he said.

"None at all."

"But I love watching you try." He kissed the curve of my neck, just below my ear. "I will remember this morning. You standing on the bank at dawn, throwing stones badly, making that face you make when you are frustrated."

"What face?"

"The one where you bite your lip and narrow your eyes. Like the stone has personally offended you."

I turned in his arms. "Teach me something I can actually do."

"You cast the net better than most men on their first try. You felt the rhythm of it." He tucked a strand of hair behind my ear. "And you make me laugh. That is a gift worth more than all the skipped stones in Galilee."

He kissed me then, slow and unhurried, tasting of river

water and morning. He raised his head and smiled at me, his dimples showed. "And that. You are very good at that. You need no teaching there."

"I am glad I am good at something useful." I suddenly felt a stirring, as gentle as a whisper beneath my ribs. I gasped and laid my hand on my belly.

"You felt her?" Andrew asked, his hand joining mine.

"Just barely."

We stood there on the bank in the morning light, our hands resting together on the swell of my belly where our child grew. The stream murmured past. Birds woke in the willows, their songs tentative at first then growing bolder. Behind us, I heard voices from camp: Simon's rumble, thick with sleep, Salome's laugh, the clatter of pots being set out for breakfast.

The day was beginning. Soon we would walk again, following Jesus toward whatever waited in Caesarea Philippi. Teaching and questions and crowds and danger lay ahead.

But not yet.

"I love this," I said quietly. "This moment. The two of us and this baby and the terrible net I cannot cast properly."

Andrew's hands cupped my face. "These are the moments we fight for," he said. "These small, ordinary, precious things."

He kissed me, and I answered with my whole mouth, my whole heart.

By the time we returned to camp, the sun had cleared the horizon. The others were already breaking fast. Jesus looked up when we approached, saw the net slung over Andrew's shoulder and the fish I carried wrapped in leaves, and smiled.

"Did you catch anything?" he asked.

"I caught everything," Andrew said, his eyes on me.

Simon took the fish from my hands and held them up. "Fresh catch. We eat well this morning." He grinned at Andrew. "Did she help at all?"

"Not with the fish," Andrew said, laughing. "But definitely with other things." I blushed and punched his shoulder.

The fish were gutted and cleaned then laid over the fire on green sticks to roast. We ate together, breaking bread in the morning light. When we finished, we gathered our few things and continued north. The road wound through hills green with late-summer growth. Wildflowers still bloomed along the edges—small white stars and purple thistles and something yellow I did not know the name of.

I walked beside Andrew, my hand in his, my palm curved over where the baby grew quiet in her walking rhythm. The promise of her waited there, small and certain.

CHAPTER 11

Caesarea Philippi, July 31, AD

THE WATERS RUSHED beneath the stone bridges of
Caesarea Philippi, tumbling from the limestone cliffs where
the great temple of Pan had been carved into the rock face.
Patches of emerald moss clung to the damp stones, and the
air hung heavy with moisture and the iron-rich scent of wet
earth. I stood at the edge of a small rise, one hand pressed to
the nagging ache in my lower back, which had become my
constant companion, the other shading my eyes against the
glare of sunlight on pale stone. Five months with child, and
my body reminded me with every breath of its changing
state. The thickening of my waist made my tunic pull tight
across my middle. The tender heaviness of my breasts made
the climb up to this place an exercise in discomfort, each
jostling step sending small shocks through tissue grown

swollen and sensitive. The occasional flutter of movement low in my belly still startled me, a fish turning in dark water.

The air here smelled of damp stone and cypress, layered with the sweet reek of burned honey and wine and, beneath that, the lingering tang of blood from the offerings worshippers had left at the pagan shrines that morning. The early-summer heat rose from the stones in shimmering waves, thickening the air until each breath felt labored. The fragrance of wild thyme and hyssop grew stronger in the heat, these plants forcing their way up through cracks in the ancient walls where nothing else would grow. Strange to be in such a place dedicated to false gods, especially with Jesus. Yet he had brought us here deliberately, to this northern boundary of our homeland where Greek and Roman influence mingled with our Jewish ways like oil and water, never truly blending despite centuries of proximity.

Andrew's shadow fell across the stones at my feet. "Should you rest?" he asked as he helped me down the path to where everyone gathered.

"I have rested enough," I replied, watching as Jesus gathered the disciples in a semicircle before him, their backs to the great stone cliff with its niches for idols. "Something is about to happen. I can feel it."

Andrew nodded, his eyes following mine to where Jesus stood. "He has been quiet these past days. I have never seen our Teacher so deep in thought."

"I have noticed too," I said. "I pray nothing is wrong."

The sun had passed its zenith when Jesus finally spoke, his voice reaching where I stood. "Who do people say that the Son of Man is?"

The disciples glanced at one another before answering.

"Some say John the Baptist," replied John.

"Others say Elijah," added James.

"Jeremiah or one of the prophets," Simon the Zealot said.

Jesus nodded, absorbing their answers, his face unreadable. Then he fixed them with a gaze that pierced through flesh and bone. "But who do you say that I am?"

Silence fell over the group. I found myself holding my breath. The question lingered in the air, unanswered. The rush of water from the caves behind them grew loud in the stillness.

Then Simon stepped forward. "You are the Messiah, the Christ," he called, his voice ringing with conviction. "The Son of the living God."

Simon's declaration rushed through the air like thunder before the rain, and I gasped, the breath catching in my chest. Though I had come to believe this truth in my heart over these months of following Jesus, to hear it proclaimed aloud, here in this place of pagan worship where stone gods stared down from their niches with blank eyes, sent a chill across my skin despite the summer heat. The hairs on my arms rose. The blood left my face and then returned in a rush of warmth.

Beside me, Andrew drew in a sharp breath, more sensation than sound. His hand found mine and squeezed it hard, his palm rough against my fingers, the pressure almost painful. His eyes shone with unshed tears that caught the light, and the muscle in his jaw worked silently, clenching and releasing. This truth that Simon now proclaimed was the very one Andrew had discovered first at the Jordan River, when he had run to find his brother with those same words on his lips. Now Simon stood in the circle of light while

Andrew remained in the shadows, his shoulders beside me rigid and drawn as tight as rope.

Everyone stood silently. Simon's words hung in the air between the stone gods staring from their niches and the living God he had just proclaimed. The water rushed from the cave mouth behind Jesus, constant and indifferent. Above us, the blank eyes of Pan looked down from the carved rock face.

Jesus's face softened with relief. "Blessed are you, Simon son of Jonah. For this was not revealed to you by flesh and blood but by my Father in heaven."

He stepped closer to Simon, placing both hands on Simon's broad shoulders. "And I tell you that you are Peter," Jesus continued, using the Greek word for *rock*, "and on this rock I will build my church, and the gates of Hades will not overcome it."

The disciples shifted uneasily, some leaning forward as if straining to hear better. The magnitude of what Jesus had just given Simon—this new name, this authority, this command to build his church—washed over all of us.

"I will give you the keys of the kingdom of heaven," Jesus told Simon Peter. "Whatever you bind on earth will be bound in heaven, and whatever you loose on earth will be loosed in heaven."

From where I stood, I could see tears forming in Simon Peter's eyes. This man, known for his impulsiveness, stood transformed before us all. Jesus's words visibly rested upon him, blessing and burden together.

Jesus raised his hands, his expression grave. "Tell no one that I am the Messiah," he commanded. "No one."

Confusion moved through the group. Next to me, Mary drew a sharp breath, her hand finding my arm.

Matthew spoke first. "Rabbi, why must we remain silent? If you are the Messiah, should not all Israel know?"

The lines around Jesus's mouth deepened. "The Messiah that most expect wears a crown and wields a sword. They wait for one who will drive out Rome with force, who will restore David's throne through conquest." He looked at each of them in turn. "That is not the kingdom I bring."

"But the prophecies—" Thomas began.

"Speak of a servant who suffers," Jesus finished. "Of one pierced for our transgressions. The people are not ready to hear this. They want liberation from Rome, not salvation from sin."

Andrew's hand came to rest on my shoulder, and I shuddered. I thought of Abba's warnings about the spies who followed Jesus everywhere and the charges being built against him. The word "Messiah" held danger I had never fully understood until now. A declaration like that would not just anger the Pharisees, it would draw Rome's attention. And Rome did not tolerate rebels.

Judas shifted restlessly. "But if we remain silent, how will people know? How will they rally to your cause?"

"When the time is right, all will be revealed. But that time is not yet. We should not linger here," Jesus said, glancing up at the pagan shrines that loomed over us. He turned to James, who managed our traveling arrangements. "We return to Galilee today."

As the disciples gathered their few possessions, I stared at Simon Peter. He had the same sun-browned face, the same strong hands, the same weathered tunic. Yet something had changed. He carried himself differently now, shoulders squared beneath a new burden. The rock on which Jesus would build his church.

Andrew appeared at my side as we began the climb down from the high place. Without a word, he offered his arm on the steeper parts of the path. Pilgrim feet had walked these stone steps for centuries, polishing them to a treacherous shine.

"The descent is harder than the climb," he murmured, his free hand hovering near the small of my back as I navigated a particularly steep section. His eyes darted to my rounded belly, concerned.

I placed my hand in his. "We are fine," I assured him with a small smile. Yet I was grateful for his steadfast presence as we descended the uneven path.

At the bottom, Matthew distributed dried figs and strips of salted fish. I accepted my portion with thanks and found a flat stone to sit upon while I ate. Andrew sat beside me, his eyes following his brother among the other disciples.

"Simon has been called many things in his life," he said. "Most of them I would not say in your presence." A faint smile crossed his lips. "It will be strange to call him Peter now. I have only ever known him as Simon."

"Yet the name fits him," I observed. "Stubborn as stone."

Andrew's laugh was brief but genuine. "That he is."

Peter broke away from the others and crossed to where we sat, his movements quick and restless. He dropped onto the ground beside Andrew and set his food on the ground next to him. For a moment, he said nothing and only stared at his hands as if he had never seen them before.

"Andrew, did you hear?" he asked finally. "Did you hear what he said?"

"We heard," Andrew said.

"The rock. He called me the rock." Peter's voice held wonder. "Upon this rock I will build my church. The keys to the kingdom, Andrew. He is giving me the keys." He looked up at his brother, his eyes shining. "Can you believe it?"

"I can believe it."

"I thought—when he asked who people say he is, and then who we say he is—I thought my heart would pound out of my chest. And then the words just came. Like they were put in my mouth." He gripped Andrew's arm. "You were the one who took me to him. You were the first to say it, that he was the Messiah. I remember that day at the Jordan. You came running, and you could barely get the words out. You were so excited."

"I remember," Andrew mumbled.

"And now he gives this to me." Peter shook his head. "The rock. Peter the rock." He laughed, the sound slightly unsteady. "Our father would have had something to say about that."

"He would have," Andrew agreed.

Peter squeezed Andrew's arm once more then stood. "I should—there are others who want to talk. But Andrew—" He paused, looking down at his brother. "We will talk later."

He strode back toward the cluster of disciples, leaving Andrew and me in silence.

I studied Andrew's profile. His jaw was tight, his eyes fixed on the middle distance. He took a piece of dried fig from his portion but did not eat it, only held it between his fingers.

"He meant well," I said softly.

"I know." Andrew set the fig aside. "He always means well."

I waited, letting the silence stretch between us. When he said nothing more, I touched his hand. "Andrew—"

"I—"

"Do you think he understands what just happened?" Salome interrupted, sitting on the ground beside us.

Andrew's mouth closed. Whatever he had been about to say retreated behind his carefully composed expression.

"I think he is still trying to," I said to Salome, though my eyes stayed on Andrew.

"Well." Salome brushed dust from her robe. "The Lord works in mysterious ways."

Mysterious, yes. And sometimes painful.

Jesus called for us to continue onward before anyone could say more. The group reassembled, and we set off.

We continued our journey southward, descending from the highlands toward Galilee. The path wound down in switchbacks, and I felt the descent in my thighs and knees, the downward pull different from climbing. Heat rose from the stones, and I caught the sharp scent of cypress when I brushed against a trunk, its resin sticky on my fingers. The child had been quiet all morning, but now with the downward slope I felt small movements, a shifting as if finding new position. Behind me, voices—Peter still talking about the keys, about being the rock, his excitement carrying back to us. Salome's low laugh at something. The scuff of sandals on stone. The usual sounds of our traveling. But something had shifted since Caesarea Philippi. I could feel it in the changed rhythm of our group, in who now walked where.

Peter moved forward through our group until he walked beside Jesus, near enough to speak without raising his voice. Andrew fell farther back with each mile, his eyes on the dusty road rather than his brother's back. He kept to himself.

I watched him from a distance, aching to know his thoughts, noting how he absently rubbed the callus at the base of his thumb, a habit I had observed whenever his mind was troubled.

When we stopped to rest near a grove of olive trees, I eased myself down onto a fallen log, the bark rough and ridged against the backs of my thighs. The pressure released from my spine, and my vertebrae settled one by one, with the ache spreading rather than concentrating in that single burning point at the base. I adjusted my position on the log, trying to ease the persistent ache in my lower back. The air here was cooler beneath the ancient trees, carrying the scent of sun-warmed olives and the bitter green of their leaves crushed underfoot. A lizard darted across a nearby stone, its scales catching the light like hammered bronze.

Tirzah eased down beside me, her hand supporting her belly, a soft grunt escaping her lips as she settled. The small sounds of her pregnancy echoed mine: the unconscious murmurs when the child moved, the altered rhythm of her breathing, the way she pressed her knuckles into the small of her back when standing too long. We had become mirrors for each other, our bodies changing in tandem.

"James noticed it too," she said without preamble, nodding toward Andrew.

"Noticed what?" I asked, though I knew.

"How the light rests differently on the brothers now." She offered me a piece of dried apple. "He says Andrew is the better fisherman, you know. More patient. Reads the water better."

I accepted the fruit with a grateful nod. "Andrew would never claim such a thing."

"Which is precisely why it is true." She bit into her own piece. "My James could learn something from your husband's humility."

The rest was cut short as Jesus called the disciples to gather once more. I drew near enough to hear, standing with the other women at the edge of the group.

"The Son of Man must go to Jerusalem and suffer many things at the hands of the elders, the chief priests and the teachers of the law," he said. "He must be killed and on the third day be raised to life."

My hand flew to my mouth. I turned to Andrew. His face had gone white.

Peter's reaction was swift and fierce. He took Jesus by the arm, drawing him aside. "Never, Lord!" I heard him exclaim. "This shall never happen to you!"

Jesus turned, his eyes flashing with an intensity that sent me back a step, my heel catching on a root. "Get behind me, Satan!" he said to Peter, his voice cutting through the afternoon heat. "You are a stumbling block to me. You do not have in mind the concerns of God but merely human concerns."

The blood left Peter's face, the sun-brown of his cheeks going ashen. His shoulders dropped, slumping forward. The hand that had reached for Jesus fell to his side, fingers curling inward. The rock upon which Jesus would build his church stood rebuked before us all. My stomach clenched.

Andrew moved to his brother's side, a supporting hand on his shoulder. Their eyes met briefly, Andrew's compassionate, Peter's shattered. In that moment, the complex bond between them transcended any rivalry.

Jesus raised his voice, gathering us all closer. "Whoever wants to be my disciple must deny themselves and take up their cross and follow me. For whoever wants to save their life will lose it, but whoever loses their life for me will find it."

Take up a cross? I laid my hand protectively over my child, feeling its restless movements. What future was this for a baby, following a Messiah marked for death?

"What good is it for someone to gain the whole world yet forfeit their soul?" Jesus continued. "For the Son of Man is going to come in his Father's glory with his angels, and then he will reward each person according to what they have done."

His final words carried a promise: "Truly I tell you, some who are standing here will not taste death before they see the Son of Man coming in his kingdom."

Judas moved closer, his face dark with disapproval. "The Messiah does not come to die," he muttered to those nearby. "He comes to rule. To drive out Rome. To restore David's throne." The rich scent of the oils he wore, expensive and foreign, drifted toward me, mingling with the sharper tang of his sweat. "This kind of talk will frighten away potential supporters. People with wealth and influence who could help our cause."

No one commented, and the rest of our journey passed in stunned silence. Peter walked alone, the fire gone from his stride. Andrew stayed close to his brother but did not speak. Even James and John, usually full of questions, kept their counsel.

Judas alone was animated, moving from disciple to disciple, whispering urgently. "He speaks in riddles," I overheard him telling Thomas as they passed near me. "When the proper time comes, you will see, he will reveal his true power. No Messiah comes to be killed. The prophets speak of victory, not defeat."

Thomas merely shrugged. "I follow what I see with my own eyes, not what I wish to see."

Judas's face tightened with frustration. Whatever future

he had imagined when joining us, it clearly did not include a Messiah who would suffer and die.

Night fell as we made camp by a tributary of the Jordan, the sky darkening from blue to purple to black, stars emerging one by one until they crowded the heavens. The moon, nearly full, cast silver light across the water, creating shimmering pathways that appeared and disappeared with the gentle current, never quite the same twice. Crickets sang in the tall grasses, their chorus rising and falling in waves, punctuated by the occasional croak of a frog and the distant call of a night bird. The mood remained subdued, Jesus's words about suffering and death hanging over us all, unspoken but present in every gesture, every averted glance.

Andrew worked to set up our sleeping area, his hands moving through the familiar rhythm of the tasks. Firelight caught his face as he moved, throwing his features into relief, and I could see the line that had formed between his brows during the afternoon, still there, unsmoothed. He checked tent pegs with the same attention he gave his nets, testing each one, making sure of the ground. But every few moments he would pause and look toward the edge of camp where Peter sat alone, hunched forward, a dark shape against the stars. Then his hands would find the next rope, pull it tight, drive the next peg into the ground, and continue.

The night air held a chill that crept through my woolen shawl, finding the gaps at my neck and wrists where the fabric could not protect me. I pulled the shawl tighter, but the cold had already worked its way beneath. I shivered as I made my way toward Andrew, the smooth river stones clicking beneath my sandals with each step, some rolling away under my weight, others shifting and settling under the pressure. The smell of the cooking fires mingled with the damp earth scent rising from the river—smoke and water and the smell of crushed grass where we had trampled paths through the growth along the bank.

I brought Andrew his portion of bread and lentil stew, the bowl still warm in my hands, the heat seeping through the clay into my palms. He took it with a distracted nod of thanks, his fingers curling around the rim but barely seeming to register the warmth, his attention already elsewhere.

"He will be all right," I said, nodding toward Peter.

Andrew looked up at me. The composure he wore in company had slipped. His brows drew together, not in anger but in genuine bewilderment, his lips parting slightly. Words seemed to gather behind his teeth but would not come. "I have never seen him so shaken. Not since our father died." He set the food aside, untouched, his fingers leaving marks in the soft bread. "All our lives, Simon has been the first to speak, the first to act, the first in all things. And I..." He trailed off, his gaze dropping to his hands where they rested on his knees.

"And you have been the one to stand beside him," I finished. "The one who steadies him when he falls."

"Yes. It is the pattern of our lives."

"And yet today, Jesus gave him a new name. A new purpose."

"The rock on which he will build his church." He was quiet for a moment, his fingers working at the callous on his thumb. "I took Simon to Jesus," he said finally. "I was the first to follow. The first to believe. And I know—" He stopped for a moment. "I know it is wrong to feel this way. Sinful, even. But I am tired, Anna. I am so tired of being second. Simon walks on water while I am not even there to see it. I find the Messiah, I run to tell him, and then he is the one who stands before Jesus and declares it to the world. He receives the keys to the kingdom." He looked at me, his eyes raw. "What does that make me? The one who finds the treasure but never gets to hold it?"

He was silent for so long I thought he might not continue. I placed my hand over his.

"I love my brother," he said, his voice rough with emotion. "I would lay down my life for him without hesitation. When I see Jesus call him the rock, part of me rejoices because I know Simon will rise to it. He always does." He paused, his thumb pressing hard into his palm. "But another part of me—the part I am ashamed of—wonders why it is always him. Why am I always the one who prepares the way but never walks it myself?" He looked at me, and in his eyes, I saw both love for his brother and the pain of a lifetime spent in shadow. "Does that make me faithless? To want what he has been given?"

"It makes you human," I said.

He nodded slowly, but his jaw remained tight. "And now Jesus speaks of death. Of crosses." His voice dropped even lower. "I am afraid, Anna. Not for myself but for you. For our child. What if this path ends in—" He could not finish.

I placed my hand over his. "I am afraid too."

"But at what cost?"

I had no answer that would satisfy either of us.

Across the camp, I noticed Tirzah watching me, her eyes full of unspoken questions. She, too, must be weighing these same concerns, with her own child growing within her. Our gazes met briefly in silent understanding before she turned back to James.

Later, as we prepared for sleep, I watched Peter finally approach Jesus. They spoke in hushed tones by the firelight,

Jesus's hand resting on Peter's shoulder, their shadows stretching long across the ground. Whatever passed between them restored something in Peter. He stood straighter as he returned to the disciples' tent.

As dawn broke, I found Andrew already awake, gazing eastward where the rising sun painted the hills gold and amber and rose. The air held the stillness of early morning, that breathless quality before the world fully wakes, cool and dew-laden, smelling of wet stone and night-blooming flowers now closing their petals with the first light. Birdsong erupted from the thickets along the riverbank, tentative at first then building to a full chorus of competing voices. I joined him silently, our shoulders touching, the warmth from his body a relief against the dawn chill. I shivered and pulled my shawl tighter.

My bare feet had gathered dew from the grass, cold and wet between my toes, and I curled them against the dampness, trying to draw heat from the earth that had not yet received the sun. My shift was wrinkled from sleep, still holding the smell of woodsmoke and sweat, my hair loose and tangled around my shoulders where it fell to my waist. I had not bothered to braid it or cover it, knowing only Andrew would see me in this state, and he had seen worse.

"I dreamed of Bethsaida last night," he said without looking at me, his eyes fixed on the eastern horizon, where light was spreading like water poured across the hills. "Of our home by the shore. Of a child learning to walk on the sand, falling and rising again, their small hands covered in grit. I could smell the lake, the scent of fish and reeds and water, feel it against my calves when I waded in at dawn to check the nets." His voice held a yearning that tightened my throat. "I heard the child's laughter. High and bright, the way children laugh when they discover their own feet."

I slipped my hand into his. "That dream may still come true."

"Perhaps." He turned to face me fully then, one hand gently coming to rest on my stomach. His fingers splayed wide, encompassing the life within. "But the path ahead is not what I imagined when we first followed him."

"No," I agreed. "It is not."

His eyes searched mine, the golden brown of them deepening in the early light to the color of the night before a storm. A muscle twitched in his cheek, just below the small scar that a fishing hook had left years before. "Yet you would still walk it? Knowing what we heard yesterday?"

"Where you go, I go."

The child moved beneath his palm.

Behind us, the camp stirred. Peter's voice called out something about breaking camp. Jesus answered him, the words too far away to hear. Andrew's hand lingered on my belly a moment longer, then he turned toward his brother's voice.

CHAPTER 12

Caesarea Philippi, September, 31 AD

THE MOUNTAIN LOOMED against the morning sky, its eastern face catching the first light while the western slopes remained in shadow. A terebinth tree stood at its base, its branches dark against the pale limestone. Mount Hermon's peaks dominated the northern horizon, where we had made camp during these summer months. Andrew stood beside me, watching three distant figures climb the rocky path—his brother Simon Peter, James, and John. Jesus had risen before first light and summoned only these three to accompany him.

"He did not say why he chose them?" I asked, one hand supporting my lower back as the weight of six months of pregnancy pulled forward against my spine.

Andrew shook his head. "No. He said only that they should go with him to pray."

He continued watching the mountain path his brother

climbed. Though Andrew never complained when Peter was chosen for such honors, his fingers worked at the edge of his belt where the leather had frayed.

The child stirred within me, and I placed my hand against the curve of my belly, feeling the firm press from within. Now there was no hiding the evidence of new life beneath my robes.

"I should help prepare the morning meal," I said, touching Andrew's arm. "The women will gather at the cooking fires."

He nodded, his gaze still fixed on the mountain. "I will join the others. Surely there are tasks to do until they return." The settlement had grown as we traveled. What had begun as our small band of followers now routinely swelled with crowds who sought Jesus for teaching or healing. Dozens of temporary shelters dotted the valley floor, and already people stirred, emerging into the cool dawn.

The morning air still held a trace of mountain cold, though the sun had begun its work of burning it away. Smoke from cooking fires drifted low across the camp, carrying with it the yeasty smell of yesterday's bread being warmed over coals and the sharper scent of green wood that had smoldered more than burned. Somewhere a child cried, and a woman sang softly to quiet him.

Tirzah met me near the central cooking fire. Her face glowed with health, as did mine, both of us flourishing as we carried new life. We exchanged knowing smiles, the shared experience of motherhood binding us together as we moved through the daily tasks of camp life.

"You have rested well?" she asked, embracing me.

"Very well," I replied. "The child grows more active each

day. Even in sleep, I feel the movements, like a reminder of the blessing I carry."

Together with Miriam and Mary, we prepared the simple morning meal. My fingers grew slick with oil as I tore the barley bread into portions, and the salt from the cheese left a gritty residue on my palms that I had to wipe against my apron. The olives had been packed in brine, and their sharp tang cut through the sweeter smell of dried figs laid out on a wooden tray. As I worked, the heat from the fire pressed against my left side while my right remained cool in the shade, and I shifted my weight to ease the ache in my lower back, all the while keeping watch on Andrew across the camp. He spoke with Philip and Nathanael, gesturing occasionally toward the mountain. Though his expression revealed nothing, his hands moved restlessly, picking up a waterskin, setting it down, and adjusting his belt.

The meal had been served and cleared, the crowds growing restless, when Thomas approached me.

"A family has arrived," he said, wiping dust from his brow. "They seek healing for their son."

I set aside the water jar I had been filling. "What ails the child?"

"A spirit seizes him. He foams at the mouth and is thrown to the ground. They say he has suffered since infancy."

I had seen such afflictions before. The rigid limbs, the violent shaking, the vacant eyes that saw nothing during the attack. I nodded. "Bring them to the shade of the terebinth tree. I will come."

Thomas hesitated. "They ask specifically for Jesus."

"Jesus is not here," I replied, gesturing toward the mountain. "The child suffers now. I may be able to offer some comfort until the Master returns."

The family huddled in the sparse shade of the ancient tree. Father, mother, and between them, a boy of perhaps twelve years. His eyes darted nervously from face to face, his thin shoulders hunched as if expecting a blow. The father rose as I approached, desperation etched into the lines around his mouth.

"My son needs healing," he said, his voice rough with exhaustion. "We heard the Teacher was here."

I sat carefully on a flat stone, arranging my robes to accommodate my swollen belly. "Jesus has gone up the mountain to pray," I explained. "He will return before nightfall. I am Anna, wife of Andrew. I have some knowledge of healing."

The mother looked at me with weary hope. "Can you help him?"

Before I could answer, the boy stiffened. Those nearest to him stepped back hastily, some making the sign against evil. His head snapped backward, eyes showing only white, and a sound like an animal's cry tore from his throat. He collapsed, limbs twisting at unnatural angles, and the unclean spirit took hold of him with a violence that made even the father struggle to keep his son from harm.

I rose and moved forward, pushing past a woman who whispered prayers to ward herself from contamination. "Turn him," I instructed the parents, gesturing to his side. The spittle on his lips had turned bloody where he had bitten his tongue, and his limbs jerked with such force that his father's strength barely held him steady.

Women led their children away. Men muttered prayers.

One called for the boy to be removed from the camp, as was done with the ritually unclean.

"When did this first afflict him?" I asked, noting the movements of the parents who had clearly done this many times before.

"Since he drew his first breath," the father answered, his knuckles white as he gripped his son's shoulders. "It has followed him like a shadow. The priests said a demon entered him at birth, punishment for some hidden sin."

The attack intensified before my eyes. The boy's breathing grew labored, his skin flushing dark with strain, and I reached for my small pouch of medicines though I knew my herbs offered little hope against such a powerful spirit.

Andrew appeared at my side, drawn by the commotion. "What troubles the child?" he asked.

"An unclean spirit," the father answered before I could speak. "We have sought every healer from Jerusalem to Damascus. None could drive it out."

Andrew's brow furrowed, and he moved forward to kneel beside the boy, whose convulsions had subsided into trembling exhaustion. I had never seen my husband attempt this before, though I knew Jesus had given his disciples this authority.

"I will try," he said.

The father's hope rekindled, his eyes fixed on Andrew.

Andrew placed his hands gently on the boy's head. "In the name of Jesus of Nazareth," he said, "I command this spirit to depart. Release this child."

A hush fell over those watching. The boy's trembling stilled momentarily, and for a breath, I thought it had worked. Then his body tensed again, a low moan escaping his lips. The spirit remained.

Andrew tried once more, his voice stronger, his hands steady on the boy, but again, nothing changed. He slowly pushed himself to his feet, his shoulders hunched forward as though bearing a weight he had not carried before, his attention fixed on the ground where the boy lay suffering still.

"I am sorry," he said.

The father's head dropped. "It is not your fault," he said, though his voice thickened with renewed despair. "No one has helped him."

My heart ached for both my husband and the father in the unending vigil over this suffering child. I had seen many illnesses yield to herbs and care, but this spirit-affliction remained beyond mortal remedy. Only God could reach into that darkness.

Andrew stepped back beside me. I touched his arm, feeling the tension in his muscles. "You tried," I whispered.

He nodded once but said nothing, and in his silence lay all the doubt and confusion of a man who had been given authority he could not wield.

The father's attention moved past us, and a flicker of hope returned to his expression. "Your companions," he said. "Perhaps they can help where others have failed."

I turned to see Nathanael, Matthew, Judas, and Thomas approaching. The boy's fit had begun to subside, his rigid muscles gradually relaxing, though slight tremors still ran through his limbs.

"This child is possessed," Thomas announced, taking a step back. "Jesus has given us authority over such spirits."

The disciples gathered around, their expressions a

mixture of confidence and uncertainty. Matthew kneeled beside the boy, placed a hand on his forehead, and said, "Unclean spirit, I command you in the name of Jesus of Nazareth, come out of him!"

Nothing happened. The boy lay still now, exhausted but otherwise unchanged.

Judas stepped forward next, his handsome features set with determination. He spoke similar words of command, his tone more forceful than Matthew's. Again, nothing happened.

Each disciple tried in turn, their commands growing louder, their gestures more emphatic as each attempt failed. A crowd gathered, drawn by the spectacle. At the edges, several men stood apart, their fine robes unstained by travel dust, watching with the stillness of merchants tallying a competitor's losses. One made a mark on a small tablet. Another spoke behind his hand to his companion, and I caught only fragments on the wind: "Cannot... failed... Jerusalem." The taste of copper filled my mouth.

The father's hope crumbled into bitter disappointment. "I should have known," he muttered. "Always the same. Promises but no help."

Andrew touched my shoulder. "Look," he said, nodding toward the mountain path.

Four figures descended toward us. Jesus led the way with Peter, James, and John following behind.

Peter's eyes were swollen, the skin around them rubbed raw. His beard was wild, his tunic askew as if he had dressed without seeing what his hands were doing. He walked like a man in a vision, his feet finding the path but his gaze turned inward toward something the rest of us could not see.

James and John flanked him, looking no better. John's lips moved soundlessly. James gripped his brother's arm with one hand while the other rested against his chest as if his heart pained him.

The crowd parted for them in silence.

Peter moved through the people like a man walking in his sleep. John passed me without recognition. James looked at the convulsing boy, at the kneeling disciples, closed his eyes briefly, his mouth twisting, then turned away.

Something had happened on that mountain.

I knew it the way I knew when fever would break or when a wound had begun to fester. Whatever had happened on that mountain had changed them. They walked among us but were not with us. They had gone up as fishermen and tax collectors and had come down as something else entirely.

Andrew saw his brother's face and went to him.

"Simon? What happened?"

Peter stood before Andrew, breathing like a man surfacing from deep water. He raised one hand toward his brother then let it drop. His mouth formed a word— perhaps Andrew's name, perhaps something else—but nothing followed. Tears came. He shook his head once, slowly.

"I cannot," Peter whispered finally. "He said... We cannot speak of it. Not yet."

"But—"

"Andrew, please." Peter gripped his brother's shoulders. "Do not ask me. I want to tell you. But I cannot. Not until —" He stopped and swallowed hard. "Not until the Son of Man has risen from the dead."

Andrew stared at his brother, his hand reaching out and then dropping back to his side, his mouth opening but no sound emerging. He stood there, close enough to touch Peter but separated by an unbridgeable distance.

The possessed boy convulsed again, his back arching, and the silence shattered. All eyes turned to Jesus, waiting. The father, seeing a last chance for his son's deliverance, pushed through the people.

"Teacher!" he cried out. "I brought my son to your disciples, but they could not heal him. He has a spirit that makes him mute. Whenever it seizes him, it throws him to the ground. He foams at the mouth, gnashes his teeth, and becomes rigid." His words tumbled out in a desperate rush. "I begged your disciples to drive out the spirit, but they could not do it."

Jesus's expression darkened as he looked from the father to his disciples, who stood with downcast eyes.

"Oh, unbelieving generation," he said, loud enough for everyone to hear. "How long shall I stay with you? How long shall I put up with you?" The rebuke fell heavily upon us all. "Bring the boy to me."

The father motioned to his wife, who helped the weakened child to his feet. As they approached Jesus, the boy's body suddenly contorted. He fell to the ground, rolling in the dust, foam once again bubbling from his lips.

"How long has he been like this?" Jesus asked the father.

"From childhood," the man replied. "It has often thrown him into fire or water to kill him. But if you can do anything, take pity on us and help us."

"'If you can'?" Jesus repeated. "Everything is possible for one who believes."

The father's voice broke. "I do believe. Help me overcome my unbelief!"

Jesus turned toward the boy, who writhed in the dirt,

heels digging furrows in the earth. The crowd drew back. Jesus's features sharpened, taking on the authority of one who commands armies.

"You deaf and mute spirit," he said, each word as distinct as hammer strikes, "I command you, come out of him and never enter him again."

The boy's scream cut through the air like metal on stone. Several women covered their ears. A child started to weep. The boy's body arched violently then collapsed into stillness so complete, I feared he had died.

"He no longer lives," an old man murmured, and others took up the whisper.

Jesus moved forward, dust rising around his ankles. Taking the boy's limp hand, he pulled gently upward. The child rose to his feet with ease, like a sleeper awakening from restful slumber. He looked at his father then his mother as if seeing them clearly for the first time.

The father gathered his son into his arms, weeping openly. The crowd erupted in praises, questions, and exclamations of wonder. Those who had backed away now came close. The scribes departed quickly from the gathering.

The sun had passed its zenith by the time the crowd finally dispersed. Jesus withdrew to the shade of the terebinth tree, and the disciples followed.

"Why could we not drive it out?" Matthew asked, shame thick in his voice.

Jesus looked at each of them. "Because you have so little faith. Truly I tell you, if you have faith as small as a mustard seed, you can say to this mountain, 'Move from here to there,' and it will move. Nothing will be impossible for you."

He paused, his gaze lingering on their chastened faces. "This kind can come out only through prayer."

The disciples fell silent. Some looked down at their feet. Others exchanged troubled glances. None questioned Jesus aloud, but their furrowed brows and tight mouths spoke for them.

~

LATER THAT AFTERNOON, I returned to the women's tasks I had abandoned during the morning's crisis. I found a place in the shade and took up the swaddling cloths I had been making, my hands grateful for familiar work after the morning's intensity.

A village woman approached, offering me a small pouch of herbs from the mountain slopes. "For when your time comes," she explained. "Mountain feverfew mixed with thyme. It grows only on these slopes.".

I accepted her gift, and we spoke briefly of birthing customs in different regions. Her knowledge was deep. She had seven children of her own and had assisted many more births.

"May the Lord grant you an easy birth and a healthy child," she said as she departed, touching my shoulder in blessing.

Throughout the day, I helped tend to those who had witnessed the boy's healing. Word spread quickly, and more people with ailments arrived at our camp. Though I could not drive out spirits as Jesus had done, my knowledge of herbs and bandages served for those with fevers and injuries.

As evening approached, Andrew found me washing blood from beneath my fingernails after lancing a shepherd's infected wound. My husband's shoulders were stiff, his mouth set in a tight line, and he had kept away from the crowds since morning, busying himself with camp tasks that required no interaction.

"Will you eat?" he asked.

I dried my hands on my apron and reached for him. His fingers closed around mine, dry and warm.

"Andrew," I said quietly, "many disciples tried and could not heal the boy. Not just you alone."

"I know." He looked over my shoulder. "The others speak of it. They wonder what they lack. What we all lack."

Before I could answer, the child stirred within me, and I guided Andrew's hand to feel it. His expression softened, hardness giving way to wonder as the small life moved beneath his palm.

"A foot?" he asked.

"Or an elbow."

A ghost of a smile crossed his lips. "Strong."

"Like his father," I said and meant it.

That evening, the disciples scattered around different fires. Peter, James, and John clustered near Jesus, speaking in hushed tones, while the others kept their distance, forming their own circle. Andrew moved between the groups but belonged fully to neither, and where once they had been a family gathered around a single table, now they resembled separate households, cautious with one another.

"They will not speak of what happened on the mountain," Andrew said, sitting down beside me. "Jesus has forbidden it until 'the Son of Man has risen from the dead.' Peter told me this much but nothing more." He shook his head. "What does that mean? Risen from the dead? Such words trouble me."

The flames crackled between us, sending sparks into the darkening sky. I waited, letting him find the words he needed.

"You wonder what they saw," I said softly.

Andrew was quiet for a long moment, watching the fire. "Jesus often takes them aside," he said at last. "Peter, James, and John. They go where the rest of us cannot follow. Today... Today they came back different. Changed. As though they had stood in the presence of something we cannot yet comprehend." He turned to me then, and in his eyes, I saw what he would not speak aloud—the ache of watching his brother cross into places he could not go, of always being on the outside looking in.

"Does it trouble you?" I asked, though I already knew the answer.

He was silent again, his honest nature warring with his desire to seem content with his portion. "Yes," he admitted finally. "Not from envy alone, though I confess that is part of it. But more than that..." He searched for words. "I wish to understand. To see what they see. To know what Peter knows."

I covered his hand with mine, feeling the solid strength that had never wavered even when others doubted. "You see with your own eyes, Andrew. Your vision is no less true for differing from your brother's."

He smiled faintly, but the words offered little comfort, and we both knew it. The truth was that some were chosen for certain things, and others were not, and no amount of faithfulness could bridge that distance.

As darkness fell, Jesus summoned Andrew and Thomas. "Tomorrow you will travel to the village of En-Rimmon," he told them. "Prepare the way for our arrival. Tell them the kingdom of God has come near."

Andrew nodded, accepting the mission as he always did, without question or complaint.

"How long?" Andrew asked.

"Three days," Jesus replied. "The village lies a full day's journey south."

I felt a flutter of anxiety. Three days was not long, yet with the growing divisions among the disciples and my advancing pregnancy, the timing troubled me. Andrew glanced at me, his brow furrowed as he measured his duty against his desire to remain.

"Anna will be well cared for," Jesus assured him, his perception uncanny as always. "Miriam and Joanna will see to her needs."

Later, in our tent, the night air cooled my skin but did nothing for the worry in my chest. The oil lamp's flame cast dancing shadows against the tent walls, making the familiar space shift and waver like water disturbed by wind. Andrew sat cross-legged on our sleeping mat, his knife in hand as he trimmed a new sandal strap—an excuse, I knew, to busy his hands while his thoughts remained tangled in the day's events.

"You do not wish to go," I said, watching him in the lamp's amber glow.

"I would prefer to stay here with you," he admitted, his hands stilling on the leather. "I failed today, Anna. I could not help that boy."

"You tried," I said, moving to sit beside him, offering what comfort I could through simple proximity. "No one succeeded but Jesus."

"We are meant to succeed. He gave us that power." He set aside his work, the leather strip curling forgotten on the wool blanket. "What if I fail again at En-Rimmon? What if I cannot do what he asks of me?"

I waited, letting the silence stretch. Outside, the wind

shifted, carrying voices from another tent.

"I do not understand what is happening," he said finally. "Jesus speaks of suffering, of death and resurrection. Peter and the others saw something on that mountain that changed them, something they cannot speak of, something that has marked them in ways I cannot fathom. And I... I could not even help one child."

"The Lord has mercy on His servants," I said. "Did not Moses also doubt his ability to speak? Did not Gideon hide in the winepress when the angel called him mighty? You are not the first to feel inadequate before God's calling."

Andrew's hands stilled, and for a long moment, the only sound was the night breeze against the tent walls and the distant crying of a desert fox hunting in the darkness.

"You will go tomorrow," I said. "And speak what you have been given to speak."

He nodded once, slowly, as though accepting a burden he did not fully understand. "I will go."

I watched the tent's shadow patterns shift as the night breeze stirred the lamp's flame, light and darkness dancing across the woven walls like the uncertainties that now danced through our days. The certainties I had once held were as changeable as those shadows. What I had known, or thought I knew, reshaped with each day's revelations. The boy's healing, Peter's transformation on the mountain, and the growing divisions among the disciples all pointed toward the approach of something that none of us could fully grasp, something that drew nearer with each passing day.

Outside, someone poured water over the last of the cooking fires. The hiss of doused embers carried to us, followed by murmured good nights. One by one, the voices around camp fell silent until only the wind remained, whispering through the valley like a breath of prophecy we could not yet interpret.

I pressed closer to Andrew, taking comfort in his solid presence beside me, in the warmth of his body and the steady rhythm of his breathing. He reached out, his hand finding mine in the dim light, and our fingers intertwined without need for words.

CHAPTER 13

Heat rose from the ground in waves that bent the air itself, turning the distant hills into something fluid and uncertain. We had arrived in Bethany beyond the Jordan two days earlier. The camp had barely been established when Jesus left with most of the disciples, Andrew among them, to the nearby villages. They would return in three or four days, perhaps sooner if the crowds were smaller than expected. Word had been sent to my father when we arrived. We were less than a day's journey from Jerusalem, and he had promised to visit before the week was out to see how I fared as my time drew closer.

I sat beneath the shade of a twisted olive tree, my back pressed against its ancient trunk, seeking relief from the relentless sun that baked the ground to dust and turned every breath into work. At seven months, my belly was round and firm beneath my tunic, pushing forward with each step, changing how I moved through the world. The child within me had grown active in recent weeks, his movements a constant presence. We had taken to calling the baby "he" and "him," both of us certain I carried a son. In quiet moments, Andrew would press his hand against my belly and whisper, "Our little Jonah." He was named for Andrew's father, who had taught his sons to fish the Galilean waters as his own father had taught him. The perfect name for a fisherman's grandson.

"And if it is a girl?" I had asked once, though neither of us truly believed it would be.

"Sarah," Andrew had answered without hesitation. "After your mother."

Two names. Two legacies we hoped to honor.

The heat sat on my skin like wool, making every breath work. Even in the shade, the air hung still and lifeless. No breeze stirred from the river, though we had camped close enough to hear its sluggish current. My feet had swollen in the morning, forcing me to loosen the straps of my sandals, and now they throbbed with each pulse of my heart. The air smelled of dust and dried grass and the acrid scent of goat dung from the nearby pens.

"You should rest inside the tent," Miriam said, pausing beside me with a waterskin in her hands.

"The breeze is better here." I accepted the water, the leather warm beneath my fingers. The water tasted strange, slightly bitter, but in this heat, any liquid was welcome.

"How is your back today?" She glanced at the way I braced myself against the tree, the baby changing my posture with each passing week.

"Like I am carrying a water jug that grows heavier by the day," I admitted. "But the baby is strong."

A firm kick pushed against my ribs. I rested my hand there, wishing Andrew could feel it too. He had been gone only two days, but the separation sat heavy on me. The tent felt emptier without him. The nights stretched longer. Even the baby's movements felt like something incomplete without him here to share them.

"Tirzah has been asking for you," Miriam said, wiping her forehead with the sleeve of her tunic. "She found wild mint near the stream and thought you might want it for your tonic."

I pushed myself up, one hand braced against the tree trunk for support, the other cradling the weight of my belly. The movement sent the world tilting sideways, sudden and disorienting. I pressed my palm flat against the rough bark until the ground steadied beneath my feet.

"Are you well?" Miriam's hand closed around my elbow.

"Just the heat," I assured her, though somewhere beneath my ribs, a whisper of warning stirred. "Where is Tirzah?"

By NIGHTFALL, the wrongness had spread through my body like poison in a stream. What began as dizziness had become cramping that bent me double on my sleeping mat, waves of it that built and receded and built again. Sweat soaked through my tunic, yet I shivered as though winter had come early.

Salome appeared at the tent opening, already carrying cloths and a waterskin. "Anna." She kneeled beside my mat, taking in the way I was curled on my side, knees drawn up as far as my belly would allow. "Miriam and Joanna have both fallen ill. Stomach cramping, fever. We think the water from the new spring has been contaminated."

She laid a cool cloth on my forehead. Another wave of pain seized me, and I could not stop the cry that escaped, my hands instinctively cradling my belly. Salome went very still. Her hand moved to my belly, waiting. When the next contraction came, her lips pressed into a thin line.

"This is not only a stomach illness," she said quietly.

"No." The word came out as barely a whisper. I gripped her arm. "Tirzah?"

"She is well. She drank from our old waterskins today, not the new spring."

Relief lasted only as long as the space between one contraction and the next. Then another wave tightened around my belly, and I knew this differed from the cramping of illness. This felt deeper, more rhythmic, like the birth pangs I had felt beneath my hands as I helped other women bring forth life. Too early. Much too early.

I grabbed Salome's wrist, my fingers digging into her flesh. "You have to save him. Salome, please. Do not let anything happen to my baby."

Her palm pressed against my cheek, steadying me. "I will do everything I can. I promise you, Anna. Everything."

She laid her other hand against my forehead, and the lines deepening around her mouth told me what she would not say aloud. But I already knew. Fever.

"Mary!" she called suddenly. "Bring clean cloths. Now!"

Mary appeared at the tent opening, her eyes widening as she took in the scene. "Is it—"

"Yes. Get Susanna. She has been fasting since sunrise and

has not drunk from the spring. Tell everyone to stop using the new well immediately. And keep Tirzah away. Her child must not be put at risk."

Her child must not be put at risk. The words echoed in my ears while the tent spun around me, colors bleeding into one another. Heat flashed through my body, then terrible cold that made my teeth chatter. Tirzah's child. Safe. Protected. What about my baby? The thought clawed at me, sharp and ugly and desperate. Another contraction seized me, harder than before.

Mary nodded, already turning. "The well water—"

"Has poisoned us. Go now."

"No." The word came out strangled. "The baby—it is too soon. Salome, please—" I could not finish. Could not say what I feared.

Another wave of pain seized me, harder than before, and this time I understood what it meant. What my body was doing.

"You have to save him," I whispered when I could speak again. "Please. Do not let anything happen to my baby."

I had seen it once before. A stillbirth in Bethsaida. Tiny fingers that would never grasp. Eyes that would never open. Lungs too fragile to draw breath in this world. The memory rose now, unbidden, and merged with the image of my own child.

"Andrew." His name tore from my throat. "Someone must go for him. Please. I need him."

Salome exchanged a glance with Mary, who had returned with clean linens. "He is a day's journey north with the others. By the time anyone could reach him..."

She leaned closer, pressing a cool cloth to my neck. "Please." I gripped her wrist, desperate for her to understand.

"He should be here. His child—" The words died. I could not finish them.

"We will send someone at first light," Salome promised, though doubt flickered in the set of her jaw. We both understood. By morning, it would already be too late.

"This is not over." Her hands clasped mine. "Fight, Anna. Fight for your child."

I nodded, grinding my teeth against another wave of contractions. Every instinct I possessed as a healer told me this should not be happening. Not yet. Not for months.

"Herbs," I gasped. "In my... pouch. Blackroot. Might stop—"

"Susanna is bringing your medicines," Mary said, her palm cool against my burning forehead. "Hold on, Anna. Just hold on. I am here."

The night stretched endlessly, a blur of agony and prayer. Susanna arrived with my medicine pouch, her expression grave as she helped prepare the bitter tincture I kept for women at risk of losing their babies. I had used it successfully before, had saved other women's children with these same herbs.

"Drink," Salome urged, lifting my head to help me swallow the dark liquid. "All of it."

I forced it down, hope flaring within me despite everything. Perhaps it was not too late. Perhaps my knowledge as a healer could save my child as it had saved others.

Hours passed. The women took turns bathing my skin with cool water, fighting the fever that raged through me. Salome placed cool cloths on my forehead while Mary worked herbs into warm oil for my cramping belly. Susanna held my hand when the contractions left me gasping.

Through it all, they spoke softly, words of comfort and courage meant to give me strength.

"It is working," I whispered as the contractions seemed to ease sometime in the darkest part of the night. "I think... I think it might be working."

But then came the blood. Too much blood. And the cramping returned sharper than before, cutting through any hope I had carefully gathered.

"No. No. Not now." I covered my belly with both hands, as if I could hold the baby in through will alone. "Please, no. Salome, make it stop!"

Her expression held a sorrow too deep for words.

"Pray, Anna," she whispered. Then louder, to the others, "Sisters, come. Pray with us."

They gathered around my mat, these women who had become my family. Susanna and Mary came closer, while Joanna and Miriam leaned weakly against the tent pole, their own illness forgotten in concern for mine. Even Tirzah pushed her way in despite Salome's earlier warning, one hand instinctively covering the child growing within her own womb. They kneeled beside me, forming a circle. Heads bowed and hands joined, some holding mine, others clasping shoulders or arms, creating an unbroken chain of sisterhood.

Salome began, her voice steady where mine could not be: "Holy One of Israel, who formed life within the womb of Sarah in her old age..."

Mary continued: "Who remembered Hannah in her barrenness and gave her Samuel..."

"Who delivered the infant Moses into safe arms..." Susanna added.

One by one, they called upon the God who had protected

mothers and children throughout our people's history. Their voices blended together, sometimes speaking as one, sometimes rising individually. The ancient words of the Psalms mingled with spontaneous pleas. In their voices, I heard centuries of women who had faced this same terror, this same anguish.

I tried to join them but could only whisper, "Please." My prayer contained everything in that one word. All my hopes, all my dreams for this child, all my love for the tiny life within me. "Please."

For a moment, wrapped in their prayers, I felt a strange peace. Perhaps God would hear us. Perhaps the combined faith of these women could accomplish what herbs and rest could not.

But then came another wave of agony, sharper than any before, and I knew.

I made desperate vows to the God of our fathers. Promised to dedicate my child to holy service like Samuel of old. Pleaded as Hannah had pleaded, as Sarah had waited, as all the barren women of our stories had cried out. If only my child would be spared.

But some battles cannot be won by will alone.

THE NIGHT DISSOLVED INTO FRAGMENTS.

The metallic smell of blood filling the small tent.

Salome's voice, growing more urgent as my fever climbed higher.

Mary's tears falling silently as she continued to lay cold cloths on my brow.

The shadow of Tirzah at the tent opening, her cry quickly muffled as someone pulled her away.

My voice, ragged and unrecognizable, calling for Andrew. Calling for my father. Calling for my mother.

And the contractions. Wave after wave of them, my body doing what it was designed to do but far too soon.

Dawn broke gray and lifeless over the camp. I lay still on my mat, aware in some distant way that I was alive but wishing I was not. The tent was quiet now. The frantic activity of the night had ceased.

Mary sat beside me, exhaustion written in every line of her body. When she saw my eyes open, she leaned forward.

"Anna? Can you hear me?"

I could, but answering seemed an impossible task. My tongue lay useless in my mouth. My limbs felt distant, as though they belonged to someone else. The emptiness in my belly had become a physical void, a hollow space that pulled at me from within. My skin alternated between burning and freezing, never finding balance. Even my eyes struggled to focus, the tent walls swimming before me in waves. And the pain. So much pain.

"She is awake," Mary called softly, and Salome appeared, carrying something wrapped in linen.

"Anna," Salome said, her voice gentle in a way I had never heard before. "Your son."

Son. The word echoed emptily. Jonah.

"You need to see him," she insisted. "You need to hold him."

"No." The single word was all I could force past my grief.

But they placed him in my arms anyway.

Time stood still. I looked down at the bundle they had laid against my breast. So small. So impossibly small and still. His face was perfectly formed, eyes closed as if in sleep.

Fingers no larger than grain kernels. My son, who would never draw breath.

My trembling finger traced the curve of his cheek. The world spun and blurred, heat pulsing behind my eyes, yet my gaze remained fixed on his face. I did not want to look yet could not turn away. My chest burned with each shallow breath, sweat and tears mingling on my skin. The weight of my hand seemed too heavy as I touched one tiny finger after another. Five on each hand. Complete yet never to grasp or reach. I searched his features despite myself—the shape of his nose, the curve of his brow—for some part of Andrew, some trace of myself, some piece of what might have been. Did he have my high cheekbones? Yes, and I thought I saw a dimple on his left cheek, or perhaps I only wanted to see it. His fingers seemed long for an infant's. Fisherman's fingers like his father's.

His father. *Where is Andrew? Why is he not here?*

A deep chill coursed through me, my body trembling beneath the blankets despite the fever that burned my skin. I had no voice for this grief, no cry that could carry the weight of what was lost. Only an emptiness spreading outward from my core, consuming everything I had ever been.

"Would you like to name him?" Mary asked.

I stared at her, unable to comprehend how she could ask such a thing. The name we had chosen burned in my throat —Jonah. How could I speak that name now? I could not.

A sob tore from me, raw and primal, the sound startling even to my own ears. Then another. And another. Until my entire body shook with them, bent over his tiny form. My tears fell onto the cloth wrapping him, my grief too vast for my body to contain.

Mary wrapped her arms around me and the baby,

rocking us both as I wept. Eventually, I ran out of tears and sat motionless, staring at my son.

"Anna, do you want more time with him?"

I said nothing. My arms went limp. They took him away.

After that, time lost meaning. Voices came and went. Hands tried to coax water between my lips. Someone spooned broth I could not taste. The fever burned through me then receded, leaving me spent and empty.

"She has not spoken since," someone said. Miriam, perhaps. "Has not eaten. Barely drinks."

"The others are recovering, but she…"

"Any word from Ephraim? About Andrew?"

"Too soon. The messenger left at dawn."

Andrew. The name drifted through my mind. Andrew should be here. The thought formed and dissolved, too heavy to hold.

I drifted in and out of awareness. The space within me where my child had grown lay empty, a hollowness that spread and deepened. It consumed my thoughts, then my feelings, until even my will to move or speak vanished. Nothing of myself remained. I floated somewhere beyond anguish, beyond life itself, untethered.

LIGHT. Too much light. My eyes closed against the brightness as the tent flap opened. A shadow fell across my face. Someone standing there. The shape of shoulders. The height.

Andrew?

My eyelids barely lifted. Not Andrew. Another face swam into focus then faded again.

But the voice that spoke my name belonged to my father.

"Anna. Oh, my daughter."

I smelled the scents of cedar and dust as he kneeled beside me. His hand, bearing the seal ring of the council, covered mine.

More voices mingled outside the tent, urgent and worried.

"Two days without food..."

"Fever returned last night..."

"Lost too much blood..."

My father's face was lined with grief and fear. When had he grown so old?

"I am taking her home," he said to someone I could not see.

"But Andrew—"

"Will follow when he returns. I have left instructions. But she cannot stay here."

Hands lifted me. The world tilted, spinning. Brightness, blinding after the dimness of the tent.

A cart. Blankets. My father's arm supporting my head.

"Stay with me, Anna," he whispered. "Just stay."

Moving. Leaving. Some part of me knew I should care. Should resist. Should wait for Andrew.

But that part was buried beneath the emptiness, beneath the broken places where my son had been. I closed my eyes against the pain.

Somewhere distant, as consciousness slipped away, I thought I heard Tirzah weeping.

Then nothing. Nothing at all.

CHAPTER 14

Arimathea, September, 31 AD

Sunlight pierced my closed eyelids. Red. Gold. Then shadow as someone moved between me and the light. The cart lurched over a stone, sending pain through my empty womb. I tasted blood in my mouth where I had bitten my lip against crying out.

"How much farther?" My father's voice called from somewhere above me.

"We arrive, my lord. See the gates ahead." I did not know the voice.

I forced my eyes open as the cart slowed. The walls of Arimathea wavered before me, seeming to breathe and pulse with my fever. Stone bleached pale by sun. My father's vineyards rippled along the hillside, green smears against dark soil. I closed my eyes as nausea rolled through me. Too bright. Too much.

Sweat beaded and then chilled on my skin, the air both scorching and freezing at once. My teeth chattered, though my forehead burned. I tried to lift my head, but the heaviness made it impossible.

The gates opened at my father's call. The cart rumbled through into the courtyard, wheels grinding over stone. The sound echoed strangely in my ears, first too loud then suddenly distant. My head throbbed with each heartbeat.

"My lord! What brings you home without..."

A gasp. Then silence.

That voice. I would know it anywhere, even through the fog of fever—Deborah. The voice that had sung away nightmares. The voice that had taught me prayers and herb lore and womanhood. I was home.

"Anna?" Her silver-streaked hair escaped her head covering as she approached the cart.

I tried to sit. Pain shot through my abdomen, fierce and sharp. The courtyard spun around me. Stone walls, faces, sky all blurred together. My father's arm braced against my back, his fingers digging into my shoulder to steady me.

"Deborah." I could barely form her name. The taste of metal filled my mouth.

She rushed to the cart, robes billowing, her sandals kicking up dust that sparkled in the sunlight. Her hands touched my face, fingers lined with years of work brushing my temples, my cheeks. They lay cool against my skin that felt like burning parchment.

"Child, what has happened to you?"

I smelled the bread on her hands, the herbs in her hair. Mint. Rosemary. Her garden... no, my garden. Where I sat with Andrew. Where is... Andrew should be here. The world rushed up to me. Why is he not here?

"Anna. You are home, Anna. I will care for you now." She brushed my sweat-laden hair back from my forehead, and her voice broke through the wall I had built against pain. I clutched at her, my hands shaking so violently I could barely grasp her tunic.

"Jonah," I gasped. The name died on my lips. "My baby... my baby..." Hot tears scalded my cheeks. "Deborah... my Jonah..."

A cry tore through me, stealing my breath. My fingers twisted in her tunic, trying to anchor myself. I could not form the words to explain. Only his name. Only my loss.

Deborah's arms encircled me, pulling me against her chest, where I had rested as a child. Her breath against my face. The thundering of her heart. Her hands trembled as they stroked my hair. Her tears dropped onto my forehead, mingling with my own.

"Oh, my child." Her voice broke on a sob. "My precious girl."

My father's voice came from somewhere beyond my tears, tight and strained. "She was with child, seven months along. The water where they made camp was tainted." The cart shifted as he climbed down. "I arrived with supplies to find many ill, but Anna..." A pause. The feel of his hand on my shoulder. "Her fever had already burned too long. The child could not survive it."

No. A wail escaped me before I could hold it back.

"My baby is gone," I sobbed against Deborah's shoulder. My tears soaked the rough fabric. My fingers clutched at her back. My body shook so violently that the cart creaked beneath us.

"I could not save him." The words tumbled out between gasping breaths. "I tried. The pain came. Blood everywhere."

"Not your fault," Deborah whispered, her lips against my hair. Her hand moved in circles on my back, gentle despite her shaking. "Not your fault, child."

I wept until my throat was raw, until my eyes burned, until my chest ached with each breath. Then nothing. Empty. My body sagged against her, too heavy to hold up.

"Andrew," I whispered, the name rising unbidden to my lips. "I need Andrew."

"Andrew is not here," my father said, his voice firm but gentle. "He is far away with the Teacher. You are home now, Anna. We will care for you."

Deborah pulled back, her lined hands framing my face. "Bring her inside," she said, her voice finding its old authority. "To her old room. I will prepare herbs for the fever."

Strong arms lifted me. The scent of my father's robes. The sensation of being carried, my head lolling against scratchy fabric. Stone walls rising around us, mercifully cool after the sun. The sound of feet on stone steps. Corridors where shadows played on whitewashed walls.

Darkness, welcoming and deep.

LIGHT FILTERED THROUGH WOVEN SHUTTERS, casting patterns on the wall. I had watched the same patterns as a child during long afternoons. The familiar wooden beams above me, darkened by years of lamp smoke. My childhood bed beneath me, the scent of cedar from the chest in the corner. My body here but my thoughts scattered, drifting between moments of clarity and confusion.

Deborah appeared in the doorway, a cup in her hand.

"You must drink," she said in the same tone she had used when I was a child refusing bitter medicine.

I did not answer. Speaking required energy I no longer possessed.

She sat beside me on the bed, one arm sliding beneath my shoulders to lift me slightly. The cup pressed against my lips. I drank because it was easier than refusing. The liquid was warm, tasting of honey and herbs.

When the cup was empty, she lowered me back against the pillows. Her hand lingered on my forehead, checking for fever.

"Your father has gone to speak with the physician," she said. "He will return soon."

I closed my eyes. I did not need a physician. There was nothing wrong with my body that time would not heal. The brokenness within me was beyond any healer's skill.

DAYS PASSED. Or perhaps it was only hours. The light changed, shadows moving across the walls, darkness giving way to light, then darkness again. I existed in a place where time had lost its meaning.

By the third day, I began to surface. Words formed in my mind again, though I rarely spoke them. Memory returned in fragments: the camp by the river, Tirzah helping me to my tent, the first waves of pain. Then my father's arrival, the journey home, the gates of Arimathea. Each memory brought fresh pain but, with it, awareness.

My father appeared at intervals, his face drawn with worry. He spoke to me, though I rarely answered. Sometimes he read from the Psalms, his voice faltering on the words of lament. Sometimes he simply sat beside my bed, his fingers working the tassels of his prayer shawl.

"Anna," he said once, setting aside his scrolls with a sigh. "You must eat something."

I turned my face to the wall. "Please, just let me be."

"No," he said firmly. "I did that for years. I left you alone when you needed me. No more."

I looked at him then, this man who had been more presence than father for much of my life. His eyes held mine, steady and determined.

"I cannot lose you as I lost your mother," he said.

His words fell into the space between us. I looked at the wall, at the familiar cracks in the limewashed stone. I tried to care about his fear, his pain. But there was nothing inside me to give him. There was only emptiness where my child had been.

"I am sorry," he said finally, his voice hoarse. "For not being there. For not protecting you from this pain."

I closed my eyes. What was there to say? It would not bring Jonah back. Nothing would.

"Andrew," I whispered, the name slipping from me unbidden. "Does he know?"

My father stiffened beside me. "We left word at the camp. Miriam promised to tell him when he returned from his mission. But he was in Galilee, teaching in the villages. The journey is long."

I did not ask more. I was not ready to think of Andrew's grief. I had lost our child.

~

Deborah moved around my room, a silent presence who appeared with food, with cool cloths for my head, with clean garments. She did not demand conversation. Did not fill the air with meaningless assurances. Instead, she hummed softly as she worked, the same melodies she had sung when I was a child.

"You should try to stand today," she said on the fourth morning. Her hand rested briefly on my forehead, then my wrist, assessing with the touch of one who had nursed many through illness.

"The fever has left you," she said with quiet satisfaction. "Your blood runs cool again. Now your body can begin to heal properly." She nodded to herself as if confirming some private calculation. "The flesh knows its way back to strength, if given time and care."

I understood her unspoken thought: The heart follows no such reliable path. Grief obeys no healer's timeline.

She held out her hand. "Just to the window and back for today."

I did not want to move. To rise meant acknowledging I still lived in a body that had betrayed me, in a world where my child did not exist.

"Anna." Her tone told me I would do what she said. "You will wither like an unwatered vine if you remain in that bed."

She held out her hand, and I took it because I lacked the will to refuse. My legs shook beneath me, weak from disuse and loss of blood. The few steps to the window seemed an impossible distance, but Deborah's arm around my waist supported me.

We stood together, looking out at the garden where I had played as a child, had learned the names and properties of plants, had dreamed of adventures beyond stone walls, never believing they might come true. The sunlight cut sharp edges against the shadows, dividing the world into certainties my heart was not ready to accept—living and dead, present and gone, here and vanished. I blinked against the harshness of it, this world that continued its course heedless of what I had lost.

"The white roses are blooming," Deborah observed, her voice as steady as the earth beneath our feet. "Later than usual this year. I thought the heat might have taken them, but they endured."

"Yes," I said, the single word all I could offer.

Below us, servants moved about their tasks with the unhurried rhythm of those for whom life had not ceased its turning. Two women toted baskets of laundry toward the drying lines, their voices carrying snatches of conversation about tomorrow's meal, a child's illness, the threat of rain—simple concerns of an ordinary world that felt impossibly distant from where I stood. Yet there was comfort in their mundane words, in the way they spoke of rain as though it were the most important thing, as though the world had not fractured beyond repair.

In the garden below, I caught sight of movement near the herb beds, where the afternoon sun had warmed the earth to perfect scratching temperature. My chickens went about their eternal work with single-minded devotion, heads bobbing as they searched the soil for whatever treasures chickens seek. Little Hannah darted between the sage plants with her usual determination, never content to scratch where the others had already been. Abigail, crooked-toed and as clever as always, found something the others had missed and clucked her satisfaction. And there, Goliath strutted among them all, neck feathers catching the light, overseeing his small kingdom with the gravity of one who takes his responsibilities seriously.

"Where is Bubbeleh?" I asked, scanning the garden for my old sheep. She should be there, grazing near the lavender as she always did, her presence as much a part of this view as the stones themselves.

Deborah's hand stilled on the windowsill. A long silence stretched between us, and in that silence, I already knew the answer before she spoke it.

"Anna..." Her voice held a gentleness that made tears threaten. "Bubbeleh died last summer. Shortly after you left for Bethsaida."

The words wove themselves into me, just one more loss layered onto the other, a smaller heartbreak laid atop the great one like stones upon a grave. I had known it would come someday. Sheep do not live forever, however much we might wish them to. But hearing it made it real in the way that knowing never quite does.

"Peacefully?" I asked.

"In her sleep. Ezra found her one morning beneath the fig tree, where the shade was deep and cool." Deborah's hand found mine, her fingers warm. "I am sorry, child. I know how much you loved her."

"She had a good life," I said at length. "Longer than most sheep get. Long enough to grow fat and lazy and impossible to move when she decided she liked where she was standing."

"She did. Because you loved her well."

Tears slid down my cheek, but these felt different. Quieter. A small grief that was safe to feel instead of the larger one that threatened to swallow me whole, a grief I could hold in my hands without being consumed by it.

"It should rain tonight," Deborah said, pointing to the clouds gathering on the western horizon, their bellies dark with promise. "The jasmine needs it. The ground has grown too hard."

Her matter-of-fact observations anchored me to the world in a way that sympathetic words could not have done, each simple statement a thread tying me back to the rhythms of life. Here was life, continuing its ancient patterns despite the void within me, indifferent to my pain yet somehow comforting in its very indifference. The jasmine would drink the rain and bloom in its season. The roses would open their petals to the sun and close them against the night. The servants would carry water from the well, tend the gardens with patient hands, and prepare food for the evening meal. Time would march forward with or without my consent, dragging me with it whether I willed it or not, pulling me back toward the land of the living even as part of me longed to remain in the shadows with my lost child.

A sudden thought pierced through my numbness. "Tirzah," I said, her name unfamiliar on my tongue after days of silence. The thought of her with child, the same as I had been, but her baby...

"I cannot go back there. Not if she—" I choked on the words as tears filled my eyes. "I cannot bear to see her still carrying her child when mine is gone."

Deborah reached for my hand. "Anna, you need not think of returning yet. Your body is still healing. Your heart, even more so."

I nodded, wiping tears with quivering fingers. I did not wish ill on Tirzah or her child, but how could I face her? How could I see her swell with the life I had lost and not break apart all over again?

Deborah seemed to understand, for she said nothing more. Instead, she pointed to a cluster of herbs growing in a sheltered corner. "The mint needs thinning. Perhaps tomorrow, if you feel stronger."

"Thank you," I said quietly, surprising myself.

Deborah's hand tightened briefly on my arm. She did not look at me, did not make more of the moment than it was. "For what?"

"For being here. For..." I swallowed. "For not treating me as if I might shatter."

She nodded, eyes still on the garden. "You are stronger than you know, Anna. You always have been."

We stood a moment longer. A bird landed on the edge of the garden wall, its red breast bright against the stone. It preened, unaware of being observed, unconcerned with grief or loss or the fragmenting of human hearts.

"Has there been any word from Andrew?" I asked, my eyes still on the garden.

"Not yet."

I nodded, watching the bird fluff its feathers against a breeze I could not feel from within these walls. "He will blame me."

She turned to face me then, her eyes meeting mine directly. "No, Anna. He will not." She spoke with such certainty that I almost believed her.

"I think I would like to try the courtyard tomorrow," I said finally. "If you will help me."

"Of course. The fresh air will do you good."

LATER THAT AFTERNOON, I dozed on my bed as rain pattered against the shutters. The sound mingled with a dream of the Jordan River, of water flowing over smooth stones, of women washing garments at the edge of the current. In the dream, I kneeled at the riverbank, my belly swollen with child. I dipped my hands into the clear water then watched in horror as it turned red, blood spreading outward from my fingers.

I woke to raised voices. For a moment, I could not place the sound. Then I realized they came from just outside my chamber, in the courtyard where my windows overlooked the fig tree.

"—should have been told before you let him in!" My father's voice rose, sharp with anger.

"She is my wife." Another voice. One I knew better than my own.

Andrew.

The knowledge pierced through the fog that had enveloped me for days. *He is here.*

I pushed myself up on my elbows, listening. My heart began to pound, the blood rushing in my ears.

"She is not well enough for visitors." My father's voice again, closer now, perhaps directly beneath my window.

"I am not a visitor. I am her husband." Andrew's voice held fury barely leashed.

"You were not there when—"

"Do not think I do not know that! Do you imagine I have thought of anything else since hearing what happened?"

I moved to the window, my bare feet silent on the cool stone floor. My legs shook beneath me, as weak as green saplings. One hand braced against the wall, fingers splayed across limestone. Every movement required thought, intention. My body felt distant, as if I moved it by force of will rather than natural impulse.

Through the latticed screen, I could see them in the courtyard below my window. The rain had slowed to a gentle mist that clung to Andrew's hair and beard, each droplet catching what light remained in the storm-dark afternoon. My father stood with his back to the house, shoulders rigid. Deborah stood to one side, her hand on my father's arm.

"She is not well," Abba said, his tone softening slightly. "She barely eats. Barely sleeps."

"She is my wife. My heart. Nothing will keep me from her side now." Andrew's voice held the same fierce certainty I had heard when he spoke of following Jesus, when he described his baptism in the Jordan. "Not walls, not guards, not all the power of Jerusalem. I will go to her."

"My lord." Deborah's voice now, as calm and firm as the earth itself. "He is right. Anna needs him."

The sight of him reached into the hollow within me, touching something I thought had died with our child. Even through the rain and lattice, I could see the way he stood—tense, exhausted, refusing to yield. His cloak hung heavy with rain, his hair plastered to his head. Mud spattered his legs to the knees, evidence of roads traveled too quickly, of a journey made without rest. But it was him. Andrew. After all these days apart, he was here.

"Andrew." His name came out as a sob, tears blurring my vision.

My voice, barely above a whisper, should not have carried to them. But Andrew's head snapped up. Our eyes met across the distance.

"Anna." He moved toward the stairs, but my father stepped into his path.

"Let him come, Abba," I said, my voice stronger now. "Please."

My father turned, looking up at me. "Anna, you should not be out of bed," he said, but there was no force behind the words.

"I need to see my husband."

Deborah placed her hand on my father's arm. "Let him go to her, my lord."

After a long moment, my father stepped aside. Andrew moved past him, taking the stairs two at a time. I backed away from the window and walked to the door, legs quaking. I heard his footsteps echoing on the stone stairs, and moved to the hall outside my room.

He reached the upper landing where I stood, his breath coming quick from the climb, his eyes never leaving mine. The narrow hallway outside my chamber suddenly felt too small to contain all that had passed between us—the days of separation, the miles he had traveled, the grief we had not yet shared. The air itself seemed to hum with unspoken words and questions that had no answers, with love that had survived even this.

"Anna," he whispered, and in that single word, I heard prayer and homecoming both.

His face held the marks of the journey—dust in the creases around his eyes, exhaustion carved into the hollow of his cheeks, new lines that had not been there before. Yet his eyes held mine with a steadfastness that tethered me.

"You came," I breathed.

"I would have walked across the sea itself," he said. "Nothing could have kept me from you."

My legs gave way beneath me.

In one step, he was there. His arms encircled me, and I

pressed my face into his neck, breathing him in—road dust and sweat and the scent of him that was more familiar than my own. My hands clutched at the rough fabric of his tunic, trying to prove he was real, that this was not some fever-dream my grief had conjured.

"I am here," he murmured against my temple, his breath warm on my skin. "I am here now."

Our hearts beat against each other, finding their rhythm again after so many days apart. His hand moved in slow circles on my back, the same gesture he had used a thousand times before, and my body remembered what my mind had almost forgotten. I was not meant to bear this alone.

"I lost our son," I whispered, the words tearing from some place that had been locked away. "Our Jonah."

"I know." His voice caught, and I felt his tears fall onto my hair. His arms tightened around me. "I know, beloved."

We stood there trembling together, our grief finally shared as it should have been from the beginning. For the first time since that terrible night, the weight I had carried in solitude now rested on both our shoulders.

"I should have been with you," he said. "By your side where I belong."

I shook my head against his chest. "Forgive me," I sobbed. "The water. I knew. I should have..." My voice cracked. "Our son, Andrew. Our Jonah. I could not save him."

"No." His hands cradled my face, tilting it so my eyes met his. "There is nothing to forgive. You could not have stopped it. No one could. Our son was in God's hands, not yours."

For a long moment, we simply looked at each other, seeing all that had been lost and all that remained. Then he lifted me into his arms and carried me toward my room.

As he laid me on the bed, his touch was gentle, careful, as though I were something fragile that might break. He brushed the hair back from my forehead, and I saw his own grief written plainly in the lines of his face—this loss was his, too, this child we would never know. He held me close, murmuring words of comfort, pouring his love into my wounded heart.

"Stay with me," I whispered, my fingers finding his, intertwining. "Please. Do not leave me."

"Always." He laid beside me on the narrow bed, our hands clasped between us. "I will be here when you wake, when you dream, when you rise. I will be here. We will not be parted again."

"Do you promise?"

"With all my heart. Rest now, love. I am here now. You are not alone.

I closed my eyes, and for the first time since losing Jonah, I slept without nightmares. Andrew's presence brought a peace no herb or potion could provide.

THE FIRST RAYS of dawn filtered through the shutters when I opened my eyes. Andrew sat in a chair beside my bed, his head bowed, eyes closed. Not in sleep but in prayer. The soft Hebrew words were barely audible—a psalm of lament followed by one of hope.

"You have turned my mourning into dancing," he whispered. "You have removed my sackcloth and clothed me with joy."

"Andrew."

His eyes opened, meeting mine. The amber flecks in his

dark irises caught the morning light. Weariness had carved new lines around his mouth, yet his eyes held that boundless strength I had always known in him.

"Anna," he said softly, reaching to brush a strand of hair from my face.

"How did you find out what happened?"

Andrew drew a deep breath before answering, his fingers tracing the knotwork of the prayer shawl's tassels.

"Miriam's messenger found us in Galilee, in a small village where we were teaching. I left that same hour." He passed his hand across his face. "Jesus would not let me go without a word for you. He said, 'Tell Anna that I weep with her. The seed that falls to the ground is not lost forever but rises in new life.'"

Tears filled my eyes at these words. Despite my grief, a small flame of hope flickered. "He truly said that?"

Andrew nodded. "And then he told me, 'Go to her now. Your wife needs you more than I do.'"

The thought of Jesus knowing our loss, acknowledging it, speaking Andrew's release from duties made it real in a new way. I had carried Jonah's death like a shameful secret. But now, our child had existed. Our child was known. Our child was mourned not just by us but by the Teacher himself.

"Did you stop at the camp?" I asked.

Andrew nodded. His hand reached for mine, his thumb brushing across my knuckles. "The messenger only said you were ill. I traveled back to find you gone." He drew a shuddering breath. "That is when they told me what happened. About our son. About your father taking you to Arimathea."

He swallowed hard. "I did not even pause to sleep. I rode through the night to reach you. The moon was so bright it cast my shadow on the road before me."

"How are the others?" I asked, unable yet to form the name I most wondered about.

"Worried about you. They all are. Miriam and Joanna were ill themselves, though not as severe. They are recovered." He hesitated. A slight tightening of his fingers around mine. "Salome can barely speak your name without tears. She says she should have done more, tried other herbs, found some way to save the child. She has not forgiven herself."

He paused again, longer this time. His eyes watched mine carefully. "Tirzah is well. She sends her love." He reached into his belt pouch and withdrew a small bundle wrapped in linen. "She sent this for you."

I hesitated before taking it, my hands suddenly unsteady.

Inside the cloth lay a tiny bracelet of blue and white threads woven together, small enough for a newborn's wrist. Tirzah had been making these for both our children, working on them during the quiet afternoons at camp.

"She finished Jonah's," Andrew said. "She said... She said he should have it, even now. That he is still your son."

I closed my fingers around the delicate band, this thing that should have circled my baby's wrist but never would. The pain was sharp yet somehow bearable. Someone else remembered him. Someone else had marked his existence with her hands.

"When you feel ready," Andrew added, "the women sent oil of myrrh and aloes. For healing."

We sat in silence as morning light crept across the room, turning the limestone walls from gray to gold, each shift of color marking the passage of time in a world that continued its turning despite our grief. So much remained unspoken between us still—questions about what would come next, whether I would return to the ministry or remain here in my father's house, how we would carry this loss through all the days ahead of us, whether the burden of it would grow lighter or simply more familiar. But for now, in this quiet space between night and day, it was enough to share the silence of mourning, our grief a bridge between us rather than a wall, connecting us in our sorrow rather than dividing us in our separate anguish.

"I brought something for you," Andrew said some time later, his voice as soft as dawn itself. He reached into the pouch at his belt, and the leather creaked slightly with the movement, releasing the scent of cedar that had been trapped within its folds.

He placed a small object in my palm with a gentleness that spoke of its significance, and I looked down to find a stone, smooth and oval, worn by water and time into something that fit perfectly against my skin. It rested there with surprising warmth, as though it had been holding heat from some distant fire, waiting to share it with me. "From the Jordan," he said, and those simple words carried with them so much of our history, our faith, the story of our people written in water and stone.

"Where I first heard the Teacher's call," he continued. "Where I saw heaven open and the Spirit descend like a dove, where I stood in water that had parted for our fathers, where prophets had walked and worked wonders, where generations of our people had crossed over from bondage into promise."

His voice carried the cadence of scripture, the rhythm of the stories we had been raised on, tales told and retold until they became part of our very bones. "I thought we might mark Jonah's passing with this," he said. "The elders teach that stones endure when we cannot, that they bear witness to what has been lost when memory fails and grief dims with the passage of years. Our people pile them in places where God has moved, where heaven has touched earth, where the boundary between this world and the next grows thin enough to see through."

I closed my fingers around the stone, feeling its solidity, its weight—small but substantial, polished but with enough texture to remind me it was real and not some phantom comfort. The Jordan, holy river of our people, boundary between wilderness and promised land, water that had witnessed more history than any of us could remember. Waters where Moses had stood on the far shore and seen what he would never enter. Waters Joshua had commanded to stand still so the people could pass over on dry ground. Waters where Elijah had struck the surface with his mantle and walked through on a path only faith could see. Waters where prophets had worked their wonders and kings had washed away their leprosy. Waters where John had baptized the penitent, calling them to turn from darkness toward light. Where Jesus himself had been proclaimed the beloved Son, where the sky had opened and the divine voice had spoken for all to hear.

This stone had witnessed Andrew's calling, had been present when his life changed forever, when he left his nets and followed a Teacher whose words would reshape the world. Now it would bear witness to our son, would hold the memory of Jonah when our own memories grew hazy with time and anguish, when the sharp edges of this loss wore smooth like water over stone.

"We could bury it in the garden," Andrew continued, his voice uncertain now, feeling his way through unfamiliar territory the way a man might feel his way through a darkened room. "Or keep it as a memorial, something to hold when we speak his name, something solid and real when everything else feels like mist and shadow. Something to remind us that though water took him from us, carried him away before we could know him, he is now beyond the Jordan, in a better land, in a place where there is no more sorrow or crying or pain, where every tear is wiped away and death has no dominion."

Tears filled my eyes again but differently now than they had filled them before. Not the violent sobs of fresh heartache or the desperate weeping of our reunion but a tender release, like rain after a long drought, like the first thaw of spring after winter's harshness. Tears of remembrance, perhaps, or even of hope—that fragile, precious thing I had thought dead within me but that now stirred like a seed beneath frozen ground, waiting for its season.

"Yes," I said, closing my fingers tightly around the stone until I could feel its edges pressing into my palm, sharp enough to feel, not enough to wound. "I want to keep it close. Always with me." I laid my hand with the stone against my heart, feeling the steady beat beneath my fingers. "Not buried. I need something of him to hold. Something solid I can touch when the pain returns. Something that will not fade like the memories."

Andrew's hand closed over mine, his palm rough and familiar against my knuckles, both of us holding the small tribute to the child we had lost together.

Outside, beyond the stone walls that sheltered us, a dove called to its mate as the sun climbed higher in the eastern sky. Its voice came pure and clear in the morning air, rising above the sounds of the household stirring to life—servants drawing water, the cook building up the morning fire, someone sweeping the courtyard stones. The world was waking to another day, and we would start the process of living.

I placed the tiny bracelet beside the Jordan stone on the small table near my bed, arranging them with care so they touched. One the promise of what might have been, as fragile as morning mist. The other, the hope of what might yet be, as solid as the foundations of the earth.

CHAPTER 15

Arimathea, October, 31 AD

"Please, I was told Anna of Arimathea could help me. The healer?"

The woman's voice carried across the courtyard, wavering on the edge of a plea. My hands stilled in the feverfew, the bitter-green scent sharp on my fingers. She stood at the estate entrance beyond the garden gate, one hand cradling her stomach, the other pressed to the small of her back. She was heavy with child, near her time, and her tunic pulled taut across the swell of her belly, the fabric catching the light where it stretched thinnest over the curve.

My hands closed tight around the feverfew, crushing leaves until the bitter oil ran between my fingers.

"I am looking for Anna," the woman said again, this time to Shira, who had appeared from the house. "My sister said she helped with her difficult birth some time ago, and I am having pains that come and go—"

I caught Shira's eye and shook my head once. "Fetch Deborah. Tell her someone needs her help."

Shira hesitated, glancing between me and the woman. "But, mistress—"

"Now, Shira."

The servant hurried toward the house. The woman turned toward where my voice had come from, her brow furrowed, scanning the garden. "But I was told Anna of Arimathea—"

I pushed through the sage and thyme before she could finish and moved deeper into the garden, where the path narrowed between shoulder-high plants, their leaves brushing my arms and releasing their scent. The garden wall at the far corner still held the sun's warmth when I laid my forehead against it, the stone solid. My knife slipped from my fingers and thudded into the soft earth. I bent to retrieve it, but my hands shook so violently I could barely close my fingers around the bone handle.

Behind me came voices at the gate, Deborah's calm tones answering the woman's higher pitch then the *creak* of wood as the gate opened wider. The sounds faded as they moved away until only the fountain remained, its endless trickle joined by bees working the late lavender.

I stood there, forehead against sun-warmed stone, counting my breaths. The sage needed pruning. That was something I could do. Something that required nothing but a sharp blade and the knowledge of what should be cut away.

I kneeled, my tunic immediately soaking up moisture from the soil Ezra had watered that morning. The hem grew heavy with damp earth, clinging to my legs. I grasped my knife—the small curved blade Abba had given me years ago, its edge honed to split a hair. The older growth was woody, silver-gray and brittle, blocking light from the tender green shoots beneath. I worked carefully, the knife biting clean through each stem with a soft snap. The sharp green scent rose with each cut, clearing my head the way it cleared congestion when steeped in boiling water, and I breathed deeply.

I see you, Anna.

The words came back to me. It had happened here, right in this place—wind carrying impossible fragrances, the latch falling from my fingers as God spoke my name. This garden. That gate just there, where I had stood one morning feeling forgotten. And He had called me by name.

My hands stilled in the sage.

If He saw me then, where was He now? Where was He when my baby came into the world too soon?

"You spoke to me here." I studied the sky, pale and empty in the midday brightness. "Where were You?"

No wind rose this time. No voice answered. Just birds calling and Ezra's axe in the distance chopping wood for winter.

My hands found the sage I had been pruning and tore it from the earth, roots and all, dirt spraying. I flung it at the wall. It hit with a soft *thud* and fell, leaving a smear of soil down the stone.

God had called me by name once. But now, when I needed Him most, He was silent.

"Destroying your garden will not bring Him closer."

Andrew stood at the garden gate, one shoulder propped against the wooden frame, arms crossed over his chest. How long he had been standing there watching me work, I could not say.

"The sage was choking itself." I brushed dirt from my hands, but it clung to my skin, worked into every line and crease. I did not meet his gaze.

He came through the gate and crossed to where I kneeled, his sandals crunching on the gravel path. When he crouched beside me, his knee touched mine, and the simple contact steadied something in me that had been shaking since I saw that pregnant woman at the gate.

"That woman," he said quietly. "She needed help."

"Deborah is perfectly capable."

"That woman came asking for you, Anna. You are the healer she wanted. Not Deborah."

"Then she can teach the woman what to do." I returned to the sage, my knife moving perhaps more forcefully than necessary. "I am not the only healer in Arimathea."

Andrew was silent for a moment. "Your father is returning. A messenger came this morning while you were out here. He is bringing my mother with him."

Something lifted, just a little. "They are traveling together?"

"So the messenger said."

"Do you think..." I hesitated. But I had seen the way Naomi looked at Abba during his visit to Bethsaida, the careful way they spoke to each other as if testing whether this unexpected connection might be something more.

"I think," Andrew said slowly, "my mother has been alone a long time. And your father has as well."

"You would not mind? If they..."

His mouth curved. "My mother deserves happiness. And your father has been kind to her."

"When do they arrive?"

"By evening, the messenger said. Before dark."

"Then I should see what needs preparing," I said. "We will want everything to be welcoming."

I started toward the house, my mind already turning to what needed doing. Shira and Tamar would handle the meal with Deborah's direction, but I should make sure a guest chamber was prepared for Naomi, that there were fresh linens and water for washing.

Andrew caught my hand before I could take more than a step, his fingers wrapping around my wrist. "Anna."

"Yes?"

"Are you well?"

"Of course. Why would I not be?" I squeezed his hand, feeling the familiar roughness of his palm. "Come. Help me make sure the courtyard is swept. If we are having guests, everything should be perfect."

He did not move, just kept looking at me. But he did not press. He never pressed.

"All right," he said finally. "But that sage might say otherwise."

THEY ARRIVED as the sun dropped toward the hills, long shadows stretching across the courtyard stones like fingers reaching for the house. I had been arranging cushions in the main room when the wagon wheels creaked to a stop outside, wood groaning against wood, leather traces jingling. Ezra's voice called out, and servants' feet hurried across the courtyard. Naomi stepped down, dust rising from her clothes as she brushed at them, her head covering askew from the journey, strands of gray hair escaping around her face. She smiled when she saw me, the lines deepening at the corners of her eyes.

I crossed to her, my arms opening. "Ima. Welcome."

She embraced me, and I breathed in road dust and the faint scent of the rosemary soap she favored. When she pulled back, her hands stayed on my shoulders, searching my face the way I searched patients for fever.

"Anna. You look well."

I smiled, tasting the lie. "I am. Come inside. You must be tired from the journey."

Abba came then, moving stiffly from hours in the wagon. He kissed my forehead, his beard scratching, dust from the road still clinging to his clothes. His hand lingered on my cheek.

"Daughter. It is good to see you."

"And you, Abba." I gestured toward the house. "Deborah has prepared lamb with your favorite spices. And we have fresh bread, and wine from last year's vintage that Ezra says is the finest yet."

We went inside where the main room glowed with lamplight, flames dancing and throwing shadows up the walls. The air hung heavy with roasted meat and warm bread, sharp with coriander and the sweetness of honey glaze. Deborah directed Shira and Tamar as they brought water for washing, clay pitchers sweating with coolness, water sloshing as they set out the meal with the efficient clatter of pottery and wood. I settled Naomi on cushions while Andrew poured wine into clay cups, the red liquid catching the lamplight like rubies, and soon we were arranged around the low table.

The lamb still steamed on its platter, the meat falling from the bone in tender chunks, the skin crispy and dark with char. Oil pooled golden in small dishes beside bread torn into rough pieces, the crust crackling, the inside soft and still warm enough to melt butter. Olives glistened dark and wrinkled, bitter-salt, the flesh slipping from the pit. I dipped bread in oil, and the taste flooded my mouth—first the richness then the pepper burn at the back of my throat.

The conversation flowed easily enough. Abba spoke of the journey, of roads grown muddy with autumn rains that sucked at the wagon wheels and made the donkeys strain in their traces. Andrew mentioned his work with Ezra, a new storage building they were constructing, and I watched his hands as he spoke, saw the new calluses forming across his palms, the wood dust still caught in the creases.

Naomi leaned forward, her face brightening. "I have news. Damaris is with her family now."

My hands stilled on the bread. "She found them?"

"Yes. Her brothers wept when they saw her." Naomi's eyes shone. "They had grieved her as lost. When she appeared at their door, they pulled her inside and would not let her go. She has a place with them again."

"She is home."

"She is home," Naomi confirmed. "She sends her love to you both. Says she prays for you every day."

I had to blink against the sudden heat behind my eyes. Damaris, who had been invisible for so long, cast out and forgotten. Now restored. Now home.

"The lamb is wonderful," Abba said, his eyes on me rather than his plate. "The herbs give it such flavor."

"The herbs are from Anna's garden," Andrew said.

"I know how much you love working in your garden," Naomi said.

Naomi studied me with an expression that saw too

much. I tore a piece of bread just to have something to do with my hands, the crust rough against my fingers, still warm enough that steam rose from the exposed crumb.

"Some things are easier to tend than others." The words came out sharper than I meant them, carrying an edge like a blade turned wrong in the hand.

Andrew's foot found mine under the table, a small pressure against my instep. I kicked it away. *Let me be.*

Abba set down his cup with a soft sound that somehow commanded attention.

"Naomi and I would like to speak with you both," he said. "After we have eaten. In the courtyard, perhaps, if the evening is mild enough."

"Yes, Abba."

The meal continued. I picked at the food on my plate while they talked. Naomi's fingers worried the edge of her cup. Abba's formal posture softened when he looked at her. They sat near enough that their sleeves nearly touched. Once I caught them exchanging a glance that held something private between them.

When Shira and Tamar began clearing the dishes, I rose, my legs stiff from sitting so long. My heart beat a little faster. Was this the moment when everything would be made official, when Abba and Naomi would speak aloud what their eyes had already said to each other?

We went out to the courtyard. Darkness wrapped around us, stars emerging one by one overhead. The evening air raised gooseflesh on my arms. I sat on the stone bench where I had sat a thousand times before, the stone still holding a ghost of the day's warmth, and Andrew sat beside me. I could feel the heat of him through our tunics.

Abba stood near the fountain, his posture formal, his

hands clasped behind his back in the way he stood when addressing the Sanhedrin. He gathered himself as if preparing to deliver a verdict. Naomi sat on the low wall across from us, her hands folded in her lap, fingers laced together.

Somewhere a bird called its evening song, a lonely sound in the gathering dusk. The fountain trickled behind Abba, water falling steady and insistent over stone, filling the silence.

"We did not come simply to visit," Abba said finally.

Andrew shifted beside me.

"Naomi and I are to be married. Three weeks hence. In Capernaum at Simon Peter's home."

Naomi's hands relaxed in her lap as if she had been holding her breath. A small smile touched her lips as she looked at Abba then turned to us, her expression uncertain, searching our faces.

I opened my mouth, but no words came. Andrew's hand found mine. Three weeks. Capernaum. All of them would be there. All of them would be waiting.

Abba leaned forward slightly, his brow creasing. "Anna? Are you not pleased?"

"Yes. Of course." The words sounded forced, but it was the best I could do.

"We are very pleased with the news," Andrew said, and I felt grateful for him, for the way he could step into the silences I left and make them less awkward.

"Who..." My voice came out thin. I swallowed and tried again. "Who will be there? Will Jesus come? The others?"

"Of course," Naomi said, smiling, the lines around her eyes deepening with pleasure. "Simon and Rachel. Jesus will officiate. And the disciples, all your friends. Everyone we love."

Everyone. For a moment, the courtyard tilted, the stones beneath my feet no longer solid, the fountain's sound suddenly too loud. I would have to face them all. Tirzah, heavy with the child I no longer carried, her belly swollen with life while mine had emptied. The women who would look at me with pity poorly disguised as sympathy, the questions no one would ask but everyone would think hovering in the air between us, smothering me. Jesus. I would have to face Jesus after abandoning everything he had taught me about faith and trust and not being afraid, after running home like a child to hide in my father's garden.

The fountain behind Abba grew louder, each trickle and splash magnified until the sound filled my ears, until I could hear nothing else, my pulse joining the rhythm—water over stone, blood through veins, both relentless.

Andrew's hand tightened on mine.

"We would like you to be there," Abba said.

"Of course we will come," Andrew said.

I turned to stare at him. He met my gaze, his expression calm, decided. Speaking for both of us as if we had discussed it. As if my answer was already known, as if he had not just committed me to the one thing I could not do.

"Anna?" Abba pulled me back, his voice cutting through the roar of water. "Will you come?"

My hands lay still in my lap. I stared at them.

"I do not know," I said.

Somewhere in the hills, a jackal called. Abba's hands stayed clasped behind his back.

"It would mean a great deal to us if you were there," Naomi said quietly.

"Perhaps you need time to consider," Abba said.

"I cannot say yes right now. I am sorry."

The words came out thin and strange, like someone else was speaking through my mouth.

"We should speak privately," Andrew said. "Anna and I. Before we give you an answer."

Abba nodded slowly, though disappointment showed in the set of his shoulders, the way his jaw tightened. "Of course. Take whatever time you need."

But Naomi did not move. She leaned forward, her elbows on her knees, and in the failing light her face showed every one of her years—the lines etched deep, the gray in her hair, the wisdom that came from loss and survival.

"Anna." Her tone was soft, but I heard the steel beneath it, the voice of a woman who had buried a husband and raised sons alone and knew what it cost to keep living. "I know you are afraid. But staying here will not protect you from the hurts of the world. It will only make the world smaller."

"You do not understand." I stood. "Excuse me."

I walked toward the garden without waiting for permission. My steps were too quick, uneven, catching on the hem of my tunic. The courtyard stones were still warm beneath my bare feet, the heat of the day bleeding away into the night but cooling fast now, degree by degree with each step. Behind me, Andrew started to follow—I heard the scrape of his sandal on stone. Then Abba's voice, low and firm, and Andrew's footsteps stopped.

The air grew cooler as I passed through the garden gate, thick with the scent of turned earth and night-blooming jasmine, their white flowers ghostly in the darkness. My breath came shallow and fast, each inhale catching somewhere high in my ribs where my heart hammered against bone. The garden was all shadows now, plants reduced to dark shapes against darker earth.

My feet found the packed earth between the beds by pure memory, avoiding the low border stones. The sage was there where I had left it that morning, silvery mounds with my knife beside it, the bone handle pale against dark soil. I dropped to my knees. The impact jarred through my bones and sent pain shooting up my thighs. My hands found the soil, still holding some warmth deep down but giving it up to the darkness, the surface already cool and dry, crumbling between my fingers.

And then the tears came.

I wept for the child I would never hold. God had given me that life and then taken it before I even knew his face. Why? Why give me something so precious only to rip it away? The world kept turning as if nothing had happened, as if my baby had never existed. And now they wanted me to leave. To go back. To face them all when I could barely breathe.

I wept into the dirt, my fingers digging deep until I hit the cooler, damper soil beneath, packing under my nails and grinding into the creases of my palms until my hands were black with it. My whole body shook. Tears streamed hot down my face, mixing with the dust on my cheeks, dripping from my chin to spot the soil dark beneath me, each drop a small stain that spread and vanished. My nose ran. I could taste salt and the grit of earth between my teeth where I had pressed my mouth to my dirt-caked hands. Sobs tore at my ribs, leaving them aching as if I had been beaten, each breath a ragged gasp that burned going in and shuddered coming out, my throat raw.

My shoulders hunched over my knees, my spine curling

until my forehead nearly touched the ground. My back ached from the force of it, muscles knotting. Somewhere a dog barked, the sound carrying lonely on the night air. The fountain still trickled behind the house, water over stone, eternal. A cricket started up nearby then stopped, then started again, its chirp absurdly cheerful. The world went on, indifferent, while I broke apart in the garden.

Time passed—how much, I could not say. Above, the stars burned their silent witness. My knees went numb against the hard ground then began to ache with a deep, bone-deep throb. My hands stiffened with cold, the soil between my fingers drying and cracking. The rage burned itself out the way a fever breaks, leaving me wrung out, pulled down into the earth as if the soil might swallow me. My face felt swollen and hot, as tight as an overfilled wineskin. My ribs ached with each breath. I had no more tears left, only emptiness where the fury had been, a void that echoed.

"Anna."

Andrew's voice came from behind me, as quiet as the night itself. He must have been standing there for some time, waiting for the storm to pass. I had not heard him approach, but when I turned my head slightly, I could see his feet, his worn sandals dark against pale earth.

I did not turn fully. "Go inside."

"No."

Footsteps soft on the garden path, barely a whisper. Then he kneeled, wrapping his arms around me, and the simple fact of his presence there beside me in the dirt made something crack open in my chest all over again.

"I thought I was better. I thought if I just gave it enough time, if I just built a life here, I could be whole again."

"You are whole."

"Look at me, Andrew. I cannot even think about going to Capernaum without feeling like I am drowning. I am terrified of a wedding. That is not whole."

He reached up, and his thumb brushed across my cheek, wiping away the tracks of tears and probably streaking dirt across my face in the process, his skin rough against mine. His hand was warm, calloused from the work with Ezra, and as gentle as a whisper.

"You are whole," he said again. "Maybe not healed fully. Not finished. But you are whole. There is a difference."

"I am afraid," I whispered.

"I know."

"What if I cannot do it? What if I go back and it destroys me?"

"Then I will be there." His other hand came up, so he held my face between both palms, and I could feel every point where his skin touched mine. "But Anna, you cannot live the rest of your life in this garden."

"Why not?" The question came out desperate and defiant. "We could stay here. Build a life. Be happy. You know we could."

"Could we?"

I wanted to say yes, but the words stuck in my throat because I knew the truth. Knew it the way I knew the bitterness of wormwood on my tongue or the feel of fever-heat beneath my palm, knowledge that lived in my body before it reached my mind.

I was not happy here.

I was only less miserable.

The woman who had followed Jesus, who had walked away from safety to serve the sick and the broken, who had found purpose in using her gifts to help others—that woman was still inside me somewhere. Buried beneath grief and fear but not dead. Not yet.

"Your mother is right," I said finally. "Staying here is making me smaller."

Andrew pulled me against his chest, his arms tight around me. I laid my face on his shoulder and breathed in the smell of him—sweat and wool, sawdust from working with Ezra caught in the weave, and beneath it all, the scent of his skin that meant home even when I was far from any physical place I recognized.

One hand came up to cup the back of my head, his fingers threading through my hair. I could feel his heartbeat against my cheek. His chest rose and fell with each breath, and gradually, without meaning to, I found my breathing slowing to match his until we breathed together.

The night had grown cold. I shivered, and he pulled me closer, sharing his warmth, his body heat seeping into mine. My knees ached where they pressed into the hard ground, a dull throb that would leave bruises by morning. My hands were filthy, soil caked under every nail. But Andrew held me anyway as if I was not covered in dirt and grief.

"We do not have to decide tonight," he said into my hair. "We can wait until morning."

But I knew already. Had known, perhaps, from the moment Abba said Capernaum. The knowing had just been buried beneath weeks of careful avoidance and false peace.

I sat back and looked up at his face, shadowed and beloved in the starlight.

"I want to say no."

"I know."

"But I am going to say yes."

His eyes searched mine. "Are you certain?"

No. Yes. I did not know.

"Ask me again in the morning," I said. "When I am less of a coward."

"You have never been a coward. You have always been brave."

I almost laughed. He had said something like that to me in those early days, when I was tending his wounds after the bandits had beaten him. "I think you are braver than I am, Anna of Arimathea." And maybe I had been then. Before I learned what it meant to lose something you loved more than your own breath.

Now I was learning bravery was just fear that had run out of places to hide.

WE EVENTUALLY ROSE, my legs shaking, pins and needles shooting through my calves as blood returned to my knees. We walked back to the house, brushing dirt from our knees, the soil falling in small streams from the folds of fabric. As we reached the garden gate, a breeze stirred the air, warm despite the night's chill, carrying something that made me freeze mid-step, my hand shooting out to grip the gate latch.

Frankincense. Honey. Cedar.

The impossible fragrances from when He spoke my name, rich and resinous, as sweet as Temple incense, nothing that grew in my garden, nothing that bloomed in Arimathea. The scent wrapped around me like arms and filled my nose and mouth until I could taste it on my tongue, as heavy as smoke.

My hand gripped the gate latch hard enough that the

wood bit into my palm. "Andrew." My voice came out strangled, choked. "Do you smell that?"

He paused beside me, and I heard him draw breath. "Smell what?"

"The wind. The scent—" I could not finish.

He breathed in again, deeper this time, audible, his chest expanding. Then he shook his head slowly. "Just the garden. The night air."

The breeze faded as quickly as it came, dissipating into simple darkness, leaving only the familiar scents of jasmine and turned earth, the distant smoke from cooking fires.

My knees weakened. I sagged against the gate, one hand pressed to my mouth, tears filling my eyes and spilling over, hot on my cold cheeks.

"Anna?" Andrew's hands grasped my arms, propping me up, his grip firm. "What is it?"

I shook my head, unable to speak. How could I explain? Hours ago in the garden, I had asked where He was, had hurled my grief at the empty sky. And now at this gate where He had first spoken my name, He had answered. Not with words or thunder or burning bushes. Just enough to say, *I am still here. I still see you. You are not forgotten.*

"He was there," I whispered, the words barely forming. "When I needed Him most. He was there."

Andrew's arms came around me. "He is still here," I said against his chest.

When we finally walked inside, I left my safety buried in the earth with the sage and the thyme. Some things had to be uprooted to survive.

CHAPTER 16

Capernaum, Late October, 31 AD

Three days north from Arimathea and the blue door of Rachel and Simon's courtyard stood before us, the same gate where Andrew and I had been betrothed only a year ago, though I had lived several lifetimes in the months between then and now. My feet would not carry me forward.

"We can wait." Andrew's hand found the small of my back, the warmth of it grounding me. "Take whatever time you need."

Deborah stood silent beside me, her presence as constant as stone. She had insisted on making the journey though I protested. "You will need me there," she had said, and she had been right, as Deborah so often was, reading what I needed before I could name it myself.

I drew a breath and tasted Capernaum. Lake water cold

and clean off the surface, fish drying on racks in the sun, the faint rot of seaweed at the shore. The scent that had once brought me such joy now felt like trying to wear a tunic I had outgrown, familiar but pulling tight across shoulders that had changed shape with grief.

"No," I said. "We should go in."

The courtyard opened before me exactly as I remembered it. Whitewashed walls catching the last golden light of day and throwing it back in soft waves, stone benches worn smooth by years of women gathering to trade gossip and news and the small intimacies that bind a community together, oil lamps already glowing in their simple clay holders as twilight deepened over the lake, their flames still pale against the lingering daylight. The air hung heavy with celebration, roasting lamb fat dripping onto hot coals and hissing into smoke, bread still radiating oven heat and filling my nose with yeast and char, wine sweetness mixing with olive oil and the green bite of mint and hyssop scattered across the ground beneath my feet.

Rachel straightened from arranging cushions on one of the benches, a pillow of embroidered linen still in her hands. For a moment, we simply looked at each other across the space between us, and her eyes held mine with a depth that needed no words, grief acknowledged and love remembered and an invitation extended and accepted in the space of a breath. Then she set down the pillow and crossed to me, her sandals whispering against the earth, and pulled me into an embrace, her arms coming around me before I had time to prepare myself for the flood of memory it would bring.

"Anna." Her voice was thick. "Welcome back."

My breath came shallow and quick. "Thank you for

hosting the wedding. I know it is a risk, with the Sanhedrin watching my father."

She looked me in the eye then, her hands firm on my shoulders. "Your father asked that we keep the gathering small. Just family and a few close friends." She glanced toward the house, where lamplight spilled golden through the doorway. "The council has spies everywhere these days, but we will be discreet. Naomi is inside, preparing. She will be glad you came."

I could only nod. Rachel turned to greet Deborah then Andrew, welcoming them with that easy warmth I remembered from before, the way she had of making everyone feel they belonged in her home. She drew Deborah toward the house, already speaking of preparations that still needed finishing, and Andrew hurried over to Simon Peter and the other men gathering near the courtyard wall, their voices a low rumble of reunion and blessing. I stood alone for a moment, catching my breath.

Mary Magdalene approached with that quality of stillness she carried always, as if she moved through water rather than air, and gathered me to her without words. Miriam came next, her arms fierce and brief, squeezing hard before releasing me just as quickly. Near the herb garden, I saw John and Matthew speaking with Thomas, their conversation soft against the preparations continuing around us.

Then Aunt Mary was there, Jesus's mother, pulling me close. I had not seen her since my wedding day.

"Anna, my beautiful girl. I have missed you."

Her voice reached some place inside me that had been holding tight. "Aunt Mary." I held her closer, breathing in wool and rosewater, letting myself be comforted for a moment. "I have missed you too."

She looked over my shoulder. "We will talk later, Anna. There is someone you need to speak with now." She kissed my cheek. "Go. You both need this."

I turned and saw Salome.

She stood near the far wall where the courtyard narrowed toward the side gate, hands twisted at her waist, fingers knotting and unknotting. Behind her, an oil lamp burned in its clay holder mounted to the whitewashed stone, the flame steady and bright, throwing her shadow long across the ground. When our eyes met, her mouth formed a smile. I tried to return it and failed, my lips refusing to give in, and her smile faltered. She started toward me, hesitated, then continued, each step seeming to require conscious thought.

I walked toward her. The distance between us felt both impossibly long and far too short.

"Anna." Salome's voice wavered when I reached her, thin and stretched too tight as if the wrong word might snap it entirely. "I did not know if you would come."

"My father is getting married. I had to come."

Tears filled my eyes, but I blinked them away. I would not cry now.

Salome's lips pressed together, her eyes glistening. She looked past me, toward where the other guests were gathering, then down at her hands, anywhere but at my face.

"I tried everything." The words burst from her like water through a crack in clay, rushing out as if she had been holding them back for months. "I was there. I held your hand. I prayed. I sent for help when the fever started. But it was not enough. I was not enough."

Laughter burst from near the food tables, where someone was telling a story, animated and joyful, the celebration building around us while we stood here in our memories, two women trying to cross a chasm neither of us knew how to bridge. The lamp behind her sputtered and smoked, sending shadows skittering across the wall before the flame caught again and burned clear and steady.

"Salome." I reached for her hand and found it cold despite the warm evening, her fingers like ice in mine. "You did all you could. I never blamed you."

"But I should have done more. I could not help you when you needed me most. I felt so helpless."

Her hand lifted, fingers trembling as they traced the line of the scar along my cheek, following the path from temple to jaw that I had carried since childhood. The touch was barely there, reverent, as if she were tracing something holy rather than the mark of old violence. "You have already endured so much," she whispered, her voice breaking on the words. "Lost so much. And I could do nothing but watch you suffer again."

The breeze shifted, bringing the smell of fresh bread from inside the house, where someone was pulling the last loaves from the oven. Behind us, voices rose in greeting and blessing, the rituals of celebration continuing despite our small pocket of sorrow.

"You stayed. When I was afraid and losing my son, you stayed with me. That mattered, Salome. Your presence mattered. You did all you could. I know that."

"I have thought of you every day." Tears pooled in her eyes and spilled over to track down her lined cheeks, following the familiar paths worn by years of joy and sadness both. "Prayed for you. Wondered if you could ever forgive me."

"There is nothing to forgive. I am sorry I am just now telling you that." I pulled her close. She wrapped her arms around me and held on for a long moment, her breath hitching against my shoulder. When we broke apart, the terrible tension that had been holding her shoulders rigid had released. She wiped her eyes with the heel of her hand then managed a small smile.

"Thank you," she whispered. "Thank you." She glanced toward where James stood with the other men, his broad back turned to us but his posture somehow watchful, the firelight throwing his profile into sharp relief. "James will be glad to see you. He worried you might not come, that it was too much to ask of you."

"How is he?"

"Afraid." A small laugh escaped her, half sob and half genuine amusement. "Tirzah is due any day now, and he has been impossible. Checking on her constantly, asking if she needs anything, hovering over her. Yesterday he tried to forbid her from coming tonight. Said the journey was too much, that she should stay home and rest. You should have seen the look she gave him."

Despite everything, my lips curved. "I can imagine."

"She is determined that this baby will be born among family." Salome glanced toward where Tirzah sat near the house, partially hidden by the cluster of women around her. The flames had grown brighter as twilight deepened into full evening, dancing in the breeze off the lake and casting moving shadows across the whitewashed walls. "She has been asking about you. Wanting to see you."

"I should speak with her." I drew a breath to calm myself, pressing my hand briefly against my stomach, where emptiness still ached. This was the moment I had been dreading most.

"Anna." Salome caught my arm, her grip surprisingly

strong. "One more thing. I want you to know, if you ever need me, if you ever want to try again..." She stopped, choosing her words with the care of someone navigating dangerous ground. "I will be there. Whatever you need. However I can help. I promise you that."

The offer settled over me like a warm cloak on a chilly night. "Thank you, Salome. I would like that. If the time comes."

I turned and saw Tirzah across the courtyard.

She sat in the narrow strip of shade cast by the house's second story, though the sun had sunk low enough now that the shade was more memory than reality. Her back was propped against the whitewashed wall, legs stretched out in front of her in that ungainly way of women at the end of pregnancy, when comfort becomes impossible to find. One hand rested on the enormous swell of her belly where life moved and kicked and pressed against her ribs. The other braced flat against the wall as if she might need to lever herself upright at any moment. Her face glistened with sweat despite the cooling evening air, and even from this distance, I could see her breathing, mouth slightly open, chest rising and falling with effort.

Our eyes met across the space. She struggled to rise, movements clumsy and awkward with the weight she carried, but I crossed to her before she could fully stand, closing the distance between us in a few swift steps.

"Do not get up," I said, kneeling beside her.

Dried herbs crushed into the dirt by passing feet released their scent beneath me, mixing with the mineral smell of sweat and the faint metallic taste of fear. Dark circles shadowed Tirzah's eyes, her lips chapped and cracked, a fine tremor running through her hands.

"Anna." Her voice sounded uncertain. "I did not know if you would want to see me. James said I should not come, that you would not want to see me…" She stopped, hand moving protectively over her belly, covering the place where life grew. "But I could not miss your father's wedding. I had to be here. I hope you understand. But I can go, if it you prefer that."

Behind us, someone started tuning a lyre, the discordant notes hanging in the air before resolving into something sweeter. Andrew approached, his shadow falling across us, and stood close behind me without speaking, his presence a quiet support.

"You were right to come."

The words surprised me even as I said them, but they were true. They had to be true, or I would break apart entirely.

I reached out and took Tirzah's hand, her palm hot and dry against mine. As I leaned closer, the baby kicked hard against her belly, the movement visible through the stretched linen. The fabric pulled tight then relaxed. Another kick, lower this time. The shape of a heel or perhaps an elbow pressed out for just a moment before it disappeared back into the mystery of her womb. *Would I ever know this again?*

A breeze came off the lake, carrying the mineral smell of water and fish and the wet earth at the shore. The guests were gathering near the chuppah, Rachel's voice calling people to their places with that calm authority she had. The lyre player found his melody and began in earnest, joined by a flute, the music weaving together into something joyful and expectant.

I sat beside Tirzah in the gathering darkness, watching life move beneath her skin, the ripple of a limb stretching, the shift of a small body turning in its watery world. Each breath

I took required conscious effort, my lungs remembering how to fill and empty, how to keep going even when everything hurt. But I was still breathing. I had not run. There was that.

"You are my friend." The words came thick, my voice barely steady. "That has not changed."

Tirzah's arms came around me in a rush and pulled me close. The swell of her belly pressed hard against my side, solid and hot through the fabric. When we finally pulled apart, her face was wet. James was watching from near the house, flame light carving deep shadows under his eyes, his jaw tight with emotion. When our eyes met, he nodded once. I nodded back.

Tirzah grimaced suddenly, her whole body tensing, hand flying to press against her side. The movement was sharp, involuntary, her face contorting briefly before relaxing again. "He kicks constantly. I have not slept properly in weeks. It hurts no matter what I do, and he seems to know when I finally find a comfortable spot and chooses that moment to move."

"Not much longer now," I said, hearing the healer in my voice despite everything, a professional assessment given even when my heart was breaking.

"I hope not." She shifted uncomfortably. The wall behind her scraped against her back through the linen. "I am ready to meet this child. To hold him in my arms instead of carrying him beneath my ribs." Her eyes widened. "I am sorry, Anna. Exhaustion is making me say things I should not."

I shook my head in dismal, and Andrew shifted closer behind me, his hand coming to rest briefly on my shoulder before falling away. The music swelled as more instruments joined in. A drum now, keeping steady time, and what sounded like a tambourine, its metallic jingle bright against the deeper tones. The smell of roasting lamb drifted on the breeze. Light pushed back the dusk, and voices rose in anticipation of the ceremony to come.

I looked up at Andrew. He had been watching me, and when our eyes met, he smiled at me.

I reached up and grabbed his hand, squeezing once in thanks.

Movement near the house drew my attention. Golden light spilled through the doorway, and my father emerged with Naomi on his arm.

He wore his finest robe, the one he saved for Sabbath and high holy days, deep-blue wool with cream embroidery at the neck and sleeves, the stitching so fine it must have taken months to complete. But despite the finery, he looked uncharacteristically nervous, adjusting the drape of fabric at his shoulder with one hand, smoothing his beard with the other, his movements restless and uncertain. The flames caught the silver in his hair, threads of age woven through the dark. Naomi glowed beside him in a robe the color of pomegranate, her face radiant, one hand resting lightly in the crook of his elbow as if she belonged there and always had.

Voices rose in greeting as they moved into the courtyard. Then my father's eyes found mine across the space, through the clusters of people and the smoke rising from the food tables, and he stopped walking. His hand went still on his beard.

I crossed to him, weaving between guests. The ground was cool beneath my feet.

When I reached him, he pulled me into his arms without

a word. He held me tightly, one hand cupping the back of my head, his palm warm against my hair. His robe smelled of myrrh oil and cedar, and his beard scratched against my temple as it always had.

"Thank you for coming." The words buried in my hair. "I know it costs you to be here."

"You are my father," I said into his chest, my voice muffled by fabric and love. "I would not be anywhere but here."

He pulled back to look at me, hands heavy on my shoulders, and his eyes searched my face with that assessment I had come to know intimately. "Are you well?"

"No." The truth came easier than a lie would have. "But I am here. That has to be enough for now."

He nodded, his grip tightening briefly on my shoulders before releasing me. Around us, others gathered to greet the bride and groom, to offer their blessings. The flames burned brighter now as full darkness settled over the courtyard, reflected in the whitewashed walls until the space seemed to glow from within, holding light like cupped hands holding water.

Then my father turned to Naomi, drawing her forward with a gentleness that made my chest both ache and sing.

Andrew stepped closer and pulled his mother into a warm embrace, his arms wrapping around her slight frame. "Congratulations, Ima. You look beautiful."

"My son." Naomi's eyes shone as she looked up at him. "I am so glad you are here."

"I would not miss this for anything." Andrew kissed her forehead then stepped back but kept one hand on her arm. The fabric of her robe was fine linen, the kind that took skilled hands months to weave. "Joseph is a good man. You will be happy together."

"I believe we will." She leaned close to me, her voice dropping to a conspiratorial whisper. "Your father has checked his prayer shawl three times already. I have never seen him so nervous."

A smile tugged at my lips despite everything, despite the grief still sitting heavily in my chest. "He was the same at my wedding. Deborah had to stop him from adjusting it a fourth time."

Naomi reached for my hand, her palm warm and dry against mine, her grip surprisingly strong for such a small woman. Then she turned back to Andrew, her expression shifting to concern. "Take care of her today."

"Always."

Rachel appeared at the edge of the gathering, clapping her hands for attention, the sharp sound cutting through the conversations. The voices died down in waves, nearest to farthest, until the courtyard held only the crackle of cooking fires and the whisper of wind through the grapevine overhead, leaves rustling secrets to each other. "Let us begin."

People moved toward the center of the courtyard, where a simple chuppah had been erected, four poles driven into the earth and holding up a prayer shawl with its blue threads at the corners. Someone had woven late-autumn flowers through the fabric, their scent drifting across the courtyard on the breeze, already beginning to fade. Chrysanthemums, I thought, and maybe the last of the wild roses from the hills above the lake.

I found myself swept along with Andrew beside me. We took our places in the loose circle forming around the chuppah. Peter and Rachel stood together near the front, Rachel's hand tucked into her husband's elbow, her head barely reaching his shoulder. Salome stood with John and James, the latter keeping one protective arm around Tirzah as she lowered herself onto a bench someone had dragged forward.

Mary Magdalene stood nearby, hands folded in front of her, her face beautiful in the firelight. Aunt Mary had positioned herself close to the chuppah where she could see everything, her eyes already bright with unshed tears. Deborah stood at my side, her shoulder brushing mine.

A quiet murmur rippled through the gathering as Jesus arrived.

He stood just inside the gate, wearing a simple robe, travel-stained and dusty from the road, marked with the signs of hard use. His hair was windblown, uncombed, and his face shadowed with several days' growth of beard. He looked like any other traveling teacher, any other rabbi making his way through Galilee on foot, teaching in synagogues and staying with whoever would offer him a meal and a place to sleep. But the conversations died completely when he entered, voices falling away into silence as if someone had blown out a flame.

When his eyes found mine across the courtyard, he smiled, just a small lifting at the corners of his mouth, and nodded. Just that. A smile and a nod. I drew a breath and felt the knot in my chest ease, slowly untying.

He moved through the crowd, and people stepped aside, creating a path as naturally as water flowing around stone. As he passed me, his hand briefly touched my shoulder, a light touch there and gone, but the feel of it remained like a blessing.

Jesus took his place under the chuppah. The courtyard existed in a pool of firelight surrounded by vast darkness, with the sky above us scattered with stars. The temperature was dropping fast the way it does in Galilee after sunset, the heat of the day bleeding away into the night sky, and I shivered despite myself. Andrew shifted closer, sharing his warmth.

My father and Naomi approached the chuppah. Naomi walked with her head held high, her face glowing in the light. My father's hands were clasped in front of him, trembling slightly despite his attempts to control them. When they reached the chuppah, they turned to face each other under the ancient prayer shawl that had covered my father through decades of Sabbaths and holy days, and the flowers woven through the fabric cast strange shadows in the flickering glow, their petals already beginning to wilt.

Jesus began to speak, his voice echoing across the courtyard, the words made holy by centuries of repetition, the traditional blessings, the same I had heard at my own wedding, the same spoken at weddings since the time of our fathers, binding each generation to the next in an unbroken chain of covenant and promise.

"Blessed are You, Lord our God, King of the universe, who has created joy and gladness, groom and bride, mirth and exultation, pleasure and delight, love, brotherhood, peace and fellowship..."

The wind picked up, stronger now, carrying the clean smell of water from the lake. The flames guttered and steadied, dancing wildly before settling again. Someone coughed softly behind me.

My father lifted Naomi's hand and slipped the ring onto her finger, the metal catching the firelight. His lips moved, speaking the words that would bind them together before God and witnesses. "Behold, you are consecrated to me with this ring according to the law of Moses and Israel."

Naomi reached up and touched my father's face, just her fingertips against his bearded cheek, and he leaned into her touch like a man who has been wandering in desert heat and finally found shade, his eyes closing briefly at the simple comfort of it.

Jesus lifted the cup of wine, a silver goblet someone had polished until it gleamed, catching and throwing back the light in bright fragments across the circle of upturned faces, and he blessed it, his voice rising and falling in the ancient rhythm that connected us to Abraham and Sarah, to Isaac and Rebecca, to all the generations that had come before and all that would come after, each blessing a thread woven into the great tapestry of our people's story. Then he handed the cup to my father. Joseph drank then offered it to Naomi. She drank, and when she lowered the cup, wine stained her lips dark in the firelight, marking her as his.

Then Jesus sang the Seven Blessings, and his voice was rough from days of teaching in dusty synagogues and preaching on hillsides and calling across crowded courtyards, but it held us all suspended in the moment, past and present and future meeting under a prayer shawl beneath the stars, time itself bending to hold this covenant, this joining of two souls who had walked separate paths and now would walk together until death parted them. Andrew's hand tightened on mine. Aunt Mary was crying openly, tears tracking silently down her face, catching light.

"Blessed are You, Lord, who gladdens the groom with the bride..."

The blessing ended. Jesus smiled at my father and Naomi, genuine joy warming his face, then stepped back from under the chuppah. For a moment, the courtyard held its breath, suspended between one thing and another. Then someone cheered, and the solemnity shattered like pottery dropped on stone.

The celebration began in earnest.

People came forward to embrace my father and Naomi, to offer blessings and congratulations and wishes for their happiness and long life together. The firelight danced across faces full of joy. My father looked younger somehow, the stern lines around his mouth softening as he smiled down at his new wife. Naomi's hand rested on his arm, and she leaned into him with a trust that made my eyes sting.

Someone began singing, the melody picked up by others until the courtyard filled with music, voices weaving together and harmonizing without planning and creating something beautiful out of individual threads. Rachel and several women brought out trays laden with roasted lamb still steaming from the fire, lentil stew thick with cumin and fragrant with herbs, fresh cheese drizzled with olive oil and scattered with za'atar, pomegranate seeds as bright as jewels in wooden bowls, almonds and pistachios roasted with honey and salt, bread still warm from the oven and releasing steam when you tore it open.

Andrew's hand found mine. He drew me toward a quieter corner near the grapevine trellis where the celebration sounds softened but did not disappear entirely, still there but muted, the voices and laughter and the rhythmic pulse of someone beating time on a drum.

The trellis formed a small alcove against the courtyard wall. Grapevines twisted thickly around the wooden frame, their leaves rustling, whispering their secrets. Someone had hung a lamp here, but it burned low, barely more than a glow, and the shadows were deep and cool. I leaned against the wall for a moment to catch my breath.

"Are you all right?" Andrew asked quietly.

"I am managing." I leaned into him. "It is strange to be back here. In this courtyard. Where we were betrothed."

"I know." His arm came around my waist, pulling me closer against his side. "I have been thinking about it too. Standing here last year, speaking our vows. How certain we were that everything would be perfect. How simple it all seemed."

"Nothing is simple anymore."

"No. Nothing is simple." His fingers traced slow circles against my side through the linen. "But we are here. We are together. And that counts for something."

"It counts for everything." The words came out fiercely. "I will never forget him. Never stop missing him."

He put his hand on my stomach, covering the place where our son had grown and died. "Neither will I. Ever."

The music shifted to something faster, more joyful, and Rachel's laugh rang out above the other voices. Miriam hurried past our alcove carrying a wine pitcher, her sandals slapping against the ground in a quick rhythm. The celebration continued, firelight and laughter and the smell of roasting lamb drifting around us, while we stood together in our grief and our survival both.

I turned in his arms to look up at him. The lamplight caught the planes of his face, throwing his features into sharp relief: the strong line of his jaw, the curve of his mouth, the eyes that had looked at me with such love from the first moment we met. I traced his face with my fingers, memorizing it all over again.

He kissed my forehead, his lips warm against my cool

skin. Then my temple, just above where my veil had slipped loose. Then he found my lips. His hand came up to cradle the back of my head, fingers threading through my hair beneath the veil. I tasted wine on his lips, the sweet date kind they were serving at the celebration, and beneath that, the taste that was just him. The stone wall pressed against my back. His chest was warm against mine, his heart beating steady beneath my palms.

When we pulled apart, I rested my forehead against his chest, listening to his breathing, the *thump* of his heart beneath my cheek. The wool of his robe was rough against my face, smelling of road dust and lamp smoke and him.

"It was right to come," I said into his chest.

"Yes." His voice rumbled beneath my ear. "Our families are truly joined now. Bound together."

We stood like that, his arms wrapped around me, holding each other in our small shelter. The grapevine shifted overhead, leaves promising to keep our story to themselves.

Andrew smiled down at me. "When did you last eat?"

"This morning, I think."

"Stay here. I will bring you something." He kissed my forehead once more and disappeared into the celebration, moving between clusters of guests.

I leaned against the wall, grateful for the moment alone, letting my breathing slow. My father stood with some of the men near the food tables, his face more relaxed than I had seen it in years. Jesus stood beside him, and whatever he was saying made my father laugh, the sound tinkling like music. Naomi sat with Rachel and Mary Magdalene, all three of them smiling as they talked, their heads bent close. Deborah and Aunt Mary had claimed a bench together, likely sharing the intimacies of old friendship.

"Anna."

I turned. Judas stood at the edge of the alcove, his hands clasped in front of him, fingers laced together. Light fell across half his face, leaving the other side in shadow, making it hard to read his expression.

"Judas. Shalom."

"I heard about your son." He stepped closer, just inside the shadow of the grapevine, the leaves rustling above him in the breeze. "I am sorry. Truly sorry."

The words were simple enough, but his voice held a roughness that made me look more closely. His hands tightened where they gripped each other, fingers laced so tight the tendons stood out.

"Thank you."

He was quiet for a moment, his jaw working as if he were chewing on words he was not sure he should speak. "I lost a son once. He was three years old."

"Judas, I did not know. I am so sorry."

"No one does. I do not speak of it often." He stopped, his shoulders sagging. "But when I heard about Jonah, about what happened to you, I thought you might understand. The pain of it. How it never really goes away, no matter how much time passes."

I moved closer, drawn by the rawness in his voice, by the recognition of shared grief. "What happened?"

"He fell. From a roof." Judas's voice went flat, the way people's voices do when they recount unbearable things, when emotion would make the telling impossible. "I was away on business in Jerusalem. Buying goods to resell in Kerioth, always chasing the next profit, the next deal. By the time word reached me and I got home, they had already buried him. I never even got to say goodbye."

"Oh, Judas."

He nodded, blinking rapidly, his eyes bright in the dim light. "My wife could not forgive me. For not being there when it happened, when she needed me most. For choosing trade over family, profit over presence. She said if I had stayed home instead of always chasing wealth, I could have stopped it somehow. She went back to her father's house. I have not seen her since."

The guilt on his face was painfully familiar. I knew those words, the if onlys that circled endlessly in the night. If I had not drunk from that spring. If I had been more careful. If I had done anything differently.

"I know what that feels like," I said. "The wondering if you could have stopped it somehow."

"Yes." He nodded. "Exactly."

We stood in silence for a moment, two people who had lost children sharing this small space of acknowledged sorrow.

"I joined the Teacher hoping I could make something of my life. I thought maybe if I served the Messiah, if I used what I am good at, managing money and organizing supplies, to help build the kingdom, maybe it would mean something. Maybe I could be forgiven for failing my son. For failing my wife."

"You are here now," I said. "That matters."

His eyes held mine for a long moment, searching for absolution, perhaps, or understanding. "Does it? Does any of it matter if I could not save my own child?"

"Yes. It matters. It must."

Andrew appeared at the edge of the alcove, carrying a plate laden with roasted lamb and fish, bread and dates glistening with honey. He stopped when he saw Judas, his eyes moving between us, his expression hardening slightly.

Judas stepped back quickly, breaking the intimacy of the moment. "I should let you eat. Again, Anna, I am sorry for your loss."

"And I for yours."

He nodded once more and disappeared toward the celebration, his figure soon swallowed by the guests.

Andrew came closer, still holding the plate, his eyes following where Judas had gone. "What did he want?"

"To offer condolences. He lost a son too. Years ago."

Andrew was quiet for a moment, his mouth tight. "Do you believe him?"

The question surprised me. "Why would he lie about something like that?"

"I do not know. But there is something about him." He stopped then held out the plate to me, his expression softening. "Never mind. I am glad he could offer you comfort."

But when his other hand found mine, he held it tighter than necessary.

I tore off a piece of bread, the warmth of it spreading through my fingers, the yeasty smell rising to fill my nose. The lamb was tender and rich, the fish flaky and sweet with herbs. I had not realized how hungry I was until I started eating. The drum kept its rhythm, and someone started singing a wedding song I remembered from my own wedding, the melody achingly familiar. Other voices joined in, the song swelling and filling the courtyard with joy and blessing.

Andrew pulled me closer, his breath stirring my hair. "Anna," he said quietly, his voice making me look up. "Look."

I followed his gaze to where Tirzah sat. Her face had gone pale, all the color drained from it, and both hands gripped the edge of the bench hard enough that her knuckles showed white against the darkened wood. As I watched, her whole body went rigid, every muscle tensing at once, and a grimace twisted her features into something unrecognizable. When our eyes met across the courtyard, her mouth formed a single word, though no sound came out: Help.

I crossed to her immediately, Andrew close behind me, and kneeled beside her. I observed the way she was breathing, shallow and panting, the sheen of sweat covering her face and neck, the tightness around her eyes. My training took over, pushing aside everything else.

"How long have the pains been coming?"

She bit her lip hard enough to draw blood. She glanced at James, who had gone very still beside her, his face draining of color. "Since this morning. But they were mild at first, irregular. I hoped they were anyway. I thought they would stop."

She gasped suddenly, her hand flying to her belly, body going rigid as stone. Her face changed with the pain, contorting, and I counted silently, marking time. Fifteen seconds. Twenty. Thirty. When it finally passed, she sagged against the wall like a sail with no wind, her chest heaving.

"They are getting stronger." Tirzah's fingers dug into my arm hard enough to leave marks I would find tomorrow, half-moons of purple pressed into my skin. "Closer together. Anna, I do not think I can wait much longer. Please help me."

Another contraction hit before she finished speaking. Tirzah screamed, unable to suppress the sound any longer, and suddenly, the celebration around us faltered as people turned to look, conversations dying, music stumbling to a halt.

James stared at the bench beneath her. Water ran dark across the wood in spreading rivers, pooling on the ground below, soaking into the dust. His face had gone the color of ash. "Anna."

We were past the point of waiting, past the point of hoping this would not happen now, here, at my father's wedding. This baby was coming.

CHAPTER 17

"There is no more time, Tirzah. This baby will not wait." The celebration had stopped. Every face turned toward us, but I focused only on her.

Rachel appeared at my shoulder. "What do you need?"

"Clean linens. Water, boiled. And Salome. Please, someone fetch Salome."

My hands trembled against Tirzah's arm. *Adonai, help me. Help me know what to do.*

Rachel nodded once and disappeared. Within moments, Salome was beside me.

"Help me get her inside. Andrew, James, support her."

We helped Tirzah to her feet. Andrew and James took either side of her, bearing most of her weight. She leaned heavily against them, breath coming in sharp gasps as another contraction hit. We half-walked, half-carried her toward the house, stopping when the pains became too strong for her to move.

Please let me remember. Please let me do this right.

Rachel met us at the door with an armful of linens. Behind her, the other women were assembling supplies, hands moving with quiet efficiency. Andrew and James helped us maneuver Tirzah through the doorway and into a small room off the main living area, barely more than a storage chamber, windowless, the air already thick with lamp oil and sweat.

The space felt too small, too hot. The walls seemed to close in around me, and I could not catch my breath. What if my hands failed? What if—

The lamp Rachel set in the corner sent shadows jumping across the plastered walls with each flicker. We helped Tirzah onto a pallet spread with fresh linens, the wool rough beneath my hands. Salome murmured soothing words, stroking Tirzah's hair. Andrew stared at me then kissed my cheek before stepping back with James toward the doorway.

I stood. My legs wobbled beneath me. The air felt thick, suffocating, pressing against my lungs until each breath required effort.

"I need—" I looked at Salome. "I just need a moment."

I pushed past the men in the doorway and into the main room. Rachel looked up from where she was organizing supplies.

"Anna? What—"

"I will be right back." My voice was unsteady.

She took one look at my face and nodded, concern plain in her eyes.

The night air hit my face when I reached the courtyard, but it was not enough. My chest constricted, ribs squeezing tight, and I pushed my hand against my breastbone, trying to force air into my lungs.

This was impossible. Holding another woman's living child in my arms. Watching her joy when I had known only loss.

Tears fell hot against my cheeks, blurring my vision. I wrapped my arms around myself. My whole body shook.

I sank onto the nearest bench, burying my face in my hands. *Father, I cannot do this. I am not strong enough. I am not—*

Footsteps approached. I knew them before he spoke.

"Anna."

Andrew sat beside me and pulled me into his arms. He did not ask what was wrong. He already knew.

"I lost him." The words came out broken. "Andrew, I lost our son. How can I help bring another woman's baby into this world when mine was born dead? I cannot bear it."

"You did not lose him. Jonah died. That was not your fault. You did everything you could."

"But what if my hands forget? What if I fail her the way I—"

"Anna." He took my face in his hands, forcing me to look at him. "You did not fail Jonah. You did not fail me. And you will not fail Tirzah."

"You do not know that."

"I know you." His thumbs brushed away my tears. "I know you are terrified. I know this feels impossible. But you are the healer in that room. Tabitha taught you. You have seen this done."

I closed my eyes, trying to breathe. Trying to believe him.

"Tirzah needs you," he said quietly. "Her baby needs you. I believe in you."

I drew a shaking breath. Another. The tightness in my chest loosened slightly.

"I am frightened."

"I know." He kissed my forehead. "Tirzah is too. She needs someone who understands what it means to be afraid."

He was right. Tirzah was in there, in pain, in danger. And I was the only one who could help her.

I stood, legs still unsteady but holding me. Andrew rose with me, his hand warm on my back.

"I am here," he said. "Right outside that door if you need me."

I nodded then turned and walked toward the house. When I stepped back into the birthing room, Salome looked up, relief crossing her face. Tirzah lay on the pallet drenched in sweat, her face twisted with pain.

"How close are the contractions?" I asked, kneeling beside her.

"Very close," Salome said. "And strong."

I took Tirzah's hand. "You are doing well. The baby will come soon."

Another contraction built. Tirzah screamed, her back arching off the pallet. I watched, trying to see how the baby was descending. The contraction seemed wrong, too long, the pressure building but not releasing.

When the pain passed, Tirzah collapsed back, gasping. Her eyes found mine. "Anna." Her voice sounded terrified. "Something is wrong. Something feels wrong."

My stomach clenched. "That is common to feel when giving birth. Most women think that at some point during labor. I am sure all is well." But even as I said it, I was placing my hands on her belly. Through the taut skin, the baby's position revealed itself. The hard curve of a skull, the angles of limbs, everything tilted oddly, wedged.

She was right.

The baby's shoulder was presenting first. Not his head, as it should be. His shoulder caught against her pelvis, stuck fast, unable to descend.

I had seen this once before. Tabitha had not been able to save them, and both mother and child were lost.

My hands went cold. This was beyond anything I had done alone. If I could not turn him, if the shoulder stayed caught, Tirzah could tear. She could bleed to death. The baby could suffocate, trapped in the birth canal. I could lose them both.

But there was no one else. Only me.

"Tirzah." I kept my voice calm, even as fear flooded through me. "Listen to me. The baby is positioned wrong. I am going to need to turn him."

"Turn him?" Her face went white, pupils dilating. "Anna, I cannot—"

"You can." I gripped her hands, forcing her to look at me. "I have done this before. I know what to do. But I need you to trust me. Can you do that?"

She stared at me for a long moment, breathing like a hunted animal. Then she nodded.

"Salome, hold her shoulders. Miriam, be ready with the oil. Rachel, keep those lamps close. I need to see what I am doing."

The women took their positions without question. Outside, the muffled voices of the men drifted in, conversations from the courtyard like sounds from another world.

I reached inside Tirzah and felt for the baby's position, mapping out in my mind what needed to happen. The heat inside her body shocked my cool hands. Blood slicked my fingers, warm and viscous. Though I told Tirzah I had done this before, the truth was I had watched Tabitha do this once. Only once. And that had not been successful.

Please, Lord. Please let me remember. Let my hands know what my mind does not know.

I worked, trying to recall exactly what Tabitha had done. The shoulder was stuck tight, bone against bone, flesh compressed in a space too narrow. Where was the rotation point? How far could I push without damaging him? Without tearing her? My fingers searched, probing, feeling the hard edge of his shoulder blade, the curve of his tiny arm.

There. The angle where pressure would turn him rather than force him.

I pushed him back slightly, felt for the rotation point, guided his head down. Push here. Ease there. Turn. Guide.

God of Abraham, let this work. Let him turn. Let them both live.

"Push when I tell you. Not before."

Another contraction built. Tirzah's scream tore through the room like fabric ripping. The sound echoed off the close walls, amplifying until it filled every corner of the small space. Salome held her shoulders, murmuring prayers in Hebrew. Miriam poured oil over my hands, slicking them, making it easier to maneuver in the tight space. The smell of it mixed with blood and sweat until the air felt thick enough to choke on.

The door opened. Deborah slipped in, taking in the scene with one glance. She moved to Tirzah's other side without being asked, picking up her hand. Her eyes met mine across the pallet. "You can do this, Anna."

The baby shifted slightly.

Thank you. Oh, thank you.

The shoulder began to give. "Push, Tirzah. Now."

She bore down with a sound that seemed torn from her very core. The baby shifted more. His shoulder finally cleared, and his body began to turn. I guided his head down. He descended properly at last.

"Push again." It was working. He was coming. They would both live.

"Almost there." My breath came as hard as hers now. "One more. One more push, and he will be here."

Tirzah gathered herself for one last effort. The contraction built to a crescendo. She pushed with everything she had left.

The baby slid into my waiting hands.

A boy, perfect limbs, perfectly formed. But he did not move. Did not cry. He lay silent and still in my palms, his body blue-tinged in the lamplight.

"It is a boy, Tirzah. You have a son."

The words came out automatically. His skin felt wrong, too cool, too slack. His limbs hung limp. No gasp for air. No reflex to cry. The blue tinge spread from his lips across his face.

Jonah. This is Jonah all over again.

"Let me see him." Tirzah's voice, breathless and eager. "Anna, let me see my son."

Her face was full of hope and exhausted joy. I could not give him to her. Not yet. Not like this.

My hands moved.

I turned him, clearing his airway with my finger. The slickness of birth coated my hands. I rubbed his back with firm strokes, each fragile rib beneath my palm.

"Breathe. Come on, little one. Breathe."

Nothing. His head lolled against my hand, body limp and terrifyingly still.

Please, Adonai, please. Do not let him die. You let me turn him. You helped me bring him out. Please. I cannot do this again.

The room went silent. No one moved. Everyone waited, suspended in that terrible moment between hope and grief.

And then—

A shudder rippled through him.

He gasped and let out a thin, wailing cry that tore through the room and through me like lightning splitting a tree.

The baby screamed. His face scrunched up, red and furious, fists the size of acorns waving in indignation at being thrust from warm darkness into cold air. His color shifted from blue to pink to red, life rushing back into him with each lusty, outraged breath. That angry cry was the most beautiful thing I had ever heard.

Relief nearly collapsed me. My hands shook as I cleaned him quickly, noting each perfect finger, each tiny toe, before wrapping him in soft linen.

"Let me see him." Tirzah was crying now, reaching out with trembling arms. "Anna, please."

I placed the baby in her arms. All the fear drained from Tirzah's face as she looked down at her son, replaced by wonder, raw and tender. James burst through the door, all propriety forgotten, falling to his knees beside the pallet.

"A son." My voice was unsteady. "You have a son."

"Zebedee." James breathed it, touching the baby's cheek with one finger as if he might break. "His name is Zebedee."

Zeb quieted at his father's touch. His small face turned

toward the sound of James's voice. He was perfect and whole and alive.

My vision blurred, and I blinked hard, trying to focus. My arms felt as heavy as wet wool, every muscle screaming from the ordeal. Sweat dripped into my eyes, stinging, and the copper taste of blood filled my mouth where I had bitten my lip without noticing. My hands looked like they belonged to someone else, still covered in blood and oil, fingers twitching. I backed away, giving them space.

"Anna." Salome was beside me, arm around my waist. "You did it. You saved them both."

The words washed over me but did not sink in. I had held him in my hands and felt that terrible moment when he would not breathe, and then—he lived.

And he was not mine. Would never be mine.

"I need air." The words came out strangled. "I need—"

Salome helped me to the door, understanding without words. I stumbled out into the courtyard. The cool night air hit my face after the stifling heat, and I gasped, pulling in breath after breath. My legs wobbled. I reached for the nearest wall to steady myself. The lamps still burned along the courtyard walls, flames wavering in the breeze. Above, stars pierced the darkness. The smell of roasted lamb still hung faintly in the air, mixing with the scents of wine and woodsmoke. Andrew's arms came around me from behind, supporting me.

I stood there for a moment, just breathing, letting my heart slow. My legs trembled with exhaustion, muscles shaking from the effort of kneeling for so long. Sweat had dried on my face, making my skin feel tight and strange. Birth still clung to me. Blood and oil coated my hands despite my attempts to wipe them clean.

When I finally looked up, they were all there, waiting.

The lamps had burned lower, their flames smaller now, casting pools of golden light that left the corners in deep shadow. My father sat on a bench with Naomi beside him, her hand clasped in his, their fingers intertwined in that unconscious way of people who have found comfort in each other. Jesus stood beneath the grapevine trellis where the leaves rustled overhead, his face serene in the firelight, completely still amid the restless movement of everyone else. Peter shifted his weight from foot to foot, and John stood with his arms crossed tight against his chest. They had been waiting, not knowing what was happening inside that small room. Their faces turned toward me, tense with worry.

"They are both well. A boy. Tirzah has borne a healthy son."

The change was immediate. Someone let out a long breath. Another murmured a prayer of thanksgiving, the Hebrew words soft and fervent. Peter's hand came up to cover his face briefly, pressing against his eyes. When he lowered it, his cheeks were wet. John smiled, the relief plain in the loosening of his shoulders.

Andrew guided me to the nearest bench, his hand firm at my elbow. My legs gave out as I sat, my knees refusing to hold me any longer. The stone was cool beneath me, almost cold now that the night had fully settled in. The chill of it seeped through my tunic, but I welcomed it after the stifling heat of the birthing chamber. My hands lay in my lap, trembling, unable to be still. The shaking ran up my arms, into my shoulders, as if my body was only now realizing what it had just endured. My fingers twitched, the muscles cramping from how tightly I had gripped Zebedee's tiny body.

He took my hands in his and held them, his eyes on

mine, his palms warm and rough against my cold fingers. The heat of his touch was startling against my chilled hands. Then he leaned forward and kissed me. "I love you. I am so proud of you."

My father appeared on my other side, sitting on the bench next to me. His arm came around my shoulders. The gesture undid the last barrier I had been holding against the flood. The wool of his robe was soft against my cheek when I leaned into him, and he smelled of myrrh oil and wine. "Anna, what is wrong?"

"The baby—" My voice broke, the words catching in my throat like briars. "The shoulder was presenting. I had to turn him. And when he came out, he was not breathing. He was blue and still and—" Tears came then. "I thought I was going to lose him."

Abba's arm tightened around me. He shifted slightly, his body angling toward Andrew, and some wordless communication passed between them in the silence that followed, that language men speak with glances and subtle movements when words would intrude on grief.

"But you did not," Andrew said.

"No." I drew a breath, still uneven. "He breathed. Finally, he breathed."

"Anna." My father's voice was thick. "What you just did—"

"I did not know whether I could." The words came tumbling out. "I watched Tabitha turn a baby once. Only once. And when Zeb did not breathe, I did everything I could. It was not enough. I kept trying, though. He would not breathe, and I thought—" The sentence died unfinished.

"But you did not stop. You fought for him. You brought that child back."

I drew another breath, this one steadier. "I am not sure I did, Abba. I think—I think Someone else breathed life into him."

"Perhaps. But He used your hands to do it."

A voice came from behind us, quiet but certain. "You did well, Anna."

I went still. My whole body tensed. I looked up to find Jesus standing a few paces away, face gentle in the lamplight. The flame caught in his eyes, making them seem lit from within.

Heat rose in my chest. I had held Zebedee in my hands tonight and fought for his life and won. But Jonah—

He glanced at my father and Andrew. "May I speak with Anna alone?"

My father kissed my forehead once then stood. Andrew hesitated, his hand lingering on mine, but then he rose as well. They moved toward the house with the others, leaving us alone. The sound of voices faded. The celebration had ended some time ago. Now, people were departing or finding places to rest for the night.

Jesus sat down next to me. I stared at my hands in my lap, unable to look at him. My whole body began to shake again, harder this time, teeth chattering despite the warm evening. The shuddering came from somewhere deep inside, beyond my control. My hands clenched into fists in my lap, nails digging into my palms.

"Where were you?"

The words came out raw and accusing, full of all the pain I had been carrying.

He reached out and took my hand, prying my fingers open gently, his palm sliding against mine.

My breath caught. The shaking stopped as if someone

had cut the strings holding me taut. My lungs expanded, ribs spreading wide, as if a weight that had been pressing down on them for weeks suddenly lifted. Air moved in and out of my chest freely, cleanly, without the crushing pressure.

I looked down at our joined hands, his skin darker than mine in the lamplight, work-roughened and warm. Then up at his face. A gust of wind stirred the grapevine leaves overhead, rustling a nighttime melody. The lamp flame near us guttered, nearly going out, then caught again and burned steadily. The breeze was cool against my tearstained face, drying the wetness on my cheeks.

"I was there, and I am with you now, Anna. I am with you even when you cannot feel me. Even when it seems I am silent, I am with you."

Tears fell hot against my chilled skin, tracking new paths through the salt already dried there. My nose was running, and I had no cloth to wipe it. "I prayed. I begged. Salome did everything she knew. And he still—" My voice broke, splintering into pieces. "He still died. You were not there."

"Anna, look at me," he said.

I raised my head and did as he asked, forcing myself to meet his eyes even though my vision blurred with tears. I drew in a shuddering breath then another, my chest hitching with the effort of controlling the sobs that wanted to break free.

"I was there. I held you while you wept. I caught every tear." His thumb moved against the back of my hand, a slow, deliberate stroke that grounded me. "And I held him, Anna. I held your son."

"But he was so small. He never even drew a breath. How can—" The words struggled through my tears, my throat closing around them. "How can life so brief matter? Sometimes it feels like he never existed at all."

"Before I formed him in the womb, I knew him. Before he drew his first breath, his days were written in my Father's book. Every single one. Even if they numbered only seven months within you. This is the blessing I gave you, and it remains true."

I stared at him, hardly daring to believe. The cricket that had been singing stopped. The only sounds were the soft hiss of the lamp flames and my ragged breathing and the distant lap of water against the shore somewhere beyond the courtyard walls. The night closed around us, the darkness beyond the lamplight absolute and complete.

"Jonah was not a mistake. He was not a punishment or a failure. He was a child, beloved by the Father, known and treasured. You carried him. You loved him. You gave him all the life he would ever have in this world. That matters, Anna. He mattered. He will always matter."

The words settled over me like oil poured into a wound, easing the burning wound that had been open for weeks. My shoulders dropped, the tension bleeding out of my clenched muscles.

"Then why?" The question tore out of me. "Why did he have to die?"

"I cannot explain all the reasons for suffering in this broken world. Not in ways that will satisfy your mind." His hand tightened on mine. "But I can tell you that death is not the end."

"What does that mean?"

A cat yowled somewhere in the street beyond the courtyard wall, the sound sharp and startling in the quiet. I jumped slightly, my free hand coming up to press against my chest.

"You will be with your son again. One day, in a place where there is no more death or mourning or crying or pain, you will hold him. He waits for you there, and he will know you. Your love for him was not wasted, Anna. It echoes into eternity."

Jonah would know me. Deep, shaking sobs came from a place I had been afraid to touch, a place so deep inside me I had not known it existed until his words opened it. My body curled forward, bowing under the weight of it. Jesus kept holding my hand, silent, letting the grief pour out of me. His grip never loosened. He put his arm across my back and pulled me to him. The lamp flames danced in their holders, making the shadows leap and sway across the white courtyard walls. The world kept turning while I fell apart and was held together all at once.

When the storm finally passed, when the sobs quieted to hiccups and then to silence, I was empty. Hollowed out. But the emptiness was clean somehow, scoured, ready to be filled again. I wiped my face with my free hand, feeling the grit of dried tears and dust against my palm.

"Grief held inside becomes a poison. But grief poured out? That becomes holy water, washing clean the wounds we carry. You needed this, Anna. Your tears know their work, even if you do not."

I nodded, unable yet to speak but understanding the truth in his words. The release had not taken away the pain, but it had made it bearable somehow, shared rather than held alone.

"I will not always be right here with you," he continued, his voice both sorrowful and certain, "but I will not leave you as an orphan. When I go, I will send the Comforter, the Spirit of truth who will be with you forever. Not standing beside you, Anna, but dwelling within you."

"Where will you be?" The question came out small, almost a whisper.

"That is for another time." He released my hand but held my gaze, and the loss of his touch rushed in like cold water. His eyes were dark in the lamplight, endless, like looking into deep water where you cannot see the bottom. "Tonight, you helped even though it terrified you. You helped bring Zebedee into the world when your own son is gone. You did not let hurt turn you away. And you will have to make that choice again and again. Some days will be harder than others. Some days the grief will feel as fresh as it did the night Jonah died."

I wrapped my arms around myself, suddenly aware of how cold the night had become. The warmth of the day was completely gone now, leached away into the clear sky above us where stars burned.

"How do I bear it?"

"You do not bear it alone. I am with you. The Father sees you. Your son is remembered." He paused, letting each word fall like stones dropped into still water, watching the ripples spread. "And one day, Anna, there will be joy again. The sorrow will not leave you. It is part of you now. But joy can hold it. You will laugh again. You will hope again. You will bring life into the world again, if that is what the Father wills. And when you do, you will do it as someone who knows how precious and fragile that life is. How sacred."

I wanted to believe him. Wanted to let those words sink in and take root in the barren soil of my heart. But doubt clung like cobwebs, sticky and persistent, catching at every attempt to move forward.

"I know what you are thinking," he told me. "But tonight, when you held Zebedee and fought for his life, you learned you can bear more than you thought. Your grief does not make you useless. It helps you understand what others cannot."

"Perhaps." I looked down at my stained hands, at the blood dried dark beneath my fingernails, the oil still slicking my palms and making them shine in the lamplight. The lines of my palms were etched in red as if someone had drawn a map there in blood. "You said, 'If that is what the Father wills.' Do you know? Will I have another child?"

Jesus smiled, and his face softened and became almost playful. "Yes, I know."

"And?"

He stood and pulled me to my feet, drawing me into an embrace. His arms were strong around me, his chest solid against my cheek. The rough weave of his robe scratched lightly against my face. His heartbeat drummed steady beneath my ear, and his breathing kept beat in the rhythm of life itself. He smelled of road dust and woodsmoke and wind over water. He leaned close, his beard brushing against my ear, his breath warm against my skin, voice barely a whisper that seemed to vibrate through my whole body.

"Name her after your mother."

The air left my lungs. My hand went to my belly.

"When?" I whispered back, my lips barely moving, the word more breath than sound.

He smiled against my hair. I felt it more than saw it, the shift of his cheek against my temple. "Shalom, little cousin."

Then he was walking back toward the house, sandals

scuffing against the flagstones with that familiar rhythm I knew so well. The sound faded into the night, swallowed by the darkness beyond the lamplight. I stood alone, watching him go until he disappeared through the doorway, until even the sound of his footsteps was gone.

My hand stayed on my belly. On the emptiness there. The linen was cool beneath my palm, my skin cold through the fabric.

A daughter.

Sarah.

CHAPTER 18

The name filled my mouth like honey, sweet and thick on my tongue. My mother's name. My daughter's name. Jesus had spoken it with such certainty, as if she already existed somewhere beyond my sight, waiting. A child not yet conceived who would bear my mother's name and grow beneath my heart and be born into my arms. The promise was impossible. I should have doubted it. But instead, I trembled, joy pushing up through grief like green shoots through winter earth.

The courtyard had grown quiet around me, voices dropping to murmurs as those who remained settled for the night. The smell of woodsmoke drifted from the banked cooking fires. My father and Naomi had already retired together. I had watched them go, his hand at the small of her back, guiding her toward their chamber. My mother's name in my mouth, his new wife at his side. The strangeness of it caught me for a moment, how life moved forward even when you thought it could not. Salome and Miriam moved between the tables, gathering the last of the serving dishes, their movements slow with exhaustion.

But I was wide awake, every part of me alive with the need to find Andrew and pour this promise into his hands. He would rejoice with me. He had been so constant through everything, so strong when I barely stood, and now I had good news, hope instead of despair. After everything we had lost, after Jonah, after the long weeks when I had nearly drowned in sorrow, we finally had more than pain to hold.

Where was he?

Peter stood near the gate with Rachel, the two of them speaking softly as they prepared to retire. I made my way toward them across the courtyard.

"Have you seen Andrew?"

Peter glanced toward the house. "In with James and Tirzah, I think. Seeing the baby."

I thanked him and turned toward the birthing chamber with the promise blooming in my chest. Andrew would be there, marveling at Zebedee the way everyone did with newborns, and I would pull him aside and whisper the news, and his face would light with happiness, and we would hold each other and finally, finally, we would have cause to celebrate instead of mourn.

I stopped in the doorway.

The small room was warm, still holding the heat of the birth despite the open door. A single lamp burned in the corner, its flame steady now, casting golden light across the walls. Tirzah lay propped against cushions on the pallet, Zebedee nestled in her arms, his face peaceful in sleep. James sat beside her, one arm around his wife, the other hand hovering near the baby as if he could not quite believe the child was real.

Andrew stood against the far wall, arms crossed over his chest, staring at Zebedee, with a frown on his face.

Tirzah looked up and saw me, her face glowing. "Anna. Come see him. He is perfect."

I moved toward the pallet and kneeled beside it. Zebedee had grown pinker in the hours since his birth, his color strong and healthy. His fist lay against Tirzah's breast, fingers splayed like stars. I reached out and touched his hand, feeling the softness of new skin.

Jonah had been smaller than this. Paler. Still.

The longing came so sharp I had to close my eyes. When I opened them, I made myself smile.

"He is beautiful. You both did well."

"We are naming him Zebedee," James said. "After my father." He looked up toward the far wall, toward Andrew. "And his middle name will be Andrew. For the man who brought the healer who saved his life."

"That is wonder—" I turned to watch Andrew receive this honor, expecting to see the way his entire face softened when he was moved.

"That is kind of you."

The words were right. The voice was not. Flat, careful, as if he were reciting lines he had rehearsed. He had not moved from the wall. He stood as far from the baby as he could, his arms still crossed, his weight pressed back against the plaster as if he needed it to hold him upright.

"Andrew?" I rose and took a step toward him.

Now the lamplight showed what the shadows had

hidden. His jaw was locked tight, a vein standing out at his temple. His fingers pressed into his arms hard enough to leave marks. His chest barely moved with each breath, and his eyes stayed fixed on Zebedee.

"Andrew."

He blinked as if waking from a trance. "Forgive me. I should let you rest. All of you." He was already moving toward the door, his gait wrong somehow, too quick and too stiff all at once. "Congratulations. He is perfect."

Then he was gone, brushing past me without meeting my eyes.

I stood frozen for a moment, torn between following him and staying with James and Tirzah.

"Is he well?" Tirzah asked, concern creasing her forehead.

"I am not sure." I turned toward the doorway. "I should go to him."

I found Andrew in the courtyard, standing with his back to me near the far wall. His shoulders hunched forward, his hands braced against the whitewashed stone.

"Andrew."

He did not turn, but his hands curled into fists. "Leave me be, Anna. I need some time. I need to walk."

"Let me come with you."

"No." The word came out sharp, and his whole body jerked with the force of it. Then softer, but still without turning, still without letting me see his face, he said, "Please. I just need to be alone for a moment."

He was already through the gate before I could stop him, disappearing into the darkness beyond. I watched him go, the news of Sarah still longing to be told but the moment all wrong. What had just happened? James had honored

Andrew by naming the baby after him. Surely that was good news. But Andrew's voice when he responded sounded nothing like him, and the way he stood so still in the birthing room, barely able to look at Zebedee, was wrong. Was he thinking of Jonah? Had the sight of the baby been too much?

Minutes passed while I paced. Finally, I went after him.

The village was dark and quiet around me, with only starlight to guide my steps. Then I heard water moving against the shore, and I knew where he had gone.

I walked down to the beach, my feet sinking into sand. The smell of fish hit me before I saw anything, laced with seaweed gone foul in the heat and the sharp tang of tar and old rope.

Then I heard the *crack* of wood breaking, sharp and violent in the quiet night. Another *crack*. Then a *splash* as debris hit the water hard. I followed the sound to where the boats were pulled up on shore.

I stopped.

Andrew was hurling pieces of driftwood into the lake with all his strength, one after another, his movements savage and desperate. Between throws, he grabbed whatever he could find: rocks, chunks of rotted planking, broken pieces of old crates left to weather near the boats. He picked up a long piece of wood and smashed it against the stones, once, twice, until it splintered in his hands. The violence was wild, uncontrolled, each throw punctuated by sounds that were half sob, half roar. His chest heaved with the effort and the grief, his whole body convulsing.

"Andrew!"

He stopped with a piece of wood in his hand, arm cocked

back to throw. For a moment, he just stood there, breath coming in gasps, the wood slipping from his fingers to fall at his feet. Then he turned to look at me. Tears streaked down his cheeks in the moonlight, his features twisted with anguish and rage. His hands hung at his sides.

"I told you not to follow me."

"I know. But I—"

"Go back." He turned away from me. "Just go back."

I stood there, unsure what to do. He had never spoken to me this way. Andrew had held me through the worst nights, had carried me when I could not walk, and had never once raised his voice to me. Now he would not even look at me. The hurt rose sharply, but beneath it was resolve.

"No." I moved closer despite the way he held himself, ready to flee. "Andrew, what is wrong? Talk to me."

He started to walk away toward the water's edge. I grabbed his arm, my fingers digging into the muscle.

"I am not going anywhere. I am your wife. You have carried my grief for weeks. Let me carry yours. Share whatever this is with me."

He stopped. For a long moment, he just stood there, his arm tense under my hand. I closed my eyes. *Adonai, please show me how to help him. Give me the right words to say.*

"Tell me." I moved my hand from his arm to his shoulder. "I can bear this. Let me be strong for you."

He jerked away and wiped his face roughly with his forearm. "Do you know what it was like? Rushing back to that camp and finding you gone? Hearing the news that you were near death and had lost the baby? Having to track you like you were livestock that had wandered off?" A horrible laugh escaped him. "And when I finally found you in Arimathea, you barely looked at me. You just lay there staring at nothing, and our son was already in the ground."

He sank to the sand, hands pressed against his face.

"I never saw him, Anna. Not once. Not his face, not his hands, nothing. He was my son, and I do not know what he looked like. If he had your eyes or mine. If his hair was dark or light. Nothing."

I kneeled beside him in the cold sand. The water lapped at the shore behind us. The smell of rot was thick in my throat, mixing with the salt air and the sound of his breathing. I laid my hand against his back, feeling the muscles knotted beneath his tunic. How many nights had he lain beside me, holding this? How many times had he swallowed down his pain so he could carry mine instead?

"I am so sorry. I am sorry for not realizing—"

"I should have been there. I should have insisted that I stay close by and not go off to teach. If I had been there, I might have tasted the water first. I might have known the spring was bad. I might have stopped you from drinking it. Our son would still be alive."

His whole body was shaking, the regret he had been carrying alone for weeks finally given voice. I wrapped my arms around him, but his words echoed in my ears. *I might have stopped you from drinking it.* The water had tasted strange, slightly wrong, and I had drunk it anyway because I was so hot and so thirsty and so tired of being pregnant in the August heat. The leather skin warm in my hand, that bitter edge against my tongue. I had ignored it. Ignored the whisper of warning and swallowed it anyway.

"The water tasted wrong," I whispered. "I knew the spring was bad, and I drank it anyway. Oh, Andrew. I am so sorry! I should have known better. I should have protected our baby." Cold flooded through me, tears sliding down my face.

"No, you could not have known. No one knew. You were not the only one who drank it."

"But I noticed. I tasted it, and I ignored—" I tried to pull away.

"Stop." He gripped my shoulders. "This is not your fault. It was never your fault. Do you hear me? You did nothing wrong."

"I hear you." A gust of wind blew in from the water, lifting my hair and drying the tears on my cheeks. "It is not your fault either. You obeyed when Jesus sent you. You came back as soon as you knew."

We sat there in silence while the waves lapped steadily against the shore. Andrew stared at the dark water, his jaw clenched, and I sat with my arms wrapped around myself, remorse and absolution warring in equal measure in my heart. We were both trapped in the same terrible place, replaying moments we could not change, torturing ourselves with what we should have done differently. He should have been there. I should have paid attention. Our son should be alive.

But he was not, and no amount of guilt would bring him back.

"They made me hold him," I said, my mind returning to the moment I had held my son for the first and only time. "I did not want to. But Salome put him in my arms and told me I needed to see him." I swallowed against the tightness in my throat. "So I did."

Andrew stared at me, his eyes filled with pain and longing.

"He had long fingers. Fisherman's fingers. Like yours."

"He did?"

"Yes. They were so small but already long, like they were meant to hold nets and mend lines." I tried to smile, but my mouth would not obey. "He would have been a fisherman like his father."

"Anna." His voice broke on my name.

"There was a dimple. Just a hint of one on his left cheek. I kept looking at it, wondering if it would have deepened when he smiled, if he would have had your smile." Tears gathered on my lower lashes, but I kept going. "His nose was yours. The shape of it. And his cheekbones. High, like mine. He was so small and perfect. He was beautiful. I should have told you before now. I am sorry I did not."

Andrew's hands came up to cover his face, and his shoulders shook with silent sobs.

I wrapped my arms around him and held on while he wept, his grief finally given permission to exist.

We sat like that for a long time until the sobs eased and his breathing steadied, and he finally lifted his head. His eyes were red and swollen, his face ravaged, but the terrible burden seemed to have eased.

"Thank you," he whispered. "Thank you for telling me now."

He put his arm around me, and I laid my head against his chest, hearing his heart beating against my cheek. "I watched James tonight. Holding Zebedee. Looking at him as if he were seeing a miracle. I will never have that. I will never hold my son." He drew a shaky breath. "The pain will never leave me. I will learn to live with it somehow. But at least now I know what he looked like. At least I have that."

I took his hand. "Jonah will always be our son. That will never change."

"No," Andrew said quietly. "It will not."

"Jesus told me two things tonight." I paused, watching his face.

He smiled briefly. "Tell me. But only if it is something good."

"It is. He said we will see Jonah again. One day, in a place where there is no more death or mourning or pain, we will hold him. He waits for us there, Andrew. You will see his face. You will hold him."

Andrew went very still. "He said this?"

"He did. He said Jonah knows us. That our love for him echoes into eternity. We will see him again."

A long breath escaped him, and fresh tears came, but these were softer somehow, as if the ice inside him had begun to melt. We sat in silence, the water lapping at the shore, his hand gripping mine.

"And the second?" he asked.

My heart began to race. I drew a breath, feeling the promise swell inside me again, warm and impossible and terrifying all at once.

"We will have another child. A daughter. He said to name her after my mother."

For a long moment, Andrew just stared at me. "A daughter?" He spoke so softly the words were almost lost in the sound of the waves.

"Sarah." I nodded.

"A daughter." Wonder broke across his face like first light touching dark water, then disappeared just as quickly. "What if we lose her too?"

The air left my lungs. Unbidden, images flooded my mind of another pregnancy, another birth, another body growing cold in my arms. I would not survive it. I would not walk through that darkness again and come out whole. The thought of hoping, of daring to love another child, of watching my belly swell and feeling life move inside me only to lose it all again. My lungs would not fill.

But beneath the terror, as steadfast as the water moving against the shore, was Jesus's promise. He had spoken Sarah's name with such certainty, had looked at me with such conviction, that even now, sitting in cold sand with exhaustion making my bones ache and fear making my hands shake, the flame still burned. I chose to believe.

"We will not lose her." I covered his hand with both of mine, holding it against my belly where Sarah would one day grow. "Andrew, Jesus told me this. He does not lie. He does not give false hope. If he says we will have a daughter, then we will have a daughter."

"But Jonah—"

"Was not a mistake. And he was not a punishment." The words came from deep within, taking shape on my tongue. "He was our son. He always will be. But his death does not mean Sarah cannot live. Grief and hope can live together."

Andrew closed his eyes, and a single tear slipped down his cheek, catching the first light of dawn where it had touched the water with fingers of pale gold.

"I want to believe you."

"Then believe. Believe with me. Choose to hope even when it terrifies you." My voice shook on the words, and the tremor ran through my whole body, the cold that had seeped into my legs from sitting so long on the damp sand, the ache in my joints and the grit of salt and tears on my skin. "It terrifies me, but I choose to hope. I cannot carry this promise alone, Andrew. I need you to hope with me."

He looked at me for a long moment, and in the growing

light, every line of this long night showed in his face, the salt-stained paths down his cheeks, the shadows beneath his eyes that spoke of grief carried too long alone. Then slowly, his fingers spread wider against my belly, his palm pressing warm through the cool linen, the calluses rough against the fabric.

"Sarah," he whispered, and the name sounded like a prayer on his lips.

CHAPTER 19

Judea, November, 31 AD

We had been traveling for nearly a month since leaving Capernaum, moving south through small villages and olive groves heavy with ripening fruit. The days had settled back into the familiar rhythm of the road.

The village clung to the hillside in terraces of pale limestone, the houses built from the same golden stone as the earth beneath them, as if they had grown from the ground itself rather than been raised by human hands. Olive groves marched in silvered rows down the slope, ancient trunks gnarled and twisted with age. The air was thick with the smell of crushed olives and fresh-pressed oil that coated the back of my throat like incense, mixed with dust and woodsmoke from cooking fires. The midday sun warmed the stones beneath our feet, pleasant after the cool of the morning road.

When we crested the final rise, the sound reached us first, children's voices as high and bright as bird calls, the rhythmic *thud* of olives hitting stretched canvas, women singing in harmony while they worked, old songs whose words I did not know but whose rhythms spoke of abundance and gratitude and seasons turning as they always had. The warmth of midday clung to the stones, radiating up through my sandals, and sweat had dried on my face and neck, leaving my skin tight with salt and grime from the road.

Children ran between the trees with woven baskets slung over small shoulders, their bare feet silent on the earth, their tunics stained from handling ripe fruit. Women moved among the branches, hands quick and sure, pulling olives free from stems heavy with fruit and dropping them into baskets that grew heavier with each passing moment. Men climbed wooden ladders propped against silver-green branches, shaking them until olives rained down like hail upon canvas sheets spread beneath, the sound of fruit striking fabric a steady percussion beneath the singing.

The village elder appeared when he saw us approaching, wiping oil-dark hands on his tunic, leaving smears of purple-black across the linen. His face was as brown as old leather, creased with years of sun and labor, and when he smiled, his eyes nearly disappeared into the folds. Oil darkened his forearms to the elbows and spattered his chest. "No travelers leave hungry when the olives are ripe. You will stay. We have food, wine, and music tonight. You will feast with us."

Jesus inclined his head, a smile touching the corners of his mouth. "We accept with gratitude."

I looked at Andrew and found him already watching me, dimples carved deep in his cheeks, his eyes bright with anticipation. A whole evening stretched before us—feast and music, rest instead of road dust, joy instead of crowds with their demands.

"This will be good," he said, his hand finding mine.

It was.

By midday, I had been conscripted into the harvest itself. A woman named Leah, round-faced and as sturdy as an olive tree herself, with arms thick from years of work and a voice that carried across the grove, handed me a basket and pointed to the low branches. "You look strong enough. Start there and work your way up."

I was uncertain this was praise.

The work proved harder than it had appeared from a distance. The basket was heavy even empty, woven reed rough against my hip where it rested. Olives hid themselves among the leaves, and I had to move branches to find them, the leaves smooth and cool on one side, slightly fuzzy on the other, releasing their scent when my hands disturbed them. The ripe ones burst when I plucked them, staining my fingers, the juice sticky and bitter when I accidentally touched my lips. My shoulders ached from reaching overhead, muscles burning across my upper back and down my arms, but it was a good ache that spoke of useful labor. Sweat trickled down my spine beneath my tunic and gathered at my temples, and dust from the shaken branches coated my skin.

But the simple rhythm satisfied. Reach into the leaves, pushing them aside with the back of my hand. Find the fruit heavy with oil, dark and firm. Pluck it clean from the stem with a slight twist. Drop it into the basket with a soft *thud* of olive against olive, the sound changing as the basket filled, becoming duller, more muffled. Reach, pluck, drop. Reach, pluck, drop. My hands remembered their own capacity for work, fingers nimble despite the stains, moving with increasing speed as the rhythm became natural, creating usefulness from what the earth provided.

Andrew appeared as I was starting my third basket, his face streaked with oil and dust in patterns, his tunic soaked dark with sweat and clinging to his chest and shoulders. He was grinning like a boy who had stolen honey cakes. "You are covered in stains."

I examined my hands, purple to the wrists, and beneath my fingernails were crescents of dark that would take days to fade, oil worked into the creases of my palms. "So are you."

"I have been at the pressing stone." He showed me his hands, slick with oil up to his elbows, gleaming gold-green in the afternoon sun, the smell of fresh-pressed oil rising from his skin sharp and peppery. "Apparently, I have good shoulders for it."

"You do have good shoulders."

"Do I?" He stepped closer, still grinning. "What else?"

"I will not feed your pride, Andrew bar Jonah."

"Why not? I am very hungry." Before I could protest, he reached out and tucked a strand of hair behind my ear, leaving a smear of oil along my jaw. "There. Now we match."

"Andrew!"

But he was already walking away, whistling some tuneless melody, his shoulders—those good shoulders—shaking with laughter. I threw an olive at him. It bounced off his back with a soft *thump*. He did not even turn around, just raised one hand in acknowledgment and kept walking, his gait easy and loose.

I picked another olive and went back to work, smiling despite the oil on my face.

The afternoon sun was still strong when Leah found me again, my fourth basket nearly full and my arms quaking with exhaustion. "Enough. The men are competing now. Come watch them make fools of themselves."

She led me to the pressing area, where a crowd had gathered, their voices rising in laughter and encouragement. Andrew and Peter stood on opposite sides of the massive grinding stone, both stripped to the waist, their skin gleaming with oil and sweat, their jaws set with that stubborn brotherly determination that would see them both injured before either admitted defeat. The stone itself was enormous, taller than a man and polished by generations of hands and shoulders, its surface dark with absorbed oil that made it gleam in the afternoon light.

"Ready?" someone called.

"Ready?" Peter threw his arms wide, his chest already heaving with anticipation. "I could push this stone with one hand! My little brother here will need both and still lose! I was born to do this!"

"You were born loud," Andrew said, his voice calm despite the slight tremor in his hands as he gripped the stone's edge. "Not strong."

The crowd roared with laughter, voices bouncing off the hillside and the stone houses.

At the signal, both brothers threw their weight against the stone, muscles bunching, their feet sliding in the green-black liquid that pooled beneath the press, their faces contorting with effort. The stone groaned like a living thing and turned, slowly at first, grinding against its bed with a deep scraping sound that vibrated up through the ground beneath my feet then faster as they found their rhythm, their bodies moving in opposition, pushing and releasing in a pattern as old as the village itself.

"Move, little brother!" Peter shouted, his face going red

then purple with exertion, the veins standing out in his neck and forehead. "Show them what a fisherman can do!"

Andrew did not waste breath on words. He simply pushed harder, his jaw locked until the muscles jumped at the hinge, sweat running in rivers down his back and chest, pooling at the waistband of his tunic, every muscle in his shoulders and arms standing out beneath the skin like carved stone. The oil made his skin gleam, highlighting every shift and flex of muscle, every straining tendon. His breath came in harsh grunts with each push, his feet planted wide for balance, toes digging into the slick earth for purchase.

The crowd was clapping now in rhythm with the stone's turning, voices rising in a wordless chant of encouragement. The stone picked up speed, moving faster than seemed possible for something so massive, the grinding sound becoming a continuous roar. Andrew's feet slipped once in the oil, but he caught himself without breaking rhythm, his balance shifting, weight redistributing. Peter was breathing like a bellows, his earlier confidence giving way to fierce concentration, his whole body shaking with effort.

Then Peter's foot went out from under him completely. He went down hard in a puddle of oil with a wet slap, cursing, and the stone ground to a halt, the sudden silence almost shocking after the continuous noise.

The crowd erupted in cheers.

Andrew stood there gasping, hands on his knees, sweat and oil dripping from his hair and chin to darken the earth beneath him. He looked over at his brother sprawled in the oil and smiled, his teeth very white in his oil-streaked face. Then he reached down and hauled Peter to his feet, their hands sliding against each other.

"I won," Andrew said between breaths.

"I slipped! That oil was everywhere—the whole stone was slick as a fish! If I had not slipped, I would have—"

"But you did."

Peter shoved him, but he was laughing, his hands leaving prints on Andrew's chest. "Next time, little brother! Next time I will push that stone so fast you will not even see me move!"

"Who wants to try next?" someone called from the crowd.

"I will." Judas stepped forward, stripping off his outer tunic to reveal a body slighter than the brothers', his muscles defined but not as heavy, built for endurance rather than raw strength.

A murmur ran through the crowd. Judas positioned himself at the stone, rolling his shoulders once, twice, before gripping the worn edge, his hands small against the massive wheel.

A villager built like an ox took the opposite side, grinning, his chest as broad as a door and arms as thick as roof beams, oil already coating his skin from an earlier turn. "Ready, friend?"

Judas nodded, his face settling into concentration.

The crowd cheered as they began, voices rising in encouragement. I clapped along, calling out, "Come on, Judas!"

The stone turned, but the villager's strength was clear from the first push. Judas pushed hard, his face going red and then white with effort, the tendons in his neck standing out like ropes, but the stone moved faster on the villager's side, grinding relentlessly against Judas's resistance, the difference in their power obvious to everyone watching. Within moments, it was over, the villager barely winded, and Judas stepped back and raised his hands in surrender, his chest heaving, sweat streaming down his face.

"Good effort!" someone called, and others laughed good-naturedly.

Judas pulled his tunic back on, shaking his head at himself but not looking defeated, managing a smile. Our eyes met across the crowd, and I waved. He gave a rueful shrug as if to say "I tried" then disappeared back into the watching crowd.

Andrew made his way to where I stood watching, his chest still working hard, each breath visible. The late-afternoon sun turned the oil and sweat on his bare skin to molten gold, highlighting every line and curve of muscle. He smelled of crushed olives and clean sweat and exertion.

"Did you see?" he asked.

"I saw your brother slip in oil."

"After I was already winning."

"He slipped. That hardly counts as winning."

"It counts. I won." He wiped sweat from his face with his forearm, leaving clean streaks through the grime and oil, revealing skin beneath. "Are you impressed?"

"With your ability to make Peter fall on his backside? Immensely."

He grinned, dimples appearing in his cheeks. "Good. That was the whole point." He caught my hand, his palm still slick with oil, our fingers sliding together. "You did not cheer as loudly for me as you did for Judas."

"You had Peter doing enough of that."

"True." He laughed, the sound easy and unguarded. "Come. They are starting the feast."

Tables had been set up in the village square as the sun touched the western hills, painting everything in shades of gold and rose and deepening purple, simple boards laid across stones and covered with the fruits of their labor. Baskets of dark, dense bread that filled the belly sat beside bowls of cured olives prepared different ways: some crushed with garlic until the smell made my mouth water, others swimming in brine sharp with herbs, still others mixed with chopped onion and coriander. The oil itself, sharp and green and so fresh it burned the throat, filled clay vessels for dipping, and when you tore the bread and dragged it through the oil, it came away glistening and dripping. Someone had roasted vegetables over coals until the onions and garlic went sweet with fire, their skins charred and splitting to reveal soft flesh beneath, and the smell of them mingled with cumin-scented lentil stew that sent up steam in the cooling air. Wine flowed freely in earthenware cups, rougher than what I was accustomed to but honest and good, warming the chest as it went down and leaving a pleasant burn at the back of the throat. The scent of it all made my stomach clench with sudden hunger.

I sat between Andrew and Salome, eating until my body was heavy with satisfaction and that good exhaustion that comes from honest work. Around me, conversations wove and overlapped, laughter bubbling up and spilling over. Jesus was telling a story that made everyone nearby lean closer, their faces intent in the firelight that had been kindled as darkness fell. Tirzah sat with James, Zeb tucked against her shoulder, the baby's fist curled in sleep against her neck, his small mouth working, even in dreams, as if nursing.

"You look happy," Salome observed, refilling my cup, the wine splashing against the clay.

"I am." I turned the thought over in my mind, examining

it from all sides like a stone picked up from the road. "I am happy."

She patted my hand, her palm warm and dry and rough with work against my stained fingers. "Good. You should be."

As darkness settled over the village like a cloak, stars appearing one by one overhead in the deepening blue, someone brought out a drum. Then a flute. The music started slow and simple, just rhythm and breath, the drum a heartbeat and the flute a voice above it, then built into wildness that made people begin to clap in time, hands striking together in rhythm. A space cleared in the center of the square, feet scuffing the earth smooth.

"Dancing!" Tirzah appeared beside me, flushed with wine and laughter, her eyes alight in the firelight. "Come on!"

She pulled me into the circle of women forming around the fire, and my heart lifted like a bird taking wing. I had danced at my wedding—my first time, my body finally free to move—and my feet remembered what joy felt like, remembered the rhythm and the release. The drum found a steady beat I felt in my chest, in my belly, in the soles of my feet. The flute joined, its clear notes weaving through the rhythm like thread through cloth, coming together in patterns that spoke without words.

The steps came naturally. Stamp and turn. Clap. Repeat. My body knew the rhythm even if my mind did not know all the words to the songs the women sang, voices rising in harmony around me. The linen of my tunic swirled around my legs with each turn, the fabric cool against my heated skin. My feet moved light across the earth, and the music pounded in my chest like a second heartbeat, driving everything else away until there was only movement and rhythm and breath and the other women spinning around me, their faces bright with joy in the firelight.

"Look at you!" Tirzah shouted over the music, laughing and breathless, her face shining with sweat.

The dance spun faster. The drum picked up speed. The flute climbed higher. Someone grabbed my hands, and we whirled until the flames became streaks of light, until the watching faces blurred into a circle of gold. The music carried me, the women's voices rising around me in songs I was learning to know, songs about harvest and blessing and abundance. Sweat dampened my back beneath my tunic, but I did not care. My body remembered—that I was strong, that I could move with grace, that my feet could dance, that my lungs could fill and empty with ease, that joy was mine to take.

Across the open space, the men had formed their own circle, stomping and clapping in their own rhythm, their voices deeper beneath the women's. I caught glimpses of Andrew between the spinning women, trying to keep pace with the other men, his feet too heavy, always half a beat behind the rhythm, his face set in concentration. Then he stopped trying altogether. He simply stood there at the edge of the circle, watching me dance, his expression open and unguarded in the firelight.

When the music finally slowed and the circles broke apart, people breathing hard and laughing, I found my way to him, breathless and smiling, my heart still racing in my chest. He was watching me with that look on his face— wonder and hunger both, his eyes dark and intent.

"You gave up," I said, trying to catch my breath.

"I was making a fool of myself."

"You were celebrating."

"I was stepping on everyone's feet." He smiled, reaching out to tuck a strand of sweat-dampened hair behind my ear. "But watching you was better anyway."

"You should learn. Here." I took his hands, positioning them properly, his palms warm and slightly rough against mine. "It is just rhythm. Feel the beat."

The drum started again, slower now, a steady pulse like a heartbeat. I tried to show him the basic steps—left, right, turn—but his feet remained stubbornly clumsy, always going in the wrong direction, his weight shifting at the wrong moments.

"No, like this—" I demonstrated, but he was laughing too hard to follow, his chest shaking with it.

"I am hopeless."

"You are good with stones. I am good at dancing."

He smiled at the memory, dimples deep in his cheeks. "You were terrible at skipping stones."

"And you are terrible at this. We are even."

"Perfectly matched." He caught my waist despite my protests about proper form, pulling me against him. "I will stay with my strengths."

I nestled close, his hand at my waist, moving together with no attempt at proper steps, just swaying in rhythm to the drum. Around us, other couples danced with actual skill, feet finding the patterns, bodies moving in unison. We did not care. His heartbeat slowed against my chest as we moved, strong beneath my palm. I rested my forehead against his shoulder, breathing in salt and clean linen beneath the day's oil and work, feeling his breath stir my hair.

"Anna."

"Mm?"

His lips moved against my hair. "I had forgotten."

"Forgotten what?"

"How to do work just for the joy of it. No mission, no teaching. Just harvesting olives and dancing badly with my wife."

I touched his face, his beard rough and slightly oily beneath my palm. "You remembered today."

"You reminded me." He turned his head to kiss my palm, his lips warm against my skin. "Come. I want to show you the view from the hill."

He led me away from the square, through the olive groves where the trees stood in patient rows, their branches heavy with remaining fruit that hung dark against the night sky. The ground was soft beneath my feet, covered in fallen leaves that rustled with each step and the canvas sheets laid out for tomorrow's work. The air was cooler here away from the fires, carrying the smell of earth and growing things and the distant scent of smoke. I noticed feverfew growing wild at the base of one ancient tree, its white flowers luminous in the starlight, almost glowing. I would gather some in the morning for headaches.

We climbed the hillside, our breath coming harder with the ascent, until we reached a flat outcropping of rock that overlooked the valley below. In the village, fires glowed like fallen stars, warm points of light against the darkness. The music drifted up to us, faint and sweet, already becoming a memory, the drum's pulse barely audible, the voices blending into a single thread of sound.

Andrew sat and pulled me down beside him, his arm coming around my shoulders, his body warm against the cooling stone. "Better?"

"Much." I leaned into his warmth, feeling his heat seep

into me where the night air had chilled my skin. "Although I was enjoying watching you make a fool of yourself."

"I was not making a fool of myself. I was celebrating."

"By pushing rocks and dancing like you had never heard music before?"

"Exactly so." He was quiet for a moment, his fingers tracing absent patterns on my shoulder, light touches that raised goose bumps on my arms. Above us, the first stars had multiplied into thousands, sharp white points against the black. "Do you know what made me happiest today?"

"Beating Peter at stone-pushing?"

"Besides that." His voice turned serious, losing its playful edge. "Watching you pick olives. Your hands were stained purple, and your basket was full. You were doing it just because you could, not because anyone needed healing or help. Just because your body was strong enough."

My eyes stung unexpectedly, hot behind my lids. "I had not thought of it that way."

"I did. I kept watching you reach into those branches, your hands filling the basket, and all I could think was how many years you could not." He turned my face toward his, his thumb gentle on my jaw, his palm cradling my cheek. "All those years your body would not let you. And now look at you."

I kissed him then, tasting wine and olives and happiness on his lips, feeling the warmth of his mouth against mine, his beard rough against my face. When we broke apart, his eyes were dark in the starlight, reflecting the distant fires.

"Come," he said, his voice rough and low. "We should go back to our tent."

Our tent stood at the edge of the camp, removed enough for privacy, the canvas pale against the darkness. Andrew lit the small lamp with a coal carried from the fire, and the space filled with warm light that turned the canvas walls golden, chasing away the shadows. He turned to me, and the lamplight caught in his eyes.

"Anna." My name was a question and a promise, rough with want.

I answered by reaching for the ties of his tunic, my stained fingers fumbling with the knots, pulling them loose. He caught my hands, stilling them, and brought them to his lips. He kissed each fingertip, one by one, tasting the bitter oil and salt and work, his lips soft and warm, his breath hot against my skin. Then his hands found the ties of my tunic, and we undressed each other slowly, carefully, savoring each moment, each revelation of skin, the lamplight turning our bodies to gold.

Afterward, we lay tangled together on our sleeping mat, the lamp burning low and sending shadows dancing across the canvas, neither of us ready for sleep. The air in the tent was warm and close, smelling of oil and salt and us. His hand rested warm against my back, his thumb moving in slow circles, barely touching, raising paths of sensation.

"Tell me a secret," he said, his voice soft and drowsy.

"What?"

"A secret. Something I do not know about you. Something small."

I thought for a moment, my mind drifting. "When I was young, I convinced one of the servants to take me to Jerusalem. I wanted to see where Abba worked, to watch the Sanhedrin. I thought if I could just see it, I would understand why he was always there instead of home."

"Did you make it?"

"Deborah found out before we even reached the gates."

The memory made me smile against his chest. "She marched me home and told me that little girls who snuck away ended up sold to caravans. I believed her for years."

Andrew chuckled, the sound vibrating through his chest beneath my cheek. "I can picture it. You, small and determined, certain you could make it all the way to Jerusalem."

"I was always certain I could do things I should not attempt." I was quiet for a moment, my fingers tracing patterns on his chest. "I missed him. He was always gone, and I thought if I could just see where he went, maybe I would understand why."

"I can understand that."

"What about you?" I lifted my head to look at him, his face soft in the lamplight. "Tell me a secret."

He was quiet for a long moment, his hand stilling on my back. "When I was young, I was terrified of the water."

"You? A fisherman?"

"I nearly drowned once. Fell off the boat when I was three or four. My father pulled me out, but after that, I would not go near the lake." He smiled at the memory, but his eyes were distant. "Simon used to tease me mercilessly. Called me a landlubber, said I should become a scribe instead."

"What changed?"

"My father made me get back in the boat. Every day, no matter how much I cried or fought. Eventually, I learned to swim. Then I learned to fish." His hand resumed its gentle movement on my back. "But I still remember that fear. How the water closed over my head, and I could not tell which way was up."

"I will always show you the way." I kissed him, tasting the words on his lips. He pulled me close, and there was only this

—his breath against my skin, my name whispered in the darkness, the lamp burning low until it guttered out and left us in warm blackness.

"Anna," he whispered.

"Hmm?"

"We should harvest olives more often."

"Yes. We should."

CHAPTER 20

Bethany, January, 32 AD

Martha's lentils were burning.

The smell drifted across the courtyard, acrid and sharp, catching at the back of my throat. I sat grinding cumin in the weak winter sunlight, the pestle warm in my hand from friction, the stone bench cold beneath me even through my tunic. The air held the kind of chill that belongs to Judea in winter—not bitter but penetrating, finding its way through wool and linen to settle against skin. My fingers were already stiff from the morning's cold, and the grinding helped warm them, down and around, down and around, the rhythm soothing even as my mind wandered.

I knew I should call out a warning before the whole pot was ruined. But Martha's voice erupted from the kitchen first, rolling across the courtyard like a wave crashing against stone.

336

"Lazarus! Did I or did I not ask you to watch the pot?"

Lazarus sprawled near the cistern as if he had not a care in the world, his long legs stretched out before him and his face tilted toward the sun, soaking up what little warmth it offered. The pale winter light turned his skin golden, highlighting the laugh lines around his closed eyes.

"You asked me to stir it," he called back, not bothering to open his eyes. "I stirred it."

"Stirring implies more than one motion of the spoon!"

"You did not specify frequency."

I laughed. For three days, I had listened to Martha and Lazarus trade barbs, and it never grew old. It reminded me of Deborah, the way she had loved me through correction and complaint, her sharp words like wool—rough but meant to keep me warm.

Martha muttered about brothers and millstones and the bottom of the sea, her voice drifting out through the kitchen doorway along with smoke and the smell of scorched lentils. A moment later, Lazarus rose and crossed to the bench across from me, ducking under the low branch of the fig tree, its bare winter branches stark against the pale sky. He settled onto the wood with a sigh, stretching his legs until his sandals nearly touched mine. Worn smooth from years of use, the bench groaned beneath his weight, the wood silvered with age.

"She loves me," he said. "Deeply. The yelling is how I know."

"Then you must be the most beloved man in Judea."

He grinned, the lines around his eyes deepening, his entire face transforming with mirth.

"You are grinding that cumin into dust," Lazarus observed.

The mortar sat heavy in my lap, the stone warm against my thighs through the fabric. He was right. The seeds had become powder so fine it would blow away at the first breath of wind. My fingers were stained yellow-brown where I gripped the pestle, the sharp scent clinging to my skin and coating the inside of my nose until I could taste it at the back of my throat. The task was a way to keep my hands busy while my thoughts wandered where they would.

"Just thinking."

"That way lies trouble." Lazarus shook his head, his expression grave. "I avoid it when I can."

"Is that why you burned your sister's lentils?"

"I did not burn them." He held up one hand in protest, palm out. "I simply let them reach a deeper color than she intended. There is a difference."

"What difference is that?"

"One is misfortune. The other is intention."

I laughed again, and Lazarus grinned as though he had accomplished great work. He stood and stretched, his shadow falling long across the courtyard stones, and sighed as though bearing the weight of the world. "I should go make peace before she poisons my portion tonight. Martha remembers every wrong like a tax collector tallies debts."

Matthew sat near the cistern and mended a sandal strap, his head bent low over his work, fingers moving with the quick precision of someone who had once worked with numbers and now worked with leather and thread. He did not look up, but his mouth twitched.

Lazarus wandered back toward the kitchen, and a moment later, the sharp edge left Martha's voice, her scolding giving way despite herself.

A dove called from somewhere beyond the courtyard

wall, its song low and mournful in the cooling air, the sound echoing off the stone. My hands slowed, the grinding forgotten, the pestle resting idle in the mortar.

There were Pharisees among us now, men with scrolls who watched and wrote down every word Jesus spoke, their faces sharp with disapproval rather than wonder, their eyes narrow and calculating. Last week on the road, there had been a man with rage carved into every line of his face as he bent for a stone, and I had watched the arc of it through the air, my breath caught, my legs locked beneath me. It struck the dirt at Jesus's feet and not his skull, but the shouts followed me into sleep. I woke in the dark with my heart hammering and the taste of fear bitter on my tongue.

But beneath the fear lay hope. The name Jesus had spoken over my empty womb. The promise I carried the way winter ground carries seed, waiting for spring.

Sarah.

My hand pressed against my belly, flat and waiting beneath my tunic. Just for a breath, I let myself imagine. A daughter who would grow there, who would move inside me and kick against my ribs and be born into my waiting arms. The wanting was sharp and immediate, lodged somewhere deep, a hole that waited to be filled.

If God willed it.

Zeb's cry cut through the afternoon, high and insistent.

Tirzah crossed the courtyard with him balanced on her hip. At three months old, he had grown fat and loud and certain that the world owed him constant attention, and from the look on Tirzah's face—jaw tight, eyes slightly wild —he had been making that opinion known for some time. His fist tangled in her braid, and she was trying to extract it without making him cry harder, her fingers working at the knot he had created. Her tunic was stained with milk down the front, white streaks dried into the blue linen, and there were shadows beneath her eyes that spoke of interrupted sleep and endless feeding.

Tirzah dropped onto the bench beside me with a sigh that seemed to come from her bones. The wood creaked under the added weight, and Zeb's crying subsided to a wet, hiccuping complaint, his small chest heaving. Her body pressed warm against my side despite the winter air, and the smell of milk and sweat and herb-scented oil rose from her hair where it had come loose from her braid.

"He has opinions today." She tried again to free her braid from his grip, wincing. "Strong ones."

"He always has opinions."

"Yes, but today they involve my hair and his apparently firm belief that it belongs to him." She finally freed his fingers from her braid, pulling a few hairs loose with them, and bounced him gently against her chest, patting his back in that automatic rhythm mothers develop. "Your aunt is no help at all, little one. She just sits there grinding spices and looking thoughtful."

My hand found his cheek, as soft as spring petals and damp with tears, hot from crying. He turned toward the touch, rooting with his mouth open, seeking.

"May I?"

Tirzah passed him over without hesitation, her arms probably grateful for the reprieve. Zeb nestled against my shoulder, solid and warm. His small body molded against mine, fitting into the hollow of my collarbone as if it had been made for him. He smelled of milk and sleep and that baby smell, clean and slightly sweet, like bread dough rising.

I closed my eyes and let him be mine just for a moment.

His chest moved against me, each breath a tiny expansion and release. My hand pressed against his small back, feeling the delicate architecture of ribs and spine beneath skin and cloth.

Jonah had never breathed.

Tears fell onto my cheeks.

Tirzah's hand found mine, and she sat with me while I wept. Grief came without asking sometimes, arriving like rain in the night.

I wiped my face with the back of my free hand, but the wetness still clung to my lashes, blurring my vision. Zeb shifted against me, oblivious to my tears, his small fist working against my shoulder.

"He should have lived," Tirzah said quietly.

"Yes. He should have."

We sat there together, the baby between us, the winter sun weak on our backs.

Two names sat in my heart. Jonah who was gone. Sarah who might yet come.

I drew a slow breath and wiped my cheeks with my palm, feeling the salt and wetness cold on my skin. My hand patted Zeb's back in that same rhythm Tirzah had used, and he nestled closer to me, his breathing evening out. I met Tirzah's eyes.

"He is easy to hold."

"I know how fortunate I am to have him, even if he is a little tyrant who screams if I set him down for even a moment." But she smiled as she said it, tired and soft and full of love despite the exhaustion written in every line of her face. She rubbed at the milk stain on her tunic, gave up when the mark refused to budge, and let her hands fall into her lap. "I am glad you are here, Anna, truly. After everything..."

She did not finish, but she did not need to. The

awkwardness that had stood between us in the weeks after Zebedee's birth had eased slowly, worn away by time and proximity and the simple fact of being together until we could sit like this without either of us apologizing or flinching. She no longer said she was sorry for having a living son, and I no longer looked away when she spoke of him.

"I am glad too."

Zeb grabbed a fistful of my tunic and tried to stuff it into his mouth, his gums working determinedly at the fabric, leaving wet marks. I laughed, and I shifted him to my other shoulder. Tirzah reached over to rescue the cloth from his grip before he could soak it completely through with his drool.

Andrew appeared from the house with a water jar balanced on his shoulder, the clay dark with moisture, condensation beading on its surface. He set it down near the cistern with a soft *thump* then crossed to where we sat. His shadow fell across us both, blocking what little warmth the sun offered. He looked at my face, still wet, still blotchy from crying, then kissed the top of my head, his lips soft against my hair, before reaching for Zeb.

"My turn."

The baby passed from my arms to his, and I felt the cold where he had been, the sudden absence of his small weight. Andrew settled him against his chest with one hand cradling the small head, his fingers spread wide and gentle against the dark fuzz of hair. His smile came then, dimples carving deep into his cheeks. "How are you faring today, little fish? Growing bigger every time I see you."

Zeb yawned, his mouth opening impossibly wide for such a small face, and grabbed Andrew's thumb with both hands, his grip surprisingly strong.

"He knows you," Tirzah said.

"Of course he does." Andrew tickled Zeb's chin gently, and the baby's eyes widened, focusing on Andrew's face. "We are old friends, are we not?"

Tirzah laughed, the sound lighter than it had been. "Old friends who see each other every day."

After a moment, Andrew handed Zeb back to Tirzah then leaned down and kissed my forehead, his breath stirring the loose strands at my temple. The gesture was simple, ordinary, but it calmed the restlessness in my chest. He smelled of clean sweat and worn wool and work. He returned to his task without another word, and I watched him go, memorizing the line of his shoulders, the way he moved with that easy strength.

By afternoon, the kitchen had claimed me. Martha and I worked shoulder to shoulder in the cramped space, the air thick with the smell of fish and garlic and heat radiating from the clay oven, the warmth of it almost oppressive after the cold courtyard. My fingers still ached from washing vegetables in the cistern's cold water earlier, the joints stiff and sore, but the oven drove the chill out slowly. Loose strands of hair stuck to my temples beneath my headscarf, damp with sweat despite the winter day outside.

Martha had been up since before dawn. I had heard her in the darkness, the soft *thump* of the kneading board being set up, the scrape of the oven door opening, the splash of water being poured into vessels, the familiar sounds of a household coming to life. Now her knife flashed as she scaled fish, the blade catching what light filtered through the high window in bright flickers. The work had a rhythm to it, her hands moving with the certainty that came from years of doing this same task, day after day, feeding whoever came through her door.

Silver scales scattered across the work surface like tiny coins, some catching in the wood's grain, where they would have to be scraped out later with a fingernail, others falling to the floor, where they would stick to our sandals and be tracked through the whole house no matter how carefully we tried to clean them up afterward.

"More garlic," she said without looking up.

My hands were already sticky when I passed it to her, the oil and flour having worked themselves into every crease of my palms, under my fingernails, between my fingers. The low worktable forced me to hunch over my task, and my lower back ached from the constant bending, a dull throb that radiated up my spine. Smoke from the oven stung my eyes, making them water, and I blinked against it, turning my head to breathe clearer air.

But there was relief in the work despite the discomfort. It gave my hands purpose when my mind wanted to wander to dangerous places. My hands knew what to do even when my thoughts drifted.

From the main room came Jesus's voice, teaching. The words were indistinct through the stone wall, muffled by distance and the crackling of the oven fire, but the cadence reached me—the starts and stops, the pause when someone asked a question, the answering flow of explanation like water finding its course. The knife slowed in my hands. I leaned toward the doorway, straining to catch even a word or two.

Martha's hands slowed too. She leaned in the same direction, her knife stilling in her grip, her whole body straining toward his voice like a plant turning toward sun. Then she shook herself and went back to scaling fish, the blade moving again with renewed vigor.

"He is teaching about the kingdom." Her voice was quiet, almost to herself. "I heard him this morning while I was kneading the bread, before the sun was even up." The knife paused again, suspended over the fish. "The way he spoke of it—like something already here, already among us, not some distant promise but present and real."

She stared at the fish in front of her, but her eyes were unfocused, seeing something else entirely, some vision I could not share.

"You should go listen." I inclined my head toward the door. "Go."

Martha shook her head, the movement sharp and decisive. "Someone has to prepare the food." She resumed working, the knife moving with fierce determination, scales flying. "Mary is listening. That is enough."

"Is it?"

Martha looked at me, her eyes full of unshed tears, the lamplight catching in them. "It has to be."

I reached over and touched her hand, stilling it. "You love us well."

She went back to the fish, blinking hard, her lips pursed.

Martha's knife slipped, catching her thumb. A thin line of red welled up, bright against her olive skin. She pressed the cut against her apron and tried to keep working, but her hands were shaking, making the knife wobble in her grip.

She set the knife down carefully on the work surface.

"I want to sit at his feet too." Her voice broke on the words. "Just once. I want to hear his words without counting loaves or wondering if the fire needs tending or calculating how many fish we need to feed everyone. I want…" She wiped her eyes with the back of her hand, leaving a smear of fish oil across her cheek. "I just want to listen."

"Then go."

Martha looked at me, her mouth opening. "Someone has to make the dinner."

"I will make the dinner."

Martha stared at me. Her mouth opened then closed. She did not seem to know what to say, caught between desire and duty.

"Go," I said again, my voice firm.

"Mary should help you." She pulled off her apron and was through the doorway before I could say more, her footsteps quick on the stone. I followed as far as the doorway.

Jesus sat on the low bench near the window where the light fell strongest. Several disciples sat around him—Peter's broad shoulders blocking part of the view, John's dark head bent in concentration, the others in shadow. And there at his feet, seated on a cushion with her knees drawn up, was Mary.

Martha crossed the room, her bare feet silent on the swept floor. I stayed near the doorway, my hands still sticky with flour, my apron streaked with blood from the scaled fish.

"Mary."

Mary glanced up, her eyes taking a moment to focus, as if being pulled from deep water. "Hmm?"

"Could you help Anna finish the meal? I want to listen."

"Let me hear the rest first." Mary's eyes were already back on Jesus, her attention sliding away like oil on water.

Martha stood there, motionless. Her bleeding thumb pressed against her tunic, leaving a dark stain that spread slowly across the fabric. The flour still dusted her arms in white streaks. She had been weeping in the kitchen moments before, and her eyes were red and swollen.

Mary's attention was already back on Jesus, her face rapt. "Lord."

Jesus looked up, his eyes finding Martha's face.

Martha's voice shook. "Lord, do you not care that my sister has left me to serve alone?"

The room went silent, conversations dying mid-word, bodies going still.

"Tell her to help me."

Mary's head snapped up, her eyes wide with shock. Peter shifted on his bench, the wood protesting beneath his weight. John studied his hands as if he had never seen them before.

Jesus watched Martha for a long moment. Then he said her name. "Martha."

She stood straighter, her chin lifting, her shoulders pulling back.

"Martha." He said it again, softer now, and rose from the bench slowly. "You are anxious and troubled about many things. And I see you. I see how faithfully you serve and how hard you work."

Her hands loosened at her sides, the tension bleeding from her fingers.

"But there is only one thing worth being concerned about." His voice was still gentle, but there was steel beneath it now, the edge of truth that could not be denied. His eyes moved to Mary. "Mary has chosen the good portion, which will not be taken away from her."

Martha was silent for a long moment. The room waited with her, the silence heavy with what Jesus had said. Then she nodded, a single sharp movement of her head, and walked back toward the kitchen. Her footsteps were slow and steady on the stone floor, one foot in front of the other, back to the place she had come from.

I followed and found her standing at the worktable with one hand braced against the stone as though she needed it to hold herself upright.

"Martha."

"He is right," she mumbled. "Of course he is right. There is need of only one thing." She looked at me over her shoulder, and her face was pale. "But someone still has to make the dinner, Anna. Someone still has to do the work. And I do not know how to stop being the one who does it."

I took my place beside her. The knife found my hand again, though my hands were tired and my back ached, and I wanted to sit down. "Maybe you are not meant to stop. Maybe you serve him by serving them. By making sure there is bread and fish and a place to rest. That matters too."

"Does it?" She looked toward the doorway, where Jesus had resumed teaching. "He said she chose the better portion. He did not say mine was good. He said hers was better."

The words sat between us, as sharp and painful as the cut on her thumb, drawing blood.

"But he also said he sees you."

Martha nodded slowly, wiping her hands on her apron though they were past being clean, the fabric already stained beyond saving. "Yes. He did say that." She took a deep breath, held it, and let it out in a long, slow stream that seemed to carry some of the tension with it. "I suppose that will have to be enough for now." She snatched up the knife again, her grip tight. "The work still needs doing. And I am still the one who will do it."

"Let me help you finish."

She nodded and handed me a fish to scale, its body cold and slippery in my hands.

We worked side by side in silence while the light faded and the kitchen grew dim and cool, the heat from the oven slowly giving way to the winter evening pushing in through the high window, bringing the smell of cold stone and coming night. The knife moved in my hands. Scrape, rinse, set aside. Scrape, rinse, set aside. I scaled the fish and gutted them, their silvery bellies opening clean under the blade, revealing pink flesh within. The onions fell away in neat pieces under my knife, reduced to translucent slivers that would melt into the stew and disappear. Oil poured golden from the jar, catching what light remained. Martha tasted the stew, her face thoughtful, adjusted it with a pinch of salt from the dish, tasted again, and nodded her approval.

The bread came out of the oven at exactly the right moment—Martha had a sense for these things, some internal clock that told her when the crust had reached perfection— and the crust cracked as it cooled, releasing steam and that smell of yeast and heat and grain that meant someone cared enough to feed you. The kitchen filled with it, familiar and good, driving out the smell of burned lentils from earlier.

Through it all, Jesus's voice carried from the other room, offering words that fed a hunger the bread could not touch. I could not make out what he said, the words lost in distance and stone, but I heard him teaching. Always teaching.

My hands worked. My heart listened. I was Martha in the kitchen with hands stained dark from onion and fish, back aching, fingers stiff from cold water. But I was Mary in my heart, too, longing to sit at his feet and drink in every word. The question was not which one to be. The question was how to be both.

When the meal was finally ready, we carried the food out together, platters balanced on our hips and in our arms. The light had faded to that soft purple-blue of winter twilight, the color of a bruise, and lamps were being lit one by one, small flames pushing back the darkness.

Mary rose from Jesus's feet to help us serve. When she took a platter from Martha, their eyes met across the clay dish still warm from the kitchen.

"I am sorry," Mary said, her voice low. "I did not mean to—"

"I know." Martha's voice was gentle, the anger gone. "It is not your fault. He is right. You chose what was needed." She touched Mary's cheek briefly, her flour-dusted fingers leaving a pale streak on her sister's skin. "I am glad one of us did."

Mary's eyes filled with tears. She nodded, unable to speak, and Martha pulled her close for just a moment, their foreheads touching.

"Does this mean you will both help with the dishes?" Lazarus asked from the doorway, his timing as impeccable as always.

Martha laughed despite herself, the sound surprised and genuine, and Mary's tears turned to laughter that shook her shoulders. Lazarus crossed to them and pulled both his sisters into his arms, one on each side.

Jesus blessed the food, his hands raised over the platters, his voice filled with the ancient words of thanksgiving, and the meal began.

Empty platters found their way back to the kitchen as people finished eating. Martha followed with the wine jars, the clay heavy in her arms.

"Go listen," she said when we set everything down on the work surface. "I can finish here."

I could see through the doorway that they were gathering closer to Jesus now that the meal was done, sitting on benches and cushions, rearranging themselves to hear better. Andrew glanced toward the kitchen, looking for me, his eyes searching.

My head shook. "You go. I will stay."

Martha looked at me, her hands stilling on the wine jar, oil from the meal coating her fingers. "Anna—"

"I want to." And it was true. The work was not finished. The platters needed washing, the floor needed sweeping, the kitchen needed to be set right for morning, the oven needed banking, and the scraps needed gathering for the dogs. Someone had to do it. Tonight it would be me. "Go. Sit with your sister."

She hesitated, her mouth opening as if to argue, then closed it. She nodded and left me there.

The sound of them carried from the other room— benches creaking under shifting weight, voices quieting to whispers and then to silence, then Jesus speaking again, his voice different now, more intimate, teaching those who had chosen to stay and listen. Something about light. About lamps that were meant to be seen, not hidden.

I carried the platters out to the courtyard, where the cistern stood, and the winter air hit me like a physical blow. The cold found every damp place on my skin—the sweat at my temples, the moisture at the back of my neck where my headscarf had slipped, the dampness on my hands from the dishwater—and turned it to ice. I drew my shawl tighter around my shoulders, but it did little good against the cold that seemed to rise from the very stones beneath my feet.

Above, the sky had darkened to the deep blue that comes just after sunset in winter, that brief moment between day and night. Stars appeared, scattered across the darkness like salt thrown across dark cloth.

I drew water from the cistern to fill the washing basin, the rope rough and cold against my palms as I pulled up the bucket, hand over hand, the muscles in my arms and shoulders protesting. The basin was heavy when I set it down on the bench, the water inside black in the darkness, reflecting nothing.

When my hands went into that water, the cold was like being stabbed. The shock of it stole my breath and made my chest seize. For a moment, I could not move, could only stand there with my hands submerged in water so cold it burned, feeling the ice of it climb from my fingers toward my wrists. Then I gasped and began to work.

I scrubbed at the platters, at the film of oil and fish and breadcrumbs that clung to the clay, my fingers moving stiffly at first, clumsy and awkward, and then with more ease as they went numb, losing sensation entirely. The oil broke apart reluctantly under my hands, needing coaxing and persistence. The water turned cloudy, with bits of food floating on the surface and catching what little moonlight there was, small dark shapes drifting and spinning in slow circles.

By the third platter, my hands seemed to be ghost hands that moved at my command but sent back no sensation. By the last, they were red when I lifted them from the water, the skin mottled and raw-looking in the moonlight. I set the platter aside to drain, the water running off it in rivulets, and dried my hands on my tunic, the rough fabric scratching against cold-numbed skin.

I lifted my gaze to the stars.

The sky was full of them now, thousands upon thousands scattered across the darkness, more appearing as my eyes adjusted. They looked sharp enough to cut, hard white points against velvet black.

Andrew came out to the courtyard, his footsteps soft on the stone. He stood beside me without speaking, looking up at the same stars, his breath visible in the cold air. Then he pulled me close, his body warm against my side, sharing his heat.

"You did well."

The water in the basin had gone still, a perfect mirror reflecting stars.

A knock sounded at the gate, sharp and insistent, and we both jumped.

Andrew crossed the courtyard and lifted the latch, the wood scraping against wood. My father stood there, travel dust on his cloak, his face weary in the lamplight spilling from the house, lines I had not seen before carved deep around his eyes and mouth.

"Anna," my father said, his eyes finding me across the courtyard.

CHAPTER 21

I CROSSED the courtyard and went into his arms, the rough
wool of his travel cloak scratching against my cheek like tree
bark, smelling of cedar soap and sweat and the dust of hard-
riding ground so deep into the fabric it seemed part of the
weave itself. His chest was solid beneath my cheek, his heartbeat steady and strong, and his arms trembled as they tightened around me.

"Abba, I did not know you were coming." I stepped back
just enough to see his face in the light spilling from Martha's
windows, my hands still gripping his cloak, the wool coarse
beneath my fingers. "Where is Naomi?"

"She is well. She stayed in Jerusalem. This journey was
not safe for her."

Another man stood beside him in the shadows near the
gate before stepping forward. He bowed, his scholar's robes
whispering against the courtyard stones. "Peace be upon this
house."

A scholar from Jerusalem—his careful diction gave him

away, each syllable as precise and measured as a scribe reading from Torah. Both men wore plain merchant cloaks over their fine robes, undyed wool too coarse and simple for men of their bearing, the fabric dulled with road dust. My father's shoulders sagged under some invisible weight, and his companion leaned heavily on his walking staff, the wood worn smooth and dark from years of use.

Andrew stepped forward and clasped my father's arm in greeting, his broad hand closing around the fine bones of a scholar's wrist. They looked at each other for a long moment, Andrew's grip tightening, my father nodding once—an exchange that needed no words.

"We heard you were in Bethany," my father said, the words coming out clipped and tight. "We came as soon as we could."

His companion's face was grave, exhaustion carving deep lines beneath his heavy brows and in the hollows of his cheeks. Whatever had brought them here in the dark, dressed as merchants when they were members of the Sanhedrin, could not wait for dawn.

Martha appeared at my elbow carrying a fresh cloth, the linen still warm from where it had been folded near the brazier. "You will stay, of course. We have room. The meal is finished, but I can bring you bread and wine. Lazarus, see to their animals."

Lazarus materialized from the shadows near the gate and led the animals away, their hooves clopping softly against the worn courtyard stones, the sound fading as he took them toward the stable at the back of the house. Martha disappeared toward the house, her voice already raised to call for Mary, already moving to fulfill the demands of hospitality.

I led my father and his companion to the washing basin

near the cistern, drawing fresh water that came up cold from the cistern's depths and smelled faintly of minerals and stone. They rinsed the dust from their hands and faces, the water turning gray-brown as it splashed into the basin, and the night air raised bumps along my arms where dampness clung to my sleeves despite my shawl pulled tight around my shoulders.

"Anna, this is Nicodemus," my father said as they dried their hands on the cloth Martha had provided, the linen coming away streaked with road dirt. "A friend from the council."

He was older than my father by perhaps a decade, his beard gone mostly gray with only a few streaks of black remaining like ink stains that had not quite washed out. His eyes were dark beneath heavy brows, watchful in the way of men who have learned that words can be weapons and silence a shield. I had never met him, but my father had spoken of him as a friend, one of the few on the council he trusted with anything that mattered, one of the handful of men in Jerusalem who still asked questions when others had stopped listening for answers.

I bowed my head slightly. "Peace be upon you. You are welcome in this house."

Nicodemus inclined his head in return but said nothing, his eyes moving past me to scan the courtyard and the gate and the dark street beyond.

"Abba, what has happened?" I kept my voice low though the courtyard was empty save for us, the night close around us. "Why are you here?"

"Not now." He glanced toward the gate again, his body as tense as a drawn bowstring. "After the others have gone to sleep. When we can speak privately."

Inside, the main room still held the remnants of evening—a few oil lamps burning low in their niches carved into the walls, the flames guttering in the drafts that crept through gaps in the shutters. The air was thick with the smell of fish and the smoke from the evening fire that had burned down to glowing embers in the brazier, and beneath that the lingering scent of garlic and wine. Most of the disciples were preparing for sleep, spreading their cloaks in the far corners, arranging bedrolls, going through the familiar rituals of men at the end of a long day. Peter and John sat with Jesus near the far wall, their voices low, words drifting across the space like smoke, too soft to hear but their tone serious.

Jesus rose when he saw my father and crossed the room in three strides. They embraced, my father's arms going tight around his nephew, his face against Jesus's shoulder for a long moment before they separated. Jesus's hand stayed on my father's arm.

"Uncle, I know," Jesus said.

My father's eyes widened then closed briefly.

Jesus guided him to where Peter and John sat, and they joined them on the cushions there. Martha brought bread and wine, setting the simple meal before them—thick slices of yesterday's bread, the crust gone slightly hard, and wine in clay cups that she filled from an earthenware jug. They ate without speaking, tearing the bread with their fingers and washing it down with wine that left their lips stained dark purple, their faces grave and as set as men preparing for battle.

When they finished, my father wiped his mouth with the back of his hand and looked at Jesus. "We need to speak." His eyes moved to Peter then to Andrew and me. "Privately."

Jesus rose without a word and moved toward the stairs,

his sandals soft against the packed earth floor. Peter and Andrew stood as well, and I followed, the hem of my tunic whispering against my ankles. Nicodemus came last, his walking staff tapping against the floor with each step. Martha withdrew ahead of us, her footsteps quick and light on the wooden stairs, and pulled the door closed behind her as we entered, the latch clicking into place.

The room was small and plain, its plastered walls bare save for the shadows that danced there in the unsteady flame of a single oil lamp sitting in a niche cut into the wall. The light guttered in the draft from the window where the shutters did not quite meet, casting more darkness than illumination, making the corners recede into blackness so complete I could not see where the walls ended. We sat on cushions arranged in a rough circle on the floor, the fabric worn smooth from years of use and smelling faintly of dust and lavender and the bodies of all who had sat there before us. I leaned back against Andrew's chest, and he wrapped his arms around me, his heart beating steady and strong against my spine, his breathing moving through me like a tide, and I tried to match my breath to his to calm the fear already rising in my throat.

The flame carved my father's face into planes of brightness and shadow, sharpening the lines around his mouth, making the hollows beneath his eyes look bruised and sunken.

From somewhere below came the *creak* of settling wood, the small sounds of a house full of people trying to sleep—a cough, the rustle of someone turning over, footsteps padding soft across the floor to the courtyard. Footsteps passed in the street outside, voices raised in conversation growing louder and then fading, and my father went rigid, his eyes fixed on the window until the street fell silent again and the only sound was the soft *hiss* of the lamp consuming oil.

"Tell him," Nicodemus said, his voice cutting through the quiet. "Tell him what Caiaphas said in the council last week."

My father drew a long breath and rubbed his hand across his jaw, the rasp of his palm against his beard loud in the small room. He looked at Jesus. "They are building a case against you. A formal case." He paused, and Andrew's heart rate quickened against my back. "They are documenting everything now. Every healing, every teaching, every word that might be construed as blasphemy. Annas keeps a scribe in the Temple courts. The man follows you when you teach there, writes down everything you say on wax tablets, copies it onto parchment when the day is done, and stores it in the Temple archives."

"We have seen him," Peter said, his voice rough. "The one who sits in the corner with the tablets."

"There are others. In every town you visit, someone reports back to Jerusalem. They know you were in Bethsaida. They know about the paralytic you healed in Capernaum, the tax collector you ate with in Jericho." My father's hands opened and closed in his lap, restless and grasping at air. "They have testimonies from the Pharisees who witnessed the Sabbath healings. Written statements, signed and sealed with wax, locked away in the Temple archives where they cannot be lost or destroyed or contradicted. They are assembling a record. Evidence for a trial."

"How many testimonies?" Andrew asked behind me, his voice rumbling in his chest, vibrating through my spine.

"Enough." Nicodemus leaned forward. "More than enough to bring formal charges before the full council."

Jesus said nothing. He sat very still, his hands resting on his knees, his face as calm and untroubled as if they were discussing the weather or the harvest.

My fingers dug into Andrew's arm hard enough that he shifted slightly beneath me.

"What charges?" Peter asked, and his voice carried an edge like flint striking steel.

Nicodemus met his eyes. "Blasphemy. Claiming to forgive sins. Claiming authority over the Temple. Calling God your father. They will argue that you make yourself equal to God."

Someone coughed in the room below, and the sound echoed up through the floorboards.

"The penalty for blasphemy—" Peter started.

"Is death," Nicodemus finished. "By stoning, according to the law of Moses."

No one moved. The light wavered, casting wild dancing patterns across the walls that made the room seem to shrink and expand, darkness closing in from all sides. A dog barked somewhere in the village, the sound carrying clear through the cold night air.

"But they cannot simply stone him," Andrew said. "There must be a trial. Witnesses who agree in their testimony. The council must vote—"

"The council will agree." My father's hands opened and closed, opened and closed. "Caiaphas has the votes. I have counted them myself, night after night in my study, going through the names of every member, marking who will vote to condemn and who might be persuaded to mercy. When they bring the charges, when they call for judgment, there are enough who will condemn him. More than enough."

The room felt smaller suddenly, the walls too close, the

air too thick and warm despite the cold draft from the window. The lamp oil burned acrid and sharp in my nostrils, mixing with the scent of sweat and fear that hung over all of us.

"Then we do not let them bring the charges," Peter said, his voice rising sharp and defiant. "We leave Judea. We go north to Galilee, where their jurisdiction ends—"

"For how long?" Nicodemus interrupted. "He cannot hide forever. Eventually, he will return to Jerusalem, and when he does, they will be waiting."

"He does not need to hide forever," my father said, and something in his voice made my chest ache. "Just long enough for this to pass. For the council to find another concern, for Caiaphas to turn his attention to some new threat—"

"Uncle." Jesus spoke for the first time, and the single word stopped my father's speech as surely as a hand pressed against his mouth. "You know it will not pass."

"It might. If you leave now, if you stay away from Jerusalem, if you stop teaching in the Temple courts where they can see you—"

"Stop teaching?"

"For a time." My father's voice cracked. "Just for a time. Until things calm. I have tried to reason with them. I point to the law, to precedent, to the testimonies that contradict each other. I argue that healing on the Sabbath is mercy, not blasphemy. That teaching in the Temple is not a crime. That crowds gathering to hear wisdom is not rebellion." His hands clenched into fists, the knuckles white. "And they dismiss me. They say I am blinded by family loyalty. That I cannot see clearly because you are my nephew. Caiaphas smiles and thanks me for my concern and calls for the next witness. Every session, they watch me more closely. Every vote I cast, they note and record and discuss in whispers when they think I cannot hear. Since the wedding—"

He stopped. The flame guttered lower, the light dimming.

"They have stopped sending me notices for certain council meetings. The private sessions where they question witnesses. Last week, Annas asked me—casually, as if discussing the weather or the price of grain—whether Anna was still traveling with your company. Whether she had been present when you healed the blind man in Jericho." His voice dropped so low I had to strain to hear it over the hiss of the lamp. "They are documenting her now too. Every town you visit. Every miracle she witnesses. I am losing ground. I cannot watch them kill you both."

My hand found Andrew's tunic, gripping the rough linen so tight my knuckles ached. The fabric was damp with his sweat despite the cold. Andrew's arms became iron bands around me, holding me so tight I could barely breathe, but I did not pull away. *Kill us both?*

Jesus reached across the space between them and laid his hand on my father's arm, his fingers pale against the dark fabric of my father's sleeve. "Uncle."

"You are like a son to me." My father's words came slowly, dragged up from some deep place in his chest. "I have watched you grow in wisdom and favor. I have listened to you teach in the Temple courts and marveled at the words that came from your mouth. I watched you heal Deborah when she was dying, watched you touch Anna's hip and make her whole. I have believed in who you are and what you came to do. I will not stand by and watch them destroy you if I can prevent it."

His eyes moved to me then back to Jesus, and tears gathered that he would not let fall. "And if they take you, if they arrest you and try you and condemn you, what do you think happens to those who follow you? To those who are known to be your disciples?" His gaze shifted to Andrew. "To their wives?"

Andrew's breath caught, his chest going still against my back for a heartbeat before he drew in air again.

"They are watching all of you," Nicodemus said. "The council knows the names of the twelve. They know about the women who travel with you, who provide for you from their own means. They know about the crowds who follow you from town to town. When they move against Jesus, they will move against all of it. Everyone will be questioned. Everyone will be watched. Some will be arrested."

The lamp oil popped and hissed. The smell of it was making me sick, acrid and chemical mixing with the stale air and the sweat of too many bodies in too small a space.

"Let them." Peter's hands were fists against his thighs, the tendons in his forearms standing out like ropes. "We have done nothing wrong. We break no laws. We heal the sick and feed the hungry and teach about the kingdom of God. If that is a crime worthy of death—"

"It is not about what is right," Nicodemus said. "It is about what is expedient. Caiaphas does not care about your innocence or your guilt. He cares about maintaining order, about keeping Rome satisfied, about preserving his own position of power. And right now, all of you threaten those things."

"How?" Andrew asked. "We preach peace. We tell people to love their enemies, to turn the other cheek, to give to

Caesar what is Caesar's and to God what is God's. We pose no threat to Rome."

"You pose a threat to the order Rome requires," Nicodemus said, the light carving deep lines in his face, making him look ancient and weary beyond measure. "Every time crowds gather to hear Jesus teach, every time people call him teacher or prophet or king, Rome sees the seeds of rebellion. And when Rome sees rebellion, Rome acts. Caiaphas knows this. He knows that Rome would rather crucify a thousand men than risk a single uprising. He would rather give Rome one man to satisfy their hunger for order than risk Rome taking all of Judea in response to a perceived threat."

Men talked outside, their voices carrying up through the window, distant at first and then growing louder, closer, passing beneath us in the street. We all went still. The voices resolved into words—a complaint about grain prices. Peter's hand moved to his knife, his fingers closing around the hilt. We waited, barely breathing, until the voices faded and died away, swallowed by the night. Only then did anyone move.

Peter's shoulders rolled back, his body coiling. "We can protect him. We have men—"

"You have nothing." Nicodemus cut him off, his voice without mercy. "Against the Sanhedrin, against Rome, you have nothing but faith."

"Then faith will have to be enough," Peter said.

"It is not," Nicodemus replied.

Jesus reached over and gripped Peter's shoulder, his fingers digging into the muscle hard enough that Peter winced and his jaw clenched. "The hour is coming. Not yet but soon. And when it comes, I will need all of you. Men and women who will do what must be done and pay whatever price is asked. Who will stand when everything in you screams to run."

"But they cannot arrest you." The words burst out before I could stop them, my voice too loud in the small room. "There must be a way to stop this."

Jesus looked at me, and in the dim light, his eyes were fathomless. "I must do what the Father has sent me to do, Anna."

"Even if it means your death?"

"Especially then."

My father made a sound—a sharp intake of breath that broke in his throat, the sound of something shattering inside him.

Jesus turned back to him. "I know what you risk by coming here. I know you have fought for me in those chambers, that you have used every argument you know and watched them dismiss you session after session. I know you would do anything to change what is coming. But you cannot change it, Uncle. This is the path the Father has set before me, and I will walk it to the end."

"Then I will walk it with you," my father said. "When they bring the charges, when they call for judgment, I will speak. I will defend you before the full council—"

"No." Jesus's voice carried absolute command, the authority of a king giving orders to his soldiers. "You will do no such thing."

"I cannot sit silent while they condemn you—"

"You can and you will." Jesus gripped my father's hands, holding them tight between his own. "Because after I am gone, someone must speak for truth in those chambers. Someone must remain who has not bowed to Caiaphas, who has not traded justice for expedience, who remembers what the law was meant to accomplish and not merely what it can be made to say. You cannot do that if you are arrested alongside me."

Arrested. My father arrested, dragged before the very council he served, stripped of his position and his honor and everything he had built over a lifetime of careful work, his name become a byword for treason and his fortune seized and his household scattered—

"Abba!"

My father looked at me. "I will be careful, Anna."

"You are here now," I said, and my voice shook despite my efforts to control it. "At night. In secret. That is not careful."

My father turned to Jesus, his hands still caught between Jesus's palms. "What good is my position if I cannot use it to save you?"

"Your position may yet save many others." Jesus released his hands and sat back. "Trust me in this, Joseph. When the time comes, you will know what to do."

The flame sputtered and nearly went out, plunging the room into near darkness before the flame caught again and steadied. The smell of burning oil was thick in my nostrils, making my head ache.

"Go and rest now," Jesus said. "For now, we go north to Galilee. We leave at first light."

Andrew's hand stayed in mine as we made our way back to our room through the house, navigating by feel and by the faint moonlight that crept through gaps in the shutters, painting silver stripes across the packed earth floor. Somewhere, a door creaked on leather hinges, and I flinched. His fingers threaded tighter through mine.

Our pallet was stuffed with wool that smelled faintly of

lavender and staleness, the familiar scent of bedding that had seen too many bodies and not enough sun. The clay brazier still glowed in the corner, its coals burned down to embers that cast a dim red light across the small room, enough to see by but not enough to read the expressions on each other's faces. But when we lay down together, neither of us slept.

Around us were the sounds of people sleeping—the rustle of bodies shifting on pallets, the creak of floorboards, someone coughing in another room, the sound harsh and wet. The night air crept in through the gaps in the shutters, cold enough to make me burrow deeper against Andrew's warmth, pressing my face against his chest, where I could hear his heartbeat and smell the familiar scent of him—fish and lake water and sweat and the faint underlying smell of the soap Naomi made from olive oil and ash.

"You are thinking too loud," Andrew murmured against my hair, his breath stirring the loose strands that had escaped my braid and tickled against my neck.

I turned in his arms until his face came into view, his features indistinct in the low light but dear enough that I could have traced them in the dark. "My father risked everything to come here. If the council finds out—"

"He knew the risk."

"That does not make it less dangerous." My fingers dug into the rough linen of his tunic, the fabric worn soft from washing but still coarse against my skin. "He will not stop, will he? Jesus. He will not stop teaching."

Andrew was silent for a long moment. "No. I do not think he will."

"What happens when they come for him? What happens to all of us?"

"I do not know."

Andrew pulled me closer, wrapping his arms around me until I could barely tell where his body ended and mine began. "Whatever comes," he said against my hair, his lips moving against my scalp, "I will keep you safe. Even if it costs me everything."

"Andrew—"

"I mean it." His arms tightened until every muscle and sinew in his forearms stood out against my ribs, the strength in his hands that came from a lifetime of hauling nets heavy with fish, of rowing against wind and current, of hard labor that had shaped his body into something solid and unbreakable. "They can take my home, my freedom, my life. But they will not take you while I breathe."

"They will not take you while I breathe either."

He pulled back enough to look at my face. "Pity you do not have your walking staff anymore. You could crack a few heads."

I almost smiled. Almost. "Andrew—"

"I know." His thumb traced my cheekbone. "My fierce Anna. I know."

My hand moved to my belly, feeling the flat plane of it through my tunic, the empty space where a child should grow. Sarah—the name Jesus had spoken over me like a promise, like a prophecy, like a gift I did not yet have the hands to hold. It felt fragile now in the face of council chambers and scribes with wax tablets and formal charges of blasphemy, as fragile and impossible as spring rain in the dead of summer.

I laid my face against Andrew's chest and listened to his heartbeat, as steady and strong and stubborn as the man himself, refusing to yield to fear or exhaustion or the weight of all that was coming.

I did not sleep.

When the first gray light crept through the gaps in the shutters, I was still awake.

We left Bethany the next morning, the ministry moving north toward the territories where the council's reach was weaker and the roads safer.

The morning was cold and clear, the sky that shade of blue that comes only in winter, pale and washed as clean as new linen. Frost still clung where the sun had not yet reached, silver and as delicate as spiderweb, catching the light and throwing it back in tiny stars that melted even as I watched them. Our breath rose in clouds that dissipated almost as quickly as they formed. My fingers were stiff as I adjusted the straps on my pack, the leather cold and unyielding beneath my hands, and I had to work the buckles twice before they would catch and hold, my fingers clumsy with cold and exhaustion.

The village was stirring around us—cooking fires sending smoke rising in thin gray columns that climbed straight up in the still air before dispersing, children running between houses on some errand or another, their voices high and bright in the morning quiet, a woman calling to her neighbor about borrowed flour, the everyday sounds of life continuing despite everything.

Martha stood at the gate with her arms crossed over her chest, her eyes wet with tears she would not let fall, her jaw set firm.

"You will come back," she said.

"We will come back."

She pulled me into an embrace that smelled of yeast and kitchens and work, of early mornings spent kneading dough and late nights spent cleaning up after meals that fed too many people with too little food, of oil lamps burning low and bread rising in covered bowls and all the quiet magic of keeping a household alive. Her arms were strong around me, her body solid and warm, and I held on longer than I should have, my face against her shoulder, breathing in the smell of her and trying to memorize it, trying to hold onto this moment.

"Take care of yourself, Anna. And that husband of yours. And—" She pulled back and looked at me, her eyes searching my face as if she could see something there I had not yet told her. "And whatever else God gives you to care for."

She smiled, a small private smile that asked no questions and demanded no answers, and said nothing more.

Lazarus appeared beside her with Mary tucked under his arm. Mary still looked half asleep, her eyes soft and unfocused in the morning light, her hair not quite tamed beneath her veil, but she leaned into her brother's side with the easy trust of a child who has never known reason to fear.

"Safe travels," Lazarus said, grinning at me with that expression he wore when he was trying to lighten a moment that had grown too heavy with things unsaid. "Try not to let Peter tell too many fish stories without me there to correct him."

"I make no promises."

He laughed, the sound warm and easy, and kissed my cheek, his beard scratching lightly against my skin, as rough as the wool on my father's cloak had been. Mary clasped my hands in her cool ones, her fingers as slender and delicate as bird bones.

"He loves you," she said softly. "Jesus. He speaks of you when you are not there. He says you are strong and brave."

I squeezed her hands, her skin soft and smooth against

mine, and turned away before the tears gathering in my eyes could spill over and run down my cheeks to freeze in the cold morning air.

Andrew was waiting by the road, his pack already shouldered, the leather straps dark against the pale linen of his tunic. Jesus and the others were ready, saying final farewells to Martha's household, their voices low and urgent. Peter stood close to Jesus, one hand resting on the knife at his belt, his body tense even here in the peaceful morning, his eyes scanning the street and the rooftops and the spaces between buildings as if expecting soldiers to appear at any moment.

Andrew reached for my hand as I approached, and I held on tighter than I needed to. Together, we joined the others filing out through Bethany's narrow streets, following the path north.

I looked back once just before the road curved.

Martha was still standing at the gate, a dark figure against the white walls of her house, one hand raised in farewell. The morning sun caught her headscarf and made it glow pale against the shadows.

I raised mine in return, holding it there until the road bent and she was gone.

CHAPTER 22

Galilee, March, 32 AD

Dust hung in the spring air, thick enough to coat my tongue with grit and turn every breath into work. We had been walking since first light, Jesus leading us toward a village whose name I had already forgotten, and behind us came the people—farmers who had left their plows standing in half-turned fields, women with infants bound against their backs and children clinging to their skirts, men whose faces bore the deep lines of hard questions and harder lives. The shuffle of feet made a sound like wind through wheat, constant and rhythmic and broken only by the occasional cry of a child or the bleat of a goat being herded along by some optimist who thought he might reach market before the crowds made the roads impassable.

Andrew's hand found mine, his palm slick with sweat.

The warmth of him anchored me against the bodies that multiplied with every mile, drawn to Jesus by hunger deeper than reason.

Three Pharisees kept to the edge of the crowd, their fine robes marking them as clearly as if they carried banners—wool dyed deep blue and purple, fabric that caught the morning sun and threw it back in rich folds while the farmers around them wore only undyed linen gone gray with age and washing. One carried a writing tablet, the wood worn smooth and dark from years of use, the wax surface scored with the marks of a stylus that had recorded who knew how many testimonies, how many accusations. Another kept his eyes fixed on Jesus with the single-minded focus of a hawk watching a hare, never turning aside, never blinking, waiting for the moment to strike. The third was younger, his beard still sparse and black without a thread of gray, and he watched not Jesus but the rest of us—the disciples, the women who traveled with us, me. His gaze met mine. Cold spread through my chest like water seeping through cracked stone.

I turned my face away, but his attention stayed on me, taking my measure.

"They are watching him," I said to Andrew, keeping my voice low enough that only he would hear above the constant noise of the people around us.

"I know."

The village appeared around a bend in the road, small and unremarkable, its mud-brick walls bleached nearly white by years of sun and wind and winter rain. A well stood in the square at the center, the stones around its mouth marked by generations of water jars and the hands that had drawn them up, and already people were gathering there, drawn by word that had somehow run ahead of us on the road. An old woman supporting a man whose right arm hung withered and useless at his side. Children hovering near a blind beggar who sat with his bowl and his stick. Two men arguing over the price of a donkey while their voices danced in the familiar rhythm of haggling that could go on for hours. And standing in the shade of an ancient fig tree whose branches spread wide and dark across half the square, four more scribes watched with arms crossed and faces stone-still, as patient as vultures.

Jesus stopped at the well. The people pushed inward, crowding close until there was barely room to move, shoulders jostling shoulders, the air growing hot and stale.I pressed as close to Andrew as the crush allowed, but they kept coming, and someone's elbow caught my ribs hard enough to drive the air from my lungs in a gasp. Andrew shifted without speaking, using his body to create space around me, and I braced my hand against the solid muscle of his back to steady myself while the smell of unwashed bodies rose around us—sweat and wool and the acrid bite of animals, the faint sweet rot of fruit gone bad somewhere nearby, all of it mingling in my nose and throat until breathing felt like swallowing wool.

A commotion erupted near the front where Jesus stood. Voices raised, sharp with alarm. Someone shouted. Over the wall of shoulders and heads I saw nothing, but people began pulling back, opening a gap.

"What is it?" I asked.

"A man," Peter called back to us. "Possessed."

The crowd shifted, and I glimpsed him through the

opening, a man perhaps thirty years old, thrashing on the packed earth while two others struggled to hold him down, to keep him from breaking his bones against the stones or lashing out at those who tried to help him. His mouth gaped open, jaw moving as he tried to force words through a throat that would not obey, but no sound emerged save a wet choking that turned my stomach. His eyes had rolled back until only the whites showed, veined and terrible, and his limbs moved with a violence impossible for human joints to sustain, bone grinding against bone while the thing inside him tried to tear its way free.

Jesus moved forward. He knelt beside the man, placed one hand on his head where sweat had plastered dark hair to his skull, and spoke words I could not distinguish over the renewed noise of people rushing forward to see. But the effect rippled through the afflicted man's body—every muscle going rigid for the space of three heartbeats, as taut as rope under strain, and then releasing all at once so that he went slack in the arms of the men who held him. His eyes rolled forward and focused. His mouth opened, and a sound came out, as hoarse and broken as a voice unused to speech but human, achingly human. The two men released their hold and helped him sit upright, where he blinked up at the sky as if seeing it for the first time.

The crowd erupted in chaos.

"He speaks!"

"Did you see what happened—"

"The demon is gone—"

"Praise be to God—"

But the scribes beneath the fig tree were not praising anything. They had drawn nearer during the healing, positioning themselves where they could see every detail, hear every word, and now they stood with heads bent together and words hissing between them. The one with the tablet had his stylus already in hand, held ready between fingers stained dark with years of ink. The younger one no longer watched Jesus. He watched me, and when I met his stare, he did not look away. His gaze moved from my face to Andrew beside me then back. Recognition sharpened his features. A hunter seeing prey.

The one with the tablet stepped forward, raising his voice to cut through the noise, and the crowd fell silent to hear him.

"By what power does this man cast out demons?"

The silence spread outward. Excitement drained from faces, replaced by uncertainty. Smiles faded. People glanced at their neighbors. Jesus turned to face the scribe, and the weariness in the line of his shoulders aged him ten years.

"By what power do you think?" Jesus asked, and his voice carried an edge that made my breath catch.

"Beelzebul. He casts out demons by the prince of demons."

The crowd drew back as if struck. Andrew's hand found my arm and closed around it, his whole body going tense beside me, ready. Around us, people were murmuring, the sound rising.

"Did he say—"

"Beelzebul—"

"In league with Satan himself—"

"That is blasphemy—"

Jesus raised one hand, and the murmuring died.

"Every kingdom divided against itself is brought to desolation," he said, and his voice carried to every corner of the square without him raising it, hard and as clear as struck bronze. "And every city or house divided against itself will not stand. If Satan casts out Satan, he is divided against himself. How then will his kingdom stand?"

The scribe opened his mouth to respond, but Jesus was not finished, and his words came faster now, building.

"And if I cast out demons by Beelzebul, by whom do your sons cast them out? Therefore, they shall be your judges. But if I cast out demons by the Spirit of God, then the kingdom of God has come upon you."

While Jesus spoke, the young scribe had begun working his way closer, using the distraction of the argument to slip between bodies, to move nearer to where Andrew and I stood with Peter and the other disciples. Too near. Close enough that only three people stood between us, and I could see that ink stained his fingers the way it stained the fingers of every scribe who spent his days recording testimonies and accusations and the names of those who would one day answer for their associations. He held my gaze deliberately. He wanted me to see him watching.

My fingers tightened on Andrew's arm until I could feel the muscle and tendon beneath the sun-warmed linen of his sleeve.

The scribe leaned toward the man beside him and whispered, his lips barely stirring, and the man glanced at me then back at the scribe before nodding slowly, a gesture of agreement or acknowledgment or perhaps simply recognition.

Jesus was still speaking. "Either make the tree good and its fruit good or make the tree corrupt and its fruit corrupt, for a tree is known by its fruit. Brood of vipers! How can you, being evil, speak good things?"

The people began to shift and separate, some nodding

and murmuring agreement with Jesus, edging forward to hear him better. Others drew back, their expressions hardening into disapproval or fear, looking between Jesus and the scribes. A flash of fine fabric to my left—another scribe with a tablet in his hands, stylus poised. Then another near the well. A third still beneath the fig tree. They were scattered throughout like sentries at their posts, watching, recording, waiting. How many were there? Too many.

The young scribe took another step toward us. Only two people stood between us now, and the number of people behind me left no room to retreat.

My fingers dug into Andrew's arm hard enough that he would carry the marks.

"Andrew," I said quietly, barely more than a breath.

"I see him."

Jesus had moved from trees and fruit to blasphemy, to sins that could be forgiven and those that could not, and his words fell sharp and unforgiving. People flinched. The older scribes drew back half a step. But the young one kept coming.

He was near enough that the acrid smell of ink reached me, mingled with his sweat and the dust that clung to his robes. He looked at me and smiled, tight and calculated.

"Joseph of Arimathea's daughter," he said, pitching his voice low enough that only those nearest could hear.

I stepped back and met Andrew's chest.

"Move away," Andrew said, angling his body to put himself fully between the scribe and me.

"I am only observing." The scribe's smile widened without warming. "Taking notes. For the council. They will want to know who keeps company with this blasphemer. Who follows him from village to village. Who enables his work." He leaned to see past Andrew. "Who on the council has family among his followers."

"You need to leave," Andrew warned.

"Or what?" The scribe laughed, the sound as brittle as old pottery. "Will you strike me? Here? In front of all these witnesses?" He gestured around us. "If you lay a hand on me, they will tear you apart themselves."

Peter pushed his way through and took his place beside Andrew, his shoulders squared. "Let them try."

The scribe's smile grew. He looked disdainfully at the three of us. "Ah. Two of the twelve defending the councilman's daughter. How very touching." He glanced down at his tablet. "The council will find this most illuminating."

My hands shook. I flattened them against my sides where he could not see.

But he had already seen. He marked it and added it to whatever list he kept of weaknesses he might use. "You appear frightened, daughter of Arimathea."

"I have broken no law."

His smile held. "Perhaps not yet. But laws are revised. Council memberships change. Your father's position grows more precarious with each passing session."

"Enough."

I turned. A Pharisee had stepped forward, younger than most of the scribes who surrounded Jesus, younger even than the one who stood threatening me. The set of his shoulders, the way he held himself slightly apart from the others—I knew him. The Temple portico in Jerusalem, months ago. The other Pharisees had stormed away from Jesus in fury, but this one had remained behind, watching with a face troubled rather than certain, with questions where the others had only answers.

"She has done nothing that warrants this harassment," he said, his voice full of authority despite his youth. "The council's business is with Jesus of Nazareth, not with women in the marketplace."

The older scribe turned slowly, deliberately. "Micah ben Gamaliel. Does your father know you defend the families of those who harbor blasphemers?"

Micah's jaw tightened. "Eleazar, I defend propriety and the law. Questioning women in public squares is beneath the dignity of—"

"The council will determine what is beneath its dignity." The young scribe who had been threatening me moved closer to Micah, his smile sharpening. "Or perhaps you would prefer to join Joseph of Arimathea in his increasingly lonely position? I am certain the high priest would be fascinated to learn that the great Gamaliel's son shares his sympathies for this Galilean troublemaker."

Micah went still. He met the younger man's stare. "Joram, you overstep your authority—"

"Do I?" Joram's expression held pure satisfaction. "Then by all means, continue your gallant defense. I am certain the full council will be most interested to hear your views."

Micah's hand moved to his prayer shawl, gripping the tasseled fabric until his knuckles showed white. His mouth opened. Closed. No words emerged.

"I thought not," Eleazar said. He turned back to me. "As we were saying, your father's position grows more precarious with every—"

"You have no authority here," Peter began, but Andrew cut across him.

"Anna. We are leaving. Now."

He took my arm and began pulling me backward, away

from the scribes, away from the well where Jesus still stood speaking. People complained as we pushed past them, their voices rising in irritation and protest, and I caught fragments of Jesus's words floating over the noise. "The sign of Jonah," "three days and three nights," "the heart of the earth." But Andrew was relentless, using his size and strength to force a path when words and apologies would not move people aside quickly enough, and I followed because there was nothing else to do, nowhere else to go except away from those ink-stained fingers and that calculating smile.

We had pushed perhaps twenty paces when a hand closed around my arm. I turned, pulling free without thinking.

Micah stood there, breathing hard as if he had run to catch us. Sweat beaded on his forehead despite the morning cool.

"Let her go," Andrew said.

Micah released me immediately, raising both hands palm-out in a gesture of peace. "I meant no harm. I only—" He shot a glance over his shoulder at the scribes. "What they did was wrong. The harassment, the threats against your father. It was beneath what we are called to be." He stopped and shook his head. "We are not all like Joram and Eleazar. Some of us still remember the Law was given to protect the weak, not to intimidate the righteous."

Andrew stepped between us. "We need to go."

Micah nodded and moved back, his hand returning to grip his prayer shawl. "I should have said more. I should have defended you properly. I am sorry for my cowardice."

"You tried," I said. "That is more than the others did."

He looked at me, and the shame in his face remained, but relief lightened it. Then he turned and disappeared among the bodies, his fine robes swallowed by simpler garments.

I looked back once before Andrew pulled me around the corner of a building.

The young scribe was still watching me, still wearing that cold smile, and his hand moved across his tablet.

Writing.

CHAPTER 23

When we reached the top of the hill, lamplight spilled from Martha's open door onto the street like a welcome made visible. She appeared in the doorway before Jesus could call out, wiping flour from her hands onto her apron, and hurried out to embrace him with the affection of a sister who had waited too long for her brother's return.

"You came!" She turned to the rest of us with the same warmth spreading across her face. "All of you, inside. Lazarus has the courtyard ready."

The house breathed roasting lamb and bread still hot from the oven, the air thick with rosemary and the sweet char of meat dripping onto coals. I stepped through the doorway, and the tightness between my shoulder blades loosened for the first time in days. Andrew's palm brushed my back as we moved into the crowded house, his touch brief.

Lazarus emerged from the back, grinning at Jesus with joy that needed no words. "Brother, you are finally here."

"The roads were slow." Jesus clasped his forearm then pulled him into an embrace that spoke of years and shared history and the love between men who had grown up knowing each other's stories. "It is good to see you."

"And you." Lazarus stepped back but kept his grip on Jesus's shoulders, studying his face the way family does when too much time has passed. "You look tired. When did you last eat properly?"

"This morning."

"You need proper food." Lazarus turned toward the kitchen, where Martha had already disappeared, her voice rising above the noise of welcome. "Martha, he needs feeding."

"I am already at work," she called back, and the sound of pottery scraping stone and water pouring into cups filled the spaces between words. "Mary, the wine—"

The house filled with the chaos of travel-worn people finding welcome after too many days on dusty roads. Disciples settling onto benches, women moving toward the kitchen, where Martha directed traffic with the ease of someone who had fed multitudes before, our voices overlapping in greeting and laughter and the relief of being somewhere safe. Tirzah put young Zebedee on her hip, the boy rubbing his eyes and fussing after the long road from Jericho. Jesus sank onto the bench beside Lazarus, and the weariness that had aged him on the road eased from his shoulders.

Mary appeared at my elbow with a cup, the wine dark and cool in the lamplight. "Here. Drink first, then I will wash your feet."

The wine was sweet on my tongue, carrying the taste of

late-summer grapes and honey. I drank half the cup while Mary kneeled with her basin and cloths, her hands gentle as she washed away the grit and dust of Jericho's roads. The water felt like mercy against blistered skin.

"How long have you been traveling?" she asked, wringing the cloth and dipping it again, her movements unhurried.

"Since dawn. We stayed in Jericho last night."

"Sleep marks your face." She dried my feet with a clean cloth that smelled of lavender. "But you will eat first. Martha has been cooking since yesterday."

The meal spread across the table in abundance that spoke of Martha's gift for hospitality. Roasted lamb came first, the meat falling from the bone at the lightest touch, rosemary and garlic clinging to the browned edges where the fat had crisped and darkened. The scent filled my mouth with water before I had taken the first bite. Lentil stew followed, thick enough to cling to bread, rich with cumin and the sweetness of carrots cooked until they surrendered their shape. Vegetables glistened with oil, soft and caramelized from long roasting. The bread was still warm when I broke it open, steam rising against my face, the crust crackling between my fingers while the tender center pulled apart in soft, fragrant layers. Dates sticky with honey sat beside figs split to show their dark-red flesh, and soft cheese melted on the tongue, leaving the taste of sheep's milk and salt.

Martha moved between kitchen and table, setting out platters and refilling cups, waving away offers of help while flour still dusted across her forearms.

I sat between Andrew and Susanna, close enough to the head of the table that Jesus and Lazarus's conversation reached me clearly over the noise of eating and laughter.

They traded stories back and forth and laughed at jokes no one else understood.

"Remember that chair you built?" Lazarus was saying, his eyes bright with mischief. "The one that collapsed under your mother?"

Jesus laughed, the sound unguarded. "I was ten."

"She landed flat on the floor. You looked ready to cry."

"I nearly did. My father said mistakes make better carpenters."

"Better carpenters." Lazarus shook his head, still grinning. "Your mother called it other things."

Around the table, other conversations wove together into the familiar music of family at table—Peter arguing with James about the healing in Jericho, John telling Mary about the blind beggar who had followed them half a mile afterward, Miriam and Martha trading complaints about men who never helped clean up after meals. The voices intermingled, overlapping and breaking apart, creating warmth that had nothing to do with the lamps burning along the walls.

Andrew tore bread and passed me half without asking if I wanted it, his knee pressing against mine under the table. I leaned into his shoulder, and he shifted to make room. We had learned this language in marriage.

"This is good," he said quietly, his voice low enough that only I could hear. "Being here."

"It is."

Across from us, Lazarus demonstrated something with both hands spread wide, making Jesus laugh again, the sound carrying over the noise. I had seen Jesus teach crowds numbering in the thousands, heal the sick who pressed close enough to steal breath, and argue with Pharisees who wanted him dead. But rarely had I seen him simply enjoy a friend's company, unburdened by the weight of what he carried everywhere else.

"He loves him," Andrew said, following my gaze to where the two men sat with their heads bent close, speaking words I could not hear.

I leaned closer into Andrew's shoulder. "He does."

Martha set down another platter of bread then paused behind Lazarus to rest her hand on his shoulder. He reached up and patted her hand without interrupting his story. Across the table, Mary smiled at something Jesus said, and Lazarus caught her eye and winked. These three siblings spoke their own language of touch and timing and love made visible through service and presence and the way they moved around each other like water finding its course.

The meal stretched into evening. Lamps were lit as darkness crept up against the open windows. Someone told a joke that made half the table laugh and the other half groan at its terrible delivery. Martha brought out honeyed nuts, and everyone ate far more than they should have, sighing with the pleasant heaviness of too much good food.

Finally, people began drifting away to prepare sleeping spaces. The disciples would spread their bedrolls in the courtyard as they usually did, claiming corners and arranging cloaks into pillows. Martha led the women toward the main room, where pallets had been laid out in neat rows.

"Anna, Andrew," she said, pausing with her hand on the doorframe. "The small room off the kitchen is yours. You will have quiet there."

It was the same room we had stayed in during our last visit, barely large enough for a sleeping pallet but private, with a door that latched and walls thick enough to muffle the sounds of a house full of people. I caught Martha's eye and saw understanding there.

"Thank you, Martha. It will be wonderful to have a room to ourselves."

Andrew caught my hand as I finished clearing dishes. "Walk with me first?"

I nodded.

We strolled through the dark streets of Bethany, leaving the lamplight and laughter behind, the path smooth and cool beneath our feet, still holding the memory of the day's warmth even as night settled over the village. Andrew's grip was steady as we picked our way between close-built houses toward the edge where homes gave way to olive groves and open sky.

The groves started where the last houses ended, trees climbing the hillside in ancient rows, their trunks twisted like the arms of old men who had been lifting prayers to heaven for longer than anyone could remember. Night had settled fully now, the sky above us thick with stars. The air carried woodsmoke from evening fires, the green scent of olive leaves, and the dusty sweetness of late harvest.

Andrew was quiet beside me, his shoulders tense and his breathing shallow in the way that meant something troubled him. Finally, he said, "You are different tonight."

"How so?"

"I cannot say. You sat at the table, and your face was—" He stopped walking and turned to face me, his hands finding mine in the darkness. "Tell me."

I had been waiting for the right moment all day, rehearsing words in my mind while we walked, while we ate, while I watched him laugh with Peter and share wine with

James. But the right moment had never arrived, and now, standing in the darkness with Andrew under the scattered stars, I found the words came without rehearsal.

"My courses have not come. It has been more than three weeks."

He went very still, his grip tightening on my hands.

"Anna—"

"Jesus promised us a daughter." The words came faster, spilling out after being held close for days. "He looked at me and said 'Sarah.' I believed him then, Andrew, and I still do. I believe this is her."

He pulled me close, his arms wrapping around me, his face buried in my hair.

"You are certain?"

"That I carry her? Not yet." I looked up at him, his face barely visible in the starlight, just the outline of cheekbone and jaw and the glint of his eyes. "But that Jesus spoke truth? Yes. I am certain of that. Are you not?"

"After Jonah—" His voice caught on the name, breaking over it the way waves break over stone. "What if—"

"That will not happen again." I touched his face, feeling the roughness of day-old beard under my palm, the warmth of his skin, the pulse beating fast in his throat. "But if it does, then we grieve again and trust again. I know losing Jonah almost broke me beyond repair, but I will not live afraid. Not anymore. Jesus promised Sarah. I choose to have faith."

He kissed me then, hard and desperate, and in that kiss lived his hope and his terror and his need to trust what I was telling him, all of it lodged between us in the darkness under stars that had watched women hope for children since Sarah laughed in her tent and Hannah wept at Shiloh. When we broke apart, we stood close, foreheads touching, breathing the same air.

"You have always been far more courageous than me, Anna of Arimathea."

"Not always." I kissed his cheek and laid my head against his chest, where his heart still beat fast. "We will have our daughter. I am sure of it."

"Sarah," he whispered, testing the name against the night air.

"Sarah."

His palms moved to my belly, flat and unchanged, and rested there as though he could feel through skin and muscle to where life might be taking root in the darkness of my womb. "When will you know for certain?"

"A few more weeks. Maybe a month." I covered his hands with mine, our fingers overlapping. "But I know already. I can feel it."

"How?"

"I cannot explain it. I just know."

Neither of us spoke. Finally, he said, "We should tell no one yet. Not until you are certain."

"I would like to tell Martha and Mary tomorrow. Just them." When he started to protest, I said, "I need to tell someone, Andrew. Women I trust. Please."

He nodded slowly. "Just them, then. For now."

"For now."

We walked back to the house hand in hand, our fingers laced together, the lamplight growing brighter as we approached until we could see our shadows stretching long across the ground before us.

Martha had left a lamp burning in the small room, and

fresh linens on the pallet, the fabric smelling of sun and wind and the lavender she kept stored with the bedding.

Andrew closed the door behind us. The wooden bar settled into place with a soft *thud*, sealing us off from the rest of the house, from curious ears, from everyone who did not yet know about Sarah. For a moment, we simply stood there in the lamplight, the weight of hope and fear and possibility filling the small space between us.

He crossed to me and began loosening my braid with careful fingers, pulling the leather tie free, combing through the plaits until my hair fell loose around my shoulders. I closed my eyes and let him work, feeling the tension of the day releasing strand by strand, my scalp tingling where his fingers moved.

When my hair hung loose, he cupped my face in both palms. "I am afraid. But I am also grateful. For you. For this. For hope."

"I am as well."

We undressed each other slowly in the lamplight, familiar now with ties and belts and the way fabric fell away to reveal skin beneath.

"She is there," I whispered. "Growing."

"I believe you."

He drew me down to the pallet, and what passed between us was prayer as much as anything else, gratitude woven through with fear, hope seeking flesh. His hands moved over me with new tenderness, learning again what he already knew—the curve of my waist, the hollow at the base of my throat where my pulse beat fast, the soft places that made me draw breath or sigh or press closer. And I learned him again—the roughness of his palms against my skin, the smooth warmth beneath my hands, the way his breathing changed when I touched him.

Afterward, I lay in his arms with his palm resting on my belly where nothing showed yet, where everything might be changing in ways too small to see, both of us breathing together in the lamp-shadows.

A bit later, I whispered, "What if my courage starts to fail?"

Andrew drew me closer, his arms around me. "Then I will be there with mine. I promised your father I would protect you. I do not mean to be parted from you this time. Rest now. I am here."

He pulled me tighter against him, and I slept without dreaming.

I woke once in the deep night to find Andrew's arm still around me, heavy with sleep, his breath even against my hair. The lamp had burned down to nothing, leaving us in darkness broken only by starlight through the small window. I lay still for a long moment, listening to the night sounds—an owl calling somewhere in the olive groves, the *creak* of the house settling. Through the window, stars scattered across the darkness like seed across black earth. The Lord had shown them to Abraham once, when he took him outside and said, "Look up into the sky and count the stars if you can. That is how many descendants you will have!"

I counted only one. Sarah.

I placed my palm where Andrew's rested on my belly.

"Lord, you opened Sarah's womb and Hannah's," I whispered into the stillness, "and now you have opened mine again. Keep Sarah safe. Let her live. Let me be strong enough to carry her."

Then I slept again.

MORNING CAME GRAY AND COOL, washing through the small window in pale light that spoke of clouds gathering over the hills. I woke to the sound of Martha already moving in the kitchen, the smell of baking bread drifting through the thin wall, and the soft scrape of a wooden spoon against pottery. Andrew still slept beside me, one arm flung over his head, his face more peaceful than waking ever allowed him.

I rose quietly, dressed in the dim light, and made my way to the kitchen, where warmth from the ovens pushed back against the morning chill.

Martha and Mary were already at work, their hands dusted with flour as they shaped bread dough on the worn wooden table that bore the marks of years of such work—flour ground into the grain, knife scars, the smooth hollow where countless palms had pressed. They looked up when I entered, and Martha gestured to the table without pausing in her rhythm.

"You are awake early. Come. Help us."

I went to stand beside them, and without comment, Martha handed me a portion of dough, still warm and soft from rising, the yeast smell strong in my nose. We worked in silence for a while, the rhythm familiar and soothing, older than memory. Fold, press, turn. The dough yielded under my hands, elastic and alive.

Mary hummed something under her breath while she worked, a melody I almost recognized but could not name. Beside me, Martha's hands never paused, moving with the grace of someone who had shaped ten thousand loaves.

"My courses have not come," I said quietly, not looking

up from the dough, watching my hands work instead. "More than three weeks now."

Both women's hands stilled. They turned to look at me.

"You think you are with child," Martha said.

"I know I am." I met their eyes, first Martha's dark and steady then Mary's soft and searching. "Jesus promised me. After I lost Jonah, after everything—he told me I would have a daughter and to name her after my mother. Sarah."

Mary reached across the table and covered my flour-dusted hands with hers, leaving white prints on my skin. "Sarah. That is a beautiful name."

Martha was quiet for a moment longer, her face unreadable in the dim light, then reached out and cupped my face with one hand, leaving a streak of flour on my cheek. "You lost Jonah, and still you choose to hope again."

"I must. Jesus promised. I believe him."

"Yes." Martha's thumb brushed my cheek, her touch gentle. "Then I believe him too. We believe him. Sarah will come, and she will be loved."

Mary came around the table to embrace me, and Martha joined us, all three of us standing in a flour-dusted huddle while bread dough waited on the table, forgotten for the moment. The ovens breathed warmth into the room, and somewhere outside, a rooster called, and I stood between these two women who had become my sisters, letting them hold me while tears I had not known were gathering spilled over and left tracks down my cheeks.

When we finally pulled apart, Mary asked, "When?"

"Early summer, I think. If all goes well."

"It will go well," Martha said with the kind of certainty that left no room for doubt. "And we will help you every step. You are not alone in this, Anna. You have sisters now."

Sisters.

I placed my hand on my stomach, where nothing showed yet, where everything might be changing. "It is too early to be certain, but my body knows. Everything feels different."

"And Andrew?" Martha asked, returning to her dough, her hands picking up the rhythm again as though they had never stopped.

"I told him last night. He is terrified and trying not to show it."

"Good man." Martha shaped the last loaf and set it aside to rise, covering it with a clean cloth. "My brother also will be glad when he learns of it. He has been asking when you and Andrew would give him little ones to spoil."

"He said that?"

"He tells me you are family now. Not guests but kin." She smiled, and the expression softened her whole face. "He takes his role as a brother very seriously."

Warmth spread through my chest. "I have never had a brother."

"You have one now," Mary said, touching my hands one more time before releasing them. "And he will be impossible when he learns about the baby. He will want to make things, ensure you have everything you need, tell everyone he meets."

A sound from the doorway made us all turn. Lazarus stood there, eyes wide, mouth slightly open. "A baby?"

We froze.

He stepped into the kitchen, looking between the three of us with growing comprehension spreading across his face. "Did I hear that right? Anna is having a baby?"

Martha recovered first, crossing her arms and fixing him with the look she had probably been using since they were children. "You were eavesdropping."

"I was coming to steal bread and heard you talking." He had the grace to look slightly ashamed. "I thought maybe something was wrong." Then his face broke into a wide grin that made him look ten years younger. "But this is not wrong. This is the best news."

"Lazarus—" I started, but he was already crossing the room with quick strides. He caught me up and spun me in a circle before setting me down, still grinning, his joy so unguarded I could not help but laugh despite myself.

"Excellent news. The very best." He held me at arm's length, his hands on my shoulders, his face alight. "When does the child come? What do you need? I will send to Jerusalem for anything—"

"Brother, calm yourself," Martha said, but she was smiling despite the rebuke. "The child will not arrive for months yet."

"Months," he repeated as though testing the word. "That gives me time to prepare. I will need to build a cradle. A good one, strong and smooth, with no rough edges. And make things for her to play with. Do babies need such things immediately or can I wait—"

"Lazarus." I caught his hands, laughing despite the tears still drying on my cheeks. "You do not need to do anything except what you are already doing."

"Nonsense. I have a duty now." He squeezed my hands, his expression shifting from joy to something more serious, more tender. "Truly, Anna. I am glad. This house loves children, and we love you. This child will be welcomed here. Always."

I held on, unable to speak past the tightness in my throat. Mary slipped her arm around my waist. "Family now."

"Yes," I managed. "Family."

Andrew appeared in the doorway, still rumpled from sleep, his hair standing in different directions and his tunic not quite straight. He took in the scene—me with flour on my cheek, the three siblings clustered around me, the bread abandoned on the table—and comprehension crossed his face.

"You told them."

"I—" I started, but Lazarus was already crossing to him.

"Brother! You are going to be a father!" He gripped Andrew's shoulders with both hands, grinning so wide his face could barely contain it. "A daughter, no less. I overheard everything. I am already planning the cradle."

Andrew looked past him to me, question in his expression, a slight furrow between his brows. I nodded once. It was all right.

His shoulders relaxed. He clasped Lazarus's forearm in return. "You cannot tell anyone. We want to keep this private for a while."

"I will tell no one," Lazarus said with exaggerated solemnity, one hand over his heart. Then his grin returned. "Except Jesus. He will be pleased."

"No!" All four of us said it at once, our voices overlapping.

He stopped, looking between us with genuine confusion. "Why not?"

"Because," Martha said with the patience of someone who had been explaining basic courtesy to her brother for thirty-some years, "Anna and Andrew should be the ones to tell people. Not you."

"Ah." He released Andrew's shoulders, consideration crossing his face. "Yes. I had not thought." Then his face lit again. "But after you tell him, I expect a full accounting of his reaction."

"After we tell him," Andrew said, "you may ask whatever questions you like."

"Good. Good." He nodded to himself then caught my eye and winked. "Congratulations, little sister."

He left whistling, and moments later, we heard him greeting someone in the courtyard with too much enthusiasm, his voice carrying through the walls.

Martha shook her head, returning to her dough. "I told you. Impossible."

We left after the midday meal, when the sun was high and warm on our shoulders despite the clouds that had gathered and dispersed without bringing rain. Jesus had already said his goodbyes to Lazarus, the two of them standing close in quiet conversation by the gate, their heads bent together in the way of men sharing words meant only for each other, before embracing one more time. Lazarus's face shone when he looked at his friend, and Jesus's palm lingered on his shoulder before letting go, reluctant to break the connection.

Martha hugged me hard at the door, her arms strong around me, flour still dusted in the creases of her sleeves and across her apron. "Take care of yourself. And Sarah. Come back soon."

I nodded, blinking against tears.

Mary pressed a small cloth bag into my hands, the fabric soft and well-worn, smelling of lavender and chamomile and something else I could not name. "For rest. When the sickness comes, brew this in hot water. It helps."

"Thank you, Mary."

Lazarus was waiting by the gate, one hand shading his eyes against the midday brightness, his face still carrying that irrepressible joy. When I approached, he pulled me into another embrace, lifting me briefly off my feet before setting me down again. "Safe travels, little sister. And remember, if you need anything, send word. I mean it."

"I promise."

"Good." He released me and turned to Andrew, gripping his forearm with both hands, his expression serious. "Take care of them both. Your wife and your daughter."

"You have my oath," Andrew said.

We joined the others and began the descent down the hill toward the road that would take us north, the dust rising pale beneath our feet and settling on the hems of our tunics, coating our sandals, working its way between our toes. The afternoon sun was warm on my shoulders, and the smell of bread and lamb from Martha's kitchen still clung to my clothes, mingling with the green scent of olive leaves and the dust of the road.

Andrew's grip tightened on mine without warning, sudden enough to make me stumble over a stone I had not seen. I steadied myself and followed his gaze to where a man stood beneath an olive tree near the village edge, his fine robes marking him even in shadow, the fabric catching light where everyone else wore homespun. A scribe. The wooden tablet in his hands caught the light as he shifted his weight, and the deliberate movement of his hand across its surface was unmistakable.

"Keep walking," Andrew said, his arm rigid where it met mine, his grip almost painful now.

The road curved ahead, descending between terraced fields where the soil lay dark and freshly turned for winter planting, the furrows running straight and deep. I did not look back again. I knew without looking that behind us, the scribe remained beneath his tree, his stylus moving across wax, recording whatever he had seen—our arrival, our departure, perhaps the house we had entered, perhaps the names of those who welcomed us. The knowledge would not shake loose, clinging like burrs to wool, even as the distance grew and Bethany's white walls faded behind the curve of the hill.

CHAPTER 24

J ERUSALEM, December, 32 AD

T HE T EMPLE LAMPS BURNED against the gray winter sky, eight flames for the eighth day of the feast, their light catching on limestone walls gone pale with cold. Thousands came to Jerusalem each winter for the Feast of Dedication, carrying with them the old stories their fathers and grandfathers had told of how Judas Maccabeus cleansed the Temple after Antiochus Epiphanes defiled it with pagan sacrifice, of how the Maccabees found only enough sacred oil to burn for one day, yet the lamps stayed lit for eight. A small miracle, the priests said each year, but one that whispered of a God who could make the impossible endure, who could stretch a day's worth of oil into a week's worth of light.

The oil still burned in the Temple even now, even as Rome occupied our land and Herod ruled by its permission. Some came to the feast with prayers for another miracle, another cleansing, another deliverance from foreign gods and foreign rule. Others came because their fathers had come, and their fathers before them, keeping the feast alive through generations of occupation and compromise and waiting that stretched longer than anyone could remember. But this year, the city felt different, drawn tight like a bowstring pulled back and trembling, waiting.

Jesus had brought all his followers to Jerusalem three days ago for the Feast of Dedication. My father insisted on housing Jesus, along with those closest to him—Andrew, Peter, James and Tirzah, John, Thomas, and me. The others found lodging where they could or camped outside the city walls, where cook fires dotted the hillsides at night like fallen stars. Naomi had prepared rooms and stocked the kitchen for our arrival.

We all knew it was dangerous. Temple guards watched Jesus when he taught, their attention as sharp as drawn blades. Pharisees clustered at the edges of crowds with their arms crossed and their eyes narrow. My father had warned us the first night, his voice low over evening bread, that Caiaphas had already spoken in council chambers about arrest warrants, that the high priest was waiting only for Jesus to give them the charge they needed. One claim too far and the guards had orders to seize him immediately.

Jesus knew. And he went to the Temple anyway.

Solomon's Portico offered some shelter from the wind that swept across the Court of the Gentiles, but even here, the December air bit through wool cloaks and worked its way beneath tunics until it seeped into bone and settled there like an ache that would not leave. I stood with the other women near one of the massive columns, my hands tucked into my sleeves for warmth, my breath rising in small clouds that vanished as quickly as prayers spoken into winter wind. Around us, hundreds had gathered, pilgrims from Galilee and Judea, from the hill country and the coastal plains, all of them pressing closer to hear Jesus teach, their breath mingling with mine in the cold air.

Jesus walked along the colonnade, his voice carrying across the courtyard as he spoke of shepherds and sheep, of hearing his voice and following where he led. I had heard him teach a hundred times now, in Galilee synagogues and on hillsides where grass grew thick, beside the sea where waves beat their rhythm against his words, but today the crowd split down the middle like cloth torn for mourning. Some leaned in with the same hunger I had seen in Galilee, that desperate thirst for words that could change everything, while others stood with arms crossed and mouths tight, watching not to learn but to catch him in error, to find the one word that would condemn him. The Pharisees and Temple authorities clustered near the eastern edge of the portico. Men whose robes marked them as belonging to the Sanhedrin, whose beards were oiled and carefully trimmed according to custom, whose hands had never known the roughness of rope or the splinters of wood or the salt-cracked skin that came from hauling nets in the cold hour before dawn. They had been there since morning, waiting for something.

I looked for my father among them but could not find him. He had left the house early, called to some council business he would not discuss even when I asked.

One of the Pharisees stepped forward, his voice loud enough to carry across the colonnade and echo off the stone. "How long will you keep us in suspense?" The challenge rang as clear as struck bronze. "If you are the Messiah, tell us plainly."

The crowd stilled. Even the wind paused in its rushing, holding its breath.

Jesus stopped walking. He turned to face the man who had spoken, and for a moment, the world narrowed to just the two of them. Teacher and accuser, prophet and priest, the one who claimed to speak for God and the one who claimed God spoke only through the Law.

"I did tell you, but you do not believe." His voice carried the same calm it always did, the steadiness that never wavered whether he spoke to thousands or to one. "The works I do in my Father's name testify about me, but you do not believe because you are not my sheep. My sheep listen to my voice. I know them, and they follow me. I give them eternal life, and they shall never perish. No one will snatch them out of my hand. My Father, who has given them to me, is greater than all. No one can snatch them out of my Father's hand."

He paused and looked up to the sky, where gray winter clouds moved slowly across the Temple mount. The world went still. The silence deepened until I could hear my own pulse beating.

"I and the Father are one."

A sharp intake of breath came from somewhere behind me. Then the scrape of sandals on stone as the Pharisees rushed forward, bending for stones from the paving, prying them loose from between the ancient blocks where rain and time had worn the mortar soft. Scribes joined them, and Temple officials, and men whose rage sent them scrambling to find weapons where moments before they had stood in prayer. They rose with rocks in their fists, their fine robes dragging in the dust they had kicked up, their carefully oiled beards catching limestone powder as they moved toward Jesus with stones raised and death in their faces.

Jesus did not move. He stood watching them come, standing there as calmly as if he were still teaching about sheep and shepherds, as if a mob with stones in their hands was no different than a crowd coming close to hear the next parable.

"I have shown you many good works from the Father," he said over the scrape of stone on stone, over the shuffle of feet and the breathing of angry men. "For which of them are you going to stone me?"

"For blasphemy!" someone shouted from the back, and others took up the cry. "You, being a man, make yourself God!"

A stone flew. It spun through the air, tumbling end over end. Jesus stepped aside as it struck the column behind him with a crack that sent chips of limestone flying like shrapnel, white dust blooming where the rock hit. Another stone followed, then another, and the air filled with the sound of them. The whistle of rocks cutting through winter wind, the *thud* when they found flesh, the sharp *crack* when they hit stone. The disciples formed a tight circle around Jesus, their bodies a wall between him and the mob. Peter's broad back took a hit that made him stagger forward. John raised his arm to shield himself as a stone grazed his shoulder and tore his sleeve.

The crowd fractured like ice breaking on a winter river. Some surged forward to help throw stones, their hands scrabbling at the paving for anything that could be hurled. Others backed away in horror, mothers pulling their children close, old men turning their faces away from what was happening in the house of God during a holy feast. A woman screamed. Children cried. People pushed and shoved in every direction.

Through the mass of bodies pressing and surging like grain in a windstorm, I saw him—Micah ben Gamaliel, standing at the edge of the mob with a stone in his hand and his arm hanging slack at his side. While the others screamed and threw and scrambled for more ammunition, he stood immobile, staring at Jesus with his face gone white.

Our eyes met across the chaos. His lips moved—words I could not hear over the shouting. He took a step toward me, his free hand rising as if to reach for something he could not quite grasp. The stone fell from his other hand and clattered onto the paving stones, rolling away into the feet of the mob.

Then someone shoved past him hard enough to send him stumbling, and he disappeared into the surging crowd.

Andrew's hand locked around my wrist, his grip tight enough that I knew he would leave marks. "Stay close."

"Where is my father—"

"I do not know. Stay with me."

More stones flew through the air like locusts swarming. The air filled with shouts and accusations and the wet sound of rocks finding flesh. Jesus spoke calmly to his attackers even as they tried to kill him, his words lost in the noise but his lips still moving, still offering them something they refused to hear. Through gaps in the surging crowd, I caught glimpses of the disciples closing ranks around Jesus. Then bodies blocked my view, and when I looked again, he was gone.

The Pharisees rushed forward, shoving through the crowd where Jesus had been standing just moments before, their heads turning left and right as they searched for him, their rage making them clumsy. More guards came running from the inner courts, their sandals slapping against stone.

"After him!" someone shouted, and the command echoed off the columns.

Andrew and I stood frozen, watching as the Pharisees ran. Temple guards joined them. Half the crowd followed, some still carrying stones, all of them pouring out of the portico like water bursting through a broken dam, flooding toward the Temple steps in pursuit of Jesus.

Then Andrew pulled me in the opposite direction, toward the outer edge of the courtyard, where the crowd was thinner and the air clearer. We stumbled over scattered stones that rolled beneath our feet, past overturned merchant tables with coins still spinning on the paving, oil spreading in dark pools between the stones, grain and dried dates crushed underfoot, through the remnants of what moments ago had been a peaceful feast day in the house of God.

My father appeared from behind a column, his blue council robes disheveled and streaked with limestone dust, more dust on his shoulders and in his beard, where it had fallen like early snow.

"Abba!"

Andrew turned me to face him, his hands gripping my shoulders hard enough that I knew he was holding on as much for himself as for me. His hands shook.

"Go with your father. Get to his house. I will come for you."

"I am not leaving you."

"Anna, the child." His eyes searched mine, urgent and wild. "Keep her safe. You need to go with him."

My father reached us then, his breath coming hard like he had run the length of the Temple courts. Andrew seized his sleeve.

"Take her. Get her to safety. She carries our child."

My father's eyes moved from Andrew to me, his mouth opening slightly, but for a moment, he could not speak.

"I must help the others escape." Andrew was already pulling away, looking back toward where the disciples were still trying to get out through the crowd, still dodging guards and angry Pharisees and pilgrims who did not know whether to help or flee. "Peter is still in there. James."

"Andrew." I tried to hold on to him, my fingers catching in his sleeve, but my father's hand closed around my arm and pulled me back.

Andrew looked at me one more time. Everything he could not say lived in that look. Fear and love and the terrible choice between staying with me and saving his brothers.

"I will come for you. I swear it."

Then he turned and ran back into the chaos, back toward where guards were still shouting and still searching for anyone who had stood with Jesus. I took a step forward to follow him into the crowd.

My father's arm locked around my middle like a vise.

"No! Andrew!"

"Come." My father's voice was iron wrapped in velvet. "We go. Now."

We did not run. My father walked with purpose but not panic, his hand firm on my arm, his council robes giving us passage where others were stopped and questioned by guards who still did not know what they were looking for or who they were trying to catch. More Temple guards rushed past us toward the portico, their spears catching winter light. Merchants gathered their scattered goods from where they had fallen when the crowd surged, counting coins with shaking hands. The feast had shattered into confusion, and no one seemed to know how to gather the pieces.

Only when we were clear of the Temple Mount and down the steps and into the narrow streets of the lower city did my father's pace slow. He led me through the maze of alleys toward home, his hand firm on my arm, his eyes watching every shadow as though Temple guards might pour from any doorway.

"Abba, I—"

"Not now," he said sharply. "Wait until we are home."

We reached the house, and the servant opened the gate immediately at my father's knock, his eyes wide with questions he did not dare ask. My father guided me into the courtyard, where the fig tree cast shadows in the afternoon light, its bare branches reaching toward a sky that had gone gray with coming rain. The air smelled of bread baking somewhere inside the house, of woodsmoke from the kitchen fire, of the bitter herbs Naomi grew in clay pots along the wall. Ordinary smells from an ordinary day, unchanged by what had just happened, unchanged by the world trying to murder God in his own Temple.

"Bar the gate. Let no one in unless I know their voice."

I reached for the wall to steady myself, my hand finding cool stone, but my father caught my arm before I could lean my weight against it and led me to the bench beneath the fig tree. The stone was cold through my cloak. I sat because my legs would not hold me anymore. I could still see the stones spinning through the air, could still hear the sound when they struck limestone. The images would not leave.

Naomi came from inside the house, Tirzah behind her with baby Zeb against her chest. Naomi's hands stilled on her shawl when she saw us.

"What happened?" She took one look at my father's dust-covered robes and ashen face, at me sitting rigid on the bench with my hands clenched in my lap, and came quickly, her footsteps quick against stone.

"They tried to stone him. In the Temple." My father sank onto the bench beside me. He sat like a man who had been carrying something too heavy for too long. "Jesus escaped, but the others, I do not know. Andrew stayed to help them."

Tirzah's face went white. "James?"

"With them," I said. "Helping to get Jesus out. He will come back, Tirzah. They all will."

Her arms tightened around Zeb. "I should go pray."

Naomi drew close and took her hand. "They will come home to us."

Tirzah nodded and hurried into the house with the baby, tears already spilling down her cheeks.

Naomi turned to me and took my hands in hers. I was shaking, my whole body trembling as if I had been standing in the December wind for hours instead of sitting in a sheltered courtyard.

"You are hurt?"

"No." The word came out as thin as stretched wool. "Just frightened."

"I will bring wine." She brushed her fingers across my cheek then stood and turned toward the house, her movements unwavering even as everything else shook apart.

She returned with a cup of wine, dark and sweet-smelling, but when she held it out, the smell turned my stomach, and bile rose in my throat like sour milk. I pushed it away before the nausea could rise any higher.

"I cannot."

She set it aside without comment and brought water instead, clear and cold from the cistern. I drank it slowly, letting the coolness spread through me, trying to wash away the taste of fear and dust. My father paced the courtyard, his footsteps restless, wearing a path from the fig tree to the gate and back again.

"They will search the city. Anyone known to be with him will be questioned. Maybe arrested." He stopped pacing long enough to look at me, really look at me for the first time since we left the Temple. "You need to rest. What we witnessed, and now that I have learned—" He looked at Naomi, and when he spoke, his voice had gentled the way it did when he talked about my mother, that softness that lived beneath all his careful control. "In the midst of this terrible day, we have joyous news. Anna is with child."

Naomi set the cup down carefully as though it might break if she moved too quickly. She turned to me and took both of my hands in hers. "Truly?"

"Yes. About three months now."

She pulled me into an embrace, her arms wrapping around me tight enough that I could smell the yeast from this morning's bread still clinging to her robe, could feel the steady beat of her heart against my cheek. When she released me, her eyes searched mine with the gaze of a woman who had tended enough births to know which questions mattered.

"Are you well? Have you been sick?"

"No sickness this time. I am well."

"And you are certain? You have felt movement?"

"Not yet. But I am certain."

Naomi studied my face. The question rose before she spoke it, the fear I had been carrying for weeks like a stone in my chest. "Is it a bad sign? That I have no sickness this time?"

She shook her head slowly. Cool relief poured through me. "No. Every pregnancy is different. Some women are sick, and some are not." Her hands tightened on mine. "You are afraid to hope again."

I nodded, afraid my voice might betray me if I tried to speak.

"I know that fear. The way hope feels like holding water in your hands. You know it will slip through your fingers, but you cup your palms anyway." She took my face in her hands, her palms warm against my cheeks. "Do not let fear steal your joy, Anna. This child is a gift. Let yourself receive it."

My father had not moved from where he stood near the fig tree, his hands clasped behind his back, watching us with an unreadable expression. Then he crossed to where I sat, and he kneeled beside the bench, lowering himself to the courtyard stones that must have been hard on his knees, but he did not seem to notice or care. He took my hand in both of his, and his palms were warm despite the December cold.

"A grandchild." His voice thickened like honey left too long in winter. "After everything, a grandchild."

"Abba, Jesus promised me a daughter. At your wedding to Naomi, he told me. He said to name her Sarah. After Ima."

"Sarah," he whispered, and the name came out like a prayer.

"Yes. I am going to have a daughter."

He bowed his head, my hand pressed to his forehead. He stayed there, silent, and I felt his breath against my wrist. When he looked up again, tears ran into his beard, catching in the gray hairs and making them dark.

"Your mother..." His voice broke on the word like pottery dropped on stone. "She would have loved this."

"I know."

Naomi spoke softly from where she stood. "It is a fine name."

My father stood, pulling me up with him, and embraced me hard enough that I had to turn my head to breathe. The Temple incense still clung to his robes from this morning's prayers, mixed now with dust and sweat and the smell of fear that had soaked into the fabric during the riot.

Naomi came and wrapped her arms around both of us, and we stood there in the courtyard while the afternoon light slanted through the fig tree's bare branches and, somewhere in the city, Andrew was still trying to escape and Jesus was running for his life and the Sanhedrin was meeting to decide what came next.

"Then she will live," he said fiercely when he released me, his hands still gripping my shoulders. "If Jesus promised, she will live." He paused, his thumb brushing against my shoulder where it rested. "And we will never forget Jonah. He was your son. He was my grandson. Sarah does not replace him." He wiped his face with the back of his hand, dragging the tears across his cheek.

I nodded, unable to speak. "No, she does not. Jonah will always live in my heart. Always."

"But you must rest. Eat properly. Stay safe. Which is why you will stay here when Andrew leaves."

Stay here. Let Andrew go without me.

"No. My place is beside my husband."

"You cannot travel in your condition."

"You can discuss it with Andrew if it pleases you. But I will not stay here without him."

My father opened his mouth to argue then decided against it. "So be it."

The afternoon crawled past with agonizing slowness. I

sat beneath the fig tree while Naomi brought bread I could barely taste and more wine I could not touch. Nausea had taken root in my belly, though whether from the baby or fear, I could not say. Every sound from the street made me look toward the gate.

"Abba, what if something has happened to him?"

My father stopped pacing. He came to sit beside me on the bench and lowered himself slowly. "Andrew is resourceful. Peter and John too. They know the city well enough to find their way out of danger."

"But the guards."

"Will be looking for Jesus, not his followers." He put his arm around me and pulled me closer to him. "Andrew will come. He gave you his word."

I wanted to believe him. But I had seen the rage in those Pharisees, the stones flying like hail, the chaos that could swallow a man whole and spit out nothing but memory.

"He will come, Anna. And when he does, we will get him out of the city before the guards know to look for him."

And me, Abba. I will not be staying here.

The courtyard fell silent except for the scrape of his sandals when he resumed pacing, wearing a path in the dust from the fig tree to the gate and back again, and the murmur of his voice when he sent the servant out through the back alley with messages to Nicodemus and others on the council who might send warning if guards were coming to search the house.

I watched the gate and listened for footsteps, my hands folded over my belly where Sarah grew, where hope lived despite everything we had seen today. The sun inched across the sky, throwing shadows that shifted and lengthened while I sat and waited and tried not to imagine what might have happened to Andrew in the hours since he ran back into the chaos.

The sun was setting when footsteps finally sounded in the street outside, quick and purposeful. The gate rattled.

"Joseph! It is Peter."

My father opened the gate, and they came through together. Peter with a bruise along his cheekbone where a stone had caught him, his tunic torn at the shoulder. John, scratched and dusty but whole, his arm cradled against his ribs. James with a torn sleeve hanging from his shoulder, Philip limping on his right leg, Thomas as pale as milk with exhaustion. And Andrew, his hair and shoulders covered in dust that had turned his dark hair gray, a cut above his eye leaking blood down the side of his head in a line that looked black in the lamplight.

I rushed to him, and he caught me in his arms, holding me tight enough that his pulse raced against mine, fast and hard like he had been running for miles.

"You are safe," he said into my hair, his breath warm against my ear. "Thank God, you are safe."

"So are you, but you are bleeding."

Tirzah rushed from the house and went straight to James, her hand finding his. He pulled her close, wrapping his arm around her shoulders, and pressed his forehead to hers for a long moment.

"It is nothing. A stone grazed me, that is all." But Andrew let me lead him to the bench where my satchel waited, set out hours ago when Naomi first brought the water, and he sat while I cleaned the cut with water from the cistern and applied strips of linen bandages.

"Jesus?" my father asked, watching me work.

"Safe. Across the Jordan by now, heading for Perea."

Peter's hands shook as he took wine from Naomi. "The guards sealed every gate after the stoning. We had to wait hours for the shift change then slip him through during the confusion."

Andrew grabbed my hand. "We got here as fast as we safely could."

"They will be looking for all of you," Abba said. "They could start at any moment."

Peter stood, setting down the wine cup with a sound like finality. "Then we need to leave before the city wakes. At dawn, before the guards start searching houses in earnest. What will we—"

A knock at the gate cut him off mid-sentence. We all froze, every person in that courtyard going still.

"Joseph." Nicodemus's voice came low and urgent through the wood. "Let me in. Quickly."

My father opened the gate just wide enough for a man to slip through, and Nicodemus came inside fast, his hood drawn low over his face even though darkness had already fallen and the streets were mostly empty. He pushed the hood back. Even in the lamplight, I could see he looked as gray as old ashes.

"The council met an hour ago. Emergency session called by Caiaphas himself." He accepted wine from Naomi but did not drink, just held the cup in both hands, warming himself against a cold that had nothing to do with December. "Caiaphas called for Jesus's immediate arrest on charges of blasphemy. They have sent guards to every gate, every known supporter, every house where he might seek shelter. They are searching for him now, and they will not stop until they find him or until they are certain he has fled the city."

"He is already across the Jordan," Andrew said. Relief washed across Nicodemus's face.

"Good. But you—" Nicodemus looked around at all of us, his gaze moving from face to dust-covered face. "You need to leave. Tonight. Before they come here looking for anyone who might know where Jesus has gone. Anyone found in this house will be arrested and questioned, and they will not be gentle in their questioning. Joseph is already suspect for his sympathies. If they find you here, they will arrest all of you and use you to draw Jesus back into their hands."

"We leave at first light," Peter said, but Nicodemus was already shaking his head.

"No." Nicodemus set down the untouched wine. "Now, before the moon sets and the streets go completely dark. You have maybe an hour, perhaps two if we are fortunate, before guards arrive to search this house."

My father turned to Andrew and me. "Come. We need to speak privately."

He led us to a corner of the courtyard, away from the others, where lamplight did not quite reach and our words would not be heard. Nicodemus watched but did not follow, giving us this small privacy even as the hour grew late.

"Anna cannot travel. She is with child. She must stay here with me in Jerusalem where she will be safe."

"No." Andrew's voice was as firm as stone. "She is my wife. I have sworn to keep her safe, and I will not leave her behind where I cannot protect her. Not again."

My father turned to me, his eyes searching mine in the dimness. "Anna—"

"I stay with Andrew. He will take care of us, Abba."

My father was silent for a long moment. All the arguments he wanted to make lived in that silence. The danger of the roads, the hardship of travel, the risk to Sarah, the safety of his house where Naomi could tend me. All of it sat between us unspoken. Finally, he said, "Andrew, she is my only child. She carries my grandchild. Sarah's grandchild." He paused on my mother's name. Years of grief caught in his voice. "You will protect her. You must."

"With my life. I will keep her and our child safe, or I will die trying."

My father closed his eyes briefly. When he opened them again, his face had changed. Not acceptance, exactly, but the kind of surrender that comes when a man realizes he cannot stop what must happen. He nodded once. "Then take what you need and go."

"Joseph, there is little time." Nicodemus's voice carried across the courtyard, urgent. "You need to leave. All of you. Now."

We moved quickly after that. Naomi and Tirzah packed bread and dried fruit, cheese wrapped in cloth and olives sealed in jars, and waterskins filled from the cistern until they were heavy enough to make shoulders ache. My father brought out a leather pouch heavy with silver and gave it to Andrew—more than I had ever seen at one time, enough for months of travel, enough to buy passage or lodging or safety if silver could still purchase such things. Warm cloaks appeared from storage chests, extra blankets that smelled of cedar and lavender, everything that could be carried without slowing us down too much.

We gathered in the courtyard as the moon rose over Jerusalem's walls, turning the limestone as white as bone. We would travel together through the night. The rest of the disciples and those who followed Jesus would leave by different routes, scatter like seeds on the wind, and meet us across the Jordan in Perea where Jesus waited.

My father pulled me aside one last time, his hands on my shoulders. "Send word when you arrive safely. If you can find a messenger who will carry it."

"I will if I can."

He embraced me then, his arms wrapping around me tight enough that I could barely breathe. He trembled slightly beneath the council robes. When he released me, he turned to Andrew and gripped his forearm. "You swore to protect them both. I will hold you to that oath, Andrew bar Jonah."

"As you should." Andrew clasped his forearm in return. "I will not fail you. I will not fail her."

Naomi pulled me close and kissed my forehead. "Be strong, daughter. Trust Jesus's promise about Sarah."

The gate opened onto a dark street where no lamps burned in the windows and no voices carried on the night air. Jerusalem slept. A handful of refugees slipped through its streets toward the eastern gate and the wilderness beyond, while the man the Sanhedrin wanted dead was already across the Jordan, moving deeper into territory where their authority did not quite reach.

We moved in silence, keeping to the shadows where the moonlight did not quite reach, where the darkness was thick enough to hide us from casual glances. Peter led us through the maze of alleys, his instinct for danger guiding each turn, each choice between taking the wider street or the narrower passage. Behind me, Tirzah walked with Zeb bundled against her chest, one hand cupped over his head to keep him warm and quiet. The streets were empty and doors barred for the night, every house shut up tight against the December cold and whatever might walk the streets after dark. Our footsteps echoed off stone walls despite our care, the sound bouncing back to us like accusations. Somewhere, a dog barked once, sharp and sudden in the stillness. I kept my hand on Andrew's arm, pushing away thoughts of Temple guards hunting through these same streets for us, pushing away images of what would happen if they found us fleeing Jerusalem like criminals running from justice.

The eastern gate loomed ahead of us, massive and dark against the star-scattered sky, its great doors already closed and barred for the night. But there was a smaller postern gate beside it, used by travelers who arrived late or left early, by merchants whose business could not wait for sunrise, by people who had reasons for coming and going when most of the city slept. A single guard stood watch there, leaning against the wall with the boneless slouch of a man who had been standing too long and was counting the hours until his relief arrived.

Peter approached him while the rest of us hung back in the shadows, pressing ourselves against walls and trying to look like nothing more than darkness itself. I could not hear what was said between them, but silver changed hands. Moonlight caught on coins as they passed from Peter's palm to the guard's. The guard weighed the silver in his hand for a long moment, considering whether it was worth the risk of letting us through. Then he unlocked the postern with a key that scraped and rattled in the lock, and stepped aside.

We filed through one by one into the cold December night, each of us ducking through the narrow opening, leaving behind the city walls and the safety they promised and stepping out onto the road that would take us away from everything familiar. The road stretched before us, pale in the moonlight like a river of milk flowing down through the hills, descending through barren slopes toward the Jordan Valley, where shadows pooled as thick as spilled wine. Behind us, Jerusalem rose white and holy on its hill, the Temple catching starlight and throwing it back like a beacon, the city where David had ruled and Solomon had built and the prophets had preached and died.

I looked back once, just once, at the city where I had been born when my mother still lived to hold me and where she had died protecting me from Roman swords when I was too young to understand what she was giving up. The city that had just tried to stone Jesus during a feast celebrating God's deliverance, that had turned the house of prayer into a place of violence and rage.

Andrew took my hand, his fingers lacing through mine. "We need to keep moving. Put distance between us and the city before dawn breaks and they discover we are gone."

I turned away from Jerusalem and toward the wilderness ahead, toward the darkness that waited beyond the reach of lamplight.

CHAPTER 25

PEREA, Across the Jordan, January, 33 AD

THE ALMOND TREES that lined the Jordan stood bare against the sky, their branches black and skeletal, waiting for spring to clothe them once more. I sat beneath a tamarisk in the winter sun, my spine pressed against bark gone smooth from wind and weather, both palms spread flat over the slight swell where Sarah grew beneath my ribs. Four months now. A small rounding that my loose tunics still concealed, a secret I carried in my body. My hands rested there, warmth of skin through wool. Soon would come what came with Jonah— that strange tumbling sensation like bubbles rising through water, the first flutter of life making itself known.

The camp around me carried on its rhythms. Women ground barley between stones, the scrape and thud steady as a heartbeat. Flies buzzed over the cooking pots where lentils simmered for the evening meal. Men sat in the shade of the date palms repairing sandals, their bronze awls punching through leather with precise sounds, or sharpening knives against whetstones, metal rasping on stone while they spoke of fishing and taxes and how long the barley would last. Under the tamarisks, small groups gathered to hear Jesus teach, their voices drifting towards me as they questioned and argued and tried to understand.

The messenger came running through our camp in the midafternoon, raising clouds with every footfall, his tunic dark with sweat across the shoulders and back.

"Andrew." I sat forward. "That is Joab. From Martha and Mary's household."

Andrew shaded his eyes, looking where I pointed. "From Bethany."

He wore travel like a second skin. His sandals had worn through, the leather cracked and splitting. Blood marked his feet where the straps had rubbed them raw. His face carried the haggard look of someone who had run far and slept little —eyes sunken deep, cheeks hollow beneath the grime, lips cracked from sun and wind. My hands went still against my belly.

Andrew helped me to my feet, and we moved closer, joining the others who had already gathered beneath the palms. Joab stood before Jesus, swaying slightly with exhaustion, barely able to stay upright.

"Peace, Joab. You have come far." Jesus steadied him with a hand on his shoulder. "Is there trouble?"

"Lord." Joab bent his head, his breathing still ragged. "Lord, the one you love is sick." He paused then gathered himself. "Lazarus. Martha and Mary sent me. They beg you —they beg you to come. Quickly."

My breath stopped. I stepped forward. "What is it? What happened?"

Joab's grimy face turned toward me. "Fever. Three days when I left Bethany. The heat pours off him like a bread oven, but he shakes with cold beneath every blanket Martha can find. He keeps nothing down—not broth, not wine, not even water half the time." His voice cracked. "When he knows us, he calls for Jesus. When he does not..." He swallowed hard. Fever madness could steal a man's mind before it took his life. "Martha sent me running. She said if Jesus did not come soon—" He stopped. "She said to run."

Three days of unbroken fever. Three days when Joab left, and how long had he been on the road? A day and a half? Two days? Lazarus could be worse now. Much worse. Or already—no. But even if we left this moment, it would take us two days to reach Bethany. Two full days.

"Jesus, we need to leave now. It cannot wait."

"We will not go now."

Joab's face went slack. "But Lord, you must come. He is dying—"

Jesus placed one hand on Joab's shoulder. "This sickness will not end in death. It is for the glory of God, so that the Son of God may be glorified through it."

Joab eyes grew round. He looked at me, desperate for an explanation I did not have.

"I have heard you." Jesus's hand tightened briefly on Joab's shoulder then released. "Rest now. Eat. You have done what they asked of you."

Mary took Joab's arm and led him toward the cooking fires, where someone would give him bread and water, where he could sit in the shade and rest his blistered feet. The others moved away slowly, glancing back at Jesus, their faces troubled, questions written in every line of their bodies. I stood rooted to that spot, unable to move, images flooding my mind. Martha laughing over something Lazarus said while her hands worked bread dough, flour dusting her sleeves white as snow. Mary sitting in their courtyard with her embroidery, her needle catching afternoon light as it rose and fell through linen. Lazarus himself, telling stories about his travels to Damascus, his voice warm with humor, teasing Mary about her sewing or Martha about burning the bread. Hoping to build Sarah a cradle.

Lazarus was dying. And Jesus stood here talking about glory.

Jesus turned toward the fires where the others had gathered, the conversation clearly finished in his mind. I stepped forward, directly into his path. He stopped.

"Why will you not go to him?"

"I know you love them, Anna." His voice gentled. "I know how much they mean to you. Martha is strong. Mary is not alone. And Lazarus—" He paused. "I love them too."

His words brought no comfort. If he loved them, then why would he not go?

"Then go to them. Today. We could leave now and be there by—"

"Anna." Andrew's voice came from behind me, his hand finding my arm.

I pulled away without looking at him, all my attention fixed on Jesus. "Martha will be managing everything alone right now. The physicians coming and going, the neighbors bringing food she has no time to cook, visitors she must receive even while her brother—" The words stuck like barley husks in my mouth. I forced them past the tightness. "And Mary. You know how she is. How deeply she feels everything.

She will be breaking apart, and no one will know how to help her because no one understands her the way you do. The way I do. She needs us there."

Jesus reached out and took my hands in his. "Do you trust me?"

The question made no sense. "Of course I trust you, but—"

"Then trust me in this."

His thumbs moved across my knuckles, then he released my hands and continued toward the fires. I stood there watching him go, thinking only that we were staying, and Lazarus was dying.

Andrew guided me back to the tamarisk tree. I went but sank down against the trunk with enough force that my teeth clicked together. Jesus moved among the people, teaching and listening, placing his hands on the sick who came to him here while refusing to go to the sick in Bethany. I dug my fingers into the dirt beside me, and the grit worked under my nails.

The sun moved across the sky, shadows lengthening across the packed earth of our camp. Evening came with its familiar rituals—fires kindled, lentils bubbling in clay pots, the smell of baking flatbread drifting through the gathering darkness. We ate, and Jesus spoke about the bread of life. I chewed flatbread that tasted like ash in my mouth, swallowed lentils gone cold in the bowl. Around me, people listened with rapt faces, nodding at his words. Questions beat against my temples until my head throbbed with them.

Joab left at first light, his shoulders bowed beneath the news he carried back to Bethany. He had rested and eaten as Jesus told him and had slept a few hours under one of the palm trees. But now he returned to tell them that Jesus was not coming. Absence where Martha and Mary had begged for his presence.

Jesus taught by the river where men still came to be baptized despite the Jordan running cold in winter, despite the chill that made them gasp when the water closed over their heads. I heard his voice across the current, speaking words of life and light. His hands lifted in blessing over each person who came up dripping and shivering from the water, the morning sun catching the drops as they fell and turning them to diamonds in the air. So much power in those hands. Power to heal with a word, with a touch. Power he was not using to heal Lazarus.

My hands found work to occupy them. Grinding barley between stones, the upper millstone heavy beneath my palms. The circular motion—push forward, lean into the weight, bring it around, push again—heated the stone until my palms grew slick with sweat despite the cool morning air. My shoulders burned. The small of my back protested. But the rhythm kept my body busy while my mind circled endlessly through images of Bethany.

When the grinding was done, I took up mending a tunic where the seam had split and pulled loose from many washings. I worked the bronze needle through the fabric, pulling each stitch tight, the metal warm from my hand. Once, I pushed too hard and the needle slipped, jabbing deep into the pad of my thumb, where blood welled up bright against my skin. I sucked the wound and kept sewing. One question beat against my skull: Why would he not go?

Two days passed. Two full days while Martha and Mary kept vigil in Bethany and Jesus kept teaching in Perea. Two days that filled me with anger.

On the third day, while grinding barley, Jesus gathered

the disciples beneath the palms. I set down the grinding stone and moved closer, my hands still white with flour.

"Let us go back to Judea."

Finally, we would go.

I caught Andrew's eye. He nodded once.

Peter's objection came swiftly. "Rabbi." He stepped forward. "The Jews tried to stone you there. You want to go back?"

"Are there not twelve hours in the day?" Jesus said. "If anyone walks in the day, he does not stumble, because he sees the light of this world. But if anyone walks in the night, he stumbles, because the light is not in him." He looked around the circle of faces. "Our friend Lazarus has fallen asleep. But I go to wake him."

Philip spoke up. "Lord, if he sleeps, he will get better."

"No, Philip. Lazarus is dead."

I gasped, both hands going to my belly. Silence fell over the circle. Jesus let it hold for a moment before continuing.

"And for your sake I am glad I was not there, for now you will really believe. But let us go to him now."

Thomas spoke, his voice flat with resignation. "Let us also go, that we may die with Jesus."

Lazarus was dead. Jesus had named it plainly, without softening, without evasion. Yet in the same breath, he spoke of going to wake him, as though death were nothing more than an afternoon nap beneath the palms.

I found Andrew among the others preparing to leave, rolling his blanket tight and securing it with cord. "He said Lazarus is dead but that he goes to wake him."

"I heard him."

"And Thomas said we may die with him." I gripped Andrew's arm. "Is it safe for me to—"

"Anna, we follow as we always have." He pulled me close, his hand warm against my back. "I will take care of you and Sarah. I will be with you every step. And Jesus said to trust him, so we must. Even when we do not understand."

"I do trust him. But you are right, I do not understand. Any of it."

"Neither do I." He pressed his forehead to mine for a moment, his breath warm against my face. "But we go anyway."

We began to pack. I folded my blanket and rolled it tight then tied it with a cord that bit into my palms as I pulled the knots secure. Andrew checked our waterskins, holding each one up to the light to see how much we had left, then set them aside to fill from the river before we left. Around us, others did the same.

AT FIRST LIGHT, we walked. Two days through country that grew greener as we climbed away from the Jordan Valley toward the hills of Judea. The winter rains had brought grass to the hillsides, tender green shoots pushing through last year's dried stalks, and wildflowers bloomed in purple and yellow patches wherever water collected in the low places. The air smelled of wet earth and new growth, that freshness that comes after rain in a dry land, so different from summer when everything turned brown and brittle.

By the second afternoon, my feet had swollen until the leather straps cut grooves into my flesh, lines that stayed white and bloodless when I loosened the ties to check. The small swell of my belly made me shift my weight differently, conscious of every stone that turned beneath my sandal, every uneven patch where the path climbed steep. Andrew walked beside me, his hand catching my elbow whenever the ground grew uncertain, steadying me over the rough places without a word, his presence as constant as my shadow.

We reached Bethany in the late afternoon, with the sun sliding toward the western hills. The olive trees cast long shadows across the path, their gnarled trunks gone black against the brightness behind them. The air had cooled, carrying the smell of cook fires and bread baking and, beneath it all, the heavy, resinous smell of myrrh and aloes, the spices used to prepare the dead.

The wailing reached us before we saw the village proper. Raw voices in the rhythmic keen of professional mourners hired for the occasion, their cries threading through the deeper, rougher sounds of anguish. The two braided together —hired sorrow and genuine sorrow, false tears and true— until telling where one ended and the other began became impossible. The sound rose and fell like waves breaking on a shore, crashing against the walls of the houses and echoing back again, filling the valley with the voice of death.

Martha must have set watchers, because she came running before we were fully into the village, her feet bare, moving fast despite her grief. Her hair hung uncovered down her back—a shocking sight, as improper as if she had stripped naked in the street, a violation of every custom of modesty and propriety that governed a woman's appearance. But Martha ran through Bethany's streets with her head uncovered and did not care who saw.

Grief had remade her face. The skin around her eyes had puffed until the lids were slits, the whites gone as pink as pomegranate flesh. Her tunic gaped at the neck where she had torn it, the linen ripped in jagged edges that exposed the hollow of her throat, and the fabric there was stiff with dried salt from days of weeping.

"Lord." The word came out raw. "If you had been here, my brother would not have died." She drew a shuddering breath, tears streaming down her face and dripping from her chin to darken the earth at Jesus's feet. "But I know that even now, God will give you whatever you ask."

I moved forward, wanting to go to her, but the crowd of mourners had followed her from the house and now pressed in around Jesus, all of them weeping. Then I saw them. Members of the Sanhedrin stood at the edges of the crowd, their faces watchful. The same men who had tried to stone Jesus stood in Martha's courtyard. We had walked straight into their hands.

Jesus lifted Martha to her feet. "Your brother will rise again."

"I know he will rise again." Martha's voice grew stronger, though tears still fell. "In the resurrection at the last day. But that does not—" She stopped and pressed her hands to her mouth, fingers digging into her cheeks as though she could physically hold back the grief that would not be contained.

"I am the resurrection and the life," Jesus said, his voice carrying through the crowd and silencing the noise around us. "The one who believes in me will live, even though they die. And whoever lives by believing in me will never die." He paused. "Do you believe this?"

Martha's face showed everything. Eyes swollen nearly shut, nose running, mouth twisted. But her eyes held that bright, fierce clarity seen in her before. The bedrock certainty that ran deeper than sorrow. "Yes, Lord. I believe that you are the Messiah, the Son of God, who is to come into the world."

"Go get your sister, Martha."

She turned and pushed back through the crowd toward the house. The mourners fell silent, their wailing suspended. People glanced at each other and shifted their weight. Time stretched as we all waited. Then Martha returned with Mary. "Lord, I told her the Teacher is here and wants to see you."

My own tears came unbidden. Martha carried grief like a wound still bleeding. Mary carried it like death itself. Her skin held no more color than old ashes, gray and lifeless. Her eyes had disappeared into swollen flesh, the lids so raw they wept clear fluid that mixed with her tears. She moved like a woman whose skeleton had turned to sand, each step uncertain, her weight leaning full into Martha's arm. When she saw Jesus, she collapsed at his feet, and the anguish that tore from her throat sounded like something living being ripped apart.

"Lord, if you had been here, my brother would not have died!"

The same words Martha spoke. Mary wept into the earth at Jesus's feet, her whole body shaking with sobs that came in waves, each one seeming to empty her out further. The crowd of mourners surged forward, wailing in response, their laments weaving together into something almost unbearable to hear.

I tried to move closer, needing to reach Mary, but hands caught at my arms. Susanna on one side, Joanna on the other, held me back. 'Not now,' Susanna whispered, her eyes on Jesus. 'Let him—

Jesus was weeping.

Tears flowed down into his beard, catching the light. His shoulders shook. Even the professional mourners fell silent.

"See how he loved him," someone said softly, and many murmured agreement.

But others whispered darker things. "Could he not have kept this man from dying? He who opened the eyes of the blind?"

Jesus wiped his face with his sleeve, a rough, impatient gesture that smeared the tears across his cheeks, then reached down to lift Mary to her feet. "Where have you laid him?"

"Come and see, Lord." Martha's voice was a whisper.

We moved through the village toward the tomb, moving slowly through streets walked before when Lazarus was alive, when this house was a place of laughter and welcome, when Martha's complaints about the cooking and Mary's dreamy distraction were the worst troubles they knew. Mary clung to Jesus's arm on one side, Martha on the other, both sisters leaning against him as though they would collapse without his support, their weight pulling at his shoulders, their grief a physical burden he carried for them. The crowd followed, a river of mourners flowing through Bethany's narrow streets. Andrew's hand stayed at my back as we walked.

The tomb stood outside the village, where all the tombs stood, cut into a hillside among the olive groves, sealed with a round stone rolled across its entrance. The opening had been hewn smooth by patient chisels years ago when the family tomb was first carved, the stone so precisely fitted that not even a sliver of darkness showed around the edges. I pictured Lazarus lying inside on a stone shelf with his ancestors, wrapped in linen on a bed of spices, myrrh and aloes layered thick to slow the decay but unable to stop it, unable to hold back the inevitable return of flesh to earth.

Lazarus, who told stories with such warmth and welcomed us into his home with wine and bread and laughter, who never tired of hearing Jesus teach, who laughed with his eyes as much as his voice. Now sealed in darkness and silence, wrapped in grave clothes, his face covered, his hands bound, his body already beginning the slow collapse back into earth.

Tears spilled down my cheeks, catching in the corners of my mouth.

Andrew's arm came around me. He bent close, his lips near my ear. "Do not lose faith," he whispered.

We gathered at the tomb. Jesus stood before the stone, his face still wet with tears that caught the slanting winter light and made tracks through the grime on his cheeks. For a long moment, he simply looked at the sealed entrance, at the massive stone that had likely taken four strong men to roll into place. The winter light slanted across the hillside, catching the pale limestone and making it glow warm against the dark earth, turning the tomb entrance to gold even while death ruled within. Somewhere in the olive grove behind us, a dove called—three clear notes that hung in the silence, pure and as sweet as a flute's voice. We waited, though for what, none of us knew.

Then Jesus spoke, breaking the silence with words clear and certain, spoken to the mourners and the curious and the Pharisees who had come to watch.

"Take away the stone."

Martha's voice rose immediately, sharp with horror. "But, Lord—" She stepped forward, her hand reaching out as though to physically stop him. "By this time, there will be a stench. He has been dead for four days."

Four days in a sealed tomb in winter. Four days for the body to begin its collapse, for the flesh to bloat and darken, for the smell of decay to fill that small space until it became unbearable.

"Did I not tell you that if you believe, you will see the glory of God?"

He nodded at the disciples. Peter, John, and James moved forward, Andrew following close behind. They positioned themselves around the massive stone, palms flat against limestone. Then they pushed. Their backs bowed with effort, muscles cording beneath their tunics. Their sandals scraped and slipped in the loose dirt as they fought for purchase, small stones skittering away under their heels. The grinding began low, a bass note that I felt in my bones before I heard it, stone grating against stone with a sound like the earth's own voice groaning, like creation itself protesting this unsealing of what should remain sealed. The stone moved. Slowly at first, just a hand's breadth, then faster as momentum took over, and the disk rolled aside with a final scrape that echoed off the hillside.

The men stepped back, chests heaving with exertion, sweat darkening their tunics across their backs and under their arms despite the winter chill. The entrance gaped black before us, a rectangle of absolute darkness against the pale limestone, deeper than shadow, deeper than night. The kind of darkness that swallowed light and gave nothing back.

Cold breathed from the opening, the temperature dropping as though we stood before a winter cistern. The air carried the musty coolness of stone and earth undisturbed, the mineral smell of limestone, the faint herbal bite of dried myrrh. No corruption. No rot. No sweet-sick reek of flesh returning to dust. Just the smell of a cave that had been sealed against the world, holding its secrets in silence.

Andrew returned to my side, and I grabbed his arm, my heart beating wildly.

Jesus lifted his eyes toward heaven, toward the pale winter sky where clouds moved slowly across the sun.

"Father, I thank you that you have heard me. I knew that you always hear me, but I said this for the benefit of the people standing here, that they may believe that you sent me."

He lowered his eyes from heaven and looked into the darkness of the tomb.

CHAPTER 26

"Lazarus, come forth!"

The words cracked across the countryside like stone splitting under a hammer, and Andrew's fingers dug into my back through layers of wool and linen while the wind stilled, leaving even the olive branches on the far hillside motionless, their silver leaves quiet against the sky. A goat bleated somewhere in the village below, thin and plaintive in the cold air, then silence fell again, absolute and waiting, before fabric rustled against stone from inside the tomb, followed by the scrape of shuffling feet on rock.

A shape emerged from the shadows, wrapped in grave clothes, linen strips binding hands to sides and feet together. Lazarus moved into the winter sunlight in small, halting steps, a grown man swaddled like an infant, the burial cloth still covering his face. That square of white linen should have been soaked through with the fluids of decay, rank with death's corruption, but the air smelled only of myrrh and aloes and cold stone, as clean as rainwater on bare rock.

Someone behind me drew breath so sharp it whistled. "God be praised!"

The shout broke whatever spell had held us, and the crowd hurried forward, hands stretching toward Lazarus, toward Jesus, desperate to touch proof that the impossible had happened. A few of the Pharisees stood frozen, faces gone as white as limestone. My knees buckled, and Andrew caught me, his arm solid around my waist, holding me upright, while he whispered a prayer of thanksgiving, his voice rough.

"Unbind him and let him go."

Jesus spoke through the noise. Peter moved to him first, his hands shaking so badly he fumbled at the linen strips, fingers slipping on knots tied in grief four days ago. Andrew shifted behind me, but I hung on to his arm and held it there. He stayed. John joined Peter, then James, the three of them unwrapping Lazarus with careful, reverent hands.

The burial cloth fell away from Lazarus's face, revealing skin as translucent as milk in the afternoon light, but his eyes were clear and aware, moving with the rhythm of breath. His eyes found Jesus across the crowd and held his gaze, then he nodded slowly while Jesus returned it. Martha and Mary reached him before the disciples had finished freeing his hands, their arms going around him, their bodies shaking with sobs that sounded like laughter, like grief transforming into joy before our eyes.

The three of them stood locked together while the linen strips fell away in pieces, littering the ground like shed snakeskin, white against winter-brown earth, and Lazarus swayed slightly before shaking his head when Martha tried to help him, standing on his own feet with shoulders straightening as color rose in his cheeks, pink spreading beneath his skin.

Andrew's hand tightened on my shoulder. "He is well. Look at him. He is well."

"I see him." My voice shook. "I see him, and I still cannot believe it."

The psalms of praise rose from the crowd, voices cracking and soaring and weaving together in a sound more beautiful than any Temple choir while others simply wept, their tears catching the thin winter sunlight. But a knot of Pharisees broke from the edge and walked fast toward the village, heads bent together, robes snapping in the wind. Peter's gaze followed them before he moved to Jesus's side, leaning close and speaking fast, and Jesus nodded once.

Martha was the first to move, pulling Lazarus toward the village road. "Come. You need to eat. You need to eat and rest and—" She could not finish.

Mary took his other arm. "And tell us everything."

The three of them started walking. We followed them back to Martha's house through air that smelled of fallow grass and distant rain. The procession rang with laughter and song. And Lazarus walked in the center of it all with his usual long stride, as natural as though he had never been gone, his sisters on either side of him like guards flanking a king.

Andrew walked close beside me. He laughed once. When I glanced up, his eyes shone with tears, watching Lazarus.

"Lazarus is alive." He shook his head and wiped his face with the back of his hand. "Four days, Anna. Four days in the tomb. And now—" He shook his head. "Death could not hold him. Jesus called, and death let go."

"I should never have doubted," I said quietly. "He asked if I trusted him. I said yes, but I—" I stopped. "I was angry we did not leave immediately. To be truthful, I wanted my own way in the matter. I did not believe in him."

Andrew's arm came around me. "You believe now."

"It is easy to believe when the proof walks before us." I watched Lazarus ruffle Mary's hair as they walked, his sister swatting his hand away while she laughed. "True faith is trusting before the tomb opens. I failed that test."

"We all did." His voice was rough. "Every one of us."

Lazarus looked over his shoulder at Jesus, who walked a few paces behind. "Brother, you took your time."

Jesus laughed. "I was giving you a chance to rest."

"Then I am well rested. And very hungry."

I smiled. There he was. Not just alive but unchanged, his humor as sharp as ever. Death had not diminished him. It had not taken the parts of him that made him Lazarus.

Thank you, Adonai, for letting me be a part of this. The words formed without my willing them. *Thank you for bringing me here, for this moment, for this mercy I do not deserve.* My hand settled on my belly where Sarah grew. *And thank you for her. For this life you have given me when I thought myself beyond such blessings. And for Andrew. For a man who stays.* Tears came then, and I wiped at them with my sleeve. Today was a day to rejoice.

At the house, the courtyard filled so quickly there was barely room to move. Bodies crowded together, the smell of unwashed wool and sweat thick in the close space, layered with olive oil and wine and the yeasty warmth of fresh bread. Lazarus saw us walk in and pulled me into an embrace, his arms strong around me, his laughter vibrating through my ribs. "Anna! It is good to see you—" Then he stopped. His arms loosened slightly. He stepped back, his hands settling on my shoulders as his gaze dropped to where my tunic pulled across my belly. "She has grown."

"Yes, she has." I laughed, wiping at my wet face with my sleeve, deciding tears were perfectly acceptable for this day.

"Well." He grinned wide. "Four days dead, and she kept growing without me."

Andrew shifted at my side, and Lazarus turned to him. "Brother. A father soon."

"Yes, I will be." Andrew's hand found Lazarus's arm. "And you were dead."

"I was." Lazarus pulled him into a hug, thumping his back hard enough to make Andrew cough. When he released Andrew, he looked at Martha, who had appeared with flour still dusting her hands. "We should have a feast."

"We will." Her voice was thick with tears and laughter woven together, a sound I had never heard from her before. She moved to my side, and her hand settled on the slight swell beneath my tunic, warm through the fabric. "You were right, Anna. We can see her now."

Mary's hand joined hers, both of them touching where my daughter grew, where life quickened and turned beneath their palms.

"Sarah," Martha said softly then looked up at me. "She will be fierce. Like her mother."

Mary smiled through her tears. "And faithful. Like her father."

Martha turned to Andrew then and gripped his forearm. "Take care of them both. Your wife and your daughter. They are part of our family now."

"With my life," Andrew promised.

Martha disappeared into her kitchen and emerged moments later with bread and fresh cheese and dried figs sticky with honey, spreading them on platters faster than seemed possible for one pair of hands. Mary brought wine, pouring cup after cup. She kept stopping to wipe her eyes then pouring again. And Lazarus sat in the center of the courtyard, already eating as though he had not been dead but merely away on a journey.

I refilled cups as Martha brought more food, weaving between the crowded bodies. The wine smelled sweet and dark, staining my fingers purple where it sloshed over cup rims. Andrew sat with Peter and John against the courtyard wall, all three of them eating bread and cheese, their eyes on Lazarus. When I poured wine for them, Andrew caught my hand and held it before I moved on.

I broke off a piece of bread for myself, and the crust crackled between my teeth, the inside soft and warm with a faint sourness. Martha's bread. I had eaten it a hundred times before, but today it tasted like manna. The kind of grace that fills empty bellies after miracles.

"This is the best bread I have ever tasted." Lazarus spoke around a mouthful, crumbs catching in his beard.

Martha laughed. "It is the same bread I always make."

"Then I have been taking it for granted." He reached for another piece and tore it with strong fingers. "I have been days without food, Martha. I thought I might die of hunger."

"You were already dead," Jesus said, and Lazarus pointed at him with a fig, the fruit dark and glistening.

"Exactly. So the hunger was even worse because I was dead and hungry." He bit into the fig and grinned. "And you. You were crying."

Jesus shook his head, but he was smiling. "I wept for my friend."

"Did your nose run?" Lazarus's eyes glinted with mischief.

"My nose did not run."

"Martha says you wept. Weeping involves nose running. It is simply a fact."

"I wept with dignity."

"There is no dignity in nose running, brother." Lazarus reached for more bread. "Though I suppose you managed it somehow."

Jesus threw a piece of bread at him. Lazarus caught it, and the courtyard erupted in laughter.

Then Lazarus went quiet. The lightness left his expression, and his mouth compressed into a line. "Thank you. For coming. For—" He stopped. His eyes shone wet in the lamplight. "For calling me back."

Jesus reached across the space between them and gripped his shoulder. "I would walk through fire for you, brother. Death is a small thing compared to that."

Lazarus nodded, unable to speak. Jesus's hand tightened briefly on his shoulder then released.

People surrounded us on all sides, everyone wanting to touch Lazarus, to see for themselves that he was truly standing before them. The heat of so many bodies made the air close, thick with too many smells layered one on top of another. My stomach turned, and I breathed through my mouth. I needed air.

I slipped through the crowd toward the gate, moving sideways between bodies until I broke free onto the street outside of Martha's house. The cold hit my face like water from a well. I leaned against the limestone wall and drew in deep breaths, letting the nausea settle. Footsteps sounded behind me. I turned.

Lazarus stood watching me. "Are you well?" His voice was quiet, stripped of the lightness he had carried inside.

"The baby." I shrugged. "Too many people. Too many smells."

"Too many people for me too." He crossed to the wall and leaned next to me against the stone. For a moment, we stood in silence. The sounds of laughter and song drifted from the courtyard.

"It is strange," he said finally. "To be here. To smell bread baking and hear my sisters' laughter and feel cold stone under my hands." He spread his fingers wide, studying his palms as though they belonged to someone else. "Four days ago, I could do none of those things."

"What was it like? Being dead."

He was quiet for so long I thought he would not answer. Then he looked out toward the hills, pale limestone against the afternoon sky.

"I cannot tell you," he said. "The language we have is not enough for it." He paused. "But I can tell you this. Jesus called, and I came. That is all you need to know. His voice reaches even there."

"Jesus told me I would see my son again," I said. "That one day, in a place where there is no more death or mourning, I would hold him. That he waits for me there."

Lazarus turned to look at me. "He does not lie."

"No." I wiped at my eyes. "But sometimes I—" The words would not come. "I miss him so much. And now, Sarah—" I laid my hand on my belly. "I am afraid. What if I lose her too? What if—"

"Anna." His hand found my shoulder. "You carry life, and you grieve the dead. One does not erase the other. This is what it means to keep living."

Tears came, and I wiped at them quickly, almost laughing. "I do not even know why I am crying. You are alive. Jesus promised me Sarah would live. I should be—" My voice caught. "I am happy. Truly."

"I know." He pulled me into a brief embrace. "Sometimes joy needs tears too."

I pulled away, wiping my face with my sleeve. "Today is for joy, not sadness."

"Today is for both." He clasped my shoulders. "And I am proof they can exist together." He smiled. "Jesus holds life and death in his hands, Anna. I have seen what comes after. Your son waits."

I nodded.

"You will see him again," Lazarus said. "Jesus promised you. And if he can call me back from four days in the tomb, then you can trust his promises about eternity."

"You are right. I can."

We stood there a moment longer, breathing the cold air. Then voices rose from inside—Martha calling for more wine, Mary's laughter.

"We should go back," Lazarus said. "Before Martha decides I have died again and begins mourning."

"That is not funny." But I smiled anyway.

"It is a little funny."

"Yes, it is," I said, laughing.

He offered me his arm. "Come."

I took his arm, and we walked back into the courtyard together. The feast continued. Martha kept bringing food from her kitchen—lentil stew thick with onions and garlic, the smell as earthy as turned soil, roasted vegetables still glistening with olive oil, olives swimming in brine that left salt on the tongue. Lazarus ate everything she put before him, making exaggerated sounds of appreciation. Martha swatted at him with her serving cloth, but her hand kept finding his shoulder, his arm, touching him as though she still could not believe he was there.

I helped where I could, carrying platters and refilling cups until my arms ached, the smell of wine sweet in my nostrils. When I took Lazarus more bread, he caught my hand. His grip was warm. "I am glad you were here to see it."

"I am glad you came back to us."

He smiled. "I did not have much choice in the matter. Jesus is very persuasive."

I laughed, and he released my hand. He was already turning to where Andrew and Peter sat nearby, their backs against the courtyard wall, sharing a wineskin between them. "You know what is strange? Being dead is less exhausting than listening to Peter talk about fishing."

Andrew choked on his wine. Peter shook his head, but he chuckled. "Wait until you hear my new theory about net weights."

"I would rather go back to the tomb."

"I have been thinking about depth and weight ratios—"

"Lazarus is right," Andrew said, wiping wine from his chin. "Death sounds preferable."

Peter elbowed him, and Andrew elbowed him back, both wearing wide smiles.

The sun had nearly set, the sky gone violet above the limestone hills, when someone near the gate froze. Then another. The quiet moved outward through the courtyard, voices dying mid-sentence, laughter trailing off. Even Lazarus stopped, his cup halfway to his lips, wine trembling in the bowl.

My father stood in the gateway with Nicodemus beside him, dust covering them both from hem to shoulder, gray coating the fine blue wool of my father's council robes while his hair hung disheveled around his face, strands escaping from his normally perfect arrangement. Sweat had drawn dark lines down his temples despite the winter cold, and Nicodemus looked no better with his robes dusty and sweat darkening the neck of his tunic, both of them breathing hard as though they had ridden without stopping.

My father's eyes found Jesus first then me. Then he looked at Lazarus, sitting there with bread in his hand and wine on his lips, his face gone pale.

"Jesus. We need to speak. Now."

Jesus stood slowly. "Uncle. Come."

They moved toward the house. My father looked at me as he passed. The muscle in his jaw jumped beneath the skin, working so hard I thought I heard his teeth grinding together. My knees weakened. Andrew came up next to me, and I grabbed his arm to steady myself, his muscles going as hard as stone beneath my fingers.

"What is it?" he whispered.

"I do not know. But it is bad."

We followed them into the house, along with Peter, John, and a few others, into dimly lit rooms where shadows pooled thick in the corners. Cold rose from the stone floor, seeping through my sandals and spreading through my feet until my toes went numb, and my father and Nicodemus stood in the center of the main room, their breathing still harsh from the ride, sweat gleaming on their temples despite the chill.

"Abba." I moved forward. "What has happened?"

"The Sanhedrin met tonight. An emergency session. Caiaphas called it himself. The Pharisees who left here—the ones who witnessed Lazarus—they went straight to the Temple. They reported everything. Within the hour, every member of the council was summoned."

Peter moved closer. The floorboards creaked under his weight. "And?"

"Caiaphas stood before the full assembly. He declared it was better for one man to die than for the entire nation to perish. He said if we let Jesus continue, Rome will see him as a threat. That they will destroy our Temple, scatter our nation, end everything we have built."

Peter shot to his feet. "This is madness! Jesus heals the sick, feeds the hungry, gives sight to the blind, and they want to kill him for it?"

"They are not killing him for healing." Nicodemus's voice was hard. "They are killing him because they are afraid. Afraid of losing power, afraid of Rome, afraid of what happens when the people follow him instead of them. Justice has nothing to do with this, Peter."

My father nodded once, and his face had gone gray in the lamplight, all color drained away. "Caiaphas called for a vote." In the silence that followed, I heard my heartbeat pounding in my ears and felt the cold from the stone floor creeping higher through my legs. "It was nearly unanimous. Only Nicodemus and I spoke against it."

He looked at his friend. They had marked themselves as enemies now, both of them, their names recorded in whatever tablet the scribe kept of those who opposed the high priest's will.

"What was the vote for?" Andrew's voice came out strained.

"Execution." My father's hands curled into fists at his sides. "The council has decreed that Jesus must be arrested and put to death. It is official now. Legal. They are waiting for the right moment. When the crowds are smaller. When they can take him without causing a riot. There was nothing we could do."

Execution. I heard someone draw breath, sharp and whistling through teeth, or perhaps it was a sob caught too late in someone's throat. I could not seem to draw enough air into my lungs. My hand found my belly and stayed there, feeling the small swell where Sarah grew, warm and alive beneath my palm while men spoke of death in the shadows.

Joanna stood with both hands pressed to her mouth, her eyes wide and wet. Peter had gone pale, the color draining from his face until even his lips looked bloodless, and beside him, John's breathing came too fast, his chest making shallow movements that made no sound. Mary swayed where she stood in the doorway, one hand braced against the frame as though without it she would collapse. Andrew's arm came around me, pulling me against his side, and I felt his heart pounding against my shoulder.

The silence stretched and stretched until I thought it would snap like an overdrawn bowstring, and still no one broke it. A lamp flame guttered somewhere in the room, the sound loud in the quiet, and shadows leaped and danced across the walls before settling again. The smell of fear hung heavy in the air, acrid and as sharp as vinegar, mingling with the dust and cold stone and the lingering scent of lamp oil.

"No." The word tore from my throat. "No, they cannot—"

"They can," Nicodemus said. "They have. It is done."

Joanna's hands dropped from her mouth. She stepped forward, her sandals scraping against stone. "I could speak to Chuza. He has Herod's ear. Perhaps—"

"Herod will not intervene in Sanhedrin business." My

father's voice was flat and dead, emptied of all hope. "He would not risk it. Not for this. Not for anyone."

"Then we fight." Peter's voice rose, desperation and fury woven together so tightly I could not tell where one ended and the other began. His hands clenched into fists at his sides. "We do not let them take him. We gather men, we arm ourselves, we—"

"We leave."

Jesus spoke quietly, but his words stopped Peter midsentence. Everyone turned to stare at him. He stood in the center of the room, lamplight catching on his face, his expression calm and certain while chaos swirled around him.

"Leave?" Peter sounded incredulous. His fists tightened until I thought I heard his knuckles crack. "You want us to run?"

"I want you to live." Jesus met his gaze and held it. "All of you. And the time is not yet come. We leave. Now."

"Where?" Andrew asked, and his voice sounded strange, hollow, as though it came from somewhere far away.

"Ephraim. A village near the wilderness. Remote enough that they will not think to look for us there."

"For how long?" The question left my mouth before I could stop it.

"Until Passover."

"That is barely two months. They will watch every gate, every road." My father stared at Jesus. "You cannot possibly —" He stopped. "Jesus. No."

Jesus crossed the room to him, his steps slow and deliberate, and the others parted to let him pass. He stopped before my father, close enough to touch. "Uncle. This is why I came."

"No. You must not return. Ever. You stay in Ephraim, or

you go north to Galilee, but you do not go to Jerusalem. You —" His voice broke. He stopped, swallowed hard, then tried again. "You have Anna to think of now. Your cousin. And her child. And the others."

"Abba, please." My voice came out thick, clogged with tears. "Do not make this about me."

He turned to look at me across the room, and the expression on his face made my chest tighten until I could not breathe. "She should not be anywhere near Jerusalem when —" He could not finish. He looked back at Jesus, his eyes desperate, pleading. "Jesus. Please."

Jesus grabbed my father's shoulders, his hands firm. "I need you to trust me. And I need you to live. You must be there after. We have spoken of this. You must do what needs to be done."

My father shook his head. "You ask too much."

"Uncle, you must." Jesus's voice was gentle but as unyielding as iron. "There is no alternative. Not now."

Silence fell again, thick and as heavy as wool, covering us all. I watched my father's face work, watched him struggle with something too large for words, too terrible to speak. Finally, he nodded once, a single sharp jerk of his head. "I will."

Jesus released him and turned to face the rest of us. His gaze moved over each face, lingering as though committing us all to memory. "Gather your things. We leave within the hour."

Peter turned and walked out, John following. The others stirred, moving slowly, their voices hushed. I stood without moving, my legs refusing to work. Passover. Two months. Sarah would be six months in my belly by then, heavy enough that I would feel every step. And Jesus would return to the city that wanted him dead. Strange, to carry life in your womb while fleeing from those who deal in death. At least Tirzah was safe in Capernaum visiting with Rachel. She would not be in danger.

Andrew's hand found mine and squeezed hard enough to hurt. "Anna. We need to go."

I nodded, but my legs had turned to stone, my feet fixed to the floor as though roots had grown through my sandals into the cold ground beneath. My father stood by the wall with Nicodemus, their heads bent close together, speaking in voices too low to hear, and Nicodemus had a hand on his arm the way one steadies a man about to fall.

"Anna." Andrew pulled gently, his other hand coming to my face, turning me toward him. "Look at me. I am with you. Whatever comes."

My father crossed the room to us. He stood looking at me, his gaze dropping to the swell of my belly beneath my tunic, and for a long moment, he simply stared as though memorizing the shape of his grandchild beneath wool and linen. Then he pulled me into an embrace.

"Stay in Ephraim," he said urgently against my hair. "When Passover comes, stay in Ephraim. Promise me."

I could not answer. We both knew I would not stay.

He released me and stepped back then turned to Andrew. "If there is trouble, come to the house in Jerusalem. You will always have shelter there. I will hire extra guards. If that is not possible, make your way to Arimathea." He paused then shook his head. "On second thought, go straight to Arimathea. No one will look for you there. It is too far from Jerusalem, and the roads—"

"Joseph." Andrew's hand came to my father's arm. "We

will be careful. I give you my word. I will protect Anna and the baby with my life."

My father nodded once then headed to where Nicodemus waited.

I broke away from Andrew and crossed the distance between us. My father turned at the sound of my footsteps, and I threw my arms around him then held him as tight as I could.

"I love you, Abba."

His arms came around me then crushed me against him. He said nothing, but his chest heaved once, twice, and I felt wetness against my hair where his face pressed into it. We stood there, neither of us willing to let go first, until finally, he pulled back and cradled my face in his hands. He looked at me for a long moment, his thumbs brushing away my tears, then kissed my forehead.

"I love you, too, little dove," he whispered then walked to Nicodemus without looking back.

We moved into the courtyard, where the feast had gone quiet, people standing in small groups with voices hushed, watching as Jesus and the disciples gathered their few belongings. Lazarus stood with Martha and Mary near the kitchen, the three of them watching us prepare to leave. When he saw me, he crossed the courtyard to where we stood.

He looked at me, and the weight of the day showed in his eyes—death and resurrection, feast and flight, all within a handful of hours. "You are leaving."

"Yes. We must."

He pulled me into an embrace, and I breathed in the smell of myrrh still clinging to his clothes from the tomb. "Take care of yourself. And our baby."

"I will."

He released me and turned to Andrew. They clasped forearms, and Lazarus leaned close, his voice dropping to a murmur I could not hear. Andrew nodded once, his hand coming to Lazarus's shoulder, and they understood each other without additional words.

Martha appeared at my side with a cloth bundle, the smell of fresh bread and sharp cheese rising from it. "It is not much," she said, handing it to me. "But you will need something for the road."

"It is perfect." I set it aside and pulled her close. Her body shook against mine, silent sobs making her shoulders tremble while her fingers dug into my back as though she could hold me there through will alone. Her hair smelled of woodsmoke and flour and the herb gardens she tended behind the house, rosemary and thyme crushed beneath her fingers a hundred times over.

"I just got him back," she whispered. "And now you are fleeing because they want to kill the man who gave him back to me."

"I know." I held her tighter. "Martha, I know. I wish we could stay longer."

"Come back." She pulled away just far enough to look at me, her face wet with tears that caught the lamplight. "When this is finished, promise me you will come back so I can meet your daughter."

"I promise."

Mary embraced me next, her arms coming around me with a fierceness that surprised me, her face already wet with tears that soaked into my tunic where her cheek rested against my shoulder. "We will pray for you," she said. "Every day. For all of you. For Sarah." Her hands came to my belly, fingers spread wide as though she could bless my daughter through skin and fabric and the waters that held her safe. "God protect this child. May she grow strong and know peace."

"Thank you. I will miss you."

Jesus stood at the gate, speaking quietly with Lazarus. Lazarus nodded, his hand on Jesus's shoulder. Then Jesus turned and began walking, and we all followed. Andrew walked close beside me, his hand at my back. When I stumbled once on a loose stone, his arm came around my waist and held me upright.

Cold worked through my cloak, finding every gap where wool met linen while my back already ached from standing too long at the feast. I looked back to see Martha and Mary standing at the gate with arms around each other, lamplight spilling out around them in a pool of gold, Lazarus beside them with one hand raised in farewell. Beyond them, my father stood alone in the shadows, watching us leave. Then we rounded the turn in the road, and they disappeared behind limestone walls and winter-bare olive trees.

CHAPTER 27

Jericho, March, 33 AD

The heat in Jericho was different from the clean, dry heat of the hills—thick and close, the air below sea level sitting heavy as wet wool against skin, carrying the fetid sweetness of the canal that brought water from the springs, the cloying perfume of roses from the gardens behind high walls.

"Ima, smell." Zebedee pointed at a garden wall where roses climbed thick and blooming.

"Yes, flowers." Tirzah kept a firm grip on his hand as he tried to pull toward them. "But we need to keep walking."

"Everything smells different here," I said. "Richer. Heavier."

"It is the air. We are so far below the hills." She glanced around at the crowded streets. "I will be glad to climb back up to Bethany."

The green rot of date palms shedding fruit onto paving stones mixed with the honey-scent of balsam blossoms that grew nowhere else in Judea. Six months pregnant, I felt the weight of it all. Sarah had not stopped moving since we entered the city gates an hour ago, kicking as though she too felt the thick air, the heaviness that sat different from the crisp spring cold of the hills.

We had come down from Ephraim at dawn, walking while the morning was still cool, but the sun had climbed and the road had filled with pilgrims heading to Jerusalem for Passover. My back ached in a way it had not ached before, a deep throb that wrapped around my spine and grabbed my hips, and my feet had swollen until my sandals cut into the flesh above my ankles. Andrew walked close beside me, a constant presence in the crowd's chaos, and though I could have managed alone, I was grateful for him there, for his steadiness when everything else felt uncertain.

The streets were impossible. Bodies pressed from all sides, pilgrims and merchants and beggars and children darting between legs, voices raised in a dozen languages, Aramaic and Greek and Latin and tongues I could not name.

A man pushed through the crowd toward us, his eyes on Jesus. "Teacher! You are the one who raised Lazarus, yes? The dead man who walks?"

Peter moved between them. "Keep moving."

"But I only want to see him! To ask—"

"I said move."

The man backed away, but others had turned to look now, heads swiveling, voices dropping to whispers. "That is him." "Jesus of Nazareth." "The Sanhedrin wants him arrested."

Someone else, louder: "He will restore the kingdom!"

The tension coiled tighter with every step.

"We should not have come." Peter's voice cut through the noise behind us. He walked with John and James, the three of them forming a loose wall between Jesus and the people that kept trying to press closer. "Every mouth in this city is speaking his name. Every eye is watching. The Sanhedrin has spies everywhere."

"Then they will watch." Jesus spoke without turning, his voice calm. "We have nothing to hide."

"Nothing to hide?" Peter's voice rose, then dropped when several heads turned. "Master, they want to kill you. We are all in danger. Coming here, walking through the center of the city during Passover week is madness."

"It is necessary."

Andrew's hand found mine, his fingers closing hard around my palm, and I returned the pressure, holding on to him while we kept walking.

The crowd grew thicker as we moved deeper into the city, bodies packed so tight I could not see more than a few paces ahead, could only follow the back of the person in front of me and trust that Andrew would not let me fall. The smell of unwashed bodies and cooking oil and animal dung was overwhelming, mixing with the sharp green scent of fresh herbs someone carried in a basket, mint and coriander crushed beneath feet, and my stomach turned. I breathed through my mouth, shallow breaths that did nothing to ease the nausea.

Then Jesus stopped.

I followed his gaze upward and saw a man perched in the branches of a sycamore tree, his fine robes hitched up around his knees, his face flushed with heat and embarrassment. He was small, this man, smaller than most, and even from the ground I could see the quality of his clothes, the gold rings on his fingers, the carefully trimmed beard, the hunger plain on his face. Wealthy, clearly, and yet people gave the tree a wide berth, as though afraid that getting too close might contaminate them.

"Zacchaeus." Jesus spoke the name clearly. "Come down. I will eat at your house today."

The tax collector's face went white, then red, his mouth opening and closing like a fish pulled from water. Around us, the crowd muttered, the sound building and spreading like ripples in a pond.

"He is going to be the guest of a sinner."

"A tax collector. Of all people."

"Does he not know what that man has done? How much he has stolen?"

Zacchaeus climbed down from the tree, his movements awkward, his fine robe catching on branches, and when he reached the ground, he simply stood there, staring at Jesus.

"Lord." His voice shook. "My house is yours. Please, come. I will prepare everything."

We followed him through streets that grew wider, the houses larger, the walls higher, until we stood before a gate of carved cedar that opened onto a courtyard tiled in mosaic, fountains playing in the corners, servants appearing from doorways with wine and bread and plates of fruit that gleamed like jewels in the afternoon light. Wealth. Everywhere, wealth, the kind bought with Roman coin and Jewish blood, and I felt Andrew stiffen beside me. Peter stood with his arms crossed, his gaze moving from the fountains to the servants to the food-laden platters. Matthew stood very still, watching Zacchaeus with eyes that had seen this wealth before, had once counted it and collected it himself.

But Jesus walked in as though this were any other house, as though the source of the money that bought the tiles and the fountains and the servants meant nothing, and he sat where Zacchaeus indicated, accepting the cup of wine offered, breaking bread with a man the rest of us would have spat on in the street.

Zacchaeus stood before him, his hands twisting together, his face working with emotion he could not quite contain. "Lord, I—" He stopped, swallowed hard, tried again. "I want to make things right. Look, here and now I give half of my possessions to the poor. And if I have cheated anybody out of anything, I will pay back four times the amount."

Silence fell. Jesus looked at him with such love, such fierce joy, that my eyes stung with tears.

"Today salvation has come to this house." Jesus's voice rang clear in the stillness. "For this man too is a son of Abraham. The Son of Man came to seek and to save the lost."

Zacchaeus dropped to his knees, his face in his hands, his shoulders shaking with sobs.

Servants brought platters of food, and we sat in Zacchaeus's courtyard while he and Jesus spoke quietly, the tax collector's transformation still fresh on his face. But the disciples stood watchful, hands never far from their belts, and outside the gate the crowd had grown, people gathering in the street, their voices loud enough to carry over the walls. The danger pressed closer with every moment we stayed. We ate quickly, the meal more obligation than refuge.

Andrew leaned close, his voice low near my ear. "Did you see Matthew's face? When he looked at Zacchaeus?"

"Like he was seeing himself."

"Yes." His hand found mine beneath the table. "Jesus does not give up on us." He paused, listening to the crowd's voices carry over the walls. "The streets are getting worse. Stay close to me when we leave."

"I will."

"I mean it, Anna. No matter what happens, you stay beside me." His grip tightened on my hand. "I will get you to Bethany. I promise."

Determination marked his face, the set of his jaw. "I know you will."

"Good." He squeezed my hand once more, then released it to reach for bread neither of us wanted.

When we left Zacchaeus's house, the day had grown late, the light turning everything sharp-edged and golden. The tax collector walked with us to the gate, his face still filled with awe, and when Jesus embraced him, several people in the crowd turned away in disgust.

We continued toward the city gate, making our way through the busy streets. Jesus lead the way with that same steady pace he always kept, unhurried and unafraid, as though he did not notice the danger crackling in the air around us.

Andrew's hand found the small of my back again. "When we tell this story later, no one will believe us."

"A tax collector in a sycamore tree? No. They will not."

"And Jesus inviting himself to dinner."

"That part they might believe." I glanced up at him. "He does that."

"True." Andrew looked ahead toward the gate. "Almost through. Then it is uphill to Bethany."

"Uphill sounds terrible."

"It does. But Martha will feed us again, and you can rest properly."

"I may sleep for three days."

"You may have to. Sarah seems determined to keep you awake."

The gate rose ahead of us, limestone arches framing the road that led to Bethany and Jerusalem beyond. We were nearly through, nearly free of the crowds, when someone shouted from the roadside, the voice hoarse and desperate, cutting through the din like a blade.

"Jesus! Son of David! Have mercy on me!"

The words stopped me where I stood. Around us, heads turned, people craning to see who had spoken. The crowd murmured, some excited, some afraid, and I felt Andrew's hand reach for mine.

"Son of David! Jesus, have mercy!"

The voice came again, louder this time, and now I could see him—a man sitting against the city wall near the gate, his robe filthy and torn, his face tilted up toward the sky in a way that made my chest tighten. Blind. His eyes were clouded white, and his hands were stretched out before him, groping at the air.

"Quiet!" someone near him hissed. "Be quiet, you fool!"

"Son of David!" the blind man shouted again, his cry cracking with desperation. "Have mercy on me!"

People around him were trying to silence him now, hands reaching to pull at his robe, their warnings sharp and urgent. "Hush! You will bring the guards!" "Stop calling out like that!" "Do you want to get us all killed?"

But he would not stop, his shouts growing louder, more desperate, drowning out those who tried to silence him. "Jesus! Son of David! Have mercy!"

Jesus stopped walking.

The crowd stilled, bodies going quiet, the noise dropping to murmurs and then to silence. Jesus turned toward the blind man, his attention complete, as though no one else existed.

"Bring him to me."

The people near the blind man hesitated, uncertain, as though waiting for someone to object, to call the guards. But no one did. After a moment, two men stepped forward and took the blind man by the arms, helping him to his feet, bringing him to where Jesus stood.

Andrew moved us forward, his arm around my waist, guiding me through the crowd until we stood near enough to see.

The blind man stood before Jesus, his head turning slightly from side to side, sightless eyes searching. "Master?"

"What do you want me to do for you?"

The blind man's head stilled. "Rabbi, I want to see."

Jesus reached out, his hands rising slowly, and then his fingers touched the blind man's eyes, covering the clouded white with his palms, and the silence deepened until I could hear nothing but the wind in the palm branches overhead.

For a long breath, nothing happened. The blind man stood frozen beneath Jesus's touch, waiting. Then Jesus stepped back, and the blind man's eyes opened. Not the clouded white they had been, but clear and brown and focused, blinking against the sudden brightness of day. He stared at Jesus, then at his own hands held up before his face, then at the faces watching him, unable to speak, tears streaming down his cheeks.

"I see," he whispered. "I see."

The crowd erupted. Shouts and cries and prayers of

thanksgiving rose from every side, people surging forward to touch the man who had been blind, to touch Jesus, hands reaching and grasping while the disciples tried to hold them back. I stood rooted where I was, watching the man who could now see spin in a slow circle, taking in everything—the walls of the city, the faces of strangers, the sky arching blue and infinite overhead.

He fell to his knees before Jesus, his hands clutching at the hem of Jesus's robe. "Thank you. Thank you, Lord. Son of David, blessed be your name."

Jesus reached down and pulled him to his feet, his hands gentle on the man's shoulders. " Bartimaeus ,your faith has healed you. Go in peace."

But the man did not go. When we began moving again, pushing through the crowd toward the city gate, he followed, his eyes never leaving Jesus, as though afraid that if he looked away this gift might be taken back, as though he could not bear to let the one who had given him sight out of his vision now that he finally had it.

The road to Bethany wound up through the hills, leaving Jericho behind in the valley below, and the air grew cooler as we climbed, carrying the clean scent of new grass and wild mustard blooming yellow along the roadside. Each uphill step pulled at muscles already worn from the long day. Andrew stayed close beside me, adjusting his pace to match mine. The disciples walked in a tight cluster around Jesus, their eyes scanning the road ahead and behind, watching for any sign of danger.

"We should not have stopped." Peter's voice was low but sharp. "We should have passed straight through."

"We stopped because we were meant to stop." Jesus did not turn, did not break his stride. "Bartimaeus needed his sight. Zacchaeus needed salvation. Would you have me pass by on the other side?"

Peter said nothing, but I could see the tension in his shoulders, the way his hand kept drifting to his belt where a knife was hidden beneath his robe.

Andrew's arm came around me, holding me close. We kept walking.

CHAPTER 28

Bethany, March, 33 AD

Six days before Passover, we returned to Bethany. The road from Ephraim wound through bare hills the color of old bone, limestone ridges cutting against a sky gone white with winter's end. Spring had not yet come to Judea, but the air had changed, no longer knife-edged with cold but heavy with damp that clung to wool and worked into skin until even walking could not shake it loose. My tunic hung sodden against my back. Each breath tasted of wet stone and the green rot of last year's grass exposed by melting snow. Six months pregnant, I walked with my hand resting on the swell of my belly, the fabric of my tunic pulled taut across it now. Sarah moved inside me, kicking with a strength that still surprised me and made me stop sometimes and press my palm to where she pushed against my skin.

We should not have been going back. Ephraim had been

safe, remote, a village so small and unremarkable that the Sanhedrin would never think to look for us there. We could have stayed hidden until after Passover, until the feast ended and Jerusalem emptied and the danger passed.

But Jesus had said we were going back. And so we went.

The road grew more traveled as we descended toward Bethany. Pilgrims heading to Jerusalem for Passover passed us in both directions, their faces alive with anticipation, their voices raised in psalms of ascent. Some recognized Jesus and called out greetings. Others walked past without a second glance, intent on their own journeys.

My back ached, a dull throb that had started an hour ago. I pushed my hand against the small of my back and stretched, trying to ease it.

"Almost there," Andrew said, nodding toward the village ahead.

We rounded the last turn, and Bethany came into view below us—limestone houses clustered on the hillside, olive groves silver-green in the afternoon light, smoke rising from cooking fires to hang in the still air. The smell of burning olive wood drifted up the road to meet us, mixed with the dusty-sweet scent of the groves. My feet ached in my sandals, the leather stiff with road dust. Six months pregnant, and every step down the slope sent a jolt through my spine.

"It looks safe," I said.

"Yes. For now." Andrew's eyes swept the street, watchful.

Martha appeared at her gate as we approached the house. She ran toward us with her tunic gathered in both fists, her hair escaping its covering, dust rising in small puffs from where her feet struck the ground. When she reached me, she wrapped her arms around me with enough force to make me gasp. She smelled of bread dough and cinnamon, of smoke and sweat and the rosemary she must have been crushing just moments before.

"You came. I was afraid—I thought maybe you would not risk it."

"We are here."

Martha stepped back and looked down at my belly. Her hands went to it immediately. "She has grown so much."

"She kicks constantly. Strong kicks. Andrew says she will be born fighting."

"Good. She will need to be strong." Martha blinked rapidly then looked past me to where Jesus walked with the disciples. "Come inside. All of you. I have been preparing since before dawn."

The courtyard smelled of roasting lamb and baking bread, garlic and rosemary thickening the air over low tables already set with bread and oil, wine cups waiting to be filled, cushions arranged in neat rows against the walls.

The abundance spread before us—bread and oil and wine, platters already arranged. "You knew we were coming."

"Jesus sent word a few weeks ago. Said he would be here for dinner six days before Passover." She managed a smile. "And that he wanted to see us before going to Jerusalem."

Her smile was almost convincing. Almost enough to make me believe this was just another meal, another visit, nothing more dangerous than pilgrims traveling to celebrate Passover.

Mary appeared from the house and embraced me, her arms gentle around my rounded middle. Her robe was damp at the shoulders, and she smelled of the courtyard well water, cool and faintly mineral. "I did not think we would see you again. Not like this. Not walking back into—" She stopped, her palm finding where Sarah grew, her hand cool against the fabric stretched over my belly. "Does she move for you?"

"Constantly. She never rests."

Martha drew close on my other side, both sisters bracketing me, their touch light and reverent. Both laughed softly when Sarah kicked, and I felt the warmth of their breath on my face, smelled the wine they had been tasting while they worked.

Lazarus crossed to me and pulled me into a careful hug. "She makes her presence known now."

"She does."

"Good. A strong daughter for Andrew. Daughters are far more dangerous than sons. Or so that is what I have been told." He glanced toward the gate where Jesus had just entered with the other disciples. "I should greet the Teacher properly. Martha has been cooking since before dawn. We will eat and drink and be together."

He patted my shoulder once then went to welcome Jesus.

Andrew helped me onto the cushions against the court-yard wall. The ache in my back had gotten worse, a band of tension across my lower spine. The cushions were sun-warm beneath me, the wool slightly scratchy against my legs. I leaned forward, bracing my hands on my knees, feeling my spine curve and pull.

"Here." Andrew shifted behind me, his hands finding the small of my back. His thumbs pressed into the knotted muscles, working slow circles. Heat spread from where he touched, and I closed my eyes and breathed, tasting lamb fat and woodsmoke on the air.

The other disciples gathered around the tables. Peter was telling a story about the fishing in Ephraim, his hands gesturing wide, his voice loud and familiar. John sat listening with that quiet smile he got when Peter grew animated, picking at a piece of bread and rolling the soft inside between his fingers. James and Matthew were discussing the crowds they had seen on the road, their voices low and serious. Even Thomas looked more at ease than he had been in weeks, a cup of wine already in his hand. Jesus sat at the center table, his presence drawing everyone like a fire draws cold travelers. The lamplight had begun to soften as afternoon faded, golden and warm on the white limestone walls.

Judas moved through the courtyard, arranging cushions and helping Martha carry wine jars. When he passed near us, I caught the scent of him—wine and sweat and something sharp underneath, like copper. He paused.

"Are you well, Anna? The journey from Ephraim was long. Perhaps you should lie down inside where it is quieter."

"She is fine." Andrew's hands stilled on my back.

Judas nodded slowly. "Of course. I only thought—"

"She does not need to lie down."

Judas looked at me, his mouth tightening, then continued on without another word.

I twisted to look at Andrew over my shoulder. "That was unkind."

"Was it?"

"He was only being considerate. He has been nothing but kind to me, and you treat him like—"

"Like what? Like a man I do not trust?"

"Yes, exactly like that. And for no reason." I faced forward again. "I do not understand why you dislike him so much."

Andrew's hands resumed their work on my back, but his movements were stiff now, harder than they had been. "You do not see what I see."

"What you think you see. What you want to see because you have decided not to trust him."

"There was a time you did not trust him either."

"I changed my mind." I pulled away and leaned back against the wall. Andrew rose and went to sit next to his brother. So be it. I grew weary of arguing about Judas.

Tirzah appeared from the house with Zebedee clinging to her hip, the boy's legs wrapped around her side. He was a sturdy toddler now, with his father's dark eyes and his mother's determined expression. When he saw me, he reached out both arms, making the insistent sound he used when he wanted something, his voice high and urgent.

"Zebedee, no. Aunt Anna cannot—" Tirzah started, but I held out my arms.

"I can hold him for a moment."

She handed him over carefully. He squirmed immediately, all solid weight and restless energy, and I settled him on my hip away from my belly. He pointed across the courtyard. 'Dat!' he declared, leaning so far forward I had to grip him tighter to keep him from tumbling off my lap. His sticky fingers grabbed at my head covering, and I caught his hand gently, redirecting it to the cord at my neck, which he found equally fascinating. 'What dat?' he asked, tugging on it.

Tirzah sat beside me and watched him for a moment, wiping her hands on her robe. "Are you afraid? Of what is coming?"

"Yes." There was no point in lying. "I am afraid all the time now."

"Do you remember when you delivered Zebedee and he would not breathe?" Tirzah smoothed his hair where it stuck up, her fingers gentle. "I thought that was the worst fear I would ever know. But this—" She looked around the courtyard where the disciples talked and laughed, where Martha moved between tables with platters, where everything seemed so normal. "This is worse. Because now I know what I could lose."

"I know." I rested my hand over Sarah. "I keep thinking about Sarah. About bringing her into—all of this."

Tirzah watched Zebedee try to grab at a lamp across the cushions, the oil inside sloshing as he reached. "I look at him and I think: I will do anything. Whatever it takes to keep him safe." She leaned over to catch his hand before he could reach too far. "But I also know I cannot keep him safe. Not truly. Not from everything that is coming."

"What if it gets worse?"

"It will get worse." Tirzah spoke with certainty. "Can you not feel it? Like a storm building over the lake."

"Yes." I did feel it. "I fear you are right."

Zebedee squirmed harder, twisting around to see the other side of the courtyard where Peter's voice rose in laughter. "Down," he demanded. I handed him back to Tirzah, who placed him on her hip. We sat without speaking, both of us holding our children—hers on her hip, mine growing inside me. The sun dropped lower, and the courtyard fell into shadow except where lamplight caught the edges of things.

Joanna and Susanna came with Mary Magdalene, all three carrying wine jars from Martha's storeroom, the clay cool and damp in their arms. They filled cups throughout the courtyard, the wine splashing dark and sweet-smelling into each vessel. Joanna poured a cup for me, the rim smooth against my palm.

"It is good to be here," she said. "Even knowing what we are walking into."

"It is," I said. "Will you see Chuza when we are in Jerusalem?"

"Yes. I plan to stay at my home while we are there." She glanced over at Jesus, lamplight catching the side of her face. "If I can." She smiled and moved on to another group, wine sloshing gently in the jar.

The meal began as the sun touched the western hills, the light gone gold and thick as honey. Martha brought platters of lamb roasted until the meat fell from the bone, the fat crisped to cracking, the smell so rich it made my mouth water and my stomach clench with sudden hunger. Lentils cooked with onions until they were soft as butter, glistening with olive oil that caught the lamplight. Fresh bread still warm from the oven, the crust shattering when I broke it, sending up a cloud of steam and the yeasty smell of wheat, the inside tender and faintly sour. Dried figs sticky with honey that clung to my fingers. Sharp cheese that crumbled on my tongue, coating my mouth with salt and cream. Olives swimming in brine, their flesh firm and bitter-rich. Wine dark and sweet sliding down my throat, warming my chest. I had missed Martha's meals.

I ate slowly, savoring each bite—the lamb falling apart on my tongue, the bread soaking up oil and meat juices, the richness of Martha's cooking settling warm in my belly. For this moment at least, surrounded by lamplight and laughter, I let myself feel safe. Andrew brought his food and came to sit next to me, his thigh warm against mine.

"I am sorry," he murmured. "I do not like to argue with you. Especially not now."

I laid my head on his shoulder. He smelled of sweat and dust and home. "I am sorry, too."

Conversation filled the courtyard. Someone laughed.

Martha refilled a platter, and Thomas smiled at something John said. The wine flowed. As dusk fell, Martha lit the lamps, and golden light pooled across the courtyard, pushing back the darkness encroached upon us again. For a moment, it felt almost normal, just friends gathered for dinner and nothing more.

The sun set, and Mary disappeared into the house.

When she returned, she carried an alabaster jar.

It was small, no larger than her palm, carved from translucent stone that glowed honey-gold in the lamplight. She held it with both hands, fingers curved around it, crossing slowly toward where Jesus reclined at the head table. Every eye followed her. Even the street sounds faded until only the soft shuffle of her feet on stone remained, the whisper of her robe against the ground.

She kneeled at his feet.

Mary's hands trembled as she turned the jar, her fingers finding the seal that held it closed.

Then she broke it.

The crack echoed through the courtyard. Then came the scent—nard, pure nard, the kind that came from the distant mountains beyond Persia, carried by traders who crossed deserts and mountains to bring it west. The air grew thick with it, coating the inside of my mouth and lungs, filling the courtyard with exotic spices and resin, with lands I would never see, with wealth so extravagant it felt obscene.

Mary tilted the jar over Jesus's feet.

The oil poured out in a thick stream, amber-gold in the lamplight, coating his skin, running between his toes to pool on the stone beneath. It kept coming, more than that small vessel should have held, viscous and endless, and the scent doubled, tripled, grew so thick I tasted resin on the back of my tongue. My eyes watered. The air turned heavy with it, and I smelled nothing but nard, tasted nothing but foreign spices and the ghost of distant mountains where such things grew.

Jesus sat very still, watching her. Tears welled in his eyes.

Mary set the broken jar aside. Then she reached up and unbound her hair.

It fell around her shoulders in dark waves, tumbling down her back to her waist. In the lamplight, it shone almost black. She bent forward until her hair brushed the floor, and then she wiped Jesus's feet with it.

The gesture was so intimate, so tender, that part of me wanted to look away. This was not a servant washing a master's feet. This felt prophetic and final. The sound of her hair against his skin whispered through the courtyard. Oil soaked into the dark strands until they clung to her neck and back, gleaming wet in the lamplight.

We all sat in silence, watching what we did not fully understand but knew in our bones was sacred.

When she finished, Mary sat back on her heels. Tears ran down her face, tracking through the lamplight. Her hair hung heavy and dark down her back, oil dripping from the ends.

She looked up at Jesus.

Jesus reached down and touched her hair, his fingers moving gently through the oil-soaked strands. "Mary." His voice broke on her name.

He cupped her face in both hands and blessed her with words too quiet for the rest of us to hear. But we saw her close her eyes beneath his touch, saw the tears come faster, saw him lean his forehead against hers for one long moment before letting her go.

Then Judas stood.

I looked up, startled. Of all the people in this courtyard, I had not expected him to break this moment.

"Why was this perfume not sold for three hundred denarii and the money given to the poor?"

The words rang across the courtyard. He gestured at the empty alabaster jar, at the oil pooled beneath Jesus's feet, at Mary's hair dripping dark and wet down her back. "Three hundred denarii. A year's wages. Wasted. Poured out on the ground when it could have fed hundreds." He stepped forward, palms spread wide. "We have a responsibility to the poor, to use our resources wisely, and this—this is the opposite of wisdom. This is extravagance. Vanity." *No, Judas. Sit back down.*

An uncomfortable silence fell over us. Peter kept his eyes fixed on his hands. John shifted his weight but said nothing. Even Thomas, who usually had an opinion on everything, sat frozen.

"The poor you will always have with you." Jesus spoke without raising his voice. "But you will not always have me."

"Always?" Judas's voice rose higher. "What does that mean? We have work to do now. People are starving now. And you sit here while—" He gestured wildly at the oil-soaked floor, at Mary. "While this—"

"Judas." Jesus held his eyes until the other man went still. "Leave her alone. She has done a beautiful thing for me. She has anointed my body beforehand for burial."

Beforehand for burial.

Someone gasped. Martha clapped her hand to her mouth. Andrew's fingers crushed mine. Around the courtyard, faces went pale. Burial. He had said it before, but here, with the funeral oil still dripping from his feet, with Mary's hair soaked in nard like a mourner at a tomb, the word became real.

Judas turned on his heel and grabbed the leather money bag from the wall.

"Where are you going?" Peter asked.

"To get air. Before I say something I should not."

Peter surged to his feet. "Leave the money."

Judas kept walking toward the gate, the bag clutched in his fist.

Peter crossed the courtyard in three strides and caught Judas's arm. "I said to leave it."

Judas jerked his arm back. "Let go."

"You are not taking—"

Judas wrenched the bag from Peter's reach, leather scraping against his palm. "It is mine to keep. I am the one who—" The words choked off. His breath came ragged, and a vein pulsed at his temple. Peter came close enough that I could see the muscle jumping in his jaw, could smell the wine on his breath mixing with the sharp salt of Judas's sweat. Neither moved. Then Judas spun toward the gate and the wood slammed behind him hard enough to rattle the hinges. The sound cracked across the courtyard like a bone breaking before dying into silence.

Silence fell over the courtyard. Peter stood staring at the gate, fists clenched at his sides. Andrew moved toward his brother but stopped, uncertain. No one spoke. No one seemed to know what to say.

The scent of nard was everywhere now, thick enough to coat the tongue, seeping into fabric and hair and skin. Mary remained kneeling at Jesus's feet, her hair still damp with oil, her face turned up to his.

Voices rose beyond the gate. Not one or two but many,

building like water against a dam. Footsteps hammered the packed earth outside. Someone slammed a fist against wood and the gate shuddered on its hinges. "Teacher!" a man shouted. "Jesus of Nazareth!" Then a woman, shrill and urgent: "Lazarus! Show us the man who came back!" More voices joined, overlapping, until individual words blurred into a roar punctuated by beating fists, trampling feet, the press of bodies shoving forward. Torchlight flickered through gaps in the slats, throwing bars of orange across the courtyard floor. The smell of unwashed bodies seeped through the cracks. Sarah shifted inside me, and I curled my arm over where she lay, as though I could shield her.

Lazarus went to peer through the gap into the darkening street, then turned back to us. His face had gone white as bone, and when he spoke, his voice came thin and high. "There must be a hundred people out there. Maybe more. They want to see me."

The noise grew louder outside, voices calling his name.

"Of course they do." Peter sounded weary. "You are the proof. The man who came back from death."

Martha appeared from the kitchen, wiping her hands on her apron, flour still dusting her sleeves. "What is happening?"

"People. In the street. They heard Jesus is here."

The gate shuddered under another assault of fists. Andrew rose and pulled me to my feet, his arm going around my waist, his body between me and the gate. "Should we leave before more arrive?"

"No." Jesus remained seated, unmoved by the chaos beyond the walls. "Let them wait. We have time yet."

"Time before what?" Lazarus asked, his hands clenched at his sides.

Jesus looked at him but gave no answer. Instead, he turned to Mary, still kneeling at his feet, her hair dripping oil. "Perhaps you should go inside now. And thank you, Mary. I will never forget what you have done for me."

Mary nodded and rose, her hair leaving dark trails across the stone as she went toward the house. The scent of nard followed her, the smell of burial in a courtyard full of life.

Then a voice called from beyond the gate. "Lazarus! It is Joseph and Nicodemus. Open the gate. Hurry!"

Lazarus pulled the gate open just wide enough for two men to slip through, then shut it against the press of bodies beyond. My father stepped in with Nicodemus beside him. Both wore their council robes, though my father's hung crooked on one shoulder, the fabric twisted at the neck as though he had dressed in haste or had been pulling at it.

Abba found Jesus first. Whatever passed between them lasted only a heartbeat before his gaze swept the courtyard and locked on me. The color drained from his face. One hand reached toward me, then fell. His jaw worked but no sound came. He stood there, one fist clenched white at his side, then his gaze returned to Jesus.

"We need to speak. All of you. Now. Inside."

Jesus stood. "Come. We will go into the house."

We moved into the main room, away from the courtyard and the people beyond the gate. Lazarus pulled the door shut behind us, and the noise from the street muffled to distant murmurs. Martha lit a lamp with hands that shook slightly, the flame catching. The light was dim after the brightness of the courtyard lamps, and I blinked as shapes resolved from shadow —the low table, the cushions arranged along the walls, the dark wool hanging that separated this room from the sleeping quarters. The smell of nard followed us in, clinging to Jesus, to

Mary's hair, seeping into the enclosed space until it mingled with lamp oil and bread and the faint mustiness of wool.

My father waited until we had all gathered, until Lazarus had checked the door latch, before he spoke.

"The Sanhedrin met again today. The chief priests held a separate session. A private one."

No one spoke. We all waited.

"They discussed the problem of—" My father stopped and looked at Lazarus. "They discussed you."

"Me?" Lazarus asked. "What about me?"

Nicodemus stepped beside my father. "They have decided you are too dangerous to let live."

The lamp flame held steady while we all held our breath. I heard it then—the absolute stillness that comes before something breaks. Martha made a sound, half gasp and half sob, clapping her hand to her mouth. The blood drained from Mary's face until she looked carved from alabaster. Lazarus stood blinking as though he had not heard correctly, the words making no sense in any language he knew.

Martha's voice came out high, thin. "What do you mean?"

My father crossed to Lazarus. "They want to kill you. For being alive. For walking and breathing and bearing witness to what Jesus can do. They want you dead."

"They have already made the decree," Nicodemus said. "It is official. Both Jesus and Lazarus are marked for execution."

Lazarus looked at Jesus. "They want to kill me. For being alive."

Martha crossed to him and grabbed his arm. "No. They will not touch you. We will leave. Tonight. We will go—"

"Where?" Mary went to Lazarus's other side, her hand finding his. "Where can we go that they will not find us?"

"Anywhere." Martha answered. "Galilee. Damascus. Egypt. Anywhere but here."

"I do not know." Lazarus stared at nothing. "I do not—I do not understand. Jesus called me back, and now they want —" He stopped. "I do not know."

Mary pulled him into an embrace, her arms tight around him. Martha joined her, both sisters clinging to their brother, their hands fisted in his robe.

Jesus went to them and put his hand on Lazarus's shoulder. The sisters stepped back slightly, but kept their hands on their brother.

"Listen to me, brother. They will not touch you. I swear it."

"How can you promise that when they want both of us dead?"

"Because I know what is coming, and it will not end in your death at the hands of the Sanhedrin."

Jesus crossed to my father and gripped his shoulder. "You know what you must do, Uncle. Be ready."

My father stared at him for a long moment. Finally, he nodded once, the movement brief and certain.

Peter surged to his feet. "You are walking into their hands."

"Yes."

"Then why walk toward death when we could flee?"

"Because the time has come." Jesus turned to face all of us. Lamplight fell on his face, casting shadows that made him look older. The smell of nard clung to him still, thick and cloying in the enclosed space, the scent of burial spices mixed with lamp oil and the salt of tears. "And all of you need to hear this."

The room went still. Even the lamplight stopped wavering.

"Tomorrow we enter Jerusalem. You know what awaits us there. You have known since we left Galilee. The Sanhedrin wants me dead. They have set the trap. And I go to do what the Father has willed. Some of you will fall away when you see what they do to me." Jesus looked at each disciple in turn, his gaze resting on Peter, on John, on James. "Some will deny you ever knew me. Some will run. Some will hide. The cost of following me is higher than any of you understand."

Sarah went still inside me, as though she too were listening. My breath caught and would not release. The air in the room had gone thin, impossible to draw deep enough into my lungs. Cold sweat broke across the back of my neck, between my shoulder blades, under my arms. Andrew's grip on my hand had gone crushing, but I barely felt it through the roaring in my ears—my own pulse, thundering so hard I tasted copper on my tongue.

Some of you will fall away. Some will deny. Some will run. Which one would I be? When they came for him, when they dragged him away, when the cost became real and not just words in a lamplight room—would I stand or would I run?

"What is coming will test every one of you. Your faith. Your courage. And your love. Everything you have said you believe about me will be tested. And some of you will not stand with me. Those that stay must be strong."

Andrew stiffened beside me. I felt the change in him, the way his body went rigid, his breathing shallow.

The words came before I could stop them. I needed to know. "How can we be strong enough?"

Jesus looked at me directly, and the lamp flame wavered. "You will not be strong enough. That is why you must cling to the Father. Your strength will fail. His will not."

He drew a breath, and when he spoke again, his words came softer, filled with tenderness. "I love you. All of you. It has been my great honor to walk with you these years. To teach you and eat with you. To watch you grow in faith and understanding. You have become more than my disciples. You are my friends. My brothers and sisters. My beloved."

Someone wept quietly. I thought it might be Mary Magdalene, or perhaps Joanna. The sound was small and broken in the stillness.

"I am telling you what is coming so that when it happens, you will remember I knew. That I chose this path knowing what it would cost for all of us." He looked at me, at my belly where Sarah grew and turned, then back to the others. "Tomorrow we walk toward what must be. And each of you will have to choose again whether to follow me into it."

Andrew's hand found mine beneath the cushions. His palm was slick with sweat, his grip crushing. I could feel his pulse racing where our wrists touched.

"I will not make you come. Any of you. If you want to leave tonight, go north, and hide until this is over. I will not stop you."

Across the room, Tirzah held Zebedee against her chest, one hand cupped over his head as though she could protect him from what was coming just by holding him close enough. Her eyes were wide. Our eyes met and held. In her face, I saw my fear reflected back at me. Then she nodded. She would go with him.

"But if you come with me tomorrow, know what you are choosing. The road is dark, and the cost is high." He paused, and in that pause I heard everything he was not saying, all the suffering and death and grief that waited for us in Jerusalem. "And trust that I know the way through to the other side."

Tomorrow. The word echoed in my head. Tomorrow we would go to Jerusalem, and then—what? How long did we have? Days? Hours? Jesus stood before me, and I understood suddenly that this might be the last quiet moment we would have together. That tomorrow everything would change. That Sarah might be born into a world where Jesus no longer walked it.

"Jesus, will you bless our child?"

Jesus looked at me for a long moment. Tears stood in his eyes. "Come, little cousin. Bring her to me."

I stood. Andrew rose with me, his arm supporting me. We started toward Jesus.

My father stepped forward from where he had been standing with Nicodemus. "Wait."

I stopped and turned to him.

"Let me be part of this." His voice caught. "Please. She is my granddaughter."

I held out my hand to him. He took it, his palm rough and warm against mine. The three of us crossed to where Jesus waited, and we kneeled before him together. The stone floor was hard beneath my knees, and my belly shifted, one hand bracing against the ground.

He placed both hands on my belly, his palms warm through the fabric of my tunic, and the scent of nard came with them. The smell of burial wrapped around me, around Sarah. I could hear the lamp flame hissing softly, someone shifting on the cushions behind me, and the distant sound of the crowd still gathered in the street beyond.

"The Father knows this daughter, Anna." His voice carried that quality I had heard so many times before, the sound of absolute certainty woven through with tenderness. "Sarah's name is written in His book beside Jonah's. The Father holds them both."

Water blurred my vision and spilled hot down my cheeks, running to my jaw. I tasted salt.

"She will be born into a time of darkness. The world will be broken and afraid. But do not fear for her. The Father has numbered every hair on her head. He knows the path she will walk."

Sarah moved beneath his palms, and then she pushed upward as though reaching for his touch.

"She will face trials you cannot shield her from. She will know grief." His hands pressed back softly against where she pushed. "But she will also know joy. And hope. And she will carry light into dark places, because the Father's light is already in her."

Sarah moved again, as though she had heard him. As though she understood.

"He will not abandon her, Anna. Or you. Be blessed, Sarah. Rest in the Father's love and safety."

Jesus's hand moved to Andrew's shoulder. "Andrew. Faithful Andrew, who brought your brother to me at the Jordan. Who has served without seeking glory. Who has loved Anna well through every season." His voice softened. "The world will remember Peter's confession, but I remember who brought Peter to the river that day. Your reward is not in men's remembering, but in the Father's. He sees what is hidden."

He paused, his hand tightening on Andrew's shoulder. "The road will take you far from Galilee. You will carry my name to places where darkness has reigned for generations. And there, in those distant lands, your faithfulness will bear fruit that will endure long after your bones return to dust. Be blessed, beloved friend."

Andrew's head bowed, and I saw his shoulders shake.

Jesus looked at my father, still kneeling beside us. He placed one hand on my father's shoulder, and my father bowed his head. A covenant, sealed without words.

"Uncle. The road ahead for your family is long. Longer than you know. You will carry the gospel to the ends of the earth, to lands where my name has never been spoken. Sarah will grow knowing many peoples, many tongues. Guard them well. All of them. The Father has need of you yet."

My father's hands were fisted in his robe.

Jesus leaned forward and kissed my forehead. His hand came up to cup my face, and his thumb brushed over the scar at my cheek. The scent of nard transferred from his fingers to my skin, and I knew I would smell it for days—the funeral oil marking me, marking Sarah, binding us both to what was coming.

"I wish we had more time, little cousin. How I wish I could meet Sarah before I leave this world."

"I wish it too," I whispered.

Jesus rose and looked at all of them. "Now, the time has come. Tomorrow we go to Jerusalem." He paused, and in that pause the lamplight steadied to perfect stillness, the flame frozen mid-waver. The air itself seemed to hold, waiting for what came next. "Who is coming with me?"

Around the room, voices rose—Peter, John, Mary Magdalene, Joanna, one by one they spoke. They would go.

My father rose to his feet, dust from the stone floor clinging to his council robes. "I will not abandon you. Not now. Not ever. I will go."

"I go with you." Andrew said as he helped me stand, his arm steady around my waist even as I felt him trembling. "Rabbi, I go wherever you go."

I wiped my face with the back of my hand. Sarah shifted inside me, as though she too were waking to what was coming. I placed my hand over where she moved and looked at Jesus.

"I go with you, too. To the end."

Jesus smiled at me. "I knew you would."

AUTHOR'S NOTE

Thank you for walking beside Anna through this season of her life—through the joy of new marriage and the wonder of carrying life, through profound revelations about who Jesus is and devastating personal loss. This book asked more of me as a writer than any I've written before. I've cried and celebrated and sat in wonder as the story took shape. Anna and Andrew are very real to me. I left a big piece of my heart on these pages.

Writing Anna's journey has changed me. Imagining what it might have been like to walk dusty roads with Jesus, to witness His miracles and hear His teachings, to struggle with faith when answers don't come—it has made Scripture breathe in ways I never expected. Anna's grief became real to me. Her questions became mine. And Jesus's presence in the midst of it all became more precious than I can express.

Anna's personal journey is woven into the larger story of Jesus's ministry as He moves steadily toward Jerusalem. The crowds. The opposition. The miracles and teachings that confound even those closest to Him. These are the days when the cost of discipleship becomes clear, when following Jesus means more than excitement and miracles—it means trust when nothing makes sense.

If you have walked through loss—of a child, a dream, a certainty you once held—I pray you found something true in these pages. Your grief is seen. And the God who wept at Lazarus's tomb walks with you still.

I've included as much as I can from the Scriptures while keeping Anna and Andrew's story front and center. I wish I had more pages to explore every disciple, every story, every word that Jesus uttered in the Gospels. I did my best. I hope you loved it.

Anna and Andrew's journey continues toward Jerusalem, toward Passion Week, and toward a morning that will change everything. Come along with them in *Anna of Calvary*, coming Fall 2026.

In Christ,
Susanne

ABOUT THE AUTHOR

Susanne Blumer is the author of *Anna of Arimathea* and *Anna of Bethsaida*, the first two books in *The Arimathea Chronicles*. She is also the owner of three magical bookstores: two nestled in the mountains of North Carolina and one in the Lowcountry of South Carolina. She cowrites the Bell Tower Bible Adventures series with her husband Cole and is the author of the Piper Periwinkle series and several other children's books. Susanne is CEO and Founder of Sassafras on Sutton, LLC, a cheerleader for Christian fiction, and adores wandering around her stores, chatting with customers and pretending she's working. She splits her time between the mountains and the coast, has more books than shelves, loves coffee more than she should and is always dreaming of the next story to tell.

Learn more about her stores at sassafraspost.com. If you're ever in Waynesville or Beaufort, stop in and say hey!

You can stay in touch with Susanne at susanneblumer.com.